Emily Climbs

L. M. Montgomery

BANTAM BOOKS

TORONTO · NEW YORK · LONDON · SYDNEY · AUCKLAND

This low-priced Bantam Book
has been completely reset in a type face
designed for easy reading, and was printed
from new plates. It contains the complete
text of the original hard-cover edition.
NOT ONE WORD HAS BEEN OMITTED.

🐓

RL 7, IL AGE 11 AND UP
EMILY CLIMBS
A Bantam Book / published by arrangement with
Harper & Row, Publishers Inc.

PRINTING HISTORY
Lippincott edition published July 1925
Bantam edition / June 1983

ISBN 0-553-23371-8

Published simultaneously in the United States and Canada

COVER PRINTED IN U.S.A.

TEXT PRINTED IN CANADA

U   0 9 8 7 6 5 4 3

To
"Pastor Felix"
in
affectionate appreciation

Contents

1
Writing Herself Out

Emily Byrd Starr was alone in her room, in the old New Moon farmhouse at Blair Water, one stormy night in a February of the olden years before the world turned upside down. She was at that moment as perfectly happy as any human being is ever permitted to be. Aunt Elizabeth, in consideration of the coldness of the night, had allowed her to have a fire in her little fireplace—a rare favour. It was burning brightly and showering a red-golden light over the small, immaculate room, with its old-time furniture and deep-set, wide-silled windows, to whose frosted, blue-white panes the snowflakes clung in little wreaths. It lent depth and mystery and allure to the mirror on the wall which reflected Emily as she sat coiled on the ottoman before the fire, writing, by the light of two tall, white candles—which were the only approved means of illumination at

New Moon—in a brand-new, glossy, black "Jimmy-book" which Cousin Jimmy had given her that day. Emily had been very glad to get it, for she had filled the one he had given her the preceding autumn, and for over a week she had suffered acute pangs of suppression because she could not write in a non-existent "diary."

Her diary had become a dominant factor in her young, vivid life. It had taken the place of certain "letters" she had written in her childhood to her dead father, in which she had been wont to "write out" her problems and worries—for even in the magic years when one is almost fourteen one has problems and worries, especially when one is under the strict and well-meant but not over-tender governance of an Aunt Elizabeth Murray. Sometimes Emily felt that if it were not for her diary she would have flown into little bits by reason of consuming her own smoke. The fat, black "Jimmy-book" seemed to her like a personal friend and a safe confidant for certain matters which burned for expression and yet were too combustible to be trusted to the ears of any living being. Now blank books of any sort were not easy to come by at New Moon, and if it had not been for Cousin Jimmy, Emily might never have had one. Certainly Aunt Elizabeth would not give her one—Aunt Elizabeth thought Emily wasted far too much time "over her scribbling nonsense" as it was—and Aunt Laura did not dare to go contrary to Aunt Elizabeth in this—more by token that Laura herself really thought Emily might be better employed. Aunt Laura was a jewel of a woman, but certain things were holden from her eyes.

Now Cousin Jimmy was never in the least frightened of Aunt Elizabeth, and when the notion occurred to him that Emily probably wanted another "blank book," that blank book materialised straightway, in defiance of Aunt Elizabeth's scornful glances. He had gone to Shrewsbury that very day, in the teeth of the rising storm, for no other reason than to get it. So Emily was happy, in her subtle and friendly firelight, while the wind howled and shrieked through the great old trees to the north of New Moon, sent huge, spectral wreaths of snow whirling across Cousin Jimmy's famous garden, drifted the sun-dial completely over, and whistled eerily through the Three Princesses—as Emily always called the three tall Lombardies in the corner of the garden.

"I love a storm like this at night when I don't have to go out in it," wrote Emily. "Cousin Jimmy and I had a splendid evening planning out our garden and choosing our seeds and plants in the catalogue. Just where the biggest drift is making, behind the summer-house, we are going to have a bed of pink asters, and we are going to give the Golden Ones—who are dreaming under four feet of snow—a background of flowering almond. I love to plan out summer days like this, in the midst of a storm. It makes me feel as if I were winning a victory over something ever so much bigger than myself, just because *I* have a brain and the storm is nothing but blind, white force—terrible, but blind. I have the same feeling when I sit here cosily by my own dear fire, and hear it raging all around me, and *laugh* at it. And *that* is just because over a hundred years ago great-great-grandfather Murray built this house and built it well. I wonder if, a hundred years from now, anybody will win a victory over anything because of something *I* left or did. It is an *inspiring thought*."

"I drew that line of italics before I thought. Mr. Carpenter says I use far too many italics. He says it is an Early Victorian obsession, and I must strive to cast it off. I concluded I would when I looked in the dictionary, for it is evidently not a nice thing to be obsessed, though it doesn't seem quite so bad as to be *possessed*. There I go again: but I think the italics are all right this time.

"I read the dictionary for a whole hour—till Aunt Elizabeth got suspicious and suggested that it would be much better for me to be knitting my ribbed stockings. She couldn't see exactly why it was wrong for me to be poring over the dictionary but she felt sure it must be because *she* never wants to do it. I *love* reading the dictionary. (Yes, those italics are *necessary*, Mr. Carpenter. An ordinary 'love' wouldn't express my feeling at all!) Words are such *fascinating* things. (I caught myself at the first syllable that time!) The very sound of some of them—'haunted'—'mystic'—for example, gives me *the flash*. (Oh, dear! But I *have* to italicize *the flash*. It isn't ordinary—it's the most extraordinary and wonderful thing in my whole life. When it comes I feel as if a door had swung open in a wall before me and given me a glimpse of—yes, of *heaven*. *More italics!* Oh, I see why Mr. Carpenter scolds! I *must* break myself of the habit.)

"Big words are never beautiful—'incriminating'—'obstreperous'—'international'—'unconstitutional.' They make me think of those horrible big dahlias and chrysanthemums Cousin Jimmy took me to see at the exhibition in Charlottetown last fall. We couldn't see anything lovely in them, though some people thought them wonderful. Cousin Jimmy's little yellow 'mums, like pale, fairy-like stars shining against the fir copse in the northwest corner of the garden, were ten times more beautiful. But I am wandering from my subject—also a bad habit of mine, according to Mr. Carpenter. He says I *must* (the italics are his this time!) learn to concentrate—another big word and a very ugly one.

"But I had a good time over that dictionary—much better than I had over the ribbed stockings. I wish I could have a pair—just one pair—of silk stockings. Ilse has three. Her father gives her everything she wants, now that he has learned to love her. But Aunt Elizabeth says silk stockings are *immoral*. I wonder why—any more than silk dresses.

"Speaking of silk dresses, Aunt Janey Milburn, at Derry Pond—she isn't any relation really, but everybody calls her that—has made a vow that she will never wear a silk dress until the whole heathen world is converted to Christianity. That is very fine. I wish I could be as good as that, but I couldn't—I love silk too much. It is so rich and sheeny. I would like to dress in it all the time, and if I could afford to I would—though I suppose every time I thought of dear old Aunt Janey and the unconverted heathen I would feel conscience-stricken. However, it will be years, if ever, before I can afford to buy even one silk dress, and meanwhile I give some of my egg money every month to missions. (I have five hens of my own now, all descended from the gray pullet Perry gave me on my twelfth birthday.) If ever I can buy that one silk dress I know what it is going to be like. Not black or brown or navy blue—sensible, serviceable colors, such as New Moon Murrays always wear—oh, dear, no! It is to be of shot silk, blue in one light, silver in others, like a twilight sky, glimpsed through a frosted window pane—with a bit of lace-foam here and there, like those little feathers of snow clinging to my windowpane. Teddy says he will paint me in it and call it 'The Ice Maiden,' and Aunt Laura smiles and says, sweetly and condescendingly, in a way I hate, even in dear Aunt Laura,

" 'What use would such a dress be to you, Emily?'

"It mightn't be of any use, but I would feel in it as if it were a part of me—that it *grew* on me and wasn't just bought and put on. I want *one* dress like that in my lifetime. And a silk petticoat underneath it—and silk stockings!

"Ilse has a silk dress now—a bright pink one. Aunt Elizabeth says Dr. Burnley dresses Ilse far too old and rich for a child. But he wants to make up for all the years he didn't dress her at all. (I don't mean she went naked, but she might have as far as Dr. Burnley was concerned. Other people had to see to her clothes.) He does everything she wants him to do now, and gives her her own way in everything. Aunt Elizabeth says it is very bad for her, but there are times when I envy Ilse a little. I know it is wicked, but I cannot help it.

"Dr. Burnley is going to send Ilse to Shrewsbury High School next fall, and after that to Montreal to study elocution. That is why I envy her—not because of the silk dress. I wish Aunt Elizabeth would let me go to Shrewsbury, but I fear she never will. She feels she can't trust me out of her sight because my mother eloped. But she need not be afraid I will ever elope. I have made up my mind that I will never marry. I shall be *wedded to my art*.

"Teddy wants to go to Shrewsbury next fall, but his mother won't let him go, either. Not that she is afraid of his eloping, but because she loves him so much she can't part with him. Teddy wants to be an artist, and Mr. Carpenter says he has genius and should have his chance, but everybody is afraid to say anything to Mrs Kent. She is a little bit of a woman—no taller than I am, really, quiet and shy—and yet every one is afraid of her. *I* am—dreadfully afraid. I've always known she didn't like me—ever since those days long ago when Ilse and I first went up to the Tansy Patch, to play with Teddy. But now she hates me—I feel sure of it—just because Teddy likes me. She can't bear to have him like anybody or anything but her. She is even jealous of his pictures. So there is not much chance of his getting to Shrewsbury. Perry is going. He hasn't a cent, but he is going to work his way through. That is why he thinks he will go to Shrewsbury in place of Queen's Academy. He thinks it will be easier to get work to do in Shrewsbury, and board is cheaper there.

" 'My old beast of an Aunt Tom has a little money,' he told me, 'but she won't give me any of it—unless —unless——'

"Then he looked at me *significantly*.

"I blushed because I couldn't help it, and then I was furious with myself for blushing, and with Perry—because he referred to something I didn't want to hear about—

that time ever so long ago when his Aunt Tom met me in Lofty John's bush and nearly frightened me to death by demanding that I promise to *marry Perry when we grew up,* in which case she would educate him. I never told anybody about it—being ashamed—except Ilse, and she said,

" 'The idea of old Aunt Tom aspiring to a Murray for Perry!'

"But then, Ilse is awfully hard on Perry and quarrels with him half the time, over things *I* only smile at. Perry never likes to be outdone by any one in anything. When we were at Amy Moore's party last week, her uncle told us a story of some remarkable freak calf he had seen, with three legs, and Perry said,

" 'Oh, *that's* nothing to a duck I saw once in Norway.'

"(Perry really was in Norway. He used to sail everywhere with his father when he was little. But I don't believe one word about that duck. He wasn't *lying*—he was just *romancing.* Dear Mr. Carpenter, I *can't* get along without italics.)

"Perry's duck had four legs, according to him—two where a proper duck's legs should be, and two sprouting from its back. And when it got tired of walking on its ordinary pair it flopped over on its back and walked on the other pair!

"Perry told this yarn with a sober face, and everybody laughed, and Amy's uncle said, 'Go up head, Perry.' But Ilse was furious and wouldn't speak to him all the way home. She said he had made a fool of himself, trying to 'show off' with a silly story like that, and that *no gentleman* would act so.

"Perry said: 'I'm no gentleman, yet, only a hired boy, but some day, Miss Ilse, I'll be a finer gentleman than any one *you* know.'

" 'Gentlemen,' said Ilse in a nasty voice, 'have to be *born*. They can't be *made*, you know.'

"Ilse has almost given up calling names, as she used to do when she quarrelled with Perry or me, and taken to saying cruel, cutting things. They hurt far worse than the names used to, but I don't really mind them—much—or long—because I know Ilse doesn't mean them and really loves me as much as I love her. But Perry says they stick in his crop. They didn't speak to each other the rest of the way home, but next day Ilse was at him again about using bad grammar and not standing up when a lady enters the room.

"'Of course you couldn't be expected to know *that*,' she said in her nastiest voice, 'but I am sure Mr. Carpenter has done his best to teach you grammar.'

"Perry didn't say one word to Ilse, but he turned to me.

"'Will *you* tell me my faults?' he said. 'I don't mind *you* doing it—it will be *you* that will have to put up with me when we're grown up, not Ilse.'

"He said that to make Ilse angry, but it made me angrier still, for it was an allusion to a *forbidden topic*. So we neither of us spoke to him for two days and he said it was a good rest from Ilse's slams anyway.

"Perry is not the only one who gets into disgrace at New Moon. I said something silly yesterday evening which makes me blush to recall it. The Ladies' Aid met here and Aunt Elizabeth gave them a supper and the husbands of the Aid came to it. Ilse and I waited on the table, which was set in the kitchen because the dining-room table wasn't long enough. It was exciting at first and then, when every one was served, it was a little dull and I began to compose some poetry in my mind as I stood by the window looking out on the garden. It was so interesting that I soon forgot everything else until suddenly I heard Aunt Elizabeth say, 'Emily,' very sharply, and then she looked significantly at Mr. Johnson, our new minister. I was confused and I snatched up the teapot and exclaimed,

"'Oh, Mr. *Cup*, will you have your *Johnson* filled?'

"Everybody roared and Aunt Elizabeth looked disgusted and Aunt Laura ashamed, and I felt as if I would sink through the floor. I couldn't sleep half the night for thinking over it. The strange thing was that I do believe I felt worse and more ashamed than I would have felt if I had done something really wrong. This is the 'Murray pride' of course, and I suppose it is very wicked. Sometimes I am afraid Aunt Ruth Dutton is right in her opinion of me after all.

"No, she isn't!

"But it is a tradition of New Moon that its women should be equal to any situation and always be graceful and dignified. Now, there was nothing graceful or dignified in asking such a question of the new minister. I am sure he will never see me again without thinking of it and I will always writhe when I catch his eye upon me.

"But now that I have written it out in my diary I don't feel so badly over it. *Nothing* ever seems as big or as terrible—oh, nor as beautiful and grand, either, alas!—when it is written out, as it does when you are thinking or feeling about it. It seems to *shrink* directly you put it into words. Even the line of poetry I had made just before I asked that absurd question won't seem half as fine when I write it down:

" '*Where the velvet feet of darkness softly go.*'

"It *doesn't*. Some bloom seems gone from it. And yet, while I was standing there, behind all those chattering, eating people, and *saw* darkness stealing so softly over the garden and the hills, like a beautiful woman robed in shadows, with stars for eyes, the *flash* came and I forgot everything but that I wanted to put something of the beauty I felt into the words of my poem. When that line came into my mind it didn't seem to me that *I* composed it at all—it seemed as if *Something Else* were trying to speak through me—and it was that *Something Else* that made the line seem wonderful—and now when it is gone the words seem flat and foolish and the

picture I tried to draw in them not so wonderful after
all.

"Oh, if I could only put things into words as I *see*
them! Mr. Carpenter says, 'Strive—strive—keep on—
words are your medium—make them your slaves—until
they will say for you what you want them to say.' That
is true—and I do try—but it seems to me there is
something *beyond* words—any words—all words— something that always escapes you when you try to grasp
it—and yet leaves something in your hand which you
wouldn't have had if you hadn't reached for it.

"I remember one day last fall when Dean and I
walked over the Delectable Mountain to the woods
beyond it—fir woods mostly, but with one corner of
splendid old pines. We sat under them and Dean read
Peveril of the Peak and some of Scott's poems to me; and
then he looked up into the big, plumy boughs and
said,

" 'The gods are talking in the pines—gods of the old
northland—of the viking sagas. Star, do you know
Emerson's lines?'

"And then he quoted them—I've remembered and
loved them ever since.

> " 'The gods talk in the breath of the wold,
>   They talk in the shaken pine,
>   And they fill the reach of the old seashore
>   With dialogue divine;
>   And the poet who overhears
>   One random word they say
>   Is the fated man of men
>   Whom the ages must obey.'

"Oh, that 'random word'—that is the *Something* that
escapes me. I'm always listening for it—I know I can
never hear it—*my* ear isn't attuned to it—but I am sure
I hear at times a little, faint, far-off echo of it—and it
makes me feel a delight that is like pain and a despair

of ever being able to translate its beauty into any words I know.

"Still, it *is* a pity I made such a goose of myself immediately after that wonderful experience.

"If I had just floated up behind Mr. Johnson, as velvet-footedly as darkness herself, and poured his tea gracefully from Great-grandmother Murray's silver tea-pot, like my shadow-woman pouring night into the white cup of Blair Valley, Aunt Elizabeth would be far better pleased with me than if I could write the most wonderful poem in the world.

"Cousin Jimmy is so different. I recited my poem to him this evening after we had finished with the cata-logue and he thought it was beautiful. (*He* couldn't know how far it fell short of what I had seen in my mind.) Cousin Jimmy composes poetry himself. He is very clever in spots. And in other spots, where his brain was hurt when Aunt Elizabeth pushed him into our New Moon well, he isn't *anything*. There's just *blankness* there. So people call him simple, and Aunt Ruth dares to say he hasn't sense enough to shoo a cat from cream. And yet if you put all his clever spots together there isn't anybody in Blair Water has half as much real cleverness as he has—not even Mr. Carpen-ter. The trouble is you can't put his clever spots together—there are always those gaps between. But I love Cousin Jimmy and I'm never in the least afraid of him when his queer spells come on him. Everybody else is—even Aunt Elizabeth, though perhaps it is remorse with her, instead of fear—except Perry. Perry always brags that he is never afraid of anything—doesn't know what fear is. I think that is very wonderful. I wish I could be so fearless. Mr. Carpenter says fear is a vile thing, and is at the bottom of almost every wrong and hatred of the world.

" 'Cast it out, Jade,' he says—'cast it out of your heart. Fear is a confession of weakness. What you fear is stronger than you, or you think it is, else you wouldn't be afraid of it. Remember your Emerson—"always do what you are afraid to do." '

"But that is a counsel of perfection, as Dean says, and I don't believe I'll ever be able to attain to it. To be honest, I am afraid of a good many *things*, but there are only two people in the word I'm truly afraid of. One is Mrs. Kent, and the other is Mad Mr. Morrison. I'm terribly afraid of him and I think almost every one is. His home is in Derry Pond, but he hardly ever stays there—he roams over the country looking for his lost bride. He was married only a few weeks when his young wife died, many years ago, and he has never been right in his mind since. He insists she is not dead, only lost, and that he will find her some time. He has grown old and bent, looking for her, but to him she is still young and fair.

"He was here one day last summer, but would not come in—just peered into the kitchen wistfully and said, 'Is Annie here?' He was quite gentle that day, but sometimes he is very wild and violent. He declares he always hears Annie calling to him—that her voice flits on before him—always before him, like my random word. His face is wrinkled and shrivelled and he looks like an old, old monkey. But the thing I hate most about him is his right hand—it is a deep blood-red all over—birth-marked. I can't tell why, but that hand fills me with horror. I could not bear to touch it. And sometimes he laughs to himself very horribly. The only living thing he seems to care for is his old black dog that always is with him. They say he will never ask for a bite of food for himself. If people do not offer it to him he goes hungry, but he will beg for his dog.

"Oh, I am terribly afraid of him, and I was so glad he didn't come into the house that day. Aunt Elizabeth looked after him, as he went away with his long, gray hair streaming in the wind, and said,

" 'Fairfax Morrison was once a fine, clever, young

man, with excellent prospects. Well, God's ways are very mysterious.'

"'That is why they are interesting,' I said.

"But Aunt Elizabeth frowned and told me not to be irreverent, as she always does when I say anything about God. I wonder why. She won't let Perry and me talk about Him, either, though Perry is really very much interested in Him and wants to find out all about Him. Aunt Elizabeth overheard me telling Perry one Sunday afternoon what I thought God was like, and she said it was scandalous.

"It wasn't! The trouble is, Aunt Elizabeth and I have different Gods, that is all. Everybody has a different God, I think. Aunt Ruth's, for instance, is one that punishes her enemies—sends 'judgments' on them. That seems to me to be about all the use He really is to her. Jim Cosgrain uses his to swear by. But Aunt Janey Milburn walks in the light of her God's countenance, every day, and shines with it.

"I have written myself out for tonight, and am going to bed. I know I have 'wasted words' in this diary— another of my literary faults, according to Mr. Carpenter.

"'You waste words, Jade—you spill them about too lavishly. Economy and restraint—that's what you need.'

"He's right, of course, and in my essays and stories I try to practise what he preaches. But in my diary, which nobody sees but myself, or ever will see until after I'm dead, I like just to let myself go."

Emily looked at her candle—it, too, was almost burned out. She knew she could not have another that night— Aunt Elizabeth's rules were as those of Mede and Persian: she put away her diary in the little right-hand cupboard above the mantel, covered her dying fire, undressed and blew out her candle. The room slowly filled with the faint, ghostly snow-light of a night when a full moon is behind the driving storm-clouds. And just as Emily was ready to slip into her high black bedstead a sudden inspiration came—a splendid new idea for a story. For a minute she shivered reluctantly: the room was getting cold. But the idea would not be denied. Emily slipped her hand between the feather tick of her bed and the chaff mattress and produced a half-burned candle, secreted there for just such an emergency.

It was not, of course, a proper thing to do. But then I have never pretended, nor ever will pretend, that Emily was a proper child. Books are not written about proper children. They would be so dull nobody would read them.

She lighted her candle, put on her stockings and a heavy coat, got out another half-filled Jimmy-book, and began to write by the single, uncertain candle which made a pale oasis of light in the shadows of the room. In that oasis Emily wrote, her black head bent over her book, as the hours of night crept away and the other occupants of New Moon slumbered soundly; she grew chill and cramped, but she was quite unconscious of it. Her eyes burned—her cheeks glowed—words came like troops of obedient genii to the call of her pen. When at last her candle went out with a sputter and a hiss in its little pool of melted tallow, she came back to reality with a sigh and a shiver. It was two, by the clock, and she was very tired and very cold; but she had finished her story and it was the best she had ever written. She crept into her cold nest with a sense of completion and victory, born of the working out of her creative impulse, and fell asleep to the lullaby of the waning storm.

2
Salad Days

This book is not going to be wholly, or even mainly, made up of extracts from Emily's diary; but, by way of linking up matters unimportant enough for a chapter in themselves, and yet necessary for a proper understanding of her personality and environment, I am going to include some more of them. Besides, when one has material ready to hand, why not use it? Emily's "diary," with all its youthful crudities and italics, really gives a better interpretation of her and of her imaginative and introspective mind, in that, her fourteenth spring, than any biographer, however sympathetic, could do. So let us take another peep into the yellowed pages of that old "Jimmy-book," written long ago in the "look-out" of New Moon.

"February 15, 19—

"I have decided that I will write down, in this journal, every day, all my good deeds and all my bad ones. I got the idea out of a book, and it appeals to me. I mean to be as honest about it as I can. It will be easy, of course, to write down the good deeds, but not so easy to record the bad ones.

"I did only one bad thing today—only one thing *I* think bad, that is. I was impertinent to Aunt Elizabeth. She thought I took too long washing the dishes. I didn't suppose there was any hurry and I was composing a story called *The Secret of the Mill*. Aunt Elizabeth looked at me and then at the clock, and said in her most disagreeable way,

" 'Is the snail your sister, Emily?'

" 'No! Snails are no relation to *me*,' I said *haughtily*.

"It was not what I said, but the way I said it that was impertinent. *And I meant it to be.* I was very angry— sarcastic speeches always aggravate me. Afterwards I was very sorry that I had been in a temper—but I was sorry because it was *foolish* and *undignified*, not because it was *wicked*. So I suppose that was not true repentance.

"As for my good deeds, I did two today. I saved two little lives. Saucy Sal had caught a poor snow-bird and I took it from her. It flew off quite briskly, and I am sure it felt wonderfully happy. Later on I went down to the cellar cupboard and found a mouse caught in a trap by its foot. The poor thing lay there, almost exhausted from struggling, with *such* a look in its black eyes. I *couldn't* endure it so I set it free, and it managed to get away quite smartly in spite of its foot. I do not feel *sure* about *this* deed. I know it was a good one from the mouse's point of view, but what about Aunt Elizabeth's?

"This evening Aunt Laura and Aunt Elizabeth read and burned a boxful of old letters. They read them aloud and commented on them, while I sat in a corner and knitted my stockings. The letters were very interesting and I learned a great deal about the Murrays I had never known before. I feel that it is quite wonderful to belong to a family like this. No wonder the Blair Water folks call us 'the Chosen People'—though *they* don't mean it as a compliment. I feel that I must live up to the traditions of my family.

"I had a long letter from Dean Priest today. He is spending the winter in Algiers. He says he is coming home in April and is going to take rooms with his sister, Mrs. Fred Evans, for the summer. I am so glad. It will be splendid to have him in Blair Water all summer. Nobody ever talks to me as Dean does. He is the nicest and most interesting old person I know.

Aunt Elizabeth says he is selfish, as all the Priests are. But then she does not like the Priests. And she always calls him Jarback, which somehow sets my teeth on edge. One of Dean's shoulders *is* a little higher than the other, but that is not his fault. I told Aunt Elizabeth once that I wished she would not call my friend that, but she only said,

" '*I* did not nickname *your friend*, Emily. His own clan have always called him Jarback. The Priests are not noted for delicacy!'

"Teddy had a letter from Dean, too, and a book—*The Lives of Great Artists*—Michael Angelo, Raphael, Velasquez, Rembrandt, Titian. He says he dare not let his mother see him reading it—she would burn it. I am sure if Teddy could only have his chance he would be as great an artist as any of them.

"February 18, 19—

"I had a lovely time with myself this evening, after school, walking on the brook road in Lofty John's bush. The sun was low and creamy and the snow so white and the shadows so slender and blue. I think there is nothing so beautiful as tree shadows. And when I came out into the garden my own shadow looked so funny—so long that it stretched right across the garden. I immediately made a poem of which two lines were,

" '*If we were as tall as our shadows
How tall our shadows would be.*'

"I think there is a good deal of *philosophy* in that.

"Tonight I wrote a story and Aunt Elizabeth knew what I was doing and was very much annoyed. She scolded me for wasting time. But it *wasn't* wasted time. I *grew* in it—I know I did. And there was something about some of the sentences I liked. '*I am afraid of the grey wood*'—that pleased me very much. And—'white and stately she walked the dark wood like a moon-beam.' I think that is rather fine. Yet Mr. Carpenter tells me that whenever I think a thing especially fine I am to cut it out. But oh, I *can't* cut that out—not yet, at least. The strange part is that about three months after Mr. Carpenter tells me to cut a thing out I come round to his point of view and feel ashamed of it. Mr. Carpenter was quite merciless over my essay today. Nothing about it suited him.

" 'Three *alas's* in one paragraph, Emily. One would have been too many in this year of grace!' '*More irresistible*—Emily, for heaven's sake, write English! That is unpardonable.'

"It *was*, too. I saw it for myself and I felt shame going all over me from head to foot like a red wave. Then, after Mr. Carpenter had blue-pencilled almost every sentence and sneered at all my fine phrases and found fault with most of my constructions and told me I was too fond of putting 'cleverisms' into everything I wrote, he flung my exercise book down, tore at his hair and said,

" 'You write! Jade, get a spoon and learn to cook!'

"Then he strode off, muttering maledictions 'not loud but deep.' I picked up my poor essay and didn't feel very badly. I *can* cook already, and I have learned a thing or two about Mr. Carpenter. The better my essays are the more he rages over them. This one must have been quite good. But it makes him so angry and impatient to see where I might have made it *still better* and didn't—through carelessness or laziness or indifference—as he thinks. And he can't tolerate a person who *could* do better and doesn't. And he wouldn't bother with me at all if he didn't think I may amount to something by and by.

"Aunt Elizabeth does not approve of Mr. Johnson. She thinks his theology is not sound. He said in his sermon last Sunday that there was some good in Buddhism.

" 'He will be saying that there is some good in Popery next,' said Aunt Elizabeth indignantly at the dinner table.

"There *may* be some good in Buddhism. I must ask Dean about it when he comes home.

"March 2, 19—
"We were all at a funeral today—old Mrs. Sarah Paul. I have always liked going to funerals. When I said that, Aunt Elizabeth looked shocked and Aunt Laura said, 'Oh, Emily *dear!*' I rather like to shock Aunt Elizabeth, but I never feel comfortable if I worry Aunt Laura—she's *such* a darling—so I explained—or tried to. It is sometimes very hard to explain things to Aunt Elizabeth.

" 'Funerals are interesting,' I said. 'And humorous, too.'

"I think I only made matters worse by saying *that*. And yet Aunt Elizabeth knew as well as I did that it was funny to see some of those relatives of Mrs. Paul, who have fought with and hated her for years—she *wasn't* amiable, if she is dead!—sitting there, holding their handkerchiefs to their faces and pretending to cry. I knew quite well what each and every one was thinking in his heart. Jake Paul was wondering if the old harridan had by any chance left him anything in her will—and Alice Paul, who knew *she* wouldn't get anything, was hoping Jake Paul wouldn't either. That would satisfy *her*. And Mrs. Charlie Paul was wondering how soon it would be decent to do the house over the way she had always wanted it and Mrs. Paul *hadn't*. And Aunty Min was worrying for fear there wouldn't be enough baked meats for such a mob of fourth cousins that they'd never expected and didn't want, and Lisette Paul was counting the people and feeling vexed because there wasn't as large an attendance as there was at Mrs. Henry Lister's funeral last week. When I told Aunt Laura this, she said gravely,

" 'All this may be true, Emily'—(she knew it was!)— 'but somehow it doesn't seem quite right for so young a girl as you, to—to—to be able to see these things, in short.'

"However, I can't help seeing them. Darling Aunt Laura is always so sorry for people that she can't see their humorous side. But I saw other things too. I saw that little Zack Fritz, whom Mrs. Paul adopted and was very kind to, was almost broken-hearted, and I saw that Martha Paul was feeling sorry and ashamed to think of her bitter old quarrel with Mrs. Paul—and I saw that Mrs. Paul's face, that looked so discontented and thwarted in life, looked peaceful and majestic and even beautiful—as if Death had *satisfied* her at last.

"Yes, funerals *are* interesting.

"March 5, 19—

"It is snowing a little tonight. I love to see the snow coming down in slanting lines against the dark trees.

"I *think* I did a good deed today. Jason Merrowby was here helping Cousin Jimmy saw wood—and I *saw him sneak into the pighouse, and take a swig from a whiskey bottle*. But I did not say one word about it to any one—that is my good deed.

"Perhaps I *ought* to tell Aunt Elizabeth, but if I did she would never have him again, and he needs all the work he can get, for his poor wife's and children's sakes. I find it is not always easy to be sure whether your deeds are good or bad.

"March 20, 19—

"Yesterday Aunt Elizabeth was very angry because I would not write an 'obituary poem' for old Peter DeGeer who died last week. Mrs. DeGeer came here and asked me to do it. I wouldn't—I felt very indignant at such a request. I felt it would be *a desecration of my art* to do such a thing—though of course I didn't say that to Mrs. DeGeer. For one thing it would have hurt her feelings, and for another she wouldn't have had the faintest idea what I meant. Even Aunt Elizabeth hadn't when I told her my reasons for refusing, after Mrs. DeGeer had gone.

" 'You are always writing yards of trash that nobody wants,' she said. 'I think you might write something that *is* wanted. It would have pleased poor old Mary DeGeer. 'Desecration of your art' indeed. If you *must* talk, Emily, why not talk sense?'

"I proceeded to talk sense.

" 'Aunt Elizabeth,' I said seriously, 'how could I write that obituary poem for her? I couldn't write an *untruthful* one to please anybody. And you know yourself that nothing good *and* truthful could be said about old Peter DeGeer!'

"Aunt Elizabeth did know it, and it posed her, but she was all the more displeased with me for that. She vexed me so much that I came up to my room and wrote an 'obituary poem' about Peter, just for my own satisfaction. It is certainly great fun to write a *truthful* obituary of some one you don't like. Not that I *dis*liked Peter DeGeer; I just despised him as everybody did. But Aunt Elizabeth had annoyed me, and when I am annoyed I can write very sarcastically. And again I felt that *Something* was writing through me—but a very different *Something* from the usual one—a malicious, mocking *Something* that *enjoyed* making fun of poor, lazy, shiftless, lying, silly, hypocritical, old Peter DeGeer. Ideas—words—rhymes—all seemed to drop into place while that *Something* chuckled.

"I thought the poem was so clever that I couldn't resist the temptation to take it to school today and show it to Mr. Carpenter. I thought he would enjoy it—and I think he *did*, too, in a way, but after he had read it he laid it down and looked at me.

"'I suppose there *is* a pleasure in satirizing a failure,' he said. 'Poor old Peter was a failure—and he is dead—and His Maker may be merciful to him, but his fellow creatures will not. When *I* am dead, Emily, will you write like this about me? You have the power—oh, yes, it's all here—this *is* very clever. You can paint the weakness and foolishness and wickedness of a character in a way that is positively uncanny, in a girl of your age. But—is it worth while, Emily?'

"'No—no,' I said. I was so ashamed and sorry that I wanted to get away and cry. It was terrible to think Mr. Carpenter imagined I would ever write so about *him*, after all he has done for me.

"'It isn't,' said Mr. Carpenter. 'There is a place for satire—there are gangrenes that can only be burned out—but leave the burning to the great geniuses. It's better to heal than hurt. We failures know that.'

"'Oh, Mr. Carpenter!' I began. I wanted to say *he* wasn't a failure—I wanted to say a hundred things—but he wouldn't let me.

"'There—there, we won't talk of it, Emily. When *I* am dead say, "He was a failure, and none knew it more truly or felt it more bitterly than himself." Be merciful to the failures, Emily. Satirise wickedness if you must—but pity weakness.'

"He stalked off then, and called school in. I've felt wretched ever since and I won't sleep tonight. But here and now I record this vow, most solemnly, in my diary, *My pen shall heal, not hurt*. And I write it in italics, Early Victorian or not, because I am tremendously in earnest.

"I didn't tear that poem up, though—I couldn't—it really *was* too good to destroy. I put it away in my literary cupboard to read over once in a while for my own enjoyment, but I will never show it to anybody.

"Oh, how I wish I hadn't hurt Mr. Carpenter!

*   *   *

"April 1, 19—

"Something I heard a visitor in Blair Water say today annoyed me very much. Mr. and Mrs. Alec Sawyer, who live in Charlottetown, were in the Post Office when I was there. Mrs. Sawyer is very handsome and fashionable and condescending. I heard her say to her husband, 'How do the natives of this sleepy place continue to live here year in and year out? *I* should go mad. *Nothing* ever happens here.'

"I would dearly have liked to tell her a few things about Blair Water. I could have been sarcastic with a vengeance. But, of course, New Moon people *do not make scenes in public*. So I contented myself with bowing *very coldly* when she spoke to me and *sweeping past* her. I heard Mr. Sawyer say, 'Who is that girl?' and Mrs. Sawyer said, 'She must be that Starr puss—she has the Murray trick of holding her head, all right.'

"The idea of saying 'nothing ever happens here'! Why, things are happening right along—*thrilling* things. I think life here is *extremely* wonderful. We have always so much to laugh and cry and talk about.

"Look at all the things that have happened in Blair Water in just the last three weeks—comedy and tragedy all mixed up together. James Baxter has suddenly stopped speaking to his wife and *nobody knows why. She* doesn't, poor soul, and she is breaking her heart about it. Old Adam Gillian, who hated pretence of any sort, died two weeks ago and his last words were, 'See that there isn't any howling and sniffling at my funeral.' So nobody howled or sniffled. Nobody wanted to, and since he had forbidden it nobody pretended to. There never was such a cheerful funeral in Blair Water. I've seen weddings that were more melancholy—Ella Brice's, for instance. What cast a cloud over hers was that she forgot to put on her white slippers when she dressed, and went down to the parlor in a pair of old, faded, bedroom shoes with holes in the toes. Really, people couldn't have talked more about it if she had gone down without *anything* on. Poor Ella cried all through the wedding supper about it.

"Old Robert Scobie and his half-sister have quarrelled, after living together for thirty years without a fuss, although she is said to be a very aggravating woman. Nothing she did or said ever provoked Robert into an outburst, but it seems that there was just one doughnut left from supper one evening recently, and Robert is very fond of doughnuts. He put it away in the pantry for a bedtime snack, and when he went to get it he found that Matilda had eaten it. He went into a terrible rage, pulled her nose, called her a *she-deviless*, and ordered her out of his house. She has gone to live with her sister at Derry Pond, and Robert is going to bach it. Neither of them will ever forgive the other, Scobie-like, and neither will ever be happy or contented again.

"George Lake was walking home from Derry Pond one moonlit evening two weeks ago, and *all at once* he saw another *very black* shadow going along beside his, on the moonlight snow.

"And there was nothing to cast that shadow.

"He rushed to the nearest house, nearly dead with fright, and they say he will never be the same man again.

"This is the most *dramatic* thing that has happened. It makes me shiver as I write of it. Of course George *must* have been mistaken. But he is a truthful man, and he doesn't drink. I don't know what to think of it.

"Arminius Scobie is a *very mean man* and always buys his wife's hats for her, lest she pay too much for them. They know this in the Shrewsbury stores, and laugh at him. One day last week he was in Jones and McCallum's, buying her a hat, and Mr. Jones told him that if he would *wear the hat* from the store to the station he would let him have it for nothing. Arminius did. It was a quarter of a mile to the station and all the small boys in Shrewsbury ran after him and hooted him. But Arminius didn't care. He had saved three dollars and forty-nine cents.

"*And*, one evening, right here at New Moon, I dropped a soft-boiled egg on Aunt Elizabeth's second-best cashmere dress. That *was* a happening. A kingdom might have been upset in Europe, and it wouldn't have made such a commotion at New Moon.

"So, Mistress Sawyer, you are vastly mistaken. Besides, apart from all happenings, the folks here are interesting in themselves. I don't *like* every one but I find every one interesting—Miss Matty Small, who is forty and wears *outrageous* colors—she wore an old-rose dress and a scarlet hat to church all last summer—old Uncle Reuben Bascom, who is so lazy that he held an umbrella over himself all one rainy night in bed, when the roof began to leak, rather than get out and move the bed—Elder McCloskey, who thought it wouldn't do to say 'pants' in a story he was telling about a missionary, at prayer-meeting, so always said politely 'the clothes of his lower parts'—Amasa Derry, who carried off four prizes at the Exhibition last fall, with vegetables he stole from Ronnie Bascom's field, while Ronnie didn't get one prize—Jimmy Joe Belle, who came here from Derry Pond yesterday to get some lumber 'to beeld a henhouse for my leetle dog'—old Luke Elliott, who is such a systematic fiend that he even draws up a schedule of the year on New Year's day, and charts down all the days he means to get drunk on—*and sticks to it*:—they're all interesting and amusing and delightful.

"There, I've proved Mrs. Alec Sawyer to be so completely wrong that I feel quite kindly towards her, even though she did call me a puss.

"Why don't I like being called a puss, when cats are such nice things? And I like being called *pussy*.

*　　*　　*

"April 28, 19—

"Two weeks ago I sent my very best poem, *Wind Song*, to a magazine in New York, and today it came back with just a little *printed slip* saying, 'We regret we cannot use this contribution.'

"I feel dreadfully. I suppose I can't really write anything that is any good.

"I *can*. That magazine will be *glad* to print my pieces some day!

"I didn't tell Mr. Carpenter I sent it. I wouldn't get any sympathy from him. *He* says that five years from now will be time enough to begin pestering editors. But I *know* that some poems I've read in that very magazine were not a bit better than *Wind Song*.

"I feel more like writing poetry in spring than at any other time. Mr. Carpenter tells me to fight against the impulse. He says spring has been responsible for more trash than anything else in the universe of God.

"Mr. Carpenter's way of talking has a *tang* to it.

"May 1, 19—

"Dean is home. He came to his sister's yesterday and this evening he was here and we walked in the garden, up and down the sun-dial walk, and talked. It was splendid to have him back, with his mysterious green eyes and his nice mouth.

"We had a long conversation. We talked of Algiers and the transmigration of souls and of being cremated and of profiles—Dean says I have a good profile—'pure Greek.' I always like Dean's compliments.

" 'Star o' Morning, how you have grown!' he said. 'I left a child last autumn—and I find a woman!'

"(I will be fourteen in three weeks, and I am tall for my age. Dean seems to be glad of this—quite unlike Aunt Laura who always sighs when she lengthens my dresses, and thinks children grow up too fast.)

" 'So goes time by,' I said, quoting the motto on the sun-dial, and feeling *quite sophisticated.*

" 'You are almost as tall as I am,' he said; and then added *bitterly,* 'to be sure Jarback Priest is of no very stately height.'

"I have always shrunk from referring to his shoulder in any way, but now I said,

"Dean, please don't sneer at yourself like that—not with me, at least. I *never* think of you as Jarback.'

"Dean took my hand and looked right into my eyes as if he were trying to *read my very soul.*

" 'Are you sure of that, Emily? Don't you often wish that I wasn't lame—and crooked?'

" 'For your sake I do,' I answered, ''but as far as I am concerned it doesn't make a bit of difference—and never will.'

" 'And never will!'' Dean repeated the words emphatically. 'If I were sure of that, Emily—if I were only sure of that.'

" 'You *can* be sure of it,' I declared quite warmly. I was vexed because he seemed to doubt it—and yet something in his expression made me feel a little uncomfortable. It suddenly made me think of the time he rescued me from the cliff on Malvern Bay and told me my life belonged to him since he had saved it. I don't like the thought of my life belonging to any one but myself—not *any one,* even Dean, much as I like him. And *in some ways* I like Dean better than any one in the world.

"When it got darker the stars came out and we studied them through Dean's splendid new field-glasses. It was very fascinating. Dean knows all about the stars—it seems to me he knows all about everything. But when I said so, he said,

" 'There is one secret I do not know—I would give everything else I *do* know for it—one secret—perhaps I shall never know it. The way to win—the way to win——'

" 'What?' I asked curiously.

" 'My heart's desire," said Dean dreamily, looking at a shimmering star that seemed to be hung on the very tip of one of the Three Princesses. 'It seems now as desirable and unobtainable as that gem-like star, Emily. But—who knows?'

"I wonder what it is Dean wants so much.

"May 4, 19—

"Dean brought me a lovely portfolio from Paris, and I have copied my favourite verse from *The Fringed Gentian* on the inside of the cover. I will read it over every day and remember my vow to 'climb the Alpine Path.' I begin to see that I will have to do a good bit of scrambling, though I once expected, I think, to soar right up to 'that far-off goal' on shining wings. Mr. Carpenter has banished that fond dream.

" 'Dig in your toes and hang on with your teeth— that's the only way,' he says.

"Last night in bed I thought out some lovely titles for the books I'm going to write in the future—*A Lady of High Degree, True to Faith and Vow, Oh, Rare Pale Margaret* (I got that from Tennyson), *The Caste of Vere de Vere* (ditto) and *A Kingdom by the Sea*.

"Now, if I can only get ideas to match the titles!

"I am writing a story called *The House Among the Rowans*—also a very good title, I think. But the love talk still bothers me. Everything of the kind I write seems so stiff and silly the minute I write it down that it infuriates me. I asked Dean if he could teach me how to write it properly because he promised long ago that he would, but he said I was too young yet—said it in that mysterious way of his which always seems to convey the idea that there is so much more in his words than the mere sound of them expresses. I wish I could speak so *significantly*, because it makes you *very interesting*.

"This evening after school Dean and I began to read

The Alhambra over again, sitting on the stone bench in the garden. That book always makes me feel as if I had opened a little door and stepped straight into fairyland.

" 'How I would love to see the Alhambra!' I said.

" 'We will go to see it sometime—together,' said Dean.

" 'Oh, that would be *lovely*,' I cried. 'Do you think we can ever manage it, Dean?'

"Before Dean could answer I heard Teddy's whistle in Lofty John's bush—the dear little whistle of two short high notes and one long low one, that is *our* signal.

" 'Excuse me—I must go—Teddy's calling me,' I said.

" 'Must you always go when Teddy calls?' asked Dean.

"I nodded and explained,

" 'He only calls like that when he wants me *especially* and I have promised I will always go if I possibly can.'

" '*I* want you *especially*!' said Dean. 'I came up this evening on purpose to read *The Alhambra* with you.'

"Suddenly I felt very unhappy. I wanted to stay with Dean dreadfully, and yet I felt as if I must go to Teddy. Dean looked at me piercingly. Then he shut up *The Alhambra*.

" 'Go,' he said.

"I went—but things seemed spoiled, somehow.

"May 10, 19—

"I have been reading three books Dean lent me this week. One was like a rose garden—very pleasant, but just a little too sweet. And one was like a pine wood on a mountain—full of balsam and tang—I loved it, and yet it filled me with a sort of despair. It was written so beautifully—I can *never* write like that, I feel sure. And one—it was just like a pig-sty. Dean gave me that one by mistake. He was very angry with himself when he found it out—angry and distressed.

" 'Star—Star—I would *never* have given you a book like that—my confounded carelessness—forgive me. That book is a faithful picture of one world—but not your world, thank God—nor any world you will ever be a citizen of. Star, promise me you will forget that book.'

" 'I'll forget it if I can,' I said.

"But I don't know if I can. It was so ugly. I have not been so happy since I read it. I feel as if my hands were soiled somehow and I couldn't wash them clean. And I have another queer feeling, as if *some gate had been shut behind me*, shutting me into a new world I don't quite understand or like, but through which I must travel.

"Tonight I tried to write a description of Dean in my Jimmy-book of character sketches. But I didn't succeed. What I wrote seemed like a photograph—not a portrait. There is something in Dean that is beyond me.

"Dean took a picture of me the other day with his new camera, but he wasn't pleased with it.

" 'It doesn't look like you,' he said, 'but of course one can never photograph starlight.'

"Then he added, quite sharply, I thought,

" 'Tell that young imp of a Teddy Kent to keep your face out of his pictures. He has no business to put *you* into every one he draws.'

" 'He doesn't!' I cried. 'Why, Teddy never made but the one picture of me—the one Aunt Nancy *stole*.'

"I said it quite viciously and unashamed, for I've never forgiven Aunt Nancy for keeping that picture.

" 'He's got *something* of you in every picture,' said Dean stubbornly—'your eyes—the curve of your neck—the tilt of your head—your personality. That's the worst—I don't mind your eyes and curves so much, but I won't have that cub putting a bit of your soul into everything he draws. Probably he doesn't know he's doing it—which makes it all the worse.'

" 'I don't understand you,' I said, *quite haughtily*. 'But Teddy is *wonderful*—Mr. Carpenter says so.'

" 'And Emily of New Moon echoes it! Oh, the kid has talent—he'll do something some day if his morbid mother doesn't ruin his life. But let him keep his pencil and brush off *my* property.'

"Dean laughed as he said it. But I held my head high. I am not anybody's 'property,' not even in fun. And I *never* will be.

"May 12, 19—

"Aunt Ruth and Uncle Wallace and Uncle Oliver were all here this afternoon. I like Uncle Oliver, but I am not much fonder of Aunt Ruth and Uncle Wallace than I ever was. They held some kind of family conclave in the parlour with Aunt Elizabeth and Aunt Laura. Cousin Jimmy was allowed in, but I was excluded, although I feel perfectly certain it had something to do with me. I think Aunt Ruth didn't get her own way, either, for she snubbed me continually all through supper, and said I was growing weedy! Aunt Ruth generally snubs me and Uncle Wallace patronises me. I prefer Aunt Ruth's snubs because I don't have to look as if I liked them. I endured them to a certain point, and then the lid flew off. Aunt Ruth said to me,

" 'Em'ly, don't contradict,' just as she might have spoken to a *mere child*. I looked her right in the eyes and said *coldly*,

" 'Aunt Ruth, I think I am too old to be spoken to in that fashion now.'

" 'You are not too old to be very rude and impertinent,' said Aunt Ruth, with a sniff, 'and if *I* were in Elizabeth's place I would give you a sound box on the ear, Miss.'

"I hate to be Em'ly'd and Miss'd and sniffed at! It seems to me that Aunt Ruth has *all* the Murray faults, and *none* of their virtues.

"Uncle Oliver's son Andrew came with him and is

going to stay for a week. He is four years older than I am.

"May 19, 19—

"This is my birthday. I am fourteen years old today. I wrote a letter 'From myself at fourteen to myself at twenty-four,' sealed it up and put it away in my cupboard, to be opened on my twenty-fourth birthday. I made some predictions in it. I wonder if they will have come to pass when I open it.

"Aunt Elizabeth gave me back all Father's books today. I was so glad. It seems to me that a part of Father is in those books. His name is in each one in his own handwriting, and the notes he made on the margins. They seem like little bits of letters from him. I have been looking over them all the evening, and Father seems so *near* to me again, and I feel both happy and sad.

"One thing spoiled the day for me. In school, when I went up to the blackboard to work a problem, everybody suddenly began to titter. I could not imagine why. Then I discovered that some one had pinned a sheet of foolscap to my back, on which was printed in big, black letters: 'Emily Byrd Starr, *Authoress of The Four-Legged Duck.*' They laughed more than ever when I snatched it off and threw it in the coal-scuttle. It infuriates me when any one ridicules my ambitions like that. I came home angry and sore. But when I had sat on the steps of the summerhouse and looked at one of Cousin Jimmy's big purple pansies for five minutes all my anger went away. Nobody can keep on being angry if she looks into the heart of a pansy for a little while.

"Besides, *the time will come when they will not laugh at me!*

"Andrew went home yesterday. Aunt Elizabeth asked me how I liked him. She never asked me how I liked any one before—my likings were not important enough.

I suppose she is beginning to realize that I am *no longer a child*.

"I said I thought he was good and kind and stupid and uninteresting.

"Aunt Elizabeth was so annoyed she would not speak to me the whole evening. Why? I had to tell the truth. And Andrew *is*.

"May 21, 19—

"Old Kelly was here today for the first time this spring, with a load of shining new tins. He brought me a bag of candies as usual—and teased me about getting married, also as usual. But he seemed to have something on his mind, and when I went to the dairy to get him the drink of milk he had asked for, he followed me.

"'Gurrl dear,' he said mysteriously. 'I met Jarback Praste in the lane. Does he be coming here much?'"

"I cocked my head at the Murray angle.

"'If you mean Mr. Dean Priest,' I said, 'he comes often. He is a particular friend of mine.'

"Old Kelly shook his head.

"'Gurrl dear—I warned ye—niver be after saying I didn't warn ye. I towld ye the day I took ye to Praste Pond niver to marry a Praste. Didn't I now?'

"'Mr. Kelly, you're too ridiculous,' I said—angry and yet feeling it was absurd to be angry with Old Jock Kelly. 'I'm not going to marry anybody. Mr. Priest is old enough to be my father, and I am just a little girl he helps in her studies.'

"Old Kelly gave his head another shake.

"'I know the Prastes, gurrl dear—and when they do be after setting their minds on a thing ye might as well try to turn the wind. This Jarback now—they tell me he's had his eye on ye iver since he fished ye up from the Malvern rocks—he's just biding his time till ye get old enough for coorting. They tell me he's an infidel, and it's well known that whin he was being christened he rached up and clawed the spectacles off av the minister. So what wud ye ixpect? I nadn't be telling ye he's lame and crooked—ye can see that for yerself. Take foolish Ould Kelly's advice and cut loose while there's time. Now, don't be looking at me like the Murrays, gurrl dear. Shure, and it's for your own good I do be spaking.'

"I walked off and left him. One *couldn't* argue with him over such a thing. I *wish* people wouldn't put such ideas into my mind. They stick there like burrs. I won't feel as comfortable with Dean for weeks now, though I know perfectly well every word Old Kelly said was nonsense.

"After Old Kelly went away I came up to my room and wrote a full description of him in a Jimmy-book.

"Ilse has got a new hat trimmed with clouds of blue tulle, and red cherries, with big blue tulle bows under the chin. I did not like it and told her so. She was furious and said I was jealous and hasn't spoken to me for two days. I thought it all over. I knew I was not jealous, but I concluded I had made a mistake. I will never again tell any one a thing like that. It was true but it was not tactful.

"I hope Ilse will have forgiven me by tomorrow. I miss her horribly when she is offended with me. She's such a dear thing and so jolly, and splendid, when she isn't vexed.

"Teddy is a little squiffy with me, too, just now. I *think* it is because Geoff North walked home with me from prayer-meeting last Wednesday night. I *hope* that is the reason. I like to feel that I *have that much power* over Teddy.

"I wonder if I ought to have written that down. But it's *true*.

"If Teddy only knew it, I have been very unhappy and ashamed over that affair. At first, when Geoff singled me out from all the girls, I was quite proud of it. It was the very first time I had had an *escort home*, and Geoff is a town boy, *very handsome and polished*, and all the older girls in Blair Water are quite foolish about him. So I sailed away from the church door with him, feeling as if I had grown up all at once. But we hadn't gone far before I was hating him. He was so *condescending*. He seemed to think I was a simple little country girl who must be quite overwhelmed with the *honour* of his company.

"And that was true at first! *That* was what stung me. To think I had been such a little fool!

"He kept saying, 'Really, you surprise me,' in an affected, drawling kind of way, whenever I made a remark. And he *bored* me. He couldn't talk sensibly about anything. Or else he wouldn't try to with me. I was quite savage by the time we got to New Moon. And then *that insufferable creature* asked me to kiss him!

"I drew myself up—oh, I was Murray clear through at that moment, all right. I *felt* I was looking exactly like Aunt Elizabeth.

" 'I do not kiss young men,' I said disdainfully.

"Geoff laughed and caught my hand.

" 'Why, you little goose, what do you suppose I came home with you for?' he said.

"I pulled my hand away from him, and walked into the house. But before I did that, I did something else.

"*I slapped his face!*

"Then I came up to my room and cried with shame over being insulted, and having been so undignified in resenting it. Dignity is a tradition of New Moon, and I felt that I had been false to it.

"But I think I 'surprised' Geoff North in right good earnest!

"May 24, 19—

"Jennie Strang told me today that Geoff North told

her brother that I was 'a regular spitfire' and he had had enough of me.

"Aunt Elizabeth has found out that Geoff came home with me, and told me today that I would not be 'trusted' to go alone to prayer-meeting again.

"May 25, 19—

"I am sitting here in my room at twilight. The window is open and the frogs are singing of something that happened very long ago. All along the middle garden walk the Gay Folk are holding up great fluted cups of ruby and gold and pearl. It is not raining now, but it rained all day—a rain scented with lilacs. I like all kinds of weather and I like rainy days—soft, misty, rainy days when the Wind Woman just shakes the tops of the spruces gently; and wild, tempestuous, streaming rainy days. I like being shut in by the rain—I like to hear it thudding on the roof, and beating on the panes and pouring off the eaves, while the Wind Woman skirls like a mad old witch in the woods, and through the garden.

"Still, if it rains when I want to go anywhere I growl just as much as anybody!

"An evening like this always makes me think of that spring Father died, three years ago, and that dear, little, old house down at Maywood. I've never been back since. I wonder if any one is living in it now. And if Adam-and-Eve and the Rooster Pine and the Praying Tree are just the same. And who is sleeping in my old room there, and if any one is loving the little birches and playing with the Wind Woman in the spruce barrens. Just as I wrote the words 'spruce barrens' an old memory came back to me. One spring evening, when I was eight years old, I was running about the barrens playing hide-and-seek with the Wind Woman, and I found a little hollow between two spruces that was just carpeted with tiny, bright-green leaves, when everything else was still brown and faded. They were so beautiful that *the flash* came as I looked at them—it was the very first time it ever came to me. I suppose that is why I remember those little green leaves so distinctly. No one else remembers them—perhaps no one else ever saw them. I have forgotten other leaves, but I remember them every spring and with each remembrance I feel again the wonder-moment they gave me."

3
In the Watches of the Night

Some of us can recall the exact time in which we reached certain milestones on life's road—the wonderful hour when we passed from childhood to girlhood—the enchanted, beautiful—or perhaps the shattering and horrible—hour when girlhood was suddenly womanhood—the chilling hour when we faced the fact that youth was definitely behind us—the peaceful, sorrowful hour of the realisation of age. Emily Starr never forgot the night when she passed the first milestone, and left childhood behind her for ever.

Every experience enriches life and the deeper such an experience, the greater the richness it brings. That night of horror and mystery and strange delight ripened her mind and heart like the passage of years.

It was a night early in July. The day had been one of intense heat. Aunt Elizabeth had suffered so much from it that she decided she would not go to prayer-meeting. Aunt Laura and Cousin Jimmy and Emily went. Before leaving Emily asked and obtained Aunt Elizabeth's permission to go home with Ilse Burnley after meeting, and spend the night. This was a rare treat. Aunt Elizabeth did not approve of all-night absences as a general thing.

But Dr. Burnley had to be away, and his housekeeper was temporarily laid up with a broken ankle. Ilse had asked Emily to come over for the night, and Emily was to be permitted to go. Ilse did not know this—hardly hoped for it, in fact—but was to be informed at prayer-meeting. If Ilse had not been late Emily would have told her before meeting "went in," and the mischances of the night would probably have been averted; but Ilse, as usual, *was* late, and everything else followed in course.

Emily sat in the Murray pew, near the top of the church by the window that looked out into the grove of fir and maple that surrounded the little white church. This prayer-meeting was not the ordinary weekly sprinkling of a faithful few. It was a "special meeting," held in view of the approaching communion Sunday, and the speaker was not young, earnest Mr. Johnson, to whom Emily always liked to listen, in spite of her blunder at the Ladies' Aid Supper, but an itinerant evangelist lent by Shrewsbury for one night. His fame brought out a churchful of people, but most of the audience declared afterwards that they would much rather have heard their own Mr. Johnson. Emily looked at him with her level, critical gaze, and decided that he was oily and unspiritual. She heard him through a prayer, and thought,

"Giving God good advice, and abusing the devil isn't praying."

She listened to his discourse for a few minutes and made up her mind that he was blatant and illogical and sensational, and then proceeded, coolly, to shut mind and ears to him and disappear into dreamland— something which she could generally do at will when anxious to escape from discordant realities.

Outside, moonlight was still sifting in a rain of silver

through the firs and maples, though an ominous bank of cloud was making up in the northwest, and repeated rumblings of thunder came on the silent air of the hot summer night—a windless night for the most part, though occasionally a sudden breath that seemed more like a sigh than a breeze brushed through the trees, and set their shadows dancing in weird companies. There was something strange about the night in its mingling of placid, accustomed beauty with the omens of rising storm, that intrigued Emily, and she spent half the time of the evangelist's address in composing a mental description of it for her Jimmy-book. The rest of the time she studied such of the audience as were within her range of vision.

This was something that Emily never wearied of, in public assemblages, and the older she grew the more she liked it. It was fascinating to study those varied faces, and speculate on the histories written in mysterious hieroglyphics over them. They had all their inner, secret lives, those men and women, known to no one but themselves and God. Others could only guess at them, and Emily loved this game of guessing. At times it seemed veritably to her that it was more than guessing—that in some intense moments she could pass into their souls and read therein hidden motives and passions that were, perhaps, a mystery even to their possessors. It was never easy for Emily to resist the temptation to do this when the power came, although she never yielded to it without an uneasy feeling that she was committing trespass. It was quite a different thing from soaring on the wings of fancy into an ideal world of creation—quite different from the exquisite, unearthly beauty of "the flash"; neither of these gave her any moments of pause or doubt. But to slip on tiptoe through some momentarily unlatched door, as it were, and catch a glimpse of masked, unuttered, unutterable things in the hearts and souls of others, was something that always brought, along with its sense of power, a sense of the forbidden—a sense even of sacrilege. Yet Emily did not know if she would ever be able to resist the allure of it—she had always peered through the door and seen the things before she realised that she was doing it. They were nearly always terrible things. Secrets are generally terrible. Beauty is not often hidden—only ugliness and deformity.

"Elder Forsyth would have been a persecutor in old times," she thought. "He has the face of one. This very minute he is loving the preacher because he is describing hell, and Elder Forsyth thinks all his enemies will go there. Yes, that is why he is looking pleased. I think Mrs. Bowes flies off on a broomstick o' nights. She *looks* it. Four hundred years ago she would have been a witch, and Elder Forsyth would have burned her at the stake. She hates everybody—it must be terrible to hate everybody—to have your soul full of hatred. I must try to describe such a person in my Jimmy-book. I wonder if hate has driven *all* love out of her soul, or if there is a little bit left in it for any one or any thing. If there is it might save her. That would be a good idea for a story. I must jot it down before I go to bed—I'll borrow a bit of paper from Ilse. No—here's a bit in my hymn-book. I'll write it now.

"I wonder what all these people would say if they were suddenly asked what they wanted most, and *had* to answer truthfully. I wonder how many of these husbands and wives would like a change? Chris Farrar and Mrs. Chris would—everybody knows that. I can't think why I feel so sure that James Beatty and *his* wife would, too. They *seem* to be quite contented with each other—but once I saw her look at him when she did not know any one was watching—oh, it seemed to me I saw right into her soul, through her eyes, and she hated him—and feared him. She is sitting there now, beside him, little and thin and dowdy, and her face is grey and her hair is faded—but she, herself, is one red flame of rebellion. What *she* wants most is to be free from him—or just to *strike back once*. That would satisfy her.

"There's Dean—I wonder what brought him to prayer meeting? His face is very solemn, but his eyes are mocking Mr. Sampson—what's that Mr. Sampson's saying?—oh, something about the wise virgins. I hate the wise virgins—I think they were horribly selfish. They *might* have given the poor foolish ones a little oil. I don't believe Jesus meant to praise them any more than He meant to praise the unjust steward—I think He was just trying to warn foolish people that they must not *be* careless, and foolish, because if they were, prudent, selfish folks would never help them out. I wonder if it's very wicked to feel that I'd rather be outside with the foolish ones trying to help and comfort them, than inside feasting with the wise ones. It would be *more interesting*, too.

"There's Mrs. Kent and Teddy. Oh, *she* wants something terribly—I don't know what it is but it's something she can never get, and the hunger for it goads her night and day. That is why she holds Teddy so closely—I know. But I don't know what it is that makes her so different from other women. I can never get a peep into *her* soul—she shuts every one out—the door is never unlatched.

"What do *I* want most? It is to climb the Alpine Path to the very top,

> "'And write upon its shining scroll
> A woman's humble name.'

"We're all hungry. We all want some bread of life—but Mr. Sampson can't give it to us. I wonder what *he* wants most? His soul is so muggy I can't see into it. He has a lot of sordid wants—he doesn't want *anything* enough to dominate him. Mr. Johnson wants to help people and preach truth—he really does. And Aunt Janey wants most of all to see the whole heathen world Christianized. Her soul hasn't any dark wishes in it. I know what Mr. Carpenter wants—his one lost chance again. Katherine Morris wants her youth back—she hates us younger girls *because* we are young. Old Malcolm Strang just wants to live—just one more year—always just one more year—just to live—just not to die. It must be horrible to have nothing to live for except just to escape dying. Yet he believes in heaven—he thinks he will go there. If he could see my flash just once he wouldn't hate the thought of dying so, poor old man. And Mary Strang wants to die—before something terrible she is afraid of tortures her to death. They say it's cancer. There's Mad Mr. Morrison up in the gallery— we all know what *he* wants—to find his Annie. Tom Sibley wants the moon, I think—and knows he can never get it—that's why people say he's not all there. Amy Crabbe wants Max Terry to come back to her— nothing else matters to her.

"I must write all these things down in my Jimmy-book tomorrow. They are fascinating—but, after all, I like writing of beautiful things better. Only—these things have a *tang* beautiful things don't have some way. Those woods out there—how wonderful they are in their silver and shadow. The moonlight is doing strange things to the tombstones—it makes even the ugly ones beautiful. But it's terribly hot—it is smothering here— and those thunder-growls are coming nearer. I hope Ilse and I will get home before the storm breaks. Oh, Mr. Sampson, Mr. Sampson, God isn't an angry God— you don't know anything about Him if you say that— He's sorrowful, I'm sure, when we're foolish and wicked, but He doesn't fly into tantrums. Your God and Ellen Green's God are exactly alike. I'd like to get up and tell you so, but it isn't a Murray tradition to sass back in church. You make God ugly—and He's beautiful. I hate you for making God ugly, you fat little man."

Whereupon Mr. Sampson, who had several times noted Emily's intent, probing gaze, and thought he was impressing her tremendously with a sense of her unsaved condition, finished with a final urgent whoop of entreaty, and sat down. The audience in the close, oppressive atmosphere of the crowded, lamplit church gave an audible sigh of relief, and scarcely waited for the hymn and benediction before crowding out to purer air. Emily, caught in the current, and parted from Aunt Laura, was swept out by way of the choir door to the left of the pulpit. It was some time before she could disentangle herself from the throng and hurry around to the front where she expected to meet Ilse. Here was another dense, though rapidly thinning crowd, in which she found no trace of Ilse. Suddenly Emily noticed that she did not have her hymnbook. Hastily she dashed back to the choir door. She must have left her hymnbook in the pew—and it would never do to leave it there. In it she had placed for safekeeping a slip of paper on which she had furtively jotted down some fragmentary notes during the last hymn—a rather biting description of scrawny Miss Potter in the choir—a couple of satiric sentences regarding Mr. Sampson himself—and a few random fancies which she desired most of all to hide because there was in them something of dream and vision which would have made the reading of them by alien eyes a sacrilege.

Old Jacob Banks, the sexton, a little blind and more than a little deaf, was turning out the lamps as she went in. He had reached the two on the wall behind the pulpit. Emily caught her hymn-book from the rack—her slip of paper was not in it. By the faint gleam of light, as Jacob Banks turned out the last lamp, she saw it on the floor, under the seat of the pew in front. She kneeled down and reached after it. As she did so Jacob went out and locked the choir door. Emily did not notice his going—the church was still faintly illuminated by the moon that as yet outrode the rapidly climbing thunderheads. That was not the right slip of paper after all—*where* could it be?—oh, here, at last. She caught it up and ran to the door which would not open.

For the first time Emily realised that Jacob Banks had gone—that she was alone in the church. She wasted time trying to open the door—then in calling Mr. Banks. Finally she ran down the aisle into the front porch. As she did so she heard the last buggy turn grindingly at the gate and drive away: at the same time the moon was suddenly swallowed up by the black clouds and the church was engulfed in darkness—close, hot, smothering, almost tangible darkness. Emily screamed in sudden panic—beat on the door—frantically twisted the handle—screamed again. Oh, everybody could not have gone—surely somebody would hear her! "Aunt Laura—"Cousin Jimmy"—"Ilse"—then finally in a wail of despair—"Oh, Teddy—Teddy!"

A blue-white stream of lightning swept the porch, followed by a crash of thunder. One of the worst storms in Blair Water annals had begun—and Emily Starr was locked alone in the dark church in the maple woods—she, who had always been afraid of thunderstorms with a reasonless, instinctive fear which she could never banish and only partially control.

She sank, quivering, on a step of the gallery stairs, and huddled there in a heap. Surely some one would come back when it was discovered she was missing. But *would* it be discovered? Who would miss her? Aunt Laura and Cousin Jimmy would suppose she was with Ilse, as had been arranged. Ilse, who had evidently gone, believing that Emily was not coming with her, would suppose she had gone home to New Moon. Nobody knew where she was—nobody would come back for her. She must stay here in this horrible, lonely, black, echoing place—for now the church she knew so well and loved for its old associations of Sunday School and song and homely faces of dear friends had become a ghostly, alien place full of haunting terrors. There was no escape. The windows could not be opened. The church was ventilated by transom-like panes near the top of them, which were opened and shut by pulling a wire. She could not get up to them, and she could not have got through them if she had.

She cowered down on the step, shuddering from head to foot. By now the thunder and lightning were almost incessant: rain blew against the windows, not in drops but sheets, and intermittent volleys of hail bombarded them. The wind had risen suddenly with the storm and shrieked around the church. It was not her old dear friend of childhood, the bat-winged, misty "Wind Woman," but a legion of yelling witches. "The Prince of the Power of the Air rules the wind," she had heard Mad Mr. Morrison say once. Why should she think of Mad Mr. Morrison now? How the windows rattled as if demon riders of the storm were shaking them! She had heard a wild tale of some one hearing the organ play in the empty church one night several years ago. *Suppose it began playing now!* No fancy seemed too grotesque or horrible to come true. Didn't the stairs creak? The blackness between the lightnings was so intense that it looked *thick.* Emily was frightened of it touching her and buried her face in her lap.

Presently, however, she got a grip on herself and began to reflect that she was not living up to Murray traditions. Murrays were not supposed to go to pieces like this. Murrays were not foolishly panicky in thunderstorms. Those old Murrays sleeping in the private graveyard across the pond would have scorned her as a degenerate descendant. Aunt Elizabeth would have said that it was the Starr coming out in her. She must be brave: after all, she had lived through worse hours than this—the night she had eaten of Lofty John's poisoned apple*—the afternoon she had fallen over the rocks of Malvern Bay. This had come so suddenly on her that she had been in the throes of terror before she

*See *Emily of New Moon.*

could brace herself against it. She *must* pick up. Nothing dreadful was going to happen to her—nothing worse than staying all night in the church. In the morning she could attract the attention of some one passing. She had been here over an hour now, and nothing had happened to her—unless indeed her hair had turned white, as she understood hair sometimes did. There had been such a funny, crinkly, crawly feeling at the roots of it at times. Emily held out her long braid, ready for the next flash. When it came she saw that her hair was still black. She sighed with relief and began to perk up. The storm was passing. The thunderpeals were growing fainter and fewer, though the rain continued to fall and the wind to drive and shriek around the church, whining through the big keyhole eerily.

Emily straightened her shoulders and cautiously let down her feet to a lower step. She thought she had better try to get back into the church. If another cloud came up, the steeple might be struck—steeples were always getting struck, she remembered: it might come crashing down on the porch right over her. She would go in and sit down in the Murray pew: she would be cool and sensible and collected: she was ashamed of her panic—but it *had* been terrible.

All around her now was a soft, heavy darkness, still with that same eerie sensation of something you could touch, born perhaps of the heat and humidity of the July night. The porch was so small and narrow—she would not feel so smothered and oppressed in the church.

She put out her hand to grasp a stair rail and pull herself to her cramped feet. Her hand touched—not the stair rail—merciful heavens, what was it?—something *hairy*—Emily's shriek of horror froze on her lips—padding footsteps passed down the steps beside her; a flash of lightning came and at the bottom of the steps was a huge black dog, which had turned and was looking up at her before he was blotted out in the returning darkness. Even then for a moment she saw his eyes blazing redly at her, like a fiend's.

Emily's hair roots began to crawl and crinkle again— a very large, very cold caterpillar began to creep slowly up her spine. She could not have moved a muscle had life depended on it. She could not even cry out. The only thing she could think of at first was the horrible demon hound of the Manx Castle in *Peveril of the Peak*. For a few minutes her terror was so great that it turned her physically sick. Then, with an effort that was unchild-like in its determination—I think it was at that moment Emily wholly ceased to be a child—she recovered her self-control. She *would not* yield to fear—she set her teeth and clenched her trembling hands; she *would* be brave—sensible. That was only a commonplace Blair Water dog which had followed its owner—some rap-scallion boy—into the gallery, and got itself left behind. The thing had happened before. A flash of lightning showed her that the porch was empty. Evidently the dog had gone into the church. Emily decided that she would stay where she was. She had recovered from her panic, but she did not want to feel the sudden touch of a cold nose or a hairy flank in the darkness. She could never forget the awfulness of the moment when she *had* touched the creature.

It must be all of twelve o'clock now—it had been ten when the meeting came out. The noise of the storm had for the most part died away. The drive and shriek of the wind came occasionally, but between its gusts there was a silence, broken only by the diminishing raindrops. Thunder still muttered faintly and lightning came at frequent intervals, but of a paler, gentler flame— not the rending glare that had seemed to wrap the very building in intolerable blue radiance, and scorch her eyes. Gradually her heart began to beat normally. The power of rational thought returned. She did not like her predicament, but she began to find dramatic possibilities in it. Oh, what a chapter for her diary—or her Jimmy-book—and, beyond it, for that novel she would write some day! It was a situation expressly shaped for the heroine—who must, of course, be rescued by the hero. Emily began constructing the scene—adding to it—intensifying it—hunting for words to express it. This was rather—interesting—after all. Only she wished she knew just where the dog was. How weirdly the pale lightning gleamed on the gravestones which she could see through the porch window opposite her! How strange the familiar valley beyond looked in the recurrent illuminations! How the wind moaned and sighed and complained—but it was her own Wind Woman again. The Wind Woman was one of her childish fancies that she had carried over into maturity, and it comforted her now, with a sense of ancient companionship. The wild riders of the storm were gone—her fairy friend had come back. Emily gave a sigh that was almost of contentment. The worst was over—and really, hadn't she behaved pretty well? She began to feel quite self-respecting again.

All at once Emily knew she was not alone!

How she knew it she could not have told. She had heard nothing—seen nothing—felt nothing: and yet she knew, beyond all doubt or dispute, that there was a Presence in the darkness above her on the stairs.

She turned and looked up. It was horrible to look, but it was less horrible to feel that—Something—was in front of you than that it was behind you. She stared with wildly dilated eyes into the darkness, but she could see nothing. Then—she heard a low laugh above her—a laugh that almost made her heart stop beating— the very dreadful, inhuman laughter of the unsound in mind. She did not need the lightning flash that came then to tell her that Mad Mr. Morrison was somewhere on the stairs above her. But it came—she saw him—she

felt as if she were sinking in some icy gulf of coldness—
she could not even scream.

The picture of him, etched on her brain by the
lightning, never left her. He was crouched five steps
above her, with his gray head thrust forward. She saw
the frenzied gleam of his eyes—the fang-like yellow
teeth exposed in a horrible smile—the long, thin, blood-
red hand outstretched towards her, almost touching
her shoulder.

Sheer panic shattered Emily's trance. She bounded
to her feet with a piercing scream of terror.

"Teddy! Teddy! Save me!" she shrieked madly.

She did not know why she called for Teddy—she did
not even realise that she *had* called him—she only
remembered it afterwards, as one might recall the
waking shriek in a nightmare—she only knew that she
must have help—that she would die if that awful hand
touched her. *It must not touch her.*

She made a mad spring down the steps, rushed into
the church, and up the aisle. She must hide before the
next flash came—but not in the Murray pew. He might
look for her there. She dived into one of the middle
pews and crouched down in its corner on the floor. Her
body was bathed in an ice-cold perspiration. She was
wholly in the grip of uncontrollable terror. All she
could think of was that it must not touch her—that
blood-red hand of the mad old man.

Moments passed that seemed like years. Presently
she heard footsteps—footsteps that came and went yet
seemed to approach her slowly. Suddenly she knew
what he was doing. He was going into every pew, not
waiting for the lightning, to feel about for her. He *was*
looking for her, then—she had heard that sometimes
he followed young girls, thinking they were Annie. If
he caught them he held them with one hand and
stroked their hair and faces fondly with the other,
mumbling foolish, senile endearments. He had never
harmed any one, but he had never let any one go until

she was rescued by some other person. It was said that Mary Paxton of Derry Pond had never been quite the same again: her nerves never recovered from the shock.

Emily knew that it was only a question of time before he would reach the pew where she crouched—feeling about with those hands! All that kept her senses in her frozen body was the thought that if she lost consciousness those hands would touch her—hold her—caress her. The next lightning flash showed him entering the adjoining pew. Emily sprang up and out and rushed to the other side of the church. She hid again: he would search her out, but she could again elude him: this might go on all night: a madman's strength would outlast hers: at last she might fall exhausted and he would pounce on her.

For what seemed hours to Emily, this mad game of hide-and-seek lasted. It was in reality about half an hour. She was hardly a rational creature at all, any more than her demented pursuer. She was merely a crouching, springing, shrieking thing of horror. Time after time he hunted her out with his cunning, implacable patience. The last time she was near one of the porch doors, and in desperation she sprang through it and slammed it in his face. With the last ounce of her strength she tried to hold the knob from turning in his grasp. And as she strove she heard—was she dreaming? —Teddy's voice calling to her from the steps outside the outer door.

"Emily—Emily—are you there?"

She did not know how he had come—she did not wonder—she only knew he *was* there!

"Teddy, I'm locked in the church!" she shrieked— "and Mad Mr. Morrison is here—oh—quick—quick— save me—save me!"

"The key of the door is hanging up in there on a nail at the right side!" shouted Teddy. "Can you get it and unlock the door? If you can't I'll smash the porch window."

The clouds broke at that moment and the porch was filled with moonlight. In it she saw plainly the big key, hanging high on the wall beside the front door. She dashed at it and caught it as Mad Mr. Morrison wrenched open the door and sprang into the porch, his dog behind him. Emily unlocked the outer door and stumbled out into Teddy's arms just in time to elude that outstretched, blood-red hand. She heard Mad Mr. Morrison give a wild, eerie shriek of despair as she escaped him.

Sobbing, shaking, she clung to Teddy.

"Oh, Teddy, take me away—take me quick—oh, don't let him touch me, Teddy—don't let him touch me!"

Teddy swung her behind him and faced Mad Mr. Morrison on the stone step.

"How dare you frighten her so?" he demanded angrily.

Mad Mr. Morrison smiled deprecatingly in the moonlight. All at once he was not wild or violent—only a heart-broken old man who sought his own.

"I want Annie," he mumbled. "Where is Annie? I thought I had found her in there. I only wanted to find my beautiful Annie."

"Annie isn't here," said Teddy, tightening his hold on Emily's cold little hand.

"Can you tell me where Annie is?" entreated Mad Mr. Morrison, wistfully. "Can you tell me where my dark-haired Annie is?"

Teddy was furious with Mad Mr. Morrison for frightening Emily, but the old man's piteous entreaty touched him—and the artist in him responded to the values of the picture presented against the background of the white, moonlit church. He thought he would like to paint Mad Mr. Morrison as he stood there, tall and gaunt, in his gray "duster" coat, with his long white hair and beard, and the ageless quest in his hollow, sunken eyes.

"No—no—I don't know where she is," he said gently, "but I think you will find her sometime."

Mad Mr. Morrison sighed.

"Oh, yes. Sometime I will overtake her. Come, my dog, we will seek her."

Followed by his old black dog he went down the steps, across the green and down the long, wet, tree-shadowed road. So going, he passed out of Emily's life. She never saw Mad Mr. Morrison again. But she looked after him understandingly, and forgave him. To himself he was not the repulsive old man he seemed to her: he was a gallant young lover seeking his lost and lovely bride. The pitiful beauty of his quest intrigued her, even in the shaking reaction from her hour of agony.

"Poor Mr. Morrison," she sobbed, as Teddy half led, half carried her to one of the old flat gravestones at the side of the church.

They sat there until Emily recovered composure and managed to tell her tale—or the outlines of it. She felt she could never tell—perhaps not even write in a Jimmy-book—the whole of its racking horror. *That* was beyond words.

"And to think," she sobbed, "that the key was there all the time. I never knew it."

"Old Jacob Banks always locks the front door with its big key on the inside, and then hangs it up on that nail," said Teddy. "He locks the choir door with a little key, which he takes home. He has always done that since the time, three years ago, when he lost the big key and was weeks before he found it."

Suddenly Emily awoke to the strangeness of Teddy's coming.

"How did you happen to come, Teddy?"

"Why, I heard you call me," he said. "You did call me, didn't you?"

"Yes," said Emily, slowly, "I called for you when I saw Mad Mr. Morrison first. But, Teddy, you couldn't have heard me—you *couldn't*. The Tansy Patch is a mile from here."

"I *did* hear you," said Teddy, stubbornly. "I was

asleep and it woke me up. You called 'Teddy, Teddy, save me'—it was your voice as plain as I ever heard it in my life. I got right up and hurried on my clothes and came here as fast as I could."

"How did you know I was here?"

"Why—I don't know," said Teddy confusedly. "I didn't stop to think—I just seemed to *know* you were in the church when I heard you calling me, and I must get here as quick as I could. It's—it's all—funny," he concluded lamely.

"It's—it's—it frightens me a little." Emily shivered. "Aunt Elizabeth says I have second sight—you remember Ilse's mother? Mr. Carpenter says I'm psychic—I don't know just what that means, but think I'd rather not be it."

She shivered again. Teddy thought she was cold and, having nothing else to put around her, put his arm—somewhat tentatively, since Murray pride and Murray dignity might be outraged. Emily was not cold in body, but a little chill had blown over her soul. Something supernatural—some mystery she could not understand—had brushed too near her in that strange summoning. Involuntarily she nestled a little closer to Teddy, acutely conscious of the boyish tenderness she sensed behind the aloofness of his boyish shyness. Suddenly she knew that she liked Teddy better than anybody—better even than Aunt Laura or Ilse or Dean.

Teddy's arm tightened a little.

"Anyhow, I'm glad I got here in time," he said. "If I hadn't that crazy old man might have frightened you to death."

They sat so for a few minutes in silence. Everything seemed very wonderful and beautiful—and a little unreal. Emily thought she must be in a dream, or in one of her own wonder tales. The storm had passed, and the moon was shining clearly once more. The cool fresh air was threaded with beguiling voices—the fitful voice of raindrops falling from the shaken boughs of

the maple woods behind them—the freakish voice of
the Wind Woman around the white church—the far-off,
intriguing voice of the sea—and, still finer and rarer,
the little, remote, detached voices of the night. Emily
heard them all, more with the ears of her soul than of
her body, it seemed, as she had never heard them
before. Beyond were fields and groves and roads,
pleasantly suggestive and elusive, as if brooding over
elfish secrets in the moonlight. Silver-white daisies
were nodding and swaying all over the graveyard above
the graves remembered and graves forgotten. An owl
laughed delightfully to itself in the old pine. At the
magical sound Emily's mystic flash swept over her,
swaying her like a strong wind. She felt as if she and
Teddy were all alone in a wonderful new world, created for themselves only out of youth and mystery and
delight. They seemed, themselves, to be part of the
faint, cool fragrance of the night, of the owl's laughter,
of the daisies blowing in the shadowy air.

As for Teddy, he was thinking that Emily looked very
sweet in the pale moonshine, with her fringed, mysterious eyes and the little dark love-curls clinging to her
ivory neck. He tightened his arm a little more—and
still Murray pride and Murray dignity made not a
particle of protest.

"Emily," whispered Teddy, "you're the sweetest girl
in the world."

The words have been said so often by so many
millions of lads to so many millions of lasses, that they
ought to be worn to tatters. But when you hear them
for the first time, in some magic hour of your teens,
they are as new and fresh and wondrous as if they had
just drifted over the hedges of Eden. Madam, whoever
you are, and however old you are, be honest, and
admit that the first time you heard those words on the
lips of some shy sweetheart, was the great moment of
your life. Emily thrilled, from the crown of her head to
the toes of her slippered feet, with a sensation of

hitherto unknown and almost terrifying sweetness—a sensation that was to sense what her "flash" was to spirit. It is quite conceivable and not totally reprehensible that the next thing that happened might have been a kiss. Emily thought Teddy was going to kiss her: Teddy knew he was: and the odds are that he wouldn't have had his face slapped as Geoff North had had.

But it was not to be. A shadow that had slipped in at the gate and drifted across the wet grass, halted beside them, and touched Teddy's shoulder, just as he bent his glossy black head. He looked up, startled. Emily looked up. Mrs. Kent was standing there, bare-headed, her scarred face clear in the moonlight, looking at them tragically.

Emily and Teddy both stood up so suddenly that they seemed veritably to have been jerked to their feet. Emily's fairy world vanished like a dissolving bubble. She was in a different world altogether—an absurd, ridiculous one. Yes, ridiculous. Everything had suddenly become ridiculous. *Could* anything be more ridiculous than to be caught here with Teddy, *by his mother,* at two o'clock at night—what was that horrid word she had lately heard for the first time?—oh, yes, *spooning*—that was it—spooning on George Horton's eighty-year-old tombstone? That was how other people would look at it. How could a thing be so beautiful one moment and so absurd the next? She was one horrible scorch of shame from head to feet. And Teddy—she knew Teddy was feeling like a fool.

To Mrs. Kent it was not ridiculous—it was dreadful. To her abnormal jealousy the incident had the most sinister significance. She looked at Emily with her hollow, hungry eyes.

"So you are trying to steal my son from me," she said. "He is all I have and you are trying to steal him."

"Oh, Mother, for goodness' sake, be sensible!" muttered Teddy.

"He—he tells me to be sensible," Mrs. Kent echoed tragically to the moon. "Sensible!"

"Yes, sensible," said Teddy angrily. "There's nothing to make such a fuss about. Emily was locked in the church by accident and Mad Mr. Morrison was there, too, and nearly frightened her to death. I came to let her out and we were sitting here for a few minutes until she got over her fright and was able to walk home. That's all."

"How did you know she was here?" demanded Mrs. Kent.

How indeed! This was a hard question to answer. The truth sounded like a silly, stupid invention. Nevertheless, Teddy told it.

"She called me," he said bluntly.

"And you heard her—a mile away. Do you expect me to believe that?" said Mrs. Kent, laughing wildly.

Emily had by this time recovered her poise. At no time in her life was Emily Byrd Starr ever disconcerted for long. She drew herself up proudly and in the dim light, in spite of her Starr features, she looked much as Elizabeth Murray must have looked over thirty years before.

"Whether you believe it or not it is true, Mrs. Kent," she said haughtily. "I am not stealing your son—I do not want him—he can go."

"I'm going to take you home first, Emily," said Teddy. He folded his arms and threw back his head and tried to look as stately as Emily. He felt that he was a dismal failure at it, but it imposed on Mrs. Kent. She began to cry.

"Go—go," she said. "Go to her—desert me."

Emily was thoroughly angry now. If this irrational woman persisted in making a scene, very well: a scene she should have.

"I won't let him take me home," she said, freezingly. "Teddy, go with your mother."

"Oh, you command him, do you? He must do as you

tell him, must he?" cried Mrs. Kent, who now seemed to lose all control of herself. Her tiny form was shaken with violent sobs. She wrung her hands.

"He shall choose for himself," she cried. "He shall go with you—or come with me. Choose, Teddy, for yourself. You shall not do her bidding. Choose!"

She was fiercely dramatic again, as she lifted her hand and pointed it at poor Teddy.

Teddy was feeling as miserable and impotently angry as any male creature does when two women are quarrelling about him in his presence. He wished himself a thousand miles away. What a mess to be in—and to be made ridiculous like this before Emily! Why on earth couldn't his mother behave like other boys' mothers? Why must she be so intense and exacting? He knew Blair Water gossip said she was "a little touched." He did not believe that. But—but—well, in short here *was* a mess. You came back to that every time. What on earth was he to do? If he took Emily home he knew his mother would cry and pray for days. On the other hand to desert Emily after her dreadful experience in the church, and leave her to traverse that lonely road alone was unthinkable. But Emily now dominated the situation. She was very angry, with the icy anger of old Hugh Murray that did not dissipate itself in idle bluster, but went straight to the point.

"You are a foolish, selfish woman," she said, "and you will make your son hate you."

"Selfish! You call me selfish," sobbed Mrs. Kent. "I live only for Teddy—he is all I have to live for."

"You *are* selfish." Emily was standing straight: her eyes had gone black: her voice was cutting: "the Murray look" was on her face, and in the pale moonlight it was a rather fearsome thing. She wondered, as she spoke, how she knew certain things. But she *did* know them. "You think you love him—it is only yourself you love. You are determined to spoil his life. You won't let him go to Shrewsbury because it will hurt you to let him go away from you. You have let your jealousy of everything he cares for eat your heart out, and master you. You won't bear a little pain for his sake. You are not a mother at all. Teddy has a great talent—every one says so. You ought to be proud of him—you ought to give him his chance. But you won't—and some day he will hate you for it—yes, he will."

"Oh, no, no," moaned Mrs. Kent. She held up her hands as if to ward off a blow and shrank back against Teddy. "Oh, you are cruel—cruel. You don't know what I've suffered—you don't know what ache is always at my heart. He is all I have—all. I have nothing else—not even a memory. You don't understand. I can't—I can't give him up."

"If you let your jealousy ruin his life you will lose him," said Emily inexorably. She had always been afraid of Mrs. Kent. Now she was suddenly no longer afraid of her—she knew she would never be afraid of her again. "You hate everything he cares for—you hate his friends and his dog and his drawing. You know you do. But you can't keep him that way, Mrs. Kent. And you will find it out when it is too late. Good-night, Teddy. Thank you again for coming to my rescue. Good-night, Mrs. Kent."

Emily's good-night was very final. She turned and stalked across the green without another glance, holding her head high. Down the wet road she marched— at first very angry—then, as anger ebbed, very tired— oh, horribly tired. She discovered that she was fairly shaking with weariness. The emotions of the night had exhausted her, and now—what to do? She did not like the idea of going home to New Moon. Emily felt that she could never face outraged Aunt Elizabeth if the various scandalous doings of this night should be discovered. She turned in at the gate of Dr. Burnley's house. His doors were never locked. Emily slipped into the front hall as the dawn began to whiten in the sky and curled up on the lounge behind the staircase.

There was no use in waking Ilse. She would tell her the whole story in the morning and bind her to secrecy—all, at least, except one thing Teddy had said, and the episode of Mrs. Kent. One was too beautiful, and the other too disagreeable to be talked about. Of course, Mrs. Kent wasn't like other women and there was no use in feeling too badly about it. Nevertheless, she had wrecked and spoiled a frail, beautiful something—she had blotched with absurdity a moment that should have been eternally lovely. And she had, of course, made poor Teddy feel like an ass. *That*, in the last analysis, was what Emily really could not forgive.

As she drifted off to sleep she recalled drowsily the events of that bewildering night—her imprisonment in the lonely church—the horror of touching the dog—the worse horror of Mad Mr. Morrison's pursuit—her rapture of relief at Teddy's voice—the brief little moonlit idyll in the graveyard—of all places for an idyll! —the tragicomic advent of poor morbid, jealous Mrs. Kent.

"I hope I wasn't too hard on her," thought Emily as she drifted into slumber. "If I was I'm sorry. I'll have to write it down as a bad deed in my diary. I feel somehow as if I'd grown up all at once tonight—yesterday seems years away. But what a chapter it will make for my diary. I'll write it all down—all but Teddy's saying I was the sweetest girl in the world. *That's* too—dear—to write. I'll—just—*remember* it."

4
"As Ithers See Us"

Emily had finished mopping up the kitchen floor at New Moon and was absorbed in sanding it in the beautiful and complicated "herring-bone pattern" which was one of the New Moon traditions, having been invented, so it was said, by great-great-grandmother of "Here I stay" fame. Aunt Laura had taught Emily how to do it and Emily was proud of her skill. Even Aunt Elizabeth had condescended to say that Emily sanded the famous pattern very well, and when Aunt Elizabeth praised, further comment was superfluous. New Moon was the only place in Blair Water where the old custom of sanding the floor was kept up; other housewives had long ago begun to use "new-fangled" devices and patent cleaners for making their floors white. But Dame Elizabeth Murray would have none of such; as long as she reigned at New Moon so long should candles burn and sanded floors gleam whitely.

Aunt Elizabeth had exasperated Emily somewhat by insisting that the latter should put on Aunt Laura's old "Mother Hubbard" while she was scrubbing the floor. A "Mother Hubbard," it may be necessary to explain to those of this generation, was a loose and shapeless garment which served principally as a sort of morning gown and was liked in its day because it was cool and easily put on. Aunt Elizabeth, it is quite unnecessary to say, disapproved entirely of Mother Hubbards. She considered them the last word in slovenliness, and Laura was never permitted to have another one. But the old one, though its original pretty lilac tint had faded to a dingy white, was still too "good" to be banished to the rag bag; and it was this which Emily had been told to put on.

Emily detested Mother Hubbards as heartily as Aunt Elizabeth herself did. They were worse, she considered, even than the hated "baby aprons" of her first summer at New Moon. She knew she looked ridiculous in Aunt Laura's Mother Hubbard, which came to her feet, and hung in loose, unbeautiful lines from her thin young shoulders; and Emily had a horror of being "ridiculous." She had once shocked Aunt Elizabeth by coolly telling her that she would "rather be bad than ridiculous." Emily had scrubbed and sanded with one eye on the door, ready to run if any stranger loomed up while she had on that hideous wrapper.

It was not, as Emily very well knew, a Murray tradition to "run." At New Moon you stood your ground, no matter what you had on—the presupposition being that you were always neatly and properly habited for the occupation of the moment. Emily recognised the propriety of this, yet was, nevertheless, foolish and young enough to feel that she would die of shame if seen by any one in Aunt Laura's Mother Hubbard. It was neat—it was clean—but it was "ridiculous." There you were!

Just as Emily finished sanding and turned to place her can of sand in the niche under the kitchen mantel, where it had been kept from time immemorial, she heard strange voices in the kitchen yard. A hasty glimpse through the window revealed to her the owners of the voices—Miss Beulah Potter, and Mrs. Ann Cyrilla Potter, calling, no doubt, in regard to the projected Ladies' Aid Social. They were coming to the back door as was the Blair Water custom when running in to see your neighbours, informally or on business; they were already past the gay platoons of hollyhocks with which Cousin Jimmy had flanked the stone path to the dairy, and of all the people in Blair Water and out of it they were the two whom Emily would least want to see her in any ridiculous plight whatever. Without stopping to think, she darted into the boot closet and shut the door.

Mrs. Ann Cyrilla knocked twice at the kitchen door, but Emily did not budge. She knew Aunt Laura was weaving in the garret—she could hear the dull thud of the treadles overhead—but she thought Aunt Elizabeth was concocting pies in the cook-house and would see or hear the callers. She would take them into the sitting-room and Emily could make her escape. And on one thing she was determined—they should not see her in that Mother Hubbard. Miss Potter was a thin, venomous, acidulated gossip who seemed to dislike everybody in general and Emily in particular; and Mrs. Ann Cyrilla was a plump, pretty, smooth, amiable gossip who, by very reason of her smoothness and amiability, did more real harm in a week than Miss Potter did in a year. Emily distrusted her even while she could not help liking her. She had so often heard Mrs. Ann Cyrilla make smiling fun of people, to whose "faces" she had been very sweet and charming, and Mrs. Ann Cyrilla, who had been one of the "dressy Wallaces" from Derry Pond, was especially fond of laughing over the peculiarities of other people's clothes.

Again the knock came—Miss Potter's this time, as Emily knew by the staccato raps. They were getting impatient. Well, they might knock there till the cows come home, vowed Emily. She would not go to the door in the Mother Hubbard. Then she heard Perry's voice outside explaining that Miss Elizabeth was away in the stumps behind the barn picking raspberries, but that he would go and get her if they would walk in and make themselves at home. To Emily's despair, this was just what they did. Miss Potter sat down with a creak and Mrs. Ann Cyrilla with a puff, and Perry's retreating footsteps died away in the yard. Emily realised that she was by way of being in a plight. It was very hot and stuffy in the tiny boot closet—where Cousin Jimmy's working clothes were kept as well as boots. She hoped earnestly that Perry would not be long in finding Aunt Elizabeth.

"My, but it's awful hot," said Mrs. Ann Cyrilla, with a large groan.

Poor Emily—no, no, we must not call her poor Emily; she does not deserve pity—she has been very silly and is served exactly right; Emily, then, already violently perspiring in her close quarters, agreed wholly with her.

"*I* don't feel the heat as fat people do," said Miss Potter. "I hope Elizabeth won't keep us waiting long. Laura's weaving—I hear the loom going in the garret. But there would be no use in seeing her—Elizabeth would override anything Laura might promise, just because it wasn't *her* arrangement. I see somebody has just finished sanding the floor. Look at those worn boards, will you? You'd think Elizabeth Murray would have a new floor laid down; but she is too mean, of course. Look at that row of candles on the chimney-piece—all that trouble and poor light because of the little extra coal-oil would cost. Well, she can't take her money with her—she'll have to leave it all behind at the golden gate even if she *is* a Murray."

Emily experienced a shock. She realised that not only was she being half suffocated in the boot closet, but that she was an eavesdropper—something she had never been since the evening at Maywood when she had hidden under the table to hear her aunts and uncles discussing her fate. To be sure, that had been voluntary, while this was compulsory—at least, the Mother Hubbard had made it compulsory. But that would not make Miss Potter's comments any pleasanter to hear. What business had she to call Aunt Elizabeth mean? Aunt Elizabeth *wasn't* mean. Emily was suddenly very angry with Miss Potter. She, herself, often criticised Aunt Elizabeth in secret, but it was intolerable that an outsider should do it. And that little sneer at the Murrays! Emily could imagine the shrewish glint in Miss Potter's eye as she uttered it. As for the candles——

"The Murrays can see farther by candlelight than *you* can by sunlight, Miss Potter," thought Emily disdainfully— or at least as disdainfully as it is possible to think when a river of perspiration is running down your back, and you have nothing to breathe but the aroma of old leather.

"I suppose it's because of the expense that she won't send Emily to school any longer than this year," said Mrs. Ann Cyrilla. "Most folks think she ought to give her a year at Shrewsbury, anyhow—you'd think she would for pride's sake, if nothing else. But I am told she has decided against it."

Emily's heart sank. She hadn't been quite sure till now that Aunt Elizabeth wouldn't send her to Shrewsbury. The tears sprang to her eyes—burning, stinging tears of disappointment.

"Emily ought to be taught something to earn a living by," said Miss Potter. "Her Father left nothing."

"He left *me*," said Emily below her breath, clenching her fists. Anger dried up her tears.

"Oh," said Mrs. Ann Cyrilla, laughing with tolerant derision, "I hear that Emily is going to make a living by writing stories—not only a living but a fortune, I believe."

She laughed again. The idea was so exquisitely ridiculous. Mrs. Ann Cyrilla hadn't heard anything so funny for a long time.

"They say she wastes half her time scribbling trash," agreed Miss Potter. "If I was her Aunt Elizabeth I would soon cure her of that nonsense."

"You mightn't find it so easy. I understand she has always been a difficult girl to manage—so very pigheaded, Murray-like. The whole clamjamfry of them are as stubborn as mules."

(*Emily, wrathfully:* "What a disrespectful way to speak of us! Oh, if I only hadn't on this Mother Hubbard I'd fling this door open and confront them.")

"She needs a tight rein, if *I* know anything of human nature," said Miss Potter. "She's going to be a flirt—any one can see that. She'll be Juliet over again. You'll see. She makes eyes at every one and her only fourteen!"

(*Emily, sarcastically:* "I do *not*! And Mother wasn't a flirt. She *could* have been, but she wasn't. *You* couldn't flirt, even if you wanted to—you respectable old female!")

"She isn't pretty as poor Juliet was, and she's very sly—sly and deep. Mrs. Dutton says she's the slyest child she ever saw. But still there are things I like about poor Emily."

Mrs. Ann Cyrilla's tone was very patronising. "Poor" Emily writhed among the boots.

"The thing *I* don't like in her is that she is always trying to be smart," said Miss Potter decidedly. "She says clever things she has read in books and passes them off as her own——"

(*Emily, outraged:* "I don't!")

"And she's very sarcastic and touchy, and of course as proud as Lucifer," concluded Miss Potter.

Mrs. Ann Cyrilla laughed pleasantly and tolerantly again.

"Oh, that goes without saying in a Murray. But their worst fault is that they think nobody can do anything right but themselves, and Emily is full of it. Why, she even thinks she can preach better than Mr. Johnson."

(*Emily:* "That is because I said he contradicted himself in one of his sermons—and he *did*. And I've heard *you* criticise dozens of sermons, Mrs. Ann Cyrilla.")

"She's jealous, too," continued Mrs. Ann Cyrilla. "She can't bear to be beaten—she wants to be first in everything. I understand she actually shed tears of mortification the night of the concert because Ilse Burnley carried off the honours in the dialogue. Emily did very poorly—she was a perfect *stick*. And she contradicts older people continually. It would be funny if it weren't so ill-bred."

"It's odd Elizabeth doesn't cure her of *that*. The Murrays think their breeding is a little above the common," said Miss Potter.

(*Emily, wrathfully, to the boots:* "It *is*, too.")

"Of course," said Mrs. Ann Cyrilla, "I think a great many of Emily's faults come from her intimacy with Ilse Burnley. She shouldn't be allowed to run about with Ilse as she does. Why, they say Ilse is as much an infidel as her father. I have always understood she doesn't believe in God at all—or the Devil either."

(*Emily:* "Which is a far worse thing in *your* eyes.")

"Oh, the doctor's training her a little better now since he found out his precious wife didn't elope with Leo Mitchell," sniffed Miss Potter. "He makes her go to Sunday School. But she's no fit associate for Emily. She swears like a trooper, I'm told. Mrs. Mark Burns was in the doctor's office one day and heard Ilse in the parlour say distinctly 'out, damned Spot!' probably to the dog."

"Dear, dear," moaned Mrs. Ann Cyrilla.

"Do you know what *I* saw her do one day last week—saw her with my own eyes!" Miss Potter was very emphatic over this. Ann Cyrilla need not suppose that she had been using any other person's eyes.

"You couldn't surprise me," gurgled Mrs. Ann Cyrilla. "Why, they say she was at the charivari at Johnson's last Tuesday night, dressed as a boy."

"Quite likely. But this happened in my own front yard. She was there with Jen Strang, who had come to get a root of my Persian rose-bush for her mother. I asked Ilse if she could sew and bake and a few other things that I thought she ought to be reminded of. Ilse said 'No' to them all, quite brazenly, and then *she* said—*what* do you think that girl said?"

"Oh, what?" breathed Mrs. Ann Cyrilla eagerly.

"She said, 'Can *you* stand on one foot and lift your other to a level with your eyes, Miss Potter? I can.'

And"—Miss Potter hushed her tone to the proper pitch of horror—*"she did it!"*

The listener in the closet stifled a spasm of laughter in Cousin Jimmy's grey jumper. How madcap Ilse did love to shock Miss Potter!

"Good gracious, were there any men around?" entreated Mrs. Ann Cyrilla.

"No—fortunately. But it's my belief she would have done it just the same no matter who was there. We were close to the road—*anybody* might have been passing. I felt so ashamed. In *my* time a young girl would have *died* before she would have done a thing like that."

"It's no worse than her and Emily bathing by moonlight up on the sands *without a stitch on,*" said Mrs. Ann Cyrilla. "*That* was the most scandalous thing. Did you hear about it?"

"Oh, yes, that story's all over Blair Water. Everybody's heard it but Elizabeth and Laura. I can't find out how it started. Were they *seen?*"

"Oh, dear no, not so bad as that. Ilse told it herself. She seemed to think it was quite a matter of course. *I* think some one ought to tell Laura and Elizabeth."

"Tell them yourself," suggested Miss Potter.

"Oh, no, *I* don't want to get in wrong with my neighbours. *I* am not responsible for Emily Starr's training, thank goodness. If I were I wouldn't let her have so much to do with Jarback Priest, either. He's the queerest of all those queer Priests. I'm sure he must have a bad influence over her. Those green eyes of his positively give me the creeps. I can't find out that he believes in any*thing.*"

(*Emily, sarcastically again:* "Not even the Devil?")

"There's a queer story going around about him and Emily," said Miss Potter. "I can't make head or tail of it. They were seen on the big hill last Wednesday evening at sunset, behaving in a most extraordinary fashion. They would walk along with their eyes fixed on the sky—then suddenly stop—grasp each other by the arm and point upward. They did it time and again. Mrs. Price was watching them from the window and she can't imagine what they were up to. It was too early for stars, and *she* couldn't see a solitary thing in the sky. She laid awake all night wondering about it."

"Well, it all comes to this—Emily Starr needs looking after," said Mrs. Ann Cyrilla. "I sometimes feel that it would be wiser to stop Muriel and Gladys from going about so much with her."

(*Emily, devoutly:* "I wish you *would*. They are so stupid and silly and they just stick around Ilse and me all the time.")

"When all is said and done, I pity her," said Miss Potter. "She's so foolish and high-minded that she'll get in wrong with every one, and no decent, sensible man will ever be bothered with her. Geoff North says he went home with her once and that was enough for *him*."

(*Emily, emphatically:* "I believe you! Geoff showed almost human intelligence in *that* remark.")

"But then she probably won't live through her teens. She looks very consumptive. Really, Ann Cyrilla, I *do* feel sorry for the poor thing."

This was the proverbial last straw for Emily. *She*, whole Starr and half Murray, to be pitied by Beulah Potter! Mother Hubbard or no Mother Hubbard, it could not be borne! The closet door suddenly opened wide and Emily stood revealed, Mother Hubbard and all, against a background of boots and jumpers. Her cheeks were crimson, her eyes black. The mouths of Mrs. Ann Cyrilla and Miss Beulah Potter fell open and stayed open; their faces turned dull red; they were dumb.

Emily looked at them steadily for a minute of scornful, eloquent silence. Then, with the air of a queen, she swept across the kitchen and vanished through the sitting-room door, just as Aunt Elizabeth came up the sandstone steps with dignified apologies for keeping them waiting. Miss Potter and Mrs. Ann Cyrilla were so dumbfounded that they were hardly able to talk about the Ladies' Aid, and got themselves confusedly away after a few jerky questions and answers. Aunt Elizabeth did not know what to make of them and thought they must have been unreasonably offended over having to wait. Then she dismissed the matter from her mind. A Murray did not care what Potters thought or did. The open closet door told no tales, and she did not know that up in the lookout chamber Emily was lying face downward across the bed crying passionately for shame and anger and humiliation. She felt degraded and hurt. It had all been the outcome of her own silly vanity in the beginning—she acknowledged that—but her punishment had been *too* severe.

She did not mind so much what Miss Potter had said, but Mrs. Ann Cyrilla's tiny barbs of malice *did* sting. She had liked pretty, pleasant Mrs. Ann Cyrilla, who had always seemed kind and friendly and had paid her many compliments. She had thought Mrs. Ann Cyrilla had really liked her. And now to find out that she would talk about her like this!

"Couldn't they have said *one* good thing of me?" she sobbed. "Oh, I feel *soiled*, somehow—between my own silliness and their malice—and all dirty and messed-up mentally. Will I ever feel *clean* again?"

She did not feel "clean" until she had written it all out in her diary. Then she took a less distorted view of it and summoned philosophy to her aid.

"Mr. Carpenter says we should make every experience teach us something," she wrote. "He says every experience, no matter whether it is pleasant or unpleasant, has something for us if we are able to view it dispassionately. 'That,' he added bitterly, 'is one of the pieces of good advice I have kept by me all my life and never been able to make any use of myself.'

"Very well, I shall try to view this dispassionately! I

suppose the way to do it is to consider all that was said of me and decide just what was *true* and what false, and what merely distorted—which is worse than the false, I think.

"To begin with: hiding in the closet at all, just out of vanity, comes under my heading of bad deeds. And I *suppose* that appearing as I did, after I *had* stayed there so long, and covering them with confusion, was another. But if so, I can't feel it 'dispassionately' yet, because I am sinfully glad I did it—yes, even if they did see me in the Mother Hubbard! I shall never forget their faces! Especially Mrs. Ann Cyrilla's. Miss Potter won't worry over it long—she will say it served me right—but Mrs. Ann Cyrilla will never, to her dying day, get over being *found out* like that.

"Now for a review of their criticisms of Emily Byrd Starr and the decision as to whether said Emily Byrd Starr deserved the said criticisms, wholly or in part. Be honest now, Emily, 'look then into thy heart' and try to see yourself, not as Miss Potter sees you or as you see yourself, but as you really are.

("I think I'm going to find this interesting!)

"In the first place, Mrs. Ann Cyrilla said I was pig-headed.

"*Am* I pig-headed?

"I know I am determined, and Aunt Elizabeth says I am stubborn. But pig-headedness is worse than either of those. Determination is a good quality and even stubbornness has a saving grace in it if you have a little gumption as well. But a pig-headed person is one who is too stupid to see or understand the foolishness of a certain course and insists on taking it—insists, in short, on running full tilt into a stone wall.

"No, I am *not* pig-headed. I accept stone walls.

"But I take a good deal of convincing that they *are* stone walls and not cardboard imitations. Therefore, I *am* a little stubborn.

"Miss Potter said I was a flirt. This is wholly untrue,

so I won't discuss it. But she also said I 'made eyes.' Now do I? I don't mean to—I know that; but it seems you can 'make eyes' without being conscious of it, so how am I going to prevent that? I can't go about all the days of my life with my eyes dropped down. Dean said the other day:

"'When you look at me like that, Star, there is nothing for me but to do as you ask.'

"And Aunt Elizabeth was quite annoyed last week because she said I was looking 'improperly' at Perry when I was coaxing him to go to the Sunday School picnic. (Perry hates Sunday School picnics.)

"Now, in both cases I thought I was only looking *beseechingly.*

"Mrs. Ann Cyrilla said I wasn't pretty. Is that true?"

Emily laid down her pen, went over to the mirror and took a "dispassionate" stock of her looks. Black of hair—smoke-purple of eye—crimson of lip. So far, not bad. Her forehead was too high, but the new way of doing her hair obviated that defect. Her skin was very white and her cheeks, which had been so pale in childhood, were now as delicately hued as a pink pearl. Her mouth was too large, but her teeth were good. Her slightly pointed ears gave her a fawn-like charm. Her neck had lines that she could not help liking. Her slender, immature figure was graceful; she knew, for Aunt Nancy had told her, that she had the Shipley ankle and instep. Emily looked very earnestly at Emily-in-the-Glass from several angles, and returned to her diary.

"I have decided that I am not pretty," she wrote. "I think I *look* quite pretty when my hair is done a certain way, but a really pretty girl would be pretty no matter how her hair was done, so Mrs. Ann Cyrilla was right. But I feel sure that I am not so plain as she implied, either.

"Then she said I was sly—and *deep.* I don't think it is any fault to be 'deep,' though she spoke as if she thought it was. I would rather be deep than shallow. But am I sly? *No.* I am *not.* Then what is it about me that makes people think I am sly? Aunt Ruth always insists that I am. *I* think it is because I have a habit, when I am bored or disgusted with people, of stepping suddenly into my own world and shutting the door. People resent this—I suppose it is only natural to resent a door being shut in your face. They call it slyness when it is only self-defence. So I won't worry over that.

"Miss Potter said an abominable thing—that I passed off clever speeches I had read in books, as my own— trying to be smart. That is *utterly false.* Honestly, I never 'try to be smart.' But—I *do* try often to see how a certain thing I've thought out sounds when it is put into words. Perhaps this is a kind of showing-off. I must be careful about it.

"Jealous: no, I'm not that. I *do* like to be first, I admit. But it wasn't because I was jealous of Ilse that I cried that night at the concert. I cried because I felt I had made a mess of my part. I *was* a stick, just as Mrs. Ann Cyrilla said. I can't *act* a part somehow. Sometimes a certain part seems to suit me and then I can *be* it, but if not I'm no good in a dialogue. I only went in it to oblige Mrs. Johnson, and I felt horribly mortified because I knew she was disappointed. And I suppose my pride suffered a bit, but I never thought of being jealous of Ilse. I was proud of her—she does magnificently in a play.

"Yes, I contradict. I admit that *is* one of my faults. But people do say such outrageous things! And why isn't it as bad for people to contradict me? They do it continually—and I am *right* just as often as they are.

"Sarcastic? Yes, I'm afraid that is another of my faults. Touchy—no, I'm *not.* I'm only *sensitive.* And proud? Well, yes, I *am* a little proud—but not nearly as proud as people think me. I can't help carrying my head at a certain angle and I can't help feeling it is a great thing to have a century of good, upright people with fine traditions and considerable brains behind you. Not like the Potters—upstarts of yesterday!

"Oh, how those women garbled things about poor Ilse. We couldn't, I suppose, expect a Potter or the wife of a Potter to recognize the sleep-walking scene from *Lady Macbeth*. I have told Ilse repeatedly that she ought to see that all doors are shut when she tries it over. She is quite wonderful in it. She *never* was at that charivari—she only said she'd *like* to go. And as for the moonlight bathing—that was true enough except that we had *some* stitches on. There was nothing dreadful about it. It was perfectly beautiful—though now it is all spoiled and degraded by being dragged about in common gossip. I wish Ilse hadn't told about it.

"We had gone away up the sandshore for a walk. It was a moonlit night and the sandshore was wonderful. The Wind Woman was rustling in the grasses on the dunes and there was a long, gentle wash of little gleaming waves on the shore. We wanted to bathe, but at first we thought we couldn't because we didn't have our bathing dresses. So we sat on the sands and talked of a hundred things. It was real conversation—not just talk. The great gulf stretched out before us, silvery, gleaming, alluring, going farther and farther into the mists of the northern sky. It was like an ocean in 'fairylands forlorn.'

"I said:

" 'I would like to get into a ship and sail straight out there—out—out—where would I land?'

" 'Anticosti, I expect,' said Ilse—a bit too prosaically, I thought.

" 'No—no—Ultima Thule, I think,' I said dreamily. 'Some beautiful unknown shore where "the rain never falls, and the wind never blows." Perhaps the country back of the North Wind where *Diamond* went. One could sail to it over that silver sea on a night like this.'

" '*That* was heaven, I think,' said Ilse.

"Then we talked about immortality, and Ilse said she was afraid of it—afraid of living for ever and for ever; she said she was sure she would get awfully tired of herself. I said I thought I liked Dean's idea of a succession of lives—I can't make out from him whether he really believes that or not—and Ilse said that might be all very well if you were sure of being born again as a decent person, but how about it if you weren't?

" 'Well, you have to take some risk in any kind of immortality,' I said.

" 'Anyhow,' said Ilse, 'whether I am myself or somebody else next time, I do hope I won't have such a dreadful temper. If I just go on being myself I'll smash my harp and tear my halo to pieces and pull all the feathers out of the other angels' wings half an hour after getting to heaven. You know I will, Emily. I can't help it. I had a fiendish quarrel with Perry yesterday again. It was all my fault—but of course he vexed me by his boasting. I *wish* I could control my temper.'

"I don't mind Ilse's rages one bit now—I know she never means anything she says in them. I never say anything back. I just smile at her and if I've a bit of paper handy I jot down the things she says. This infuriates her so that she chokes with anger and can't say anything more. At all other times Ilse is a darling and such good fun.

" 'You can't control your rages because you like going into them,' I said.

"Ilse stared at me.

" 'I don't—I don't.'

" 'You do. You enjoy them,' I insisted.

" 'Well, of course,' said Ilse, grinning, 'I *do* have a good time while they last. It's awfully *satisfying* to say the most insulting things and call the worst names. I believe you're right, Emily. I *do* enjoy them. Queer I never thought of it. I suppose if I really were unhappy in them I wouldn't go into them. But after they're over—I'm so remorseful. I cried for an hour yesterday after fighting with Perry.'

" 'Yes, and you enjoyed that, too—didn't you?'

"Ilse reflected.

" 'I guess so, Emily; you're an uncanny thing. I won't talk about it any more. Let's go bathing. No dresses? What does it matter. There isn't a soul for miles. I can't resist those waves. They're *calling* me.'

"I felt just as she did, and bathing by moonlight seemed such a lovely, romantic thing—and it *is*, when the Potters of the world don't know of it. When they do, they smudge it. We undressed in a little hollow among the dunes—that was like a bowl of silver in the moonlight—but we kept our petticoats on. We had the loveliest time splashing and swimming about in that silver-blue water and those creamy little waves, like mermaids or sea nymphs. It was like living in a poem or a fairy tale. And when we came out I held out my hands to Ilse and said:

> " 'Come unto these yellow sands,
> Curtseyed when we have and kissed,
> The wild winds whist,
> Foot it featly here and there
> And, sweet sprites, the burden bear.'

"Ilse took my hands and we danced in rings over the moonlit sands, and then we went up to the silver bowl and dressed and went home perfectly happy. Only, of course, we had to carry our wet petticoats rolled up under our arms, so we looked rather slinky, but nobody saw us. And *that* is what Blair Water is so scandalised about.

"All the same, I hope Aunt Elizabeth won't hear of it.

"It is too bad Mrs. Price lost so much sleep over Dean and me. We were not performing any weird incantations—we were simply walking over the Delectable Mountain and tracing pictures in the clouds. Perhaps it was childish—but it was great fun. That is one thing I like about Dean—he isn't afraid of doing something harmless and pleasant just because it's childish. One cloud he pointed out to me looked exactly like an angel flying along the pale, shining sky and carrying a baby in its arms. There was a filmy blue veil over its head with a faint, first star gleaming through it. Its wings were tipped with gold and its white robe flecked with crimson.

"'There goes the Angel of the Evening Star with tomorrow in its arms,' said Dean.

"It was so beautiful that it gave me one of my wonder moments. But ten seconds later it had changed into something that looked like a camel with an exaggerated hump!

"We had a wonderful half hour, even if Mrs. Price, who couldn't see anything in the sky, did think us quite mad.

"Well, it all comes to this, there's no use trying to live in other people's opinions. The only thing to do is to live in your own. After all, I believe in myself. I'm not so bad and silly as they think me, and I'm not consumptive, and I *can* write. Now that I've written it all out I feel differently about it. The only thing that still aggravates me is that Miss Potter *pitied* me—pitied by a Potter!

"I looked out of my window just now and saw Cousin Jimmy's nasturtium bed—and suddenly the flash came—and Miss Potter and her pity, and her malicious tongue seemed to matter not at all. Nasturtiums, who colored you, you wonderful, glowing things? You must have been fashioned out of summer sunsets.

"I help Cousin Jimmy a great deal with his garden this summer. I think I love it as much as he does. Every day we make new discoveries of bud and bloom.

"So Aunt Elizabeth won't send me to Shrewsbury! Oh, I feel as disappointed as if I'd really hoped she would. Every door in life seems shut to me.

"Still, after all, I've lots to be thankful for. Aunt

Elizabeth will let me go to school another year here, I think, and Mr. Carpenter can teach me heaps yet; I'm not hideous; moonlight is still a fair thing; I'm going to do something with my pen some day—*and* I've got a lovely, grey, moon-faced cat who has just jumped up on my table and poked my pen with his nose as a signal that I've written enough for one sitting.

"The only real cat is a grey cat!"

5
Half a Loaf

O ne late August evening Emily heard Teddy's signal whistle from the Tomorrow Road, and slipped out to join him. He had news—that was evident from his shining eyes.

"Emily," he cried excitedly, "I'm going to Shrewsbury after all! Mother told me this evening she had made up her mind to let me go!"

Emily was glad—with a queer sorriness underneath, for which she reproached herself. How lonesome it would be at New Moon when her three old pals were gone! She had not realised until that moment how much she had counted on Teddy's companionship. He had always been there in the background of her thoughts of the coming year. She had always taken Teddy for granted. Now there would be nobody— not even Dean, for Dean was going away for the winter as usual—to Egypt or Japan, as he might decide at the last moment. What would she do? Would all the Jimmy-books in the world take the place of her flesh-and-blood chums?

"If you were only going, too!" said Teddy, as they

walked along the Tomorrow Road—which was almost a Today Road now, so fast and so tall had the leafy young maples grown.

"There's no use wishing it—don't speak of it—it makes me unhappy," said Emily jerkily.

"Well, we'll have week-ends anyhow. And it's you I have to thank for going. It was what you said to Mother that night in the graveyard that made her let me go. I know she's been thinking of it ever since, by things she would say every once in a while. One day last week I heard her muttering: 'It's awful to be a mother—awful to be a mother and suffer like this. Yet she called me selfish!' And another time she said, 'Is it selfish to want to keep the only thing you have left in the world?' But she was lovely tonight when she told me I could go. I know folks say Mother isn't quite right in her mind—and sometimes she *is* a little queer. But it's only when other people are around. You've no idea, Emily, how nice and dear she is when we're alone. I hate to leave her. But I *must* get some education!"

"I'm very glad if what I said has made her change her mind, but she will never forgive me for it. She has hated me ever since—you know she has. You know how she *looks* at me whenever I'm at the Tansy Patch—oh, she's very polite to me. But her eyes, Teddy."

"I know," said Teddy, uncomfortably. "But don't be hard on Mother, Emily. I'm sure she wasn't always like that—though she has been ever since I can remember. I don't know *anything* of her before that. She never tells me anything—I don't know a thing about my Father. She won't talk about him. I don't even know how she got that scar on her face."

"I don't think there's anything the matter with your Mother's mind, really," said Emily slowly. "But I think there's something troubling it—always troubling it— something she can't forget or throw off. Teddy, I'm sure your mother is *haunted*. Of course, I don't mean by a ghost or anything silly like that. But by some terrible *thought*."

"She isn't happy, I know," said Teddy, "and, of course, we're poor. Mother said tonight she could only send me to Shrewsbury for three years—that was all she could afford. But that will give me a start—I'll get on somehow after that. I *know* I can. I'll make it up to her yet."

"You will be a great artist some day," said Emily dreamily.

They had come to the end of the Tomorrow Road. Before them was the pond pasture, whitened over with a drift of daisies. Farmers hate the daisies as a pestiferous weed, but a field white with them on a summer twilight is a vision from the Land of Lost Delight. Beneath them Blair Water shone like a great golden lily. Up on the eastern hill the little Disappointed House crouched amid its shadows, dreaming, perhaps, of the false bride that had never come to it. There was no light at the Tansy Patch. Was lonely Mrs. Kent crying there in the darkness, with only her secret, tormenting heart-hunger for companion?

Emily was looking at the sunset sky—her eyes rapt, her face pale and seeking. She felt no longer blue or depressed—somehow she never could feel that way long in Teddy's company. In all the world there was no music like his voice. All good things seemed suddenly possible with him. She could not go to Shrewsbury— but she could work and study at New Moon—oh, how she would work and study. Another year with Mr. Carpenter would do a great deal for her—as much as Shrewsbury, perhaps. She, too, had her Alpine Path to climb—she *would* climb it, no matter what the obstacles in the way—no matter whether there was any one to help her or not.

"When I am I'll paint you just as you're looking now," said Teddy, "and call it Joan of Arc—with a face all spirit—listening to her voices."

In spite of her voices Emily went to bed that night feeling rather down-hearted—and woke in the morning with an unaccountable conviction that some good news was coming to her that day—a conviction that did not lessen as the hours passed by in the commonplace fashion of Saturday hours at New Moon—busy hours in which the house was made immaculate for Sunday, and the pantry replenished. It was a cool, damp day when the fogs were coming up from the shore on the east wind, and New Moon and its old garden were veiled in mist.

At twilight a thin, grey rain began to fall, and still the good news had not come. Emily had just finished scouring the brass candlesticks and composing a poem called *Rain Song*, simultaneously, when Aunt Laura told her that Aunt Elizabeth wanted to see her in the parlour.

Emily's recollections of parlour interviews with Aunt Elizabeth were not especially pleasant. She could not recall any recent deed, done or left undone, which would justify this summons, yet she walked into the parlour quakingly: whatever Aunt Elizabeth was going to say to her it must have some special significance or it would not be said in the parlour. This was just one of Aunt Elizabeth's little ways. Daffy, her big cat, slipped in beside her like a noiseless, grey shadow. She hoped Aunt Elizabeth would not shoo him out: his presence was a certain comfort: a cat is a good backer when he is on your side!

Aunt Elizabeth was knitting; she looked solemn but not offended or angry. She ignored Daff, but thought that Emily seemed very tall in the old, stately, twilit room. How quickly children grew up! It seemed but the other day since fair, pretty Juliet—Elizabeth Murray shut her thoughts off with a click.

"Sit down, Emily," she said. "I want to have a talk with you."

Emily sat down. So did Daffy, wreathing his tail comfortably about his paws. Emily suddenly felt that her hands were clammy and her mouth dry. She wished that she had knitting, too. It was nasty to sit there, unoccupied, and wonder what was coming. What *did* come was the one thing she had never thought of. Aunt Elizabeth, after knitting a deliberate round on her stocking, said directly:

"Emily, would you like to go to Shrewsbury next week?"

Go to Shrewsbury? Had she heard aright?

"Oh, Aunt Elizabeth!" she said.

"I have been talking the matter over with your uncles and aunts," said Aunt Elizabeth. "They agree with me that you should have some further education. It will be a considerable expense, of course—no, don't interrupt. I don't like interruptions—but Ruth will board you for half-price, as her contribution to your upbringing—Emily, I will *not* be interrupted! Your Uncle Oliver will pay the other half; your Uncle Wallace will provide your books, and I will see to your clothes. You will, of course, help your Aunt Ruth about the house in every way possible as some return for her kindness. You may go to Shrewsbury for three years on a certain condition."

What was the condition? Emily, who wanted to dance and sing and laugh through the old parlour as no Murray, not even her mother, had ever ventured to dance and laugh before, constrained herself to sit rigidly on her ottoman and ask herself that question. Behind her suspense she felt that the moment was quite dramatic.

"Three years at Shrewsbury," Aunt Elizabeth went on, "will do as much for you as three at Queen's—except, of course, that you don't get a teacher's license, which doesn't matter in your case, as you are not under the necessity of working for your living. But, as I have said, there is a condition."

Why didn't Aunt Elizabeth name the condition? Emily felt that the suspense was unendurable. Could it be possible that Aunt Elizabeth was a little *afraid* to name it? It was not like her to talk for time. Was it so very terrible?

"You must promise," said Aunt Elizabeth sternly, "that for the three years you are at Shrewsbury you will give up entirely this writing nonsense of yours—*entirely*, except in so far as school compositions may be required."

Emily sat very still—and cold. No Shrewsbury on the one hand—on the other no more poems, no more stories and "studies," no more delightful Jimmy-books of miscellany. She did not take more than one instant to make up her mind.

"I can't promise that, Aunt Elizabeth," she said resolutely.

Aunt Elizabeth dropped her knitting in amazement. She had not expected this. She had thought Emily was so set on going to Shrewsbury that she would do anything that might be asked of her in order to go—especially such a trifling thing as this—which, so Aunt Elizabeth thought, involved only a surrender of stubbornness.

"Do you mean to say you won't give up your foolish scribbling for the sake of the education you've always pretended to want so much?" she demanded.

"Not that I *won't*—it's just that I *can't*," said Emily despairingly. She knew Aunt Elizabeth could not understand—Aunt Elizabeth never had understood *this*. "I *can't* help writing, Aunt Elizabeth. It's in my blood. There's no use in asking me. I *do* want an education—it isn't pretending—but I can't give up my writing to get it. I *couldn't* keep such a promise—so what use would there be in making it?"

"Then you can stay home," said Aunt Elizabeth angrily.

Emily expected to see her get up and walk out of the room. Instead, Aunt Elizabeth picked up her stocking and wrathfully resumed her knitting. To tell the truth, Aunt Elizabeth was absurdly taken aback. She really wanted to send Emily to Shrewsbury. Tradition required so much of her, and all the clan were of the opinion she should be sent. This condition had been her own idea. She thought it a good chance to break Emily of a silly un-Murray-like habit of wasting time and paper, and she had never doubted that her plan would succeed, for she knew how much Emily wanted to go. And now this senseless, unreasoning, ungrateful obstinacy—"the Starr coming out," thought Aunt Elizabeth rancorously, forgetful of the Shipley inheritance! What was to be done? She knew too well from past experience that there would be no moving Emily once she had taken up a position, and she knew that Wallace and Oliver and Ruth, though they thought Emily's craze for writing as silly and untraditional as she did, would not back her—Elizabeth—up in her demand. Elizabeth Murray foresaw a complete right-about-face before her, and Elizabeth Murray did not like the prospect. She could have shaken, with a right good will, the slim, pale thing sitting before her on the ottoman. The creature was so slight—and young—and indomitable. For over three years Elizabeth Murray had tried to cure Emily of this foolishness of writing and for over three years she, who had never failed in anything before, had failed in this. One couldn't starve her into submission—and nothing short of it would seem to be efficacious.

Elizabeth knitted furiously in her vexation, and Emily sat motionless, struggling with her bitter disappointment and sense of injustice. She was determined she would not cry before Aunt Elizabeth, but it was hard to keep the tears back. She wished Daff wouldn't purr with such resounding satisfaction, as if everything were perfectly delicious from a grey cat's point of view. She wished Aunt Elizabeth would tell her to go. But Aunt Elizabeth only knitted furiously and said nothing. It all seemed rather nightmarish. The wind was rising and the rain began to drive against the pane, and the dead-and-gone Murrays looked down accusingly from their dark frames. *They* had no sympathy with flashes and Jimmy-books and Alpine paths—with the pursuit of unwon, alluring divinities. Yet Emily couldn't help thinking, under all her disappointment, what an excellent setting it would make for some tragic scene in a novel.

The door opened and Cousin Jimmy slipped in. Cousin Jimmy knew what was in the wind and had been coolly and deliberately listening outside the door. *He* knew Emily would never promise such a thing—he had told Elizabeth so at the family council ten days before. *He* was only simple Jimmy Murray, but he understood what sensible Elizabeth Murray could not understand.

"What is wrong?" he asked, looking from one to the other.

"Nothing is wrong," said Aunt Elizabeth haughtily. "I have offered Emily an education and she has refused it. She is free to do so, of course."

"No one can be free who has a thousand ancestors," said Cousin Jimmy in the eerie tone in which he generally said such things. It always made Elizabeth shiver—she could never forget that his eeriness was *her* fault. "Emily can't promise what you want. Can you, Emily?"

"No." In spite of herself a couple of big tears rolled down Emily's cheeks.

"If you *could*," said Cousin Jimmy, "you *would* promise it for *me*, wouldn't you?"

Emily nodded.

"You've asked too much, Elizabeth," said Cousin Jimmy to the angry lady of the knitting-needles. "You've asked her to give up *all* her writing—now, if you'd just asked her to give up *some*—Emily, what if she just asked you to give up *some*? You might be able to do that, mightn't you?"

"What *some*?" asked Emily cautiously.

"Well, anything that wasn't *true*, for instance." Cousin Jimmy sidled over to Emily and put a beseeching hand on her shoulder. Elizabeth did not stop knitting, but the needles went more slowly. "*Stories*, for instance, Emily. She doesn't like your writing stories, especially. She thinks they're lies. She doesn't mind other things so much. Don't you think, Emily, you could give up writing stories for three years? An education is a great thing. Your grandmother Archibald would have lived on herring tails to get an education—many a time I've heard her say it. Come, Emily?"

Emily thought rapidly. She loved writing stories: it would be a hard thing to give them up. But if she could still write air-born fancies in verse—and weird little Jimmy-book sketches of character—and accounts of everyday events—witty—satirical—tragic—as the humour took her—she might be able to get along.

"Try her—try her," whispered Cousin Jimmy. "Propitiate her a little. You do owe her a great deal, Emily. Meet her half-way."

"Aunt Elizabeth," said Emily tremulously, "if you will send me to Shrewsbury I promise you that for three years I won't write anything that isn't *true*. Will that do? Because it's *all* I can promise."

Elizabeth knitted two rounds before deigning to reply. Cousin Jimmy and Emily thought she was not going to reply at all. Suddenly she folded up her knitting and rose.

"Very well. I will let it go at that. It is, of course, your stories I object to most: as for the rest, I fancy Ruth will see to it that you have not much time to waste on it."

Aunt Elizabeth swept out, much relieved in her secret heart that she had not been utterly routed, but had been enabled to retreat from a perplexing position with some of the honours of war. Cousin Jimmy patted Emily's black head.

"That's good, Emily. Mustn't be too stubborn, you know. And three years isn't a lifetime, pussy."

No: but it seems like one at fourteen. Emily cried herself to sleep when she went to bed—and woke again at three by the clock, of that windy, dark-grey night on the old north shore—rose—lighted a candle—sat down at her table and described the whole scene in her Jimmy-book: being exceedingly careful to write therein no word that was not strictly true!

6
Shrewsbury Beginnings

Teddy and Ilse and Perry whooped for joy when Emily told them she was going to Shrewsbury. Emily, thinking it over, was reasonably happy. The great thing was that she was going to High School. She did not like the idea of boarding with Aunt Ruth. This was unexpected. She had supposed Aunt Ruth would never be willing to have *her* about and that, if Aunt Elizabeth *did* decide to send her to Shrewsbury, she would board elsewhere—probably with Ilse. Certainly, she would have greatly preferred this. She knew quite well that life would not be very easy under Aunt Ruth's roof. And then she must write no more stories.

To feel within her the creative urge and be forbidden to express it—to tingle with delight in the conception of humorous or dramatic characters, and be forbidden to bring them into existence—to be suddenly seized with the idea of a capital plot and realise immediately afterward that you couldn't develop it. All this was a torture which no one who has not been born with the fatal itch for writing can realise. The Aunt Elizabeths of the world can never understand it. To them, it is merely foolishness.

Those last two weeks of August were busy ones at New Moon. Elizabeth and Laura held long conferences over Emily's clothes. She must have an outfit that would cast no discredit on the Murrays, but common sense and not fashion was to give the casting vote. Emily herself had no say in the matter. Laura and Elizabeth argued "from noon to dewy eve" one day as to whether Emily might have a taffeta silk blouse—Ilse had three—and decided against it, much to Emily's disappointment. But Laura had her way in regard to what she dared not call an "evening dress," since the name would have doomed it in Elizabeth's opinion: it was a very pretty crêpe thing, of a pinkish-grey—the shade, I think, which was then called ashes-of-roses—and was made collarless—a great concession on Elizabeth's part—with the big puffed sleeves that look very absurd today, but which, like every other fashion, were pretty and piquant when worn by the youth and beauty of their time. It was the prettiest dress Emily had ever had—and the longest, which meant much in those days, when you could not be grown up until you had put on "long" dresses. It came to her pretty ankles.

She put it on one evening, when Laura and Elizabeth were away, because she wanted Dean to see her in it. He had come up to spend the evening with her—he was off the next day, having decided on Egypt—and they walked in the garden. Emily felt quite old and sophisticated because she had to lift her shimmering skirt clear of the ribbon grasses. She had a little greyish-pink scarf wound around her head and looked more like a star than ever, Dean thought. The cats were in attendance—Daffy, sleek and striped, Saucy Sal, who still reigned supreme in the New Moon barns. Cats might come and cats might go, but Saucy Sal went on for ever. They frisked over the grass plots and pounced on each other from flowery jungles and rolled insinuatingly around Emily's feet. Dean was going to

Egypt but he knew that nowhere, even amid the strange charm of forgotten empires, would he see anything he liked better than the pretty picture Emily and her little cats made in the prim, stately, scented old garden of New Moon.

They did not talk as much as usual and the silences did queer things to both of them. Dean had one or two mad impulses to throw up the trip to Egypt and stay home for the winter—go to Shrewsbury perhaps; he shrugged his shoulders and laughed at himself. This child did not need his looking after—the ladies of New Moon were competent guardians. She was only a child yet—in spite of her slim height and her unfathomable eyes. But how perfect the white line of her throat—how kissable the sweet red curve of her mouth. She would be a woman soon—but not for him—not for lame Jarback Priest of her father's generation. For the hundredth time Dean told himself that he was not going to be a fool. He must be content with what fate had given him—the friendship and affection of this exquisite, starry creature. In the years to come her love would be a wonderful thing—for some other man. No doubt, thought Dean cynically, she would waste it on some good-looking young manikin who wasn't half worthy of it.

Emily was thinking how dreadfully she was going to miss Dean—more than she had ever missed him before. They had been such good pals that summer. She had never had a talk with him, even if it were only for a few minutes, without feeling that life was richer. His wise, witty, humorous, satiric sayings were educative. They stimulated—stung—inspired her. And his occasional compliments gave her self-confidence. He had a certain strange fascination for her that no one else in the world possessed. She felt it though she could not analyse it. Teddy, now—she knew perfectly well why she liked Teddy. It was just because of his Teddyness. And Perry—Perry was a jolly, sunburned, outspoken, boastful rogue you couldn't help liking. But Dean was different. Was his charm the allure of the unknown—of experience—of subtle knowledge—of a mind grown wise on bitterness—of things Dean knew that she could never know? Emily couldn't tell. She only knew that everybody tasted a little flat after Dean—even Teddy, though she liked him best. Oh, yes, Emily never had any doubt at all that she liked Teddy best. And yet Dean seemed to satisfy some part of her subtle and intricate nature that always went hungry without him.

"Thank you for all you've taught me, Dean," she said as they stood by the sundial.

"Do you think you have taught me nothing, Star?"

"How could I? I'm so young—so ignorant——"

"You've taught me how to laugh without bitterness. I hope you'll never realise what a boon that is. Don't let them spoil you at Shrewsbury, Star. You're so pleased over going that I don't want to throw cold water. But you'd be just as well off—better—here at New Moon."

"Dean! I want *some* education——"

"Education! Education isn't being spoon-fed with algebra and second-rate Latin. Old Carpenter could teach you more and better than the college cubs, male and female, in Shrewsbury High School."

"I can't go to school any more here," protested Emily. "I'd be all alone. All the pupils of my age are going to Queen's or Shrewsbury or staying home. I don't understand you, Dean. I thought you'd be so glad they're letting me go to Shrewsbury."

"I *am* glad—since it pleases you. Only—the lore I wished for you isn't learned in High Schools or measured by terminal exams. Whatever of worth you get at any school you'll dig out for yourself. Don't let them make anything of you but yourself, that's all. I don't think they will."

"No, they won't," said Emily decidedly. "I'm like Kipling's cat—I walk by my wild lone and wave my wild tail where so it pleases me. That's why the Murrays look askance at me. They think I should only run with the pack. Oh, Dean, you'll write me often, won't you? Nobody understands like you. And you've got to be such a habit with me I can't do without you."

Emily said—and meant—it lightly enough; but Dean's thin face flushed darkly. They did not say good-bye—that was an old compact of theirs. Dean waved his hand at her.

"May every day be kind to you," he said.

Emily gave him only her slow, mysterious smile—he was gone. The garden seemed very lonely in the faint blue twilight, with the ghostly blossoms of the white phlox here and there. She was glad when she heard Teddy's whistle in Lofty John's Bush.

On her last evening at home she went to see Mr. Carpenter and get his opinion regarding some manuscripts she had left with him for criticism the preceding week. Among them were her latest stories, written before Aunt Elizabeth's ultimatum. Criticism was something Mr. Carpenter could give with a right good will and he never minced matters; but he was just, and Emily had confidence in his verdicts, even when he said things that raised temporary blisters on her soul.

"This love story is no good," he said bluntly.

"I know that it isn't what I wanted to make it," sighed Emily.

"No story ever is," said Mr. Carpenter. "You'll never write anything that really satisfies you though it may satisfy other people. As for love stories, you can't write them because you can't feel them. Don't try to write anything you can't feel—it will be a failure—'echoes nothing worth.' This other yarn now—about this old woman. It's not bad. The dialogue is clever—the climax simple and effective. And thank the Lord you've got a sense of humor. *That's* mainly why you're no good at love stories, I believe. Nobody with any real sense of humor *can* write a love story."

Emily didn't see why this should be. She liked writing love stories—and terribly sentimental, tragical stories they were.

"Shakespeare could," she said defiantly.

"You're hardly in the Shakespeare class," said Mr. Carpenter drily.

Emily blushed scorchingly.

"I *know* I'm not. But you said *nobody.*"

"And maintain it. Shakespeare is the exception that proves the rule. Though *his* sense of humor was certainly in abeyance when he wrote *Romeo and Juliet.* However, let's come back to Emily of New Moon. *This* story—well, a young person might read it without contamination."

Emily knew by the inflection of Mr. Carpenter's voice that he was not praising her story. She kept silence and Mr. Carpenter went on, flicking her precious manuscripts aside irreverently.

"This one sounds like a weak imitation of Kipling. Been reading him lately?"

"Yes."

"I thought so. Don't try to imitate Kipling. If you *must* imitate, imitate Laura Jean Libbey. Nothing good about this but its title. A priggish little yarn. And *Hidden Riches* is not a story—it's a machine. It creaks. It never made me forget for one instant that it *was* a story. Hence it *isn't* a story."

"I was trying to write something very true to life," protested Emily.

"Ah, that's why. We all see life through an illusion— even the most disillusioned of us. That's why things aren't convincing if they're too true to life. Let me see—*The Madden Family*—another attempt at realism. But it's only photography—not portraiture."

"What a lot of disagreeable things you've said," sighed Emily.

"It might be a nice world if nobody ever said a disagreeable thing, but it would be a dangerous one," retorted Mr. Carpenter. "You told me you wanted criticism, not taffy. However, here's a bit of taffy for you. I kept it for the last. *Something Different* is comparatively good and if I wasn't afraid of ruining you I'd say it was absolutely good. Ten years from now you can rewrite it and make something of it. Yes, ten years—don't screw up your face, Jade. You have talent—and you've got a wonderful feeling for words—you get the inevitable one every time—that's a priceless thing. But you have some vile faults, too. Those cursed italics—forswear them, Jade, forswear them. And your imagination needs a curb when you get away from realism."

"It's to have one now," said Emily, gloomily.

She told him of her compact with Aunt Elizabeth. Mr. Carpenter nodded.

"Excellent."

"Excellent!" echoed Emily blankly.

"Yes. It's just what you need. It will teach you restraint and economy. Stick to facts for three years and see what you can make of them. Leave the realm of imagination severely alone and confine yourself to ordinary life."

"There isn't any such thing as ordinary life," said Emily.

Mr. Carpenter looked at her for a moment.

"You're right—there isn't," he said slowly. "But one wonders a little how you know it. Well, go on—go on—walk in your chosen path—and 'thank whatever gods there be' that you're free to walk it."

"Cousin Jimmy says nobody can be free who has a thousand ancestors."

"And yet people call that man simple," muttered Mr. Carpenter. "However, your ancestors don't seem to have wished any special curse on you. They've simply laid it on you to aim for the heights and they'll give you no peace if you don't. Call it ambition—aspiration— *cacoëthes scribendi*—any name you will. Under its sting—

or allure—one has to go on climbing—until one fails—or——"

"Succeeds," said Emily, flinging back her dark head.

"Amen," said Mr. Carpenter.

Emily wrote a poem that night—*Farewell to New Moon*—and shed tears over it. She felt every line of it. It was all very well to be going to school—but to leave dear New Moon! Everything at New Moon was linked with her life and thoughts—was a part of her.

"It's not only that I love my room and trees and hills—they love me," she thought.

Her little black trunk was packed. Aunt Elizabeth had seen that everything necessary was in it, and Aunt Laura and Cousin Jimmy had seen that one or two unnecessary things were in it. Aunt Laura had told Emily that she would find a pair of black lace stockings inside her strap slippers—even Laura did not dare go so far as silk stockings—and Cousin Jimmy had given her three Jimmy-books and an envelope with a five-dollar bill in it.

"To get anything you want with, Pussy. I'd have made it ten but five was all Elizabeth would advance me on next month's wages. I think she suspected."

"Can I spend a dollar of it for American stamps if I can find a way to get them?" whispered Emily anxiously.

"Anything you like," repeated Cousin Jimmy loyally—though even to him it did appear an unaccountable thing that any one should want to buy American stamps. But if dear little Emily wanted American stamps, American stamps she should have.

The next day seemed rather dream-like to Emily—the bird she heard singing rapturously in Lofty John's bush when she woke at dawn—the drive to Shrewsbury in the early crisp September morning—Aunt Ruth's cool welcome—the hours at a strange school—the organisation of the "Prep" classes—home to supper—surely it must all have taken more than a day.

Aunt Ruth's house was at the end of a residential side street—almost out in the country. Emily thought it a very ugly house, covered as it was with gingerbread-work of various kinds. But a house with white wooden lace on its roof and its bay windows was the last word of elegance in Shrewsbury. There was no garden—nothing but a bare, prim, little lawn; but one thing rejoiced Emily's eyes. Behind the house was a big plantation of tall, slender fir trees—the tallest, straightest, slenderest firs she had ever seen, stretching back into long, green, gossamered vistas.

Aunt Elizabeth had spent the day in Shrewsbury and went home after supper. She shook hands with Emily on the doorstep and told her to be a good girl and do exactly as Aunt Ruth bade her. She did not kiss Emily, but her tone was very gentle for Aunt Elizabeth. Emily choked up and stood tearfully on the doorstep to watch Aunt Elizabeth out of sight—Aunt Elizabeth going back to dear New Moon.

"Come in," said Aunt Ruth, "and *please* don't slam the door."

Now, Emily never slammed doors.

"We will wash the supper dishes," said Aunt Ruth. "You will always do that after this. I will show you where everything is put. I suppose Elizabeth told you I would expect you to do a few chores for your board."

"Yes," said Emily briefly.

She did not mind doing chores, any number of them—but it was Aunt Ruth's *tone*.

"Of course your being here will mean a great deal of extra expense for me," continued Aunt Ruth. "But it is only fair that we should all contribute something to your bringing up. *I* think, and I have always thought, that it would have been much better to send you to Queen's to get a teacher's license."

"I wanted that, too," said Emily.

"M—m." Aunt Ruth pursed her mouth. "So you tell me. In that case I don't see why Elizabeth didn't send you to Queen's. She has pampered you enough in other ways, I'm sure—I would expect her to give in about this, too, if she thought you really wanted it. You will sleep in the kitchen chamber. It is warmer in winter than the other rooms. There is no gas in it but I could not afford to let you have gas to study by in any case. You must use candles—you can burn two at a time. I shall expect you to keep your room neat and tidy and to be here at my exact hours for meals. I am very particular about that. And there is another thing you might as well understand at once. You must not bring your friends here. I do not propose to entertain them."

"Not Ilse—or Perry—or Teddy?"

"Well, Ilse is a Burnley and a distant connection. She might come in once in a while—I can't have her running in at all times. From all I hear of her she isn't a very suitable companion for you. As for the boys— certainly not. I know nothing of Teddy Kent—and you ought to be too proud to associate with Perry Miller."

"I'm too proud *not* to associate with him," retorted Emily.

"Don't be pert with *me*, Em'ly. You might as well understand right away that you are not going to have things all your own way, *here*, as you had at New Moon. You have been badly spoiled. But I will not have hired boys calling on my niece. I don't know where you get your low tastes from, I'm sure. Even your father *seemed* like a gentleman. Go upstairs and unpack your trunk. Then do your lessons. We go to bed at nine o'clock!"

Emily felt very indignant. Even Aunt Elizabeth had never dreamed of forbidding Teddy to come to New Moon. She shut herself in her room and unpacked drearily. The room was such an ugly one. She hated it at sight. The door wouldn't shut tight; the slanting ceiling was rain stained, and came down so close to the bed that she could touch it with her hand. On the bare floor was a large "hooked" mat which made Emily's eyes ache. It was not in Murray taste—nor in Ruth

Dutton's taste either, to be just. A country cousin of the deceased Mr. Dutton had given it to her. The centre, of a crude, glaring scarlet, was surrounded by scrolls of militant orange and violent green. In the corners were bunches of purple ferns and blue roses.

The woodwork was painted a hideous chocolate brown, and the walls were covered with paper of still more hideous design. The pictures were in keeping, especially a chromo of Queen Alexandra, gorgeously bedizened with jewels, hung at such an angle that it seemed the royal lady must certainly fall over on her face. Not even a chromo could make Queen Alexandra ugly or vulgar, but it came piteously near it. On a narrow, chocolate shelf sat a vase filled with paper flowers that had been paper flowers for twenty years. One couldn't believe that *anything* could be as ugly and depressing as they were.

"This room is unfriendly—it doesn't want me—I can *never* feel at home here," said Emily.

She was horribly homesick. She wanted the New Moon candle-lights shining out on the birch trees—the scent of hop-vines in the dew—her purring pussy cats—her own dear room, full of dreams—the silences and shadows of the old garden—the grand anthems of wind and billow in the gulf—that sonorous old music she missed so much in this inland silence. She missed even the little graveyard where slept the New Moon dead.

"I'm *not* going to cry." Emily clenched her hands. "Aunt Ruth will laugh at me. There's nothing *in* this room I can ever love. Is there anything *out* of it?"

She pushed up the window. It looked south into the fir grove and its balsam blew in to her like a caress. To the left there was an opening in the trees like a green, arched window, and one saw an enchanting little moon-lit landscape through it. And it would let in the splendour of sunset. To the right was a view of the hillside along which West Shrewsbury straggled: the hill was dotted with lights in the autumn dusk, and had a fairy-like loveliness., Somewhere near by there was a drowsy twittering, as of little, sleepy birds swinging on a shadowy bough.

"Oh, *this* is beautiful," breathed Emily, bending out to drink in the balsam-scented air. "Father told me once that one could find something beautiful to love *everywhere*. I'll love this."

Aunt Ruth poked her head in at the door, unannounced.

"Em'ly, why did you leave that antimacassar crooked on the sofa in the dining-room?"

"I—don't—know," said Emily confusedly. She hadn't even known she had disarranged the antimacassar. Why did Aunt Ruth ask such a question, as if she suspected her of some dark, deep, sinister design?

"Go down and put it straight."

As Emily turned obediently Aunt Ruth exclaimed,

"Em'ly Starr, put that window down at once! Are you crazy?"

"The room is so close," pleaded Emily.

"You can air it in the daytime but *never* have that window open after sundown. *I* am responsible for your health now. You must know that consumptives have to avoid night air and draughts."

"I'm not a consumptive," cried Emily rebelliously.

"Contradict, of course."

"And if I *were*, fresh air *any* time is the best thing for me. Dr. Burnley says so. I *hate* being smothered."

" 'Young people *think* old people to be fools and old people *know* young people to be fools.' " Aunt Ruth felt that the proverb left nothing to be said. "Go and straighten that antimacassar, Em'ly."

"Em'ly" swallowed something and went. The offending antimacassar was mathematically corrected.

Emily stood for a moment and looked about her. Aunt Ruth's dining-room was much more splendid and "up-to-date" than the "sitting-room" at New Moon where they had "company" meals. Hardwood floor—Wilton rug—Early English oak furniture. But it was not half as "friendly" as the old New Moon room, Emily thought. She was more homesick than ever. She did not believe she was going to like *anything* in Shrewsbury—living with Aunt Ruth, or going to school. The teachers all seemed flat and insipid after pungent Mr. Carpenter and there was a girl in the Junior class she had hated at sight. And she had thought it would be all so delightful—living in pretty Shrewsbury and going to High School. Well, nothing ever *is* exactly like what you expect it to be, Emily told herself in temporary pessimism as she went back to her room. Hadn't Dean told her once that he had dreamed all his life of rowing in a gondola through the canals of Venice on a moonlit night? And when he did he was almost eaten alive by mosquitoes.

Emily set her teeth as she crept into bed.

"I shall just have to fix my thoughts on the moonlight and romance and ignore the mosquitoes," she thought. "Only—Aunt Ruth *does* sting so."

7
Pot-pourri

"September 20, 19—

"I have been neglecting my diary of late. One does not have a great deal of spare time at Aunt Ruth's. But it is Friday night and I couldn't go home for the week-end so I come to my diary for comforting. I can spend only alternate week-ends at New Moon. Aunt Ruth wants me every other Saturday to help 'houseclean.' We go over this house from top to bottom whether it needs it or not, as the tramp said when he washed his face every month, and then rest from our labours for Sunday.

"There is a hint of frost in the air tonight. I am afraid the garden at New Moon will suffer. Aunt Elizabeth will begin to think it is time to give up the cookhouse for the season and move the Waterloo back into the kitchen. Cousin Jimmy will be boiling the pigs' potatoes in the old orchard and reciting his poetry. Likely Teddy and Ilse and Perry—who have all gone home, lucky creatures—will be there and Daff will be prowling about. But I must not think of it. That way homesickness lies.

"I am beginning to like Shrewsbury and Shrewsbury school and Shrewsbury teachers—though Dean was right when he said I would not find any one here like Mr. Carpenter. The Seniors and Juniors look down on the Preps and are very condescending. Some of them condescended to *me*, but I do not think they will try it again—except Evelyn Blake, who condescends every time we meet, as we do quite often, because her chum, Mary Carswell, rooms with Ilse at Mrs. Adamson's boarding-house.

"I hate Evelyn Blake. There is no doubt at all about that. And there is as little doubt that she hates me. We are instinctive enemies—we looked at each other the first time we met like two strange cats, and that was enough. I never really hated any one before. I thought I did but now I know it was only dislike. Hate is rather interesting for a change. Evelyn is a Junior—tall, clever, rather handsome. Has long, bright, *treacherous* brown eyes and talks through her nose. She has *literary ambitions*, I understand, and considers herself the best dressed girl in High School. Perhaps she is; but somehow her clothes seem to make more impression on you than *she* does. People criticise Ilse for dressing too richly and too *old* but she *dominates* her clothes for all that. Evelyn doesn't. You always think of her clothes before you think of her. The difference seems to be that Evelyn dresses for other people and Ilse dresses for herself. I must write a character sketch of her when I have studied her a little more. What a satisfaction that will be!

"I met her first in Ilse's room and Mary Carswell introduced us. Evelyn looked down at me—she is a little taller, being a year older—and said,

"'Oh, yes, Miss Starr? I've heard my aunt, Mrs. Henry Blake, talking about you.'

"Mrs. Henry Blake was once Miss Brownell. I looked straight into Evelyn's eyes and said,

"'No doubt Mrs. Henry Blake painted a very flattering picture of me.'

"Evelyn laughed—with a kind of laugh I don't like. It gives you the feeling that she is laughing at *you*, not at what you've said.

"'You didn't get on very well with her, did you? I understand you are quite literary. What papers do you write for?'

"She asked the question sweetly but she knew perfectly well that I don't write for any—yet.

"'The Charlottetown *Enterprise* and the Shrewsbury *Weekly Times*,' I said with a wicked grin. 'I've just made a bargain with them. I'm to get two cents for every news item I send the *Enterprise* and twenty-five cents a week for a society letter for the *Times*.'

"My grin worried Evelyn. Preps aren't supposed to grin like that at Juniors. It isn't done.

"'Oh, yes, I understand you are working for your board,' she said. 'I suppose every little helps. But I meant real literary periodicals.'

"'The Quill?' I asked with another grin.

"The Quill is the High School paper, appearing monthly. It is edited by the members of the *Skull and Owl*, a 'literary society' to which only Juniors and Seniors are eligible. The contents of The Quill are written by the students and in theory any student can contribute but in practice hardly anything is ever accepted from a Prep. Evelyn is a Skull and Owlite and her cousin is editor of *The Quill*. She evidently thought I was waxing sarcastic at her expense and ignored me for the rest of her call, except for one dear little jab when dress came up for discussion.

" 'I want one of the new ties,' she said. 'There are some sweet ones at Jones and McCallum's and they are awfully smart. The little black velvet ribbon you are wearing around your neck, Miss Starr, is rather becoming. I used to wear one myself when they were in style.'

"I couldn't think of anything clever to say in retort. I can think of clever things so easily when there is no one to say them to. So I said nothing but merely smiled *very* slowly and *disdainfully*. That seemed to annoy Evelyn more than speech, for I heard she said afterwards that 'that Emily Starr' had a very affected smile.

"Note:—One can do a great deal with appropriate smiles. I must study the subject carefully. The friendly smile—the scornful smile—the detached smile—the entreating smile—the common or garden grin.

"As for Miss Brownell—or rather Mrs. Blake—I met *her* on the street a few days ago. After she passed she said something to her companion and they both laughed. Very bad manners, *I* think.

"I like Shrewsbury and I like school but I shall never like Aunt Ruth's house. It has a disagreeable personality. Houses are like people—some you like and some you don't like—and once in a while there is one you love. Outside, this house is covered with frippery. I feel like getting a broom and sweeping it off. Inside, its rooms are all square and proper and soulless. Nothing you could put into them would ever seem to belong to them. There are no nice romantic corners in it, as there are at New Moon. My room hasn't improved on acquaintance, either. The ceiling oppresses me—it comes down so low over my bed—and Aunt Ruth won't let me move the bed. She looked amazed when I suggested it.

" 'The bed has *always* been in that corner,' she said, just as she might have said, 'The sun has always risen in the east.'

"But the pictures are really the worst thing about this room—chromos of the most aggravated description. Once I turned them all to the wall and of course Aunt Ruth walked in—she *never* knocks—and noticed them at once.

" 'Em'ly, why have you meddled with the pictures?'

"Aunt Ruth is always asking 'why' I do this and that. Sometimes I can explain and sometimes I can't. This was one of the times I couldn't. But of course I had to answer Aunt Ruth's question. No disdainful smile would do here.

" 'Queen Alexandra's dog collar gets on my nerves,' I said, 'and Byron's expression on his death-bed at Missolonghi hinders me from studying.'

" 'Em'ly,' said Aunt Ruth, 'you might try to show a *little* gratitude.'

"I wanted to say,

" 'To whom—Queen Alexandra or Lord Byron?' but of course I didn't. Instead I meekly turned all the pictures right side out again.

" 'You haven't told me the real reason why you turned those pictures,' said Aunt Ruth sternly. 'I suppose you don't mean to tell me. Deep and sly—deep and sly—I always said you were. The very first time I saw you at Maywood I said you were the slyest child I have ever seen.'

" 'Aunt Ruth, why do you say such things to me?' I said, in exasperation. 'Is it because you love me and want to improve me—or hate me and want to hurt me—or just because you can't help it?'

" 'Miss Impertinence, please remember that this is *my* house. And you will leave *my* pictures alone after this. I will forgive you for meddling with them this time but don't let it happen again. I will find out yet your motive in turning them around, clever as you think yourself.'

"Aunt Ruth stalked out but I know she listened on the landing quite a while to find out if I would begin talking to myself. She is always watching me—even when she says nothing—does nothing—I know she is watching me. I feel like a little fly under a microscope. Not a word or action escapes her criticism, and, though she can't read my thoughts, she attributes thoughts to me that I never had any idea of thinking. I hate that worse than anything else.

"Can't I say anything good of Aunt Ruth? Of course I can.

"She is honest and virtuous and truthful and industrious and of her pantry she needeth not to be ashamed. But she hasn't any lovable virtues—and she will never give up trying to find out why I turned the pictures. She will never believe that I told her the simple truth.

"Of course, things 'might be worse.' As Teddy says, it might have been Queen Victoria instead of Queen Alexandra.

"I have some pictures of my own pinned up that save me—some lovely sketches of New Moon and the old orchard that Teddy made for me, and an engraving Dean gave me. It is a picture in soft, dim colours of palms around a desert well and a train of camels passing across the sands against a black sky gemmed with stars. It is full of lure and mystery and when I look at it I forget Queen Alexandra's jewelry and Lord Byron's lugubrious face, and my soul slips out—out—through a little gateway into a great, vast world of freedom and dream.

"Aunt Ruth asked me where I got that picture. When I told her she sniffed and said,

" 'I can't understand how you have such a liking for Jarback Priest. He's a man I've no use for.'

"I shouldn't think she would have.

"But if the house is ugly and my room unfriendly, the Land of Uprightness is beautiful and saves my soul alive. The Land of Uprightness is the fir grove behind the house. I call it that because the firs are all so exceedingly tall and slender and straight. There is a pool in it, veiled with ferns, with a big grey boulder beside it. It is reached by a little, winding, capricious path so narrow that only one can walk in it. When I'm tired or lonely or angry or too ambitious I go there and sit for a few minutes. Nobody can keep an upset mind looking at those slender, crossed tips against the sky. I go there to study on fine evenings, though Aunt Ruth is suspicious and thinks it is just another manifestation of my slyness. Soon it will be dark too early to study there and I'll be so sorry. Somehow, my books have a *meaning* there they never have anywhere else.

"There are so many dear, green corners in the Land of Uprightness, full of the aroma of sun-steeped ferns, and grassy, open spaces where pale asters feather the grass, swaying gently towards each other when the Wind Woman runs among them. And just to the left of my window there is a group of tall old firs that look, in moonlight or twilight, like a group of witches weaving spells of sorcery. When I first saw them, one windy night against the red sunset, with the reflection of my candle, like a weird, signal flame, suspended in the air among their boughs, the *flash* came—for the first time in Shrewsbury—and I felt so happy that nothing else mattered. I have written a poem about them.

"But oh, I burn to write stories. I knew it would be hard to keep my promise to Aunt Elizabeth but I didn't know it would be *so* hard. Every day it seems harder—such splendid ideas for plots pop into my mind. Then I have to fall back on character studies of the people I know. I have written several of them. I always feel so strongly tempted to *touch them up a bit*—deepen the shadows—bring out the highlights a little more vividly. But I remember that I promised Aunt Elizabeth never to write anything that wasn't true so I stay my hand and try to paint them exactly as they are.

"I have written one of Aunt Ruth. Interesting but dangerous. I never leave my Jimmy-book or my diary in my room. I know Aunt Ruth rummages through it when I'm out. So I always carry them in my book-bag.

"Ilse was up this evening and we did our lessons together. Aunt Ruth frowns on this—and, to be strictly just, I don't know that she is wrong. Ilse is so jolly and comical that we laugh more than we study, I'm afraid. We don't do as well in class next day—and besides, this house disapproves of laughter.

"Perry and Teddy like the High School. Perry earns his lodging by looking after the furnace and grounds and his board by waiting on the table. Besides, he gets twenty-five cents an hour for doing odd jobs. I don't see much of him or Teddy, except in the week-ends home, for it is against the school rules for boys and girls to walk together to and from school. Lots *do* it, though. I had several chances to but I concluded that it would not be in keeping with New Moon traditions to break the rule. Besides, Aunt Ruth asks me every blessed night when I come home from school if I've walked with anybody. I think she's sometimes a little disappointed when I say 'No.'

"Besides, I didn't much fancy any of the boys who wanted to walk with me.

                              "October 20, 19—

"My room is full of boiled cabbage smells tonight but I dare not open my window. Too much night air outside. I would risk it for a little while if Aunt Ruth hadn't been in a very bad humor all day. Yesterday was my Sunday in Shrewsbury and when we went to church I sat in the corner of the pew. I did not know that Aunt Ruth must always sit there but she thought I did it on purpose. She read her Bible all the afternoon.

I *felt* she was reading it *at* me, though I couldn't imagine why. This morning she asked me why I did it.

" 'Did what?' I said in bewilderment.

" 'Em'ly, you know what you did. I will not tolerate this slyness. What was your motive?'

" 'Aunt Ruth, I haven't the slightest idea what you mean,' I said—quite haughtily, for I felt I was not being treated fairly.

" 'Em'ly, you sat in the corner of the pew yesterday just to keep me out of it. *Why* did you do it?"

"I looked down at Aunt Ruth—I am taller than she is now and I can do it. She doesn't like it, either. I was angry and I *think* I had a little of the Murray look on my face. The whole thing seemed so contemptible to be making a fuss over.

" 'If I did it to keep you out of it, isn't that *why*?' I said as contemptuously as I felt. I picked up my book-bag and stalked to the door. There I stopped. It occurred to me that, whatever the Murrays might or might not do, I was not behaving as a Starr should. Father wouldn't have approved of my behaviour. So I turned and said, very politely,

" 'I should not have spoken like that, Aunt Ruth, and I beg your pardon. I didn't mean anything by sitting in the corner. It was just because I happened to go into the pew first. I didn't know you preferred the corner.'

"Perhaps I overdid the politeness. At any rate, my apology only seemed to irritate Aunt Ruth the more. She sniffed and said,

" 'I will forgive you this time, but don't let it happen again. Of course I didn't expect you would tell me your reason. You are too sly for that.'

"Aunt Ruth, Aunt Ruth! If you keep on calling me sly you'll drive me into being sly in reality and *then* watch out. If I choose to be sly I can twist you round my finger! It's only because I'm straightforward that you can manage me at all.

"I have to go to bed every night at nine o'clock—

'people who are threatened with consumption require a great deal of sleep.' When I come from school there are chores to be done and I must study in the evenings. So I haven't a moment of time for writing anything. I know Aunt Elizabeth and Aunt Ruth have had a conference on the subject. But I *have* to write. So I get up in the morning as soon as it is daylight, dress, and put on a coat—for the mornings are cold now—sit down and scribble for a priceless hour. I didn't choose that Aunt Ruth should discover it and call me sly so I told her I was doing it. She gave me to understand that I was mentally unsound and would make a bad end in some asylum, but she didn't actually forbid me—probably because she thought it would be of no use. It wouldn't. I've *got* to write, that is all there is to it. That hour in the grey morning is the most delightful one in the day for me.

"Lately, being forbidden to write stories, I've been *thinking* them out. But one day it struck me that I was breaking my compact with Aunt Elizabeth in spirit if not in letter. So I have stopped it.

"I wrote a character study of Ilse today. Very fascinating. It is difficult to analyse her. She is so different and unexpectable. (I coined that word myself.) She doesn't even get mad like anybody else. I enjoy her tantrums. She doesn't say so many awful things in them as she used to but she is *piquant*. (Piquant is a new word for me. I like using a new word. I never think I really own a word until I've spoken or written it.)

"I am writing by my window. I love to watch the Shrewsbury lights twinkle out in the dusk over that long hill.

"I had a letter from Dean today. He is in Egypt—among ruined shrines of old gods and the tombs of old kings. I saw that strange land through his eyes—I seemed to go back with him through the old centuries—I knew the magic of its skies. I was Emily of Karnak or

Thebes—not Emily of Shrewsbury at all. That is a trick Dean has.

"Aunt Ruth insisted on seeing his letter and when she read it she said it was impious!

"I should never have thought of that adjective.

"October 21, 19—

"I climbed the steep little wooded hill in the Land of Uprightness tonight and had an exultation on its crest. There's always something satisfying in climbing to the top of a hill. There was a fine tang of frost in the air, the view over Shrewsbury Harbour was very wonderful, and the woods all about me were expecting something to happen soon—at least that is the only way I can describe the effect they had on me. I forgot *everything*—Aunt Ruth's stings and Evelyn Blake's patronage and Queen Alexandra's dog collar—everything in life that isn't just right. Lovely thoughts came flying to meet me like birds. They weren't *my* thoughts. I couldn't think anything half so exquisite. They *came* from somewhere.

"Coming back, on that dark little path, where the air was full of nice, whispering sounds, I heard a chuckle of laughter in a fir copse just behind me. I was startled—and a little bit alarmed. I knew at once it wasn't human laughter—it was more like the Puckish mirth of fairy folk, with just a faint hint of malice in it. I can no longer believe in wood elves—alas, one loses so much when one becomes incredulous—so this laughter puzzled me—and, yes, a horrid, crawly feeling began in my spine. Then, suddenly, I thought of owls and knew it for what it was—a truly delightful sound, as if some survival of the Golden Age were chuckling to himself there in the dark. There were two of them, I think, and they were certainly having a good time over some owlish joke. I must write a poem about it—though I'll never be able to put into words half the charm and devilry of it.

"Ilse was up on the carpet in the principal's room yesterday for walking home from school with Guy Lindsay. Something Mr. Hardy said made her so furious that she snatched up a vase of chrysanthemums that was on his desk and hurled it against the wall, where of course it was smashed to pieces.

"'If I hadn't thrown it at the wall I'd have had to have thrown it at *you*,' she told him.

"It would have gone hard with some girls but Mr. Hardy is a friend of Dr. Burnley's. Besides, there is something about those yellow eyes of Ilse's that do things to you. I know exactly how she would look at Mr. Hardy after she had smashed the vase. All her rage would be gone and her eyes would be laughing and daring—impudent, Aunt Ruth would call it. Mr. Hardy merely told her she was acting like a baby and would have to pay for the vase, since it was school property. That rather squelched Ilse; she thought it a tame ending to her heroics.

"I scolded her roundly. Really, somebody *has* to bring Ilse up and nobody but me seems to feel any responsibility in the matter. Dr. Burnley will just roar with laughter when she tells him. But I might as well have scolded the Wind Woman. Ilse just laughed and hugged me.

"'Honey, it made such a jolly smash. When I heard it I wasn't a bit mad any more.'

"Ilse recited at our school concert last week and everybody thought her wonderful.

"Aunt Ruth told me today that she expected me to be a star pupil. She wasn't punning on my name—oh, no, Aunt Ruth hasn't a nodding acquaintance with puns. All the pupils who make ninety per cent. average at the Christmas exams and do not fall below eighty in any subject are called 'Star' pupils and are given a gold star-pin to wear for the rest of the term. It is a coveted distinction and of course not many win it. If I fail Aunt Ruth will rub it in to the bone. I must *not* fail.

          "October 30, 19—

"The November *Quill* came out today. I sent my owl poem in to the editor a week ago but he didn't use it. And he *did* use one of Evelyn Blake's—a silly, simpering little rhyme about *Autumn Leaves*—very much the sort of thing *I* wrote three years ago.

"And Evelyn *condoled* with me before the whole roomful of girls because *my* poem hadn't been taken. I suppose Tom Blake had told her about it.

" 'You mustn't feel badly about it, Miss Starr. Tom said it wasn't half bad but of course not up to *The Quill's* standard. Likely in another year or two you'll be able to get in. Keep on trying.'

" 'Thanks,' I said. 'I'm not feeling badly. Why should I? I didn't make "beam" rhyme with "green" in *my* poem. If I had I'd be feeling very badly indeed.'

"Evelyn coloured to her eyes.

" 'Don't show your disappointment so plainly, *child*,' she said.

"But I noticed she dropped the subject after that.

"For my own satisfaction I wrote a criticism of Evelyn's poem in my Jimmy-book as soon as I came from school. I modelled it on Macaulay's essay on poor Robert Montgomery, and I got so much fun out of it that I didn't feel sore and humiliated any more. I must show it to Mr. Carpenter when I go home. He'll chuckle over it.

          "November 6, 19—

"I noticed this evening in glancing over my journal that I soon gave up recording my good and bad deeds. I suppose it was because so many of my doings were half-and-half. I never could decide in what class they belonged.

"We are expected to answer roll call with a quotation on Monday mornings. This morning I repeated a verse from my own poem *A Window that Faces the Sea*. When I left Assembly to go down to the Prep classroom Miss Aylmer, the Vice-Principal, stopped me.

" 'Emily, that was a beautiful verse you gave at roll call. Where did you get it? And do you know the whole poem?'

"I was so elated I could hardly answer,

" 'Yes, Miss Aylmer,' *very* demurely.

" 'I would like a copy of it,' said Miss Aylmer. 'Could you write me off one? And who is the author?'

" 'The author,' I said laughing, 'is Emily Byrd Starr. The truth is, Miss Aylmer, that I forgot to look up a quotation for roll call and couldn't think of any in a hurry, so just fell back on a bit of my own.'

"Miss Alymer didn't say anything for a moment. She just looked at me. She is a stout, middle-aged woman with a square face and nice, wide, grey eyes.

" 'Do you still want the poem, Miss Aylmer?' I said, smiling.

" 'Yes,' she said, still looking at me in that funny way, as if she had never seen me before. 'Yes—and autograph it, please.'

"I promised and went on down the stairs. At the foot I glanced back. She was still looking after me. Something in her look made me feel glad and proud and happy and humble—and—and—*prayerful*. Yes, that was just how I felt.

"Oh, this has been a wonderful day. What care I now for *The Quill* or Evelyn Blake?

"This evening Aunt Ruth marched up town to see Uncle Oliver's Andrew, who is in the bank here now. She made me go along. She gave Andrew lots of good advice about his morals and his meals and his under-clothes and asked him to come down for an evening whenever he wished. Andrew is a Murray, you see, and can therefore rush in where Teddy and Perry dare not tread. He is quite good-looking, with straight, well-groomed, red hair. But he always looks as if he'd just been starched and ironed.

"I thought the evening not wholly wasted, for Mrs. Garden, his landlady, has an interesting cat who made certain advances to me. But when Andrew patted him and called him 'Poor pussy' the intelligent animal hissed at him.

"'You mustn't be too familiar with a cat,' I advised Andrew. 'And you must speak respectfully *to* and *of* him.'

"'Piffle!' said Aunt Ruth.

"But a cat's a cat for a' that.

"November 8, 19—

"The nights are cold now. When I came back Monday I brought one of the New Moon gin jars for my comforting. I cuddle down with it in bed and enjoy the contrasting roars of the storm wind outside in the Land of Uprightness, and the rain whirling over the roof. Aunt Ruth worries for fear the cork will come out and deluge the bed. That would be almost as bad as what really did happen night before last. I woke up about midnight with the most wonderful idea for a story. I felt that I must rise at once and jot it down in a Jimmy-book before I forgot it. Then I could keep it until my three years are up and I am free to write it.

"I hopped out of bed and, in pawing around my table to find my candle, I upset my ink bottle. Then of course I went mad and couldn't find *anything!* Matches—candles—everything had disappeared. I set the ink bottle up, but I knew there was a pool of ink on the table. I had ink all over my fingers and dare not touch anything in the dark and couldn't find anything to wipe it off. And all the time I heard that ink drip-dripping on the floor.

"In desperation I opened the door—with my *toes* because I dare not touch it with my inky hands—and went downstairs where I wiped my hands on the stove rag and got some matches. By this time, of course, Aunt Ruth was up, demanding whys and motives. She took my matches, lighted her candle, and marched me upstairs. Oh, 'twas a gruesome sight! How could a small stone ink-bottle hold a quart of ink? There *must* have been a quart to have made the mess it did.

"I felt like the old Scotch emigrant who came home one evening, found his house burned down and his entire family scalped by Indians and said, 'This is pairfectly redeeclous.' The table cover was ruined—the carpet was soaked—even the wall paper was bespattered. But Queen Alexandra smiled benignly over all and Bryon went on dying.

"Aunt Ruth and I had an hour's seance with salt and vinegar. Aunt Ruth wouldn't believe me when I said I got up to jot down the plot of a story. She knew I had some other motive and it was just some more of my deepness and slyness. She also said a few other things which I won't write down. Of course I deserved a scolding for leaving that ink bottle uncorked; but I *didn't* deserve all she said. However, I took it all very meekly. For one thing I *had* been careless: and for another I had my bedroom shoes on. Any one can overcrow me when I'm wearing bedroom shoes. Then she wound up by saying she would forgive me this time, but it was not to happen again.

"Perry won the mile race in the school sports and broke the record. He bragged too much about it and Ilse raged at him.

"November 11, 19—
"Last night Aunt Ruth found me reading *David Copper-field* and crying over *Davy's* alienation from his mother, with

a black rage against *Mr. Murdstone* in my heart. She must know *why* I was crying and wouldn't believe me when I told her.

" 'Crying over people who never existed!' said my Aunt Ruth incredulously.

" 'Oh, but they *do* exist,' I said. 'Why, they are as real as *you* are, Aunt Ruth. Do you mean to say that Miss Betsy Trotwood is a delusion?'

"I thought perhaps I could have *real* tea when I came to Shrewsbury, but Aunt Ruth says it is not healthy. So I drink cold water for I will *not* drink cambric tea any longer. As if I were a child!

"November 30, 19—

"Andrew was in tonight. He always comes the Friday night I don't go to New Moon. Aunt Ruth left us alone in the parlour and went out to a meeting of the Ladies' Aid. Andrew, being a Murray, can be trusted.

"I don't dislike Andrew. It would be impossible to dislike so harmless a being. He is one of those good, talkative, awkward dears who goad you irresistibly into tormenting them. Then you feel remorseful afterwards because they *are* so good.

"Tonight, Aunt Ruth being out, I tried to discover how little I could really say to Andrew, while I pursued my own train of thought. I discovered that I could get along with very few words—'Yes'—'No'—in several inflections, with or without a little laugh—'I don't know' —'Really?'—'Well, well'—'How wonderful!'—es-pecially the last. Andrew talked on, and when he stopped for breath I stuck in 'How wonderful.' I did it exactly eleven times. Andrew liked it. I know it gave him a nice, flattering feeling that *he* was wonderful, and his conversation wonderful. Meanwhile I was living a splen-did imaginary dream life by the River of Egypt in the days of Thotmes I.

"So we were both very happy. I think I'll try it again. Andrew is too stupid to catch me at it.

"When Aunt Ruth came home she asked, 'Well, how did you and Andrew get along?'

"She asks that every time he comes down. I *know why*. I know the little scheme that is understood among the Murrays, even though I don't believe any of them have ever put it into words.

" 'Beautifully,' I said. 'Andrew is improving. He said *one* interesting thing tonight, and he hadn't so many feet and hands as usual.'

"I don't know *why* I say things like that to Aunt Ruth occasionally. It would be so much better for me if I didn't. But *something*—whether it's Murray or Starr or Shipley or Burnley, or just pure cussedness I know not—*makes* me say them before I've time to reflect.

" 'No doubt you would find more congenial company in Stovepipe Town,' said Aunt Ruth."

8
Not Proven

Emily regretfully left the "Booke Shoppe," where the aroma of books and new magazines was as the savour of sweet incense in her nostrils, and hastened down cold and blustery Prince Street. Whenever possible she slipped into the Booke Shoppe and took hungry dips into magazines she could not afford to buy, avid to learn what kind of stuff they published—especially poetry. She could not see that many of the verses in them were any better than some of her own, yet editors sent hers back religiously. Emily had already used a considerable portion of the American stamps she had bought with Cousin Jimmy's dollar in paying the homeward way of her fledglings, accompanied by only the cold comfort of rejection slips. Her *Owl's Laughter* had already been returned six times, but Emily had not wholly lost faith in it yet. That very morning she had dropped it again into the letter-box at the Shoppe.

"The seventh time brings luck," she thought as she turned down the street leading to Ilse's boarding-house. She had her examination in English at eleven o'clock and she wanted to glance over Ilse's note-book before she went for it. The Preps were almost through their terminal examinations, taking them by fits and starts when the class-rooms were free from Seniors and Juniors—a thing that always made the Preps furious. Emily felt comfortably certain she would get her star pin. The examinations in her hardest subjects were over and she did not believe she had fallen below eighty in any of them. Today was English, in which she ought to go well over ninety. Remained only history, which she also loved. Everybody expected her to win the star pin. Cousin Jimmy was intensely excited over it, and Dean had sent her premature congratulations from the top of a pyramid, so sure was he of her success. His letter had come the previous day, along with the packet containing his Christmas gift.

"I send you a little gold necklace that was taken from the mummy of a dead princess of the nineteenth dynasty," wrote Dean. "Her name was Mena and it said in her epitaph that she was 'sweet of heart.' So I think she fared well in the Hall of Judgment and that the dread old gods smiled indulgently upon her. This little amulet lay on her dead breast for thousands of years. I send it to you weighted with centuries of love. I think it must have been a love gift. Else why should it have rested on her heart all this time? It must have been her own choice. Others would have put a finer thing on the neck of a king's daughter."

The little trinket intrigued Emily with its charm and mystery, yet she was almost afraid of it. She gave a slight ghostly shudder as she clasped it around her slim white throat and wondered about the royal girl who had worn it in those days of a dead empire. What was its history and its secret?

Naturally Aunt Ruth had disapproved. What business had Emily to be getting Christmas presents from Jarback Priest?

"At least he might have sent you something *new* if he had to send anything," she said.

"A souvenir of Cairo, made in Germany," suggested Emily gravely.

"Something like that," agreed Aunt Ruth unsuspiciously. "Mrs. Ayers has a handsome, gold-mounted glass paper-weight with a picture of the Sphinx in it that her brother brought *her* from Egypt. That battered thing looks positively cheap."

"Cheap! Aunt Ruth, do you realise that this necklace was made by hand and worn by an Egyptian princess before the days of Moses?"

"Oh, well—if you want to believe Jarback Priest's fairy tales," said Aunt Ruth, much amused. "I wouldn't wear it in public if I were you, Em'ly. The Murrays never wear shabby jewelry. You're not going to leave it on tonight, child?"

"Of course I am. The last time it was worn was probably at the court of Pharaoh in the days of the oppression. Now, it will go to Kit Barrett's snowshoe dance. What a difference! I hope the ghost of Princess Mena won't haunt me tonight. She may resent my sacrilege—who knows? But it was not I who rifled her tomb, and somebody would have this if I didn't— somebody who mightn't think of the little princess at all. I'm sure she would rather that it was warm and shining about my neck than in some grim museum for thousands of curious, cold eyes to stare at. She was 'sweet of heart,' Dean says—she won't grudge me her pretty pendant. Lady of Egypt, whose kingdom has been poured on the desert sands like spilled wine, I salute you across the gulf of time."

Emily bowed deeply and waved her hand adown the vistas of dead centuries.

"Such high-falutin' language is very foolish," sniffed Aunt Ruth.

"Oh, most of that last sentence was a quotation from Dean's letter," said Emily candidly.

"Sounds like him," was Aunt Ruth's contemptuous agreement. "Well, *I* think your Venetian beads would be better than that heathenish-looking thing. Now, mind you don't stay too late, Em'ly. Make Andrew bring you home not later than twelve."

Emily was going with Andrew to Kitty Barrett's dance—a privilege quite graciously accorded since Andrew was one of the elect people. Even when she did not get home until one o'clock Aunt Ruth overlooked it. But it left Emily rather sleepy for the day, especially as she had studied late the two previous nights. Aunt Ruth relaxed her rigid rules in examination time and permitted an extra allowance of candles. What she would have said had she known that Emily used some of the extra candlelight to write a poem on *Shadows* I do not know and cannot record. But no doubt she would have considered it an added proof of slyness. Perhaps it was sly. Remember that I am only Emily's biographer, not her apologist.

Emily found Evelyn Blake in Ilse's room and Evelyn Blake was secretly much annoyed because *she* had not been invited to the snowshoe dance and Emily Starr had. Therefore Evelyn, sitting on Ilse's table and swinging her high, silken-sheathed instep flauntingly in the face of girls who had no silk stockings, was prepared to be disagreeable.

"I'm glad you've come, trusty and well-beloved," moaned Ilse. "Evelyn has been clapper-clawing me all the morning. Perhaps she'll whirl in at you now and give me a rest."

"I have been telling her that she should learn to control her temper," said Evelyn virtuously. "Don't you agree with me, Miss Starr?"

"What have you been doing now, Ilse?" asked Emily.

"Oh, I had a large quarrel with Mrs. Adamson this morning. It was bound to come sooner or later. I've been good so long there was an awful lot of wickedness bottled up in me. Mary knew that, didn't you, Mary? Mary felt quite sure an explosion was due to happen. Mrs. Adamson began it by asking disagreeable questions. She's always doing that—isn't she, Mary? After that she started in scolding—and finally she cried. *Then* I slapped her face."

"You see," said Evelyn, significantly.

"I couldn't help it," grinned Ilse. "I could have endured her impertinence and her scolding—but when she began to cry—she's so *ugly* when she cries—well, I just slapped her."

"I suppose you felt better after that," said Emily, determined not to show any disapproval before Evelyn.

Ilse burst out laughing.

"Yes, at first. It stopped her yowling, anyway. But afterwards came remorse. I'll apologise to her, of course. I *do* feel real sorry—but I'm quite likely to do it again. If Mary here weren't so good I wouldn't be half as bad. I have to even the balance up a bit. Mary is meek and humble and Mrs. Adamson walks all over her. You should hear her scold Mary if Mary goes out more than one evening a week."

"She is right," said Evelyn. "It would be much better if *you* went out less. You're getting talked about, Ilse."

"You weren't out last night, anyhow, were you, dear?" asked Ilse with another unholy grin.

Evelyn coloured and was haughtily silent. Emily buried herself in her note-book and Mary and Ilse went out. Emily wished Evelyn would go, too. But Evelyn had no intention of going.

"Why don't you make Ilse behave herself?" she began in a hatefully confidential sort of way.

"*I* have no authority over Ilse," said Emily coldly. "Besides, I don't think she misbehaves."

"Oh, my dear girl—why, you heard her yourself saying she slapped Mrs. Adamson."

"Mrs. Adamson *needed* it. She's an odious woman— *always* crying when there's no need in the world for her to cry. There's nothing more aggravating."

"Well, Ilse skipped French *again* yesterday afternoon and went for a walk up-river with Ronnie Gibson. If she does that too often she's going to get caught."

"Ilse is very popular with the boys," said Emily, who knew that Evelyn wanted to be.

"She's popular in the wrong quarters." Evelyn was condescending now, knowing by instinct that Emily Starr hated to be condescended to. "She always has a ruck of wild boys after her—the nice ones don't bother with her, you notice."

"Ronnie Gibson's nice, isn't he?"

"Well, what do you say to Marshall Orde?"

"Ilse has nothing to do with Marshall Orde."

"Oh, hasn't she! She was driving with him till twelve o'clock last Tuesday night—and he was drunk when he got the horse from the livery stable."

"I don't believe a word of it! Ilse never went driving with Marsh Orde." Emily was white-lipped with indignation.

"I was told by a person who *saw* them. Ilse is being talked about *everywhere*. Perhaps you have no authority over her but surely you have some *influence*. Though *you* do foolish things yourself sometimes, don't you? Not meaning any harm perhaps. That time you went bathing on the Blair Water sands without any clothes on, for instance? *That's* known all through the school. I heard Marsh's brother laughing about it. Now, *wasn't* that foolish, my dear?"

Emily blushed with anger and shame—though quite as much over being my-deared by Evelyn Blake as anything else. That beautiful bathing by moonlight— what a thing of desecration it had been made by the world! She would *not* discuss it with Evelyn—she would not even tell Evelyn they had their petticoats on. Let her think what she would.

"I don't think you quite understand some things, Miss Blake," she said, with a certain fine, detached irony of tone and manner which made very commonplace words seem charged with meanings unutterable.

"Oh, you belong to the Chosen People, don't you?" Evelyn laughed her malicious little laugh.

"I do," said Emily calmly, refusing to withdraw her eyes from her note-book.

"Well, don't get so vexed, dear. I only spoke because I thought it a pity to see poor Ilse getting in wrong everywhere. I rather like her, poor soul. And I wish she would tone down her taste in colours a bit. That scarlet evening dress she wore at the Prep concert— really, you know, it's weird."

"She looked like a tall golden lily in a scarlet sheath, *I* thought," said Emily.

"What a loyal friend you are, dear. I wonder if Ilse would stand up for *you* like that. Well, I suppose I ought to let you study. You have English at ten, haven't you? Mr. Scoville is going to watch the room—Mr. Travers is sick. Don't you think Mr. Scoville's hair is wonderful? Speaking of hair, dear, why don't you dress yours low enough at the sides to hide your ears—the tips, anyway? I think it would become you so much better."

Emily decided that if Evelyn Blake called her "dear" again she would throw an ink-bottle at her. *Why* didn't she go away and let her study?

Evelyn had another shot in her locker.

"That callow young friend of yours from Stovepipe Town has been trying to get into *The Quill*. He sent in a patriotic poem. Tom showed it to me. It was a scream. One line especially was delicious—'Canada, like a *maiden*, welcomes back her sons.' You should have heard Tom howl."

Emily could hardly help smiling herself, though she was horribly annoyed with Perry for making such a target of himself. *Why* couldn't he learn his limitations and understand that the slopes of Parnassus were not for him?

"I do not think the editor of *The Quill* has any business to show rejected contributions to outsiders," she said coldly.

"Oh, Tom doesn't look on *me* as an outsider. And that really *was* too good to keep. Well, I think I'll run down to the Shoppe."

Emily sighed with relief as Evelyn took her departure. Presently Ilse returned.

"Evelyn gone? Sweet temper she was in this morning. I can't understand what Mary sees in her. Mary's a decent sort though she isn't exciting."

"Ilse," said Emily seriously. "Were you out driving with Marsh Orde one night last week?"

Ilse stared.

"No, you dear young ass, I wasn't. I can guess where you heard *that* yarn. I don't know who the girl was."

"But you cut French and went up-river with Ronnie Gibson?"

"Peccavi."

"Ilse—you shouldn't—really——"

"Now, don't make me mad, Emily!" said Ilse shortly. "You're getting too smug—something ought to be done to cure you before it gets chronic. I hate prunes and prisms. I'm off—I want to run round to the Shoppe before I go to the school."

Ilse gathered up her books pettishly and flounced

out. Emily yawned and decided she was through with the notebook. She had half an hour yet before it was necessary to go to the school. She would lie down on Ilse's bed for just a moment.

It seemed the next minute when she found herself sitting up, staring with dismayed face at Mary Carswell's clock. Five minutes to eleven—five minutes to cover a quarter of a mile and be at her desk for examination. Emily flung on coat and cap, caught up her note-books and fled. She arrived at the High School out of breath, with a nasty subconsciousness that people had looked at her queerly as she tore through the streets, hung up her wraps without a glance at the mirror, and hurried into the class-room.

A stare of amazement followed by a ripple of laughter went over the room. Mr. Scoville, tall, slim, elegant, was giving out the examination papers. He laid one down before Emily and said gravely,

"Did you look in your mirror before you came to class, Miss Starr?"

"No," said Emily resentfully, sensing something fearfully wrong somewhere.

"I—think—I would look—now—if I were—you." Mr. Scoville seemed to be speaking with difficulty.

Emily got up and went back to the girls' dressing-room. She met Principal Hardy in the Hall and Principal Hardy stared at her. Why Principal Hardy stared—why the Preps had laughed—Emily understood when she confronted the dressing-room looking-glass.

Drawn skilfully and blackly across her upper lip and her cheeks was a moustache—a flamboyant, very black moustache, with fantastically curled ends. For a moment Emily gaped at herself in blank horror—why—what—*who* had done it?

She whirled furiously about. Evelyn Blake had just entered the room.

"*You*—you did this!" panted Emily.

Evelyn stared for a moment—then went off into a peal of laughter.

"Emily Starr! You look like a nightmare. Do you mean to tell me you went into class with *that* on your face?"

Emily clenched her hands.

"*You* did it," she said again.

Evelyn drew herself up very haughtily.

"Really, Miss Starr, I hope you don't think I'd *stoop* to such a trick. I suppose your dear friend Ilse thought she'd play a joke on you—she was chuckling over something when she came in a few minutes ago."

"Ilse never did it," cried Emily.

Evelyn shrugged her shoulders.

"I'd wash it off first and find out who did it afterward," she said with a twitching face as she went out.

Emily, trembling from head to foot with anger, shame, and the most intense humiliation she had ever suffered, washed the moustache off her face. Her first impulse was to go home—she could not face that roomful of Preps again. Then she set her teeth and went back, holding her black head very high as she walked down the aisle to her desk. Her face was burning and her spirit was aflame. In the corner she saw Ilse's yellow head bent over her paper. The others were smiling and tittering. Mr. Scoville was insultingly grave. Emily took up her pen but her hand shook over her paper.

If she could have had a good cry there and then her shame and anger would have found a saving vent. But that was impossible. She would *not* cry. She would not let them see the depths of her humiliation. If Emily could have laughed off the malicious joke it would have been better for her. Being Emily—and being one of the proud Murrays—she could not. She resented the indignity to the very core of her passionate soul.

As far as the English paper was concerned she might almost as well have gone home. She had lost twenty minutes already. It was ten minutes more before she could steady her hand sufficiently to write. Her thoughts she could not command at all. The paper was a difficult one, as Mr. Travers' papers always were. Her mind seemed a chaos of jostling ideas spinning around a fixed point of torturing shame. When she handed in her paper and left the class-room she knew she had lost her star. That paper would be no more than a pass, if it were that. But in her turmoil of feeling she did not care. She hurried home to her unfriendly room, thankful that Aunt Ruth was out, threw herself on the bed and wept. She felt sore, beaten, bruised—and under all her pain was a horrible, teasing little doubt.

Did Ilse do it—no, she *didn't*—she *couldn't* have. Who then? Mary? The idea was absurd. It must have been Evelyn—Evelyn had come back and played that cruel trick on her out of spite and pique. Yet she had denied it, with seemingly insulted indignation, and eyes that were perhaps a shade too innocent. *What* had Ilse said—"You are getting positively smug—something ought to be done to cure you before it gets chronic." Had Ilse taken that abominable way of curing her?

"No—no—no!" Emily sobbed fiercely into her pillow. But the doubt persisted.

Aunt Ruth had no doubt. Aunt Ruth was calling on her friend, Mrs. Ball, and her friend, Mrs. Ball, had a daughter who was a Prep. Anita Ball came home with the tale that had been well laughed over in Prep and Junior and Senior classes, and Anita Ball said that Evelyn Blake had said Ilse Burnley had done the deed.

"Well," said Aunt Ruth, invading Emily's room on her return home, "I hear Ilse Burnley decorated you beautifully today. I hope you realise what she is now."

"Ilse didn't do it," said Emily.

"Have you asked her?"

"No. I wouldn't insult her with such a question."

"Well, I believe she did do it. And she is not to come here again. Understand that."

"Aunt Ruth——"

"You've heard what I said, Em'ly. Ilse Burnley is no fit associate for you. I've heard too many tales about her lately. But this is unpardonable."

"Aunt Ruth, if I ask Ilse if she did it and she says she did not, won't you believe her?"

"No, I wouldn't believe any girl brought up as Ilse Burnley was. It's my belief she'd do anything and say anything. Don't let me see her in my house again."

Emily stood up and tried to summon the Murray look into a face distorted by weeping.

"Of course, Aunt Ruth," she said coldly, "I won't bring Ilse here if she is not welcome. But I shall go to see her. And if you forbid me—I'll—I'll go home to New Moon. I feel as if I wanted to go anyhow now. Only—I *won't* let Evelyn Blake drive me away."

Aunt Ruth knew quite well that the New Moon folks would not agree to a complete divorce between Emily and Ilse. They were too good friends with the doctor for that. Mrs. Dutton had never liked Dr. Burnley. She had to be content with the excuse for keeping Ilse away from her house, for which she had long hankered. Her own annoyance over the matter was not born out of any sympathy with Emily but solely from anger at a Murray being made ridiculous.

"I would have thought you'd had enough of going to see Ilse. As for Evelyn Blake, she is too clever and sensible a girl to have played a silly trick like that. I know the Blakes. They are an excellent family and Evelyn's father is well-to-do. Now, stop crying. A pretty face you've got. What sense is there in crying?"

"None at all," agreed Emily drearily, "only I can't help it. I can't *bear* to be made ridiculous. I can endure anything but that. Oh, Aunt Ruth, *please* leave me alone. I can't eat any supper."

"You've got yourself all worked up—Starr-like. We Murrays conceal our feelings."

"I don't believe you've any to conceal—some of you," thought Emily rebelliously.

"Keep away from Ilse Burnley after this, and you'll not be so likely to be publicly disgraced," was Aunt Ruth's parting advice.

Emily, after a sleepless night—during which it seemed to her that if she couldn't push that ceiling farther from her face she would surely smother—went to see Ilse the next day and reluctantly told her what Aunt Ruth had said. Ilse was furious—but Emily noted with a pang that she did not assert any innocence of the crayon trick.

"Ilse, you—you didn't really do that?" she faltered. She *knew* Ilse hadn't—she was *sure* of it—but she wanted to hear her say so. To her surprise, a sudden blush swept over Ilse's face.

"Is thy servant a dog?" she said, rather confusedly. It was very unlike straightforward, outspoken Ilse to be so confused. She turned her face away and began fumbling aimlessly with her book-bag. "You don't suppose I'd do anything like that to you, Emily?"

"No, of course not," said Emily, slowly. The subject was dropped. But the little doubt and distrust at the bottom of Emily's mind came out of its lurking-place and declared itself. Even yet she couldn't believe Ilse could do such a thing—and lie about it afterward. But why was she so confused and shamefaced? Would not an innocent Ilse have stormed about according to form, berated Emily, roundly, for mere suspicion, and aired the subject generally until all the venom had been blown out of it?

It was not referred to again. But the shadow was there and spoiled, to a certain extent, the Christmas holidays at New Moon. Outwardly, the girls were the friends they had always been, but Emily was acutely conscious of a sudden rift between them. Strive as she would she could not bridge it. The seeming unconsciousness of any such severance on Ilse's part served to deepen it. Hadn't Ilse cared enough for her and her friendship to *feel* the chill that had come over it? Could she be so shallow and indifferent as not to perceive it? Emily brooded and grew morbid over it. A thing like that—a dim, poisonous thing that lurked in shadow and dared not come into the open—always played havoc with her sensitive and passionate temperament. No open quarrel with Ilse could have affected her like this—she had quarrelled with Ilse scores of times and made up the next minute with no bitterness or backward glance. *This* was different. The more Emily brooded over it the more monstrous it grew. She was unhappy, absent, restless. Aunt Laura and Cousin Jimmy noticed it but attributed it to her disappointment over the star pin. She had told them she was sure she would not win. But Emily had ceased to care about the star pin.

To be sure, she had a bad time of it, when she went back to High School and the examination results were announced. She was not one of the envied four who flaunted star pins and Aunt Ruth rubbed it in for weeks. Aunt Ruth felt that she had lost family prestige in Emily's failure and she was very bitter about it. Altogether Emily felt that the New Year had come in very inauspiciously for her. The first month of it was a time she never liked to recall. She was very lonely. Ilse could not come to see her, and though she made herself go to see Ilse the subtle little rift between them was slowly widening. Ilse still gave no sign of feeling it; but then, somehow, she was seldom alone with Ilse now. The room was always filled with girls, and there was a good deal of noise and laughter and jokes and school gossip—all very harmless and even jolly, but very different from the old intimacy and understanding comradeship with Ilse. Formerly it used to be a chummy jest between them that they could walk or sit for hours together and say no word and yet feel that they had had a splendid time. There were no such silences now: when they did happen to be alone together they both chattered gaily and shallowly, as if each were secretly afraid that there might come a moment for the silence that betrays.

Emily's heart ached over their lost friendship: every night her pillow was wet with tears. Yet there was nothing she could do: she could not, try as she would, banish the doubt that possessed her. She made many an honest effort to do so. She told herself every day that Ilse Burnley could never have played that trick— that she was constitutionally incapable of it—and went straightway to Ilse with the firm determination to be just what she had always been to her. With the result that she was unnaturally cordial and friendly—even gushing—and no more like her real self than she was like Evelyn Blake. Ilse was just as cordial and friendly— and the rift was wider still.

"Ilse never goes into a tantrum with me now," Emily reflected sadly.

It was quite true. Ilse was always good-tempered with Emily, presenting a baffling front of politeness unbroken by a single flash of her old wild spirit. Emily felt that nothing could have been more welcome than one of Ilse's stormy rages. It might break the ice that was forming so relentlessly between them, and release the pent-up flood of old affection.

One of the keenest stings in the situation was that Evelyn Blake was quite well aware of the state of affairs between Ilse and Emily. The mockery of her long brown eyes and the hidden sneer in her casual sentences betrayed her knowledge and her enjoyment of it. This was gall and wormwood to Emily, who felt that she had no defence against it. Evelyn was a girl whom intimacies between other girls annoyed, and the friendship between Ilse and Emily had annoyed her especially. It had been so complete—so absorbing. There had been no place in it for any one else. And Evelyn did not like to feel that she was barred out—that there was some garden enclosed, into which she might not enter. She was therefore hugely delighted to think that this vexingly beautiful friendship between two girls she secretly hated was at an end.

9
A Supreme Moment

Emily came downstairs laggingly, feeling that all the colour and music had somehow gone out of life, and that it stretched before her in unbroken greyness. Ten minutes later she was encompassed by rainbows and the desert of her future had blossomed like the rose.

The cause of this miracle of transformation was a thin letter which Aunt Ruth handed to her with an Aunt Ruthian sniff. There was a magazine, too, but Emily did not at first regard it. She saw the address of a floral firm on the corner of the envelope, and sensed at touch the promising thinness of it—so different from the plump letters full of rejected verses.

Her heart beat violently as she tore it open and glanced over the typewritten sheet.

"Miss Emily B. Starr,
"Shrewsbury, P.E. Island,
"Can.

"Dear Miss Starr:
   "It gives us great pleasure to tell you that your poem, *Owl's Laughter* has been found available for use in *Garden and Woodland*. It appears in the current issue of our magazine, a copy of which we are sending you. Your verses have the true ring and we shall be glad to see more of your work.

"It is not our custom to pay cash for our contributions but you may select two dollars' worth of seeds or plants from our catalogue to be sent to your address prepaid.

"Thanking you,

"We remain,
"Yours truly,
"THOS. E. CARLTON & CO."

Emily dropped the letter and seized upon the magazine with trembling fingers. She grew dizzy—the letters danced before her eyes—she felt a curious sensation of choking—for there on the front page, in a fine border of curlicues, was her poem—*Owl's Laughter*, by Emily Byrd Starr.

It was the first sweet bubble on the cup of success and we must not think her silly if it intoxicated her. She carried the letter and magazine off to her room to gloat over it, blissfully unconscious that Aunt Ruth was doing an extra deal of sniffing. Aunt Ruth felt very suspicious of suddenly crimsoned cheek and glowing eye and general air of rapture and detachment from earth.

In her room Emily sat down and read her poem as if she had never seen it before. There was, to be sure, a printer's error in it that made the flesh creep on her bones—it was awful to have *hunter's moon* come out as *hunter's moan*—but it was her poem—*hers*—accepted by and printed in a *real* magazine.

And *paid* for! To be sure a check would have been more acceptable—two dollars all her own, earned by her own pen, would have seemed like riches to Emily. But what fun she and Cousin Jimmy would have selecting the seeds! She could see in imagination that beautiful flowerbed next summer in the New Moon garden—a glory of crimson and purple and blue and gold.

And what was it the letter said?

"Your verses have the true ring and we shall be glad to see more of your work."

Oh, bliss—oh, rapture! The world was hers—the *Alpine Path* was as good as climbed—what signified a few more scrambles to the summit?

Emily could not remain in that dark little room with its oppressive ceiling and unfriendly furniture. Lord Byron's funereal expression was an insult to her happiness. She threw on her wraps and hurried out to the Land of Uprightness.

As she went through the kitchen, Aunt Ruth, naturally more suspicious than ever, inquired with markedly bland sarcasm,

"Is the house on fire? Or the harbour?"

"Neither. It's my soul that's on fire," said Emily with an inscrutable smile. She shut the door behind her and at once forgot Aunt Ruth and every other disagreeable thing and person. How beautiful the world was—how beautiful life was—how wonderful the Land of Uprightness was! The young firs along the narrow path were lightly powdered with snow, as if, thought Emily, a veil of aërial lace had been tricksily flung over austere young Druid priestesses foresworn to all such frivolities of vain adornment. Emily decided she would write that sentence down in her Jimmy-book when she went back. On and on she flitted to the crest of the hill. She felt as if she were flying—her feet *couldn't* really be touching the earth. On the hill she paused and stood, a rapt, ecstatic figure with clasped hands and eyes of dream. It was just after sunset. Out, over the ice-bound harbour, great clouds piled themselves up in dazzling, iridescent masses. Beyond were gleaming white hills with early stars over them. Between the dark trunks of the old fir trees to her right, far away through the crystal evening air, rose a great, round, full moon.

" 'It has the true ring,' " murmured Emily, tasting the

incredible words anew. "They want to see more of my work! Oh, if only Father could see my verses in print!"

Years before, in the old house at Maywood, her Father, bending over her as she slept had said, "She will love deeply—suffer terribly—she will have glorious moments to compensate."

This was one of her glorious moments. She felt a wonderful lightness of spirit—a soul-stirring joy in mere existence. The creative faculty, dormant through the wretched month just passed, suddenly burned in her soul again like a purifying flame. It swept away all morbid, poisonous, rankling things. All at once Emily *knew* that Ilse had never done *that*. She laughed joyously—amusedly.

"What a little fool I've been! Oh, *such* a little fool! Of course, Ilse never did it. There's nothing between us now—it's gone—gone—gone. I'll go right to her and tell her so."

Emily hurried back adown her little path. The Land of Uprightness lay all about her, mysterious in the moonlight, wrapped in the exquisite reticence of winter woods. She seemed one with its beauty and charm and mystery. With a sudden sigh of the Wind Woman through the shadowy aisles came "the flash" and Emily went dancing to Ilse with the afterglow of it in her soul.

She found Ilse alone—threw her arms around her—hugged her fiercely.

"Ilse, do forgive me," she cried. "I shouldn't have doubted you—I *did* doubt you—but now I know—I *know*. You *will* forgive me?"

"You young goat," said Ilse.

Emily loved to be called a young goat. This was the old Ilse—*her* Ilse.

"Oh, Ilse, I've been so unhappy."

"Well, don't bawl over it," said Ilse. "I haven't been very hilarious myself. Look here, Emily, I've got something to tell you. Shut up and listen. That day I met

Evelyn at the Shoppe and we went back for some book she wanted and we found you sound asleep—so sound asleep that you never stirred when I pinched your cheek. Then, just for devilment I picked up a black crayon and said, 'I'm going to draw a moustache on her'—shut up! Evelyn pulled a long face and said, 'Oh, no! that would be *mean*, don't you think?' I hadn't had the slightest intention of doing it—I'd only spoken in fun—but that shrimp Evelyn's ungodly affectation of righteousness made me so mad that I decided I would do it—shut *up!*—I meant to wake you right up and hold a glass before you, that was all. But before I could do it Kate Errol came in and wanted us to go along with her and I threw down the chalk and went out. That's all, Emily, honest to Caesar. But it made me feel ashamed and silly later on—I'd say a bit conscience-stricken if I had such a thing as a conscience, because I felt that *I* must have put the idea into the head of whoever did do it, and so was responsible in a way. And then I saw you distrusted me—and that made me mad—not tempery-mad, you see, but a nasty, cold, *inside* sort of madness. I thought you had no business even to suspect that I could have done such a thing as let you go to class like that. And I thought, since you did, you could go on doing it—*I* wouldn't say one word to put matters straight. Golly, but I'm glad you're through with seein' things."

"Do you think Evelyn Blake did it?"

"No. Oh, she's quite capable of it, of course, but I don't see how it could have been she. She went to the Shoppe with Kate and me and we left her there. She was in class fifteen minutes later, so I don't think she'd have had time to go back and do it. I really think it was that little devil of a May Hilson. She'd do anything and she was in the hall when I was flourishing the crayon. She'd 'take the suggestion as a cat laps milk.' But it couldn't have been Evelyn."

Emily retained her belief that it could have been and

was. But the only thing that mattered now was the fact that Aunt Ruth still believed Ilse guilty and would continue so to believe.

"Well, that's a rotten shame," said Ilse. "We can't have any real chum-talks here—Mary always has such a mob in and E. B. pervades the place."

"I'll find out who did it yet,' said Emily darkly, "and *make* Aunt Ruth give in."

On the next afternoon Evelyn Blake found Ilse and Emily in a beautiful row. At least Ilse was rowing while Emily sat with her legs crossed and a bored, haughty expression in her insolently half-shut eyes. It should have been a welcome sight to a girl who disliked the intimacies of other girls. But Evelyn Blake was not rejoiced. Ilse was quarrelling with Emily again—*ergo*, Ilse and Emily were on good terms once more.

"I'm so glad to see you've forgiven Ilse for that mean trick," she said sweetly to Emily the next day. "Of course, it was just pure thoughtlessness on her part— I've always insisted on *that*—she never stopped to think what ridicule she was letting you in for. Poor Ilse is like that. You know I tried to stop her—I didn't tell you this before, of course—*I* didn't want to make any more trouble than there was—but I *told* her it was a horribly mean thing to do to a friend. I thought I *had* put her off. It's sweet of you to forgive her, Emily dear. You *are* better-hearted than I am. I'm afraid I could *never* pardon any one who had made me such a laughing stock."

"Why didn't you slay her in her tracks?" said Ilse when she heard of it from Emily.

"I simply half-shut my eyes and looked at her like a Murray," said Emily, "and that was more bitter than death."

10
The Madness of an Hour

The High School concert in aid of the school library was an annual event in Shrewsbury, coming off in early April, before it was necessary to settle down to hard study for spring examinations. This year it was at first intended to have the usual programme of music and readings with a short dialogue. Emily was asked to take part in the latter and agreed, after securing Aunt Ruth's very grudging consent, which would probably never have been secured if Miss Aylmer had not come in person to plead for it. Miss Aylmer was a granddaughter of Senator Aylmer and Aunt Ruth yielded to family what she would have yielded to nothing else. Then Miss Aylmer suggested cutting out most of the music and all of the readings and having a short play instead. This found favour in the eyes of the students and the change was made forthwith. Emily was cast for a part that suited her, so she became keenly interested in the matter and enjoyed the practises, which were held in the school building two evenings of the week under the chaperonage of Miss Aylmer.

The play created quite a stir in Shrewsbury. Nothing so ambitious had been undertaken by the High School students before: it became known that many of the Queen's Academy students were coming up from Charlottetown on the evening train to see it. This drove the performers half wild. The Queen's students were old hands at putting on plays. Of course they came to criticise. It became a fixed obsession with each member of the cast to make the play as good as any of the Queen's Academy plays had been, and every nerve was strained to that end. Kate Errol's sister, who was a graduate of a school of oratory, coached them, and when the evening of the performance arrived there was burning excitement in the various homes and boarding-houses of Shrewsbury.

Emily, in her small, candle-lighted room, looked at Emily-in-the-Glass with considerable satisfaction—a satisfaction that was quite justifiable. The scarlet flush of her cheeks, the deepening darkness of her grey eyes, came out brilliantly above the ashes-of-roses gown, and the little wreath of silver leaves, twisted around her black hair, made her look like a young dryad. She did not, however, *feel* like a dryad. Aunt Ruth had made her take off her lace stockings and put on cashmere ones—had tried, indeed, to make her put on woollen ones, but had gone down in defeat on that point retrieving her position, however, by insisting on a flannel petticoat.

"Horrid bunchy thing," thought Emily resentfully—meaning the petticoat, of course. But the skirts of the day were full and Emily's slenderness could carry even a thick flannel petticoat.

She was just fastening her Egyptian chain around her neck when Aunt Ruth stalked in.

One glance was sufficient to reveal that Aunt Ruth was very angry.

"Em'ly, Mrs. Ball has just called. She told me something that amazed me. Is this a *play* you're taking part in tonight?"

Emily stared.

"Of course it's a play, Aunt Ruth. Surely you knew that."

"When you asked my permission to take part in this concert you told me it was a *dialogue*," said Aunt Ruth icily.

"O-o-h—but Miss Aylmer decided to have a little

play in place of it. I *thought* you knew, Aunt Ruth—truly I did. I thought I mentioned it to you."

"You didn't think anything of the kind, Em'ly—you deliberately kept me in ignorance because you knew I wouldn't have allowed you to take part in a *play*."

"Indeed, no, Aunt Ruth," pleaded Emily, gravely. "I never thought of hiding it. Of course, I didn't feel like talking much to you about it because I knew you didn't approve of the concert at all."

When Emily spoke gravely Aunt Ruth always thought she was impudent.

"This crowns all, Em'ly. Sly as I've always known you to be I wouldn't have believed you could be as sly as this."

"There was nothing of the kind about it, Aunt Ruth!" said Emily impatiently. "It would have been silly of me to try to hide the fact that we were getting up a play when all Shrewsbury is talking of it. I don't see how you could *help* hearing of it."

"You knew I wasn't going anywhere because of my bronchitis. Oh, I see through it all, Em'ly. You cannot deceive *me*."

"I haven't tried to deceive you. I thought you knew—that is all there is to it. I thought the reason you never spoke of it was because you were opposed to the whole thing. That is the truth, Aunt Ruth. What difference is there between a dialogue and a play?"

"There is *every* difference," said Aunt Ruth. "Plays are wicked."

"But this is such a *little* one," pleaded Emily despairingly—and then laughed because it sounded so ridiculously like the nursemaid's excuse in *Midshipman Easy.* Her sense of humour was untimely; her laughter infuriated Aunt Ruth.

"Little or big, you are not going to take part in it."

Emily stared again, paling a little.

"Aunt Ruth—I *must*—why, the play would be ruined."

"Better a play ruined than a soul ruined," retorted Aunt Ruth.

Emily dared not smile. The issue at stake was too serious.

"Don't be so—so—indignant, Aunt Ruth"—she had nearly said unjust. "I am sorry you don't approve of plays—I won't take part in any more—but you can see I *must* do it tonight."

"Oh, my dear Em'ly, I don't think you are quite as indispensable as all *that*."

Certainly Aunt Ruth was very maddening. How disagreeable the word "dear" could be! Still was Emily patient.

"I really am—tonight. You see, they couldn't get a substitute at the last moment. Miss Aylmer would never forgive me."

"Do you care more about Miss Aylmer's forgiveness than God's?" demanded Aunt Ruth with the air of one stating a decisive position.

"Yes—than *your* God's," muttered Emily, unable to keep her patience under such insensate questions.

"Have you no respect for your forefathers?" was Aunt Ruth's next relevant query. "Why, if they knew a descendant of theirs was play-acting they would turn over in their graves!"

Emily favoured Aunt Ruth with a sample of the Murray look.

"It would be excellent exercise for them. I am going to take my part in the play tonight, Aunt Ruth."

Emily spoke quietly, looking down from her young height with resolute eyes. Aunt Ruth felt a nasty sense of helplessness: there was no lock to Emily's door—and she couldn't detain her by physical force.

"If you go, you needn't come back here tonight," she said, pale with rage. "This house is locked at nine o'clock."

"If I don't come back here tonight, I won't come at all." Emily was too angry over Aunt Ruth's unreasonable attitude to care for consequences. "If you lock me out I'll go back to New Moon. *They* know all about the play there—even Aunt Elizabeth was willing for me to take part."

She caught up her coat and jammed the little red-feather hat, which Uncle Oliver's wife had given her at Christmas, down on her head. Aunt Addie's taste was not approved at New Moon but the hat was very becoming and Emily loved it. Aunt Ruth suddenly realised that Emily looked oddly mature and grown-up in it. But the knowledge did not as yet dampen her anger. Em'ly was gone—Em'ly had dared to defy her and disobey her—sly, underhand Em'ly—Em'ly must be taught a lesson.

At nine o'clock a stubborn, outraged Aunt Ruth locked all the doors and went to bed.

The play was a big success. Even the Queen's students admitted that and applauded generously. Emily threw herself into her part with a fire and energy generated by her encounter with Aunt Ruth, which swept away all hampering consciousness of flannel petticoats and agreeably astonished Miss Errol, whose one criticism of Emily's acting had been that she was rather cold and reserved in a part that called for more abandon. Emily was showered with compliments at the close of the performance. Even Evelyn Blake said graciously,

"Really, dear, you are quite wonderful—a star actress—a poet—a budding novelist—what surprise will you give us next?"

Thought Emily, "Condescending, insufferable creature!"

Said Emily, "*Thank* you!"

There was a happy, triumphant walk home with Teddy, a gay good-night at the gate, and then—the locked door.

Emily's anger, which had been sublimated during the evening into energy and ambition, suddenly flared up again, sweeping everything before it. It was unbearable to be treated thus. She had endured enough at Aunt Ruth's hands—this was the proverbial last straw. One could not put up with *everything*, even to get an education. One owed *something* to one's dignity and self-respect.

There were three things she could do. She could thump the old-fashioned brass knocker on the door until Aunt Ruth came down and let her in, as she had done once before—and then endure weeks of slurs because of it. She could fly up-street and down-street to Ilse's boarding-house—the girls wouldn't be in bed yet—as she had likewise done once before, and as no doubt Aunt Ruth would expect her to do now; and then Mary Carswell would tell Evelyn Blake and Evelyn Blake would laugh maliciously and tell it all through the school. Emily had no intention of doing either of these things; she knew from the moment she found the door locked just what she would do. She would walk to New Moon—and stay there! Months of suppressed chafing under Aunt Ruth's perpetual stings burst into a conflagration of revolt. Emily marched out of the gate, slammed it shut behind her with no Murray dignity but plenty of Starr passion, and started on her seven-mile walk through the midnight. Had it been three times seven she would have started just the same.

So angry was she, and so angry she continued to be, that the walk did not seem long, nor, though she had no wrap save her cloth coat, did she feel the cold of the sharp April night.

The winter's snow had gone but the bare road was hard-frozen and rough—no dainty footing for the thin kid slippers of Cousin Jimmy's Christmas box. Emily reflected with what she considered a grim, sarcastic laugh that it was well, after all, that Aunt Ruth had insisted on cashmere stockings and flannel petticoat.

There was a moon that night, but the sky was covered with curdled grey clouds, and the harsh, bleak landscape lay dourly in the pallid grey light. The wind came across it in sudden, moaning gusts. Emily felt with considerable dramatic satisfaction that the night harmonised with her stormy, tragic mood.

She would *never* go back to Aunt Ruth's that was certain. No matter what Aunt Elizabeth might say—and she *would* say aplenty, no doubt of that—no matter what any one would say. If Aunt Elizabeth would not let her go anywhere else to board she would give up school altogether. She knew it would cause a tremendous upheaval at New Moon. Never mind. In her very reckless mood upheavals seemed welcome things. It was time somebody upheaved. She would not humiliate herself another day—that she would not! Aunt Ruth had gone too far at last. You could not safely drive a Starr to desperation.

"I have done with Ruth Dutton forever," vowed Emily, feeling a tremendous satisfaction in leaving off the "Aunt."

As she drew near home the clouds cleared away suddenly, and when she turned into the New Moon lane the austere beauty of the three tall Lombardies against the moonlit sky made her catch her breath. Oh, how wonderful! For a moment she almost forgot her wrongs and Aunt Ruth. Then bitterness rushed over her soul again—not even the magic of the Three Princesses could charm it away.

There was a light shining out of the New Moon kitchen window, falling on the tall, white birches in Lofty John's bush with spectral effect. Emily wondered who could be up at New Moon: she had expected to find it in darkness and had meant to slip in by the front door and up to her own dear room, leaving explanations to the morning. Aunt Elizabeth always locked and barred the kitchen door every night with great ceremony before retiring, but the front door was never locked. Tramps and burglars would surely never be so ill-mannered as to come to the front door of New Moon.

Emily crossed the garden and peeped through the kitchen window. Cousin Jimmy was there alone, sitting by the table, with two candles for company. On the table was a stoneware crock and just as Emily looked in he absently put his hand into it and drew out a chubby doughnut. Cousin Jimmy's eyes were fixed on a big beef ham pendent from the ceiling and Cousin Jimmy's lips moved soundlessly. There was no reasonable doubt that Cousin Jimmy was composing poetry, though why he was doing it at that hour o' night was a puzzle.

Emily slipped around the house, opened the kitchen door gently, and walked in. Poor Cousin Jimmy in his amazement tried to swallow half a doughnut whole and then couldn't speak for several seconds. Was *this* Emily—or an apparition? Emily in a dark-blue coat, an enchanting little red-feather hat—Emily with wind-blown night-black hair and tragic eyes—Emily with tattered kid slippers on her feet—Emily in this plight at New Moon when she should have been sound asleep on her maiden couch in Shrewsbury?

Cousin Jimmy seized the cold hands Emily held out to him.

"Emily, dear child, what has happened?"

"Well, just to jump into the middle of things—I've left Aunt Ruth's and I'm not going back."

Cousin Jimmy didn't say anything for a few moments. But he did a few things. First he tiptoed across the kitchen and carefully shut the sitting-room door; then he gently filled the stove up with wood, drew a chair up to it, pushed Emily into it and lifted her cold, ragged feet to the hearth. Then he lighted two more candles and put them on the chimney-piece. Finally he sat down in his chair again and put his hands on his knees.

"Now, tell me all about it."

Emily, still in the throes of rebellion and indignation, told it pretty fully.

As soon as Cousin Jimmy got an inkling of what had

really happened he began to shake his head slowly—continued to shake it—shook it so long and gravely that Emily began to feel an uncomfortable conviction that instead of being a wronged, dramatic figure she was by way of being a bit of a little fool. The longer Cousin Jimmy shook his head the smaller grew her heroics. When she had finished her story with a defiant, conclusive "I'm *not* going back to Aunt Ruth's, *anyhow*," Cousin Jimmy gave a final wag to his head and pushed the crock across the table.

"Have a doughnut, pussy."

Emily hesitated. She was very fond of doughnuts—and it had been a long time since she had her supper. But doughnuts seemed out of keeping with rebellion and tumult. They were decidedly reactionary in their tendencies. Some vague glimmering of this made Emily refuse the doughnut.

Cousin Jimmy took one himself.

"So you're not going back to Shrewsbury?"

"Not to Aunt Ruth's," said Emily.

"It's the same thing," said Cousin Jimmy.

Emily knew it was. She knew it was of no use to hope that Aunt Elizabeth would let her board elsewhere.

"And you walked all the way home over those roads." Cousin Jimmy shook his head. "Well, you *have* spunk. Heaps of it," he added meditatively between bites.

"Do you blame me?" demanded Emily passionately—all the more passionately because she felt some inward support had been shaken away by Cousin Jimmy's head.

"No-o-o, it was a durn mean shame to lock you out—just like Ruth Dutton."

"And you see—don't you—that I can't go back after such an insult?"

Cousin Jimmy nibbled at the doughnut cautiously, as if bent on trying to see how near he could nibble to the hole without actually breaking through.

"I don't think any of your grandmothers would have given up a chance for an education so easily," he said. "Not on the Murray side, anyhow," he added after a moment's reflection, which apparently reminded him that he knew too little about the Starrs to dogmatise concerning them.

Emily sat very still. As Teddy would have said in cricket parlance, Cousin Jimmy had got her middle wicket with the first ball. She felt at once that when Cousin Jimmy, in that diabolical fit of inspiration, dragged her grandmothers in, everything was over but the precise terms of surrender. She could see them all around her—the dear, dead ladies of New Moon—Mary Shipley and Elizabeth Burnley and all the rest—mild, determined, restrained, looking down with something of contemptuous pity on her, their foolish, impulsive descendant. Cousin Jimmy appeared to think there might be some weakness on the Starr side. Well, there wasn't—she would show him!

She *had* expected more sympathy from Cousin Jimmy. She had known Aunt Elizabeth would condemn her and even Aunt Laura would look disappointed question. But she had counted on Cousin Jimmy taking her part. He always had before.

"My grandmothers never had to put up with Aunt Ruth," she flung at him.

"They had to put up with your grandfathers." Cousin Jimmy appeared to think that this was conclusive— as any one who had known Archibald and Hugh Murray might have very well thought.

"Cousin Jimmy, do you think I ought to go back and accept Aunt Ruth's scolding and go on as if this had never happened?"

"What do *you* think about it?" asked Cousin Jimmy. "*Do* take a doughnut, pussy."

This time Emily took the doughnut. She might as well have some comfort. Now, you can't eat doughnuts and remain dramatic. Try it.

Emily slipped from her peak of tragedy to the valley of petulance.

"Aunt Ruth has been *abominable* these past two months—ever since her bronchitis has prevented her from going out. You don't know *what* it's been like."

"Oh, I do—I do. Ruth Dutton never made any one feel better pleased with herself. Feet getting warm, Emily?"

"I *hate* her," cried Emily, still grasping after self-justification. "It's horrible to live in the same house with any one you hate——"

"Poisonous," agreed Cousin Jimmy.

"And it *isn't* my fault. I *have* tried to like her—tried to please her—she's always twitting me—she attributes mean motives to everything I do or say—or *don't* do or say. I've never heard the last of sitting in the corner of the pew—and failing to get a star pin. She's always *hinting* insults to my father and mother. And she's always *forgiving* me for things I haven't done—or that don't need forgiveness."

"Aggravating—very," conceded Cousin Jimmy.

"Aggravating—you're right. I know if I go back she'll say 'I'll forgive you this time, but don't let it happen again.' And she will *sniff*—oh, Aunt Ruth's sniff is the hatefulest sound in the world!"

"Ever hear a dull knife sawing through thick cardboard?" murmured Cousin Jimmy.

Emily ignored him and swept on.

"I can't be *always* in the wrong—but Aunt Ruth thinks I am—and says she has 'to make allowances' for me. She doses me with cod-liver oil—she never lets me go out in the evening if she can help it—'consumptives should never be out after eight o'clock.' If *she* is cold, *I* must put on an extra petticoat. She is always asking disagreeable questions and refusing to believe my answers. She believes and always will believe that I kept this play a secret from her because of slyness. I never thought of such a thing. Why, the Shrewsbury *Times* referred to it last week. Aunt Ruth doesn't often miss anything in the *Times*. She twitted me for days because she found a composition of mine that I had signed 'Emilie.' 'Better try to spell your name after some unheard-of twist,' she sneered!"

"Well, wasn't it a bit silly, pussy?"

"Oh, I suppose my grandmothers wouldn't have done it! But Aunt Ruth needn't have kept it up as she did. *That* is what is so dreadful—if she'd speak her mind on a thing and have done with it. Why, I got a little spot of iron-rust on my white petticoat and Aunt Ruth harped on it for weeks. She was determined to find out *when* it was rusted and *how*—and I hadn't the least idea. Really, Cousin Jimmy, when this had gone on for three weeks I thought I'd have to scream if she mentioned it again."

"*Any* proper person would feel the same," said Cousin Jimmy to the beef ham.

"Oh, any *one* of these things is only a pin-prick, I know—and you think I'm silly to mind it—but——"

"No, no. A hundred pin-pricks would be harder to put up with than a broken leg. *I*'d sooner be knocked on the head and be done with it."

"Yes, that's it—nothing but pin-pricks all the time. She won't let Ilse come to the house—or Teddy, or Perry—nobody but that stupid Andrew. I'm so tired of him. She wouldn't let me go to the Prep dance. They had a sleigh drive and supper at the Brown Teapot Inn and a little dance—everybody went but me—it was the event of the winter. If I go for a walk in the Land of Uprightness at sunset she is sure there is something sinister in it—*she* never wants to walk in the Land of Uprightness, so why should *I*? She says I have got too high an opinion of myself. I *haven't*—*have* I, Cousin Jimmy?"

"No," said Cousin Jimmy thoughtfully. "High—but not *too* high."

"She says I'm always displacing things—if I look out

of a window she'll trot across the room and mathematically match the corners of the curtains again. And it's 'Why—why—why'—all the time, *all* the time, Cousin Jimmy."

"I know you feel a lot better now that you've got all that out of your system," said Cousin Jimmy. "'Nother doughnut?'"

Emily, with a sigh of surrender, took her feet off the stove and moved over to the table. The crock of doughnuts was between her and Cousin Jimmy. She *was* very hungry.

"Ruth give you enough to eat?" queried Cousin Jimmy anxiously.

"Oh, yes. Aunt Ruth keeps up one New Moon tradish at least. She has a good table. But there are no snacks."

"And you always liked a tasty bite at bed-time, didn't you? But you took a box back last time you were home?"

"Aunt Ruth confiscated it. That is, she put it in the pantry and served its contents up at meal times. These doughnuts *are* good. And there is always something exciting and lawless about eating at unearthly hours like this, isn't there? How did you happen to be up, Cousin Jimmy?"

"A sick cow. Thought I'd better sit up and look after her."

"It was lucky for me you were. Oh, I'm in my proper senses again, Cousin Jimmy. Of course, I know you think I've been a little fool."

"Everybody's a fool in some particular," said Cousin Jimmy.

"Well, I'll go back and bite the sour apple without a grimace."

"Lie down on the sofa and have a nap. I'll hitch up the grey mare and drive you back as soon as it begins to be daylight."

"No, that won't do at all. Several reasons. In the first

place, the roads aren't fit for wheels or runners. In the second place we couldn't drive away from here without Aunt Elizabeth hearing us, and then she'd find out all about it and I don't want her to. We'll keep my foolishness a dark and deadly secret between you and me, Cousin Jimmy."

"Then how are you going to get back to Shrewsbury?"

"Walk."

"Walk? To Shrewsbury? At this hour of the night?"

"Haven't I just walked from Shrewsbury at this hour? I can do it again and it won't be any harder than bumping over those awful roads behind the grey mare. Of course, I'll put something on my feet that will be a little more protection than kid slippers. I've ruined your Christmas present in my brain-storm. There is a pair of my old boots in the closet there. I'll put them on—and my old ulster. I'll be back in Shrewsbury by daylight. I'll start as soon as we finish the doughnuts. Let's lick the platter clean, Cousin Jimmy."

Cousin Jimmy yielded. After all, Emily was young and wiry, the night was fine, and the less Elizabeth knew about some things the better for all concerned. With a sigh of relief that the affair had turned out so well—he had really been afraid at first that Emily's underlying "stubbornness" had been reached and then, whew!—Cousin Jimmy settled down to doughnuts.

"How's the writing coming on?" he asked.

"I've written a good deal lately—though it's pretty cold in my room mornings, but I love it so—it's my dearest dream to do something worth while some day."

"So you will. *You* haven't been pushed down a well," said Cousin Jimmy.

Emily patted his hand. None realised better than she what Cousin Jimmy might have done if *he* had not been pushed down a well.

When the doughnuts were finished Emily donned her old boots and ulster. It was a very shabby garment but her young-moon beauty shone over it like a star in the old, dim, candle-lighted room.

Cousin Jimmy looked up at her. He thought that she was a gifted, beautiful, joyous creature and that some things were a shame.

"Tall and stately—tall and stately like all our women," he murmured dreamily. "Except Aunt Ruth," he added.

Emily laughed—and "made a face."

"Aunt Ruth will make the most of her inches in our forthcoming interview. This will last her the rest of the year. But don't worry, Cousin darling, I won't do any more foolish things for quite a long time now. This has cleared the air. Aunt Elizabeth will think it was dreadful of you to eat a whole crockful of doughnuts yourself, you greedy Cousin Jimmy."

"Do you want another blank-book?"

"Not yet. The last one you gave me is only half-full yet. A blank-book lasts me quite a while when I can't write stories. Oh, I wish I could, Cousin Jimmy."

"The time will come—the time will come," said Cousin Jimmy encouragingly. "Wait a while—just wait a while. If we don't chase things—sometimes the things following us can catch up. 'Through wisdom is an house builded, and by understanding is it established. And by knowledge shall the chambers be filled with all precious and pleasant riches'—all precious and pleasant riches, Emily. Proverbs twenty-fourth, third and fifth."

He let Emily out and bolted the door. He put out all the candles but one. He glared at it for a few moments, then, satisfied that Elizabeth could not hear him, Cousin Jimmy said fervently,

"Ruth Dutton can go to—to—to—" Cousin Jimmy's courage failed him. "—to heaven!"

Emily went back to Shrewsbury through the clear moonlight. She had expected the walk to be dreary and weary, robbed of the impetus anger and rebellion had given. But she found that it had become transmuted into a thing of beauty—and Emily was one of "the eternal slaves of beauty," of whom Carman sings, who are yet "masters of the world." She was tired, but her tiredness showed itself in a certain exaltation of feeling and imagination such as she often experienced when over-fatigued. Thought was quick and active. She had a series of brilliant imaginary conversations and thought out so many epigrams that she was agreeably surprised at herself. It was good to feel vivid and interesting and all-alive once more. She was alone but not lonely.

As she walked along she dramatised the night. There was about it a wild, lawless charm that appealed to a certain wild, lawless strain hidden deep in Emily's nature—a strain that wished to walk where it would with no guidance but its own—the strain of the gypsy and the poet, the genius and the fool.

The big fir trees, released from their burden of snow, were tossing their arms freely and wildly and gladly across the moonlit fields. Was ever anything so beautiful as the shadows of those grey, clean-limbed maples on the road at her feet? The houses she passed were full of intriguing mystery. She liked to think of the people who lay there dreaming and saw in sleep what waking life denied them—of little children's dear hands folded in exquisite slumber—of hearts that, perhaps, kept sorrowful, wakeful vigils—of lonely arms that reached out in the emptiness of the night—all while she, Emily, flitted by like a shadowy wraith of the small hours.

And it was easy to think, too, that other things were abroad—things that were not mortal or human. She always lived on the edge of fairyland and now she stepped right over it. The Wind Woman was really whistling eerily in the reeds of the swamp—she was sure she heard the dear, diabolical chuckles of owls in the spruce copses—something frisked across her path— it might be a rabbit or it might be a Little Grey Person:

the trees put on half pleasing, half terrifying shapes they never wore by day. The dead thistles of last year were goblin groups along the fences: that shaggy, old yellow birch was some satyr of the woodland: the footsteps of the old gods echoed around her: those gnarled stumps on the hill field were surely Pan piping through moonlight and shadow with his troop of laughing fauns. It was delightful to believe they were.

"One loses so much when one becomes incredulous," said Emily—and then thought that was a rather clever remark and wished she had a Jimmy-book to write it down.

So, having washed her soul free from bitterness in the aërial bath of the spring night and tingling from head to foot with the wild, strange, sweet life of the spirit, she came to Aunt Ruth's when the faint, purplish hills east of the harbour were growing clear under a whitening sky. She had expected to find the door still locked; but the knob turned as she tried it and she went in.

Aunt Ruth was up and was lighting the kitchen fire.

On the way from New Moon Emily had thought over a dozen different ways of saying what she meant to say—and now she used not one of them. At the last moment an impish inspiration came to her. Before Aunt Ruth could—or would—speak Emily said,

"Aunt Ruth, I've come back to tell you that I forgive you, but that this must not happen again."

To tell the truth, Mistress Ruth Dutton was considerably relieved that Emily *had* come back. She had been afraid of Elizabeth and Laura—Murray family rows were bitter things—and truly a little afraid of the results to Emily herself if she had really gone to New Moon in those thin shoes and that insufficient coat. For Ruth Dutton was not a fiend—only a rather stupid, stubborn little barnyard fowl trying to train up a skylark. She was honestly afraid that Emily might catch a cold and go into consumption. And if Emily took it into her head *not* to come back to Shrewsbury—well, that would "make talk" and Ruth Dutton hated "talk" when she or her doings was the subject. So, all things considered, she decided to ignore the impertinence of Emily's greeting.

"Did you spend the night on the streets?" she asked grimly.

"Oh, dear no—I went out to New Moon—had a chat with Cousin Jimmy and some lunch—then walked back."

"Did Elizabeth see you? Or Laura?"

"No. They were asleep."

Mrs. Dutton reflected that this was just as well.

"Well," she said coldly, "you have been guilty of great ingratitude, Em'ly, but I'll forgive you this time"—then stopped abruptly. Hadn't that been said already this morning? Before she could think of a substitute remark Emily had vanished upstairs. Mistress Ruth Dutton was left with the unpleasant sensation that, somehow or other, she had not come out of the affair quite as triumphantly as she should have.

11
Heights and Hollows

"Shrewsbury,
"April 28, 19—

"This was my week-end at New Moon and I came back this morning. Consequently this is blue Monday and I'm homesick. Aunt Ruth, too, is always a little more *unlivable* on Mondays—or seems so by contrast with Aunt Laura and Aunt Elizabeth. Cousin

Jimmy wasn't quite so nice this week-end as he usually is. He had several of his queer spells and was a bit grumpy for two reasons: in the first place, several of his young apple trees are dying because they were girdled by mice in the winter; and in the second place he can't induce Aunt Elizabeth to try the new creamers that every one else is using. For my own part I am secretly glad that she won't. I don't want our beautiful old dairy and the glossy brown milk pans to be improved out of existence. I can't think of New Moon without a dairy.

"When I could get Cousin Jimmy's mind off his grievances we explored the Carlton catalogue and discussed the best selections to make for my two dollars' worth of owl's laughter. We planned a dozen different combinations and beds, and got several hundred dollars' worth of fun out of it, but finally settled on a long, narrow bed full of asters—lavender down the middle, white around it and a border of pale pink, with clumps of deep purple for sentinels at the four corners. I am sure it will be beautiful: and I shall look at its September loveliness and think, '*This* came out of my head!'

"I have taken another step in the Alpine Path. Last week the *Ladies' Own Journal* accepted my poem, *The Wind Woman,* and gave me two subscriptions to the *Journal* for it. No cash—but that may come yet. I *must* make enough money before very long to pay Aunt Ruth every cent my living with her has cost her. Then she won't be able to twit me with the expense I am to her. She hardly misses a day without some hint of it—'No, Mrs. Beatty, I feel I can't give quite as much to missions this year as usual—my expenses have been much heavier, you know'—'Oh, no, Mr. Morrison, your new goods are beautiful but I can't afford a silk dress *this* spring'—'This davenport should really be upholstered again—it's getting fearfully shabby—but it's out of the question now for a year or two.' So it goes.

"But my soul doesn't belong to Aunt Ruth.

"*Owl's Laughter* was copied in the Shrewsbury *Times*—'hunter's moan' and all. Evelyn Blake, I understand, says she doesn't believe I wrote it at all—she's *sure* she read something exactly like it somewhere some years ago.

"Dear Evelyn!

"Aunt Elizabeth said nothing at all about it, but Cousin Jimmy told me she cut it out and put it in the Bible she keeps on the stand by her bed. When I told her I was to get two dollars' worth of seeds for it she said I'd likely find when I sent for them that the firm had gone bankrupt!

"I have a notion to send that little story about the child that Mr. Carpenter liked to *Golden Hours*. I wish I could get it typewritten, but that is impossible, so I shall have to write it very plainly. I wonder if I *dare*. They would surely pay for a story.

"Dean will soon be home. How glad I will be to see him! I wonder if he will think I have changed much. I have certainly grown taller. Aunt Laura says I will soon have to have really long dresses and put my hair up, but Aunt Elizabeth says fifteen is too young for that. She says girls are not so womanly at fifteen nowadays as they were in *her* time. Aunt Elizabeth is really frightened, I know, that if she lets me grow up I'll be eloping—'like Juliet.' But I'm in no hurry to grow up. It's nicer to be just like this—betwixt-and-between. Then, if I want to be childish I can be, none daring to make me ashamed; and if I want to behave maturely I have the authority of my extra inches.

"It's a gentle, rainy evening tonight. There are pussy willows out in the swamp and some young birches in the Land of Uprightness have cast a veil of transparent purple over their bare limbs. I think I will write a poem on *A Vision of Spring*.

"May 5, 19—

"There has been quite an outbreak of spring poetry in High School. Evelyn has one in the May *Quill* on *Flowers*. Very wobbly rhymes.

"And Perry! He also felt the annual spring urge, as Mr. Carpenter calls it, and wrote a dreadful thing called *The Old Farmer Sows His Seed*. He sent it to *The Quill* and *The Quill* actually printed it—in the 'jokes' column. Perry is quite proud of it and doesn't realise that he has made an ass of himself. Ilse turned pale with fury when she read it and hasn't spoken to him since. She says he isn't fit to associate with. Ilse is far too hard on Perry. And yet, when I read the thing, especially the verse,

> " 'I've ploughed and harrowed and sown—
> I've done my best,
> Now I'll leave the crop alone
> And let God do the rest.'

I wanted to murder him myself. Perry can't understand what is wrong with it.

" 'It rhymes, doesn't it?'

"Oh, yes, it rhymes!

"Ilse has also been raging at Perry lately because he has been coming to school with all but one button off his coat. I couldn't endure it myself, so when we came out of class I whispered to Perry to meet me for five minutes by the Fern Pool at sunset. I slipped out with needle, thread and buttons and sewed them on. He didn't see why it wouldn't have done to wait till Friday night and have Aunt Tom sew them on. I said,

" 'Why didn't you sew them on yourself, Perry?'

" 'I've no buttons and no money to buy any,' he said,

'but never mind, some day I will have gold buttons if I want them.'

"Aunt Ruth saw me coming in with thread and scissors, etc., and of course wanted to know where, what, and why. I told her the whole tale and she said,

" 'You'd better let Perry Miller's friends sew his buttons on for him.'

" 'I'm the best friend he's got,' I said.

" 'I don't know where you get your low tastes from,' said Aunt Ruth.

"May 7, 19—

"This afternoon after school Teddy rowed Ilse and me across the harbour to pick May-flowers in the spruce barrens up the Green River. We got basketfuls, and spent a perfect hour wandering about the barrens with the friendly murmur of the little fir trees all around us. As somebody said of strawberries so say I of May-flowers, 'God might have made a sweeter blossom, but never did.'

"When we left for home a thick white fog had come in over the bar and filled the harbour. But Teddy rowed in the direction of the train whistles, so we hadn't any trouble really and I thought the experience quite wonderful. We seemed to be floating over a white sea in an unbroken calm. There was no sound save the faint moan of the bar, the deep-sea call beyond, and the low dip of the oars in the glassy water. We were alone in a world of mist on a veiled, shoreless sea. Now and then, for just a moment, a cool air current lifted the mist curtain and dim coasts loomed phantom-like around us. Then the blank whiteness shut down again. It was as though we sought some strange, enchanted shore that ever receded farther and farther. I was really sorry when we got to the wharf, but when I reached home I found Aunt Ruth all worked up on account of the fog.

" 'I knew I shouldn't have allowed you to go,' she said.

" 'There wasn't any danger really, Aunt Ruth,' I protested, 'and look at my lovely May-flowers.'

"Aunt Ruth wouldn't look at the May-flowers.

" 'No danger—in a white fog! Suppose you had got lost and a wind had come up before you reached land?'

" 'How could one get lost on little Shrewsbury harbour, Aunt Ruth?' I said. 'The fog was wonderful—wonderful. It just seemed as if we were voyaging over the planet's rim into the depth of space.'

"I spoke enthusiastically and I suppose I looked a bit wild with mist drops on my hair, for Aunt Ruth said coldly, pityingly,

" 'It is unfortunate that you are *so excitable*, Emily.'

"It is maddening to be frozen and pitied, so I answered recklessly,

" 'But think of the fun you miss when you're nonexcitable, Aunt Ruth. There is nothing more wonderful than dancing around a blazing fire. What matter if it end in ashes?'

" 'When you are as old as I am,' said Aunt Ruth, 'you will have more sense than to go into ecstasies over white fogs.'

"It seems to me impossible that I shall either grow old or die. I *know* I will, of course, but I don't *believe* it. I didn't make any answer to Aunt Ruth, so she started on another tack.

" 'I was watching Ilse go past. Em'ly, does that girl wear *any* petticoats?'

" '*Her clothing is silk and purple*,' I murmured, quoting the Bible verse simply because there is something in it that charms me. One couldn't imagine a finer or simpler description of a gorgeously dressed woman. I don't think Aunt Ruth recognised the quotation: she thought I was just trying to be smart.

" 'If you mean that she wears a purple silk petticoat,

Em'ly, say so in plain English. Silk petticoats, indeed. If *I* had anything to do with her I'd silk petticoat her.'

" 'Some day *I* am going to wear silk petticoats,' I said.

" 'Oh, indeed, miss. And may I ask what *you* have got to get silk petticoats with?'

" 'I've got a *future*,' I said, as proudly as the Murrayest of all Murrays could have said it.

"Aunt Ruth sniffed.

"I have filled my room with May-flowers and even Lord Byron looks as if there might be a chance of recovery.

"May 13, 19—

"I have made the plunge and sent my story *Something Different* to *Golden Hours*. I actually trembled as I dropped it into the box at the Shoppe. Oh, if it should be accepted!

"Perry has set the school laughing again. He said in class that France *exported fashions*. Ilse walked up to him when class came out and said, 'You *spawn!*' She hasn't spoken to him since.

"Evelyn continues to say sweet cutting things and laugh. I might forgive her the cutting things but never the laugh.

"May 15, 19—

"We had our Prep 'Pow-wow' last night. It always comes off in May. We had it in the Assembly room of the school and when we got there we found we couldn't light the gas. We didn't know what was the matter but suspected the Juniors. (Today we discovered they had cut off the gas in the basement and locked the basement doors.) At first we didn't know what to do: then I remembered that Aunt Elizabeth had brought Aunt Ruth a big box of candles last week for my use. I tore home and got them—Aunt Ruth being out—and we stuck them all around the room. So we had our Pow-wow after all and it was a brilliant success. We had such fun improvising candle holders that we got off to a good start, and somehow the candle-light was so much more friendly and inspiring than gas. We all seemed to be able to think of wittier things to say. Everybody was supposed to make a speech on any subject he or she wished. Perry made the speech of the evening. He had prepared a speech on 'Canadian History' —very sensible and, I suspect, dull; but at the last minute he changed his mind and spoke on 'candles' —just making it up as he went along, telling of all the candles he saw in different lands when he was a little boy sailing with his father. It was so witty and interesting that we sat enthralled and I think the students will forget about French fashions and the old farmer who left the hoeing and weeding to God.

"Aunt Ruth hasn't found out about the candles yet, as the old box isn't quite empty. When I go to New Moon tomorrow night I'll coax Aunt Laura to give me another box—I know she will—and I'll bring them to Aunt Ruth.

                                      "May 22, 19—
"Today there was a hateful, long, fat envelope for me in the mail. *Golden Hours* had sent my story back. The accompanying rejection slip said:

"'We have read your story with keen interest, and regret to say that we cannot accept it for publication at the present time.'

"At first I tried to extract a little comfort from the fact that they had read it with 'keen interest.' Then it came home to me that the rejection slip was a printed one, so of course it is just what they send with *all* rejected manuscripts.

"The worst of it was that Aunt Ruth had seen the packet before I got home from school and had opened it. It was humiliating to have *her* know of my failure.

"'I hope *this* will convince you that you'd better waste no more stamps on such nonsense, Em'ly. The idea of your thinking *you* could write a story fit to be published.'

"'I've had two poems published,' I cried.

"Aunt Ruth sniffed.

"'Oh, *poems*. Of course they have to have something to fill up the corners.'

"Perhaps it's so. I felt very flat as I crawled off to my room with my poor story. I was quite 'content to fill a little space' then. You could have packed me in a thimble.

"My story is all dog-eared and smells of tobacco. I've a notion to burn it.

"No, I *won't*!! I'll copy it out again and try somewhere else. I *will* succeed!

"I think, from glancing over the recent pages of this journal, that I am beginning to be able to do without italics. But sometimes they are necessary.

"New Moon, Blair Water.
"May 24, 19—

"'For lo, the winter is past: the rain is over and gone: the flowers appear on the earth: the time of the singing of birds has come.'

"I'm sitting on the sill of my open window in my own dear room. It's so lovely to get back to it every now and then. Out there, over Lofty John's bush, is a soft yellow sky and one very white little star is just visible where the pale yellow shades off into paler green. Far off, down in the south 'in regions mild of calm and serene air' are great cloud-palaces of rosy marble. Leaning over the fence is a choke-cherry tree that is a mass of blossoms like creamy caterpillars. Everything is so lovely—'the eye is not satisfied with seeing nor the ear with hearing.'

"Sometimes I think it really isn't worth while to try to write anything when everything is already so well expressed in the Bible. That verse I've just quoted for instance—it makes me feel like a pigmy in the presence of a giant. Only twelve simple words—yet a dozen pages couldn't have better expressed the feeling one has in spring.

"This afternoon Cousin Jimmy and I sowed our aster bed. The seeds came promptly. Evidently the firm has not gone bankrupt yet. But Aunt Elizabeth thinks they are old stock and won't grow.

"Dean is home; he was down to see me last night—dear old Dean. He hasn't changed a bit. His green eyes are as green as ever and his nice mouth as nice as ever and his interesting face as interesting as ever. He took both my hands and looked earnestly at me.

" '*You* have changed, Star,' he said. 'You look more like spring than ever. But don't grow any taller,' he went on. 'I don't want to have you looking down on me.'

"I don't want to, either. I'd hate to be taller than Dean. It wouldn't seem right at all.

"Teddy is an inch taller than I am. Dean says he has improved greatly in his drawing this past year. Mrs. Kent still hates me. I met her tonight, when I was out for a walk with myself in the spring twilight, and she would not even stop to speak to me—just slipped by me like a shadow in the twilight. She looked at me for a second as she passed me, and her eyes were pools of hatred. I think she grows more unhappy every year.

"In my walk I went and said good-evening to the Disappointed House. I am always so sorry for it—it is a house that has never lived—that has not fulfilled its destiny. Its blind windows seem peering wistfully from its face as if seeking vainly for what they cannot find. No homelight has ever gleamed through them in summer dusk or winter darkness. And yet I feel, somehow, that the little house has kept its dream and that sometime it will come true.

"I wish I owned it.

"I dandered around all my old haunts tonight—Lofty John's bush—Emily's Bower—the old orchard—the pond graveyard—the Today Road—I love that little road. It's like a personal friend to me.

"I think 'dandering' is a lovely word of its kind—not in itself exactly, like some words, but because it is so perfectly expressive of its own meaning. Even if you'd never heard it before you'd know exactly what it meant— *dandering* could mean *only* dandering.

"The discovery of beautiful and interesting words always gives me joy. When I find a new, charming word I exult as a jewel-seeker and am unhappy until I've set it in a sentence.

"May 29, 19—

"Tonight Aunt Ruth came home with a portentous face.

"'Em'ly, what does this story mean that is all over Shrewsbury—that you were seen standing on Queen Street last night *with a man's arms around you, kissing him?*'

"I knew in a minute what had happened. I wanted to stamp—I wanted to laugh—I wanted to tear my hair. The whole thing was so absurd and ludicrous. But I had to keep a grave face and explain to Aunt Ruth.

"This is the dark, unholy tale.

"Ilse and I were 'dandering' along Queen Street last night at dusk. Just by the old Taylor house we met a man. I do not know the man—not likely I shall ever know him. I do not know if he was tall or short, old or young, handsome or ugly, black or white, Jew or Gentile, bond or free. But I *do* know he hadn't shaved that day!

"He was walking at a brisk pace. Then something happened which passed in the wink of an eye, but takes several seconds to describe. I stepped aside to let him pass—he stepped in the same direction—I darted the other way—so did he—then I thought I saw a chance of getting past and I made a wild dash—he made a dash—with the result that I ran full tilt against him. He had thrown out his arms when he realised a collision was unavoidable—I went right between them—and in the shock of the encounter they involuntarily closed around me for a moment while my nose came into violent contact with his chin.

" 'I—I—beg your pardon,' the poor creature gasped, dropped me as if I were a hot coal, and tore off around the corner.

"Ilse was in fits. She said she had never seen anything so funny in her life. It had all passed so quickly that to a by-stander it looked exactly as if that man and I had stopped, gazed at each other for a moment, and then rushed madly into each other's arms.

"My nose ached for blocks. Ilse said she saw Miss Taylor peering from the window just as it happened. Of course that old gossip has spread the story with her own interpretation of it.

"I explained all this to Aunt Ruth, who remained incredulous and seemed to consider it a very limping tale indeed.

" 'It's a *very* strange thing that on a sidewalk twelve feet wide you couldn't get past a man without embracing him,' she said.

" 'Come now, Aunt Ruth,' I said, 'I know you think me sly and deep and foolish and ungrateful. But you know I am half Murray, and *do* you think any one with *any* Murray in her would embrace a gentleman friend on the public street?'

" 'Oh, I *did* think you could hardly be so brazen,'

admitted Aunt Ruth. 'But Miss Taylor said she *saw* it. Every one has heard it. I do *not* like to have one of my family talked about like that. It would not have occurred if you had not been out with Ilse Burnley in defiance of my advice. Don't let anything like this happen again.'

" 'Things like that don't happen,' I said. 'They are foreordained.'

"June 3, 19—

"The Land of Uprightness is a thing of beauty. I can go to the Fern Pool to write again. Aunt Ruth is very suspicious of this performance. She has never forgotten that I 'met Perry' there one evening. The Pool is very lovely now, under its new young ferns. I look into it and imagine it is the legendary pool in which one could see the future. I picture myself tiptoeing to it at midnight by full o' moon—casting something precious into it—then looking timidly at what I saw.

"What *would* it show me? The Alpine Path gloriously climbed? Or failure?

"No, never failure!

"June 9, 19—

"Last week Aunt Ruth had a birthday and I gave her a centre-piece which I had embroidered. She thanked me rather stiffly and didn't seem to care anything about it.

"Tonight I was sitting in the bay window recess of the dining-room, doing my algebra by the last light. The folding-doors were open and Aunt Ruth was talking to Mrs. Ince in the parlour. I thought they knew I was in the bay, but I suppose the curtains hid me. All at once I heard my name. Aunt Ruth was showing the centre-piece to Mrs. Ince—quite proudly.

" 'My niece Em'ly gave me this on my birthday. See

how beautifully it is done—she is very skilful with her needle.'

"Could this be Aunt Ruth? I was so petrified with amazement that I could neither move nor speak.

" 'She is clever with more than her needle,' said Mrs. Ince. "I hear Principal Hardy expects her to head her class in the terminal examinations.'

" 'Her mother—my sister Juliet—was a *very* clever girl,' said Aunt Ruth.

" 'And she's quite pretty, too,' said Mrs. Ince.

" 'Her father, Douglas Starr, was a remarkably handsome man,' said Aunt Ruth.

"They went out then. For once an eavesdropper heard something good of herself!

"But from Aunt Ruth!!

                                              "June 17, 19—

"My 'candle goeth not out by night' now—at least not until quite late. Aunt Ruth lets me sit up because the terminal examinations are on. Perry infuriated Mr. Travers by writing at the end of his algebra paper, Matthew 7:5. When Mr. Travers turned it up he read: 'Thou hypocrite, first cast out the beam out of thine own eye, and then shalt thou see clearly to cast out the mote out of thy brother's eye.' Mr. Travers is credited with knowing much less about mathematics than he pretends to. So he was furious and threw Perry's paper out 'as a punishment for impertinence.' The truth is poor Perry made a mistake. He *meant* to write Matthew 5:7. 'Blessed are the merciful for they shall obtain mercy.' He went and explained to Mr. Travers but Mr. Travers wouldn't listen. Then Ilse bearded the lion in his den—that is, went to Principal Hardy, told him the tale and induced him to intercede with Mr. Travers. As a result Perry got his marks, but was warned not to juggle with Scripture texts again.

* * *

"June 28, 19—

"School's out. I have won my star pin. It has been a great old year of fun and study and *stings*. And now I'm going back to dear New Moon for two splendid months of freedom and happiness.

"I'm going to write a Garden Book in vacation. The idea has been sizzling in my brain for some time and since I can't write stories I shall try my hand at a series of essays on Cousin Jimmy's garden, with a poem for a tail-piece to each essay. It will be good practice and will please Cousin Jimmy."

12
At the Sign of the Haystack

"Why do you want to do a thing like that?" said Aunt Ruth—sniffing, of course. A sniff may always be taken for granted with each of Aunt Ruth's remarks, even when the present biographer omits mention of it.

"To poke some dollars into my slim purse," said Emily.

Holidays were over—the Garden Book had been written and read in instalments to Cousin Jimmy, in the dusks of July and August, to his great delight; and now it was September, with its return to school and studies, the Land of Uprightness, and Aunt Ruth. Emily, with skirts a fraction longer and her hair clubbed up so high in the "Cadogan Braid" of those days, that it really was almost "up," was back in Shrewsbury for her Junior year; and she had just told Aunt Ruth what she meant to do on her Shrewsbury Saturdays, for the autumn.

The editor of the Shrewsbury *Times* was planning a special illustrated Shrewsbury edition and Emily was going to canvass as much of the country as she could cover for subscriptions to it. She had wrung a rather reluctant consent from Aunt Elizabeth—a consent which could never have been extorted if Aunt Elizabeth had been paying all Emily's expenses at school. But there was Wallace paying for her books and tuition fees, and occasionally hinting to Elizabeth that he was a very fine, generous fellow to do so. Elizabeth, in her secret heart, was not overfond of her brother Wallace and resented his splendid airs over the little help he was extending to Emily. So, when Emily pointed out that she could easily earn, during the fall, at least half enough to pay for her books for the whole year, Elizabeth yielded. Wallace would have been offended if *she*, Elizabeth, had insisted on paying Emily's expenses when *he* took a notion to do it, but he could not reasonably resent Emily earning part for herself. He was always preaching that girls should be self-reliant, and able to earn their own way in life.

Aunt Ruth could not refuse when Elizabeth had assented, but she did not approve.

"The idea of your wandering over the country alone!"

"Oh, I'll not be alone. Ilse is going with me," said Emily.

Aunt Ruth did not seem to consider this much of an improvement.

"We're going to begin Thursday," said Emily. "There is no school Friday, owing to the death of Principal Hardy's father, and our classes are over at three on Thursday afternoon. We are going to canvass the Western Road that evening."

"May I ask if you intend to camp on the side of the road?"

"Oh, no. We'll spend the night with Ilse's aunt at Wiltney. Then, on Friday, we'll cut back to the Western Road, finish it that day and spend Friday night with

Mary Carswell's people at St. Clair—then work home Saturday by the River Road."

"It's perfectly absurd," said Aunt Ruth. "No Murray ever did such a thing. I'm surprised at Elizabeth. It simply isn't decent for two young girls like you and Ilse to be wandering alone over the country for three days."

"What do you suppose could happen to us?" asked Emily.

"A good many things might happen," said Aunt Ruth severely.

She was right. A good many things might—and did—happen in that excursion; but Emily and Ilse set off in high spirits Thursday afternoon, two graceless school girls with an eye for the funny side of everything and a determination to have a good time. Emily especially was feeling uplifted. There had been another thin letter in the mail that day, with the address of a third-rate magazine in the corner, offering her three subscriptions to the said magazine for her poem *Night in the Garden*, which had formed the conclusion of her Garden Book and was considered both by herself and Cousin Jimmy to be the gem of the volume. Emily had left the Garden Book locked up in the mantel cupboard of her room at New Moon, but she meant to send copies of its "tail pieces" to various publications during the fall. It augured well that the first one sent had been accepted so promptly.

"Well, we're off," she said, " 'over the hills and far away'—what an alluring old phrase! *Anything* may be beyond those hills ahead of us."

"I hope we'll get lots of material for our essays," said Ilse practically.

Principal Hardy had informed the Junior English class that he would require several essays from them during the fall term and Emily and Ilse had decided that one at least of their essays should recount their experiences in canvassing for subscriptions, from their separate points of view. Thus they had two strings to their bow.

"I suggest we work along the Western Road and its branches as far as Hunter's Creek, tonight," said Emily. "We ought to get there by sunset. Then we can hit the gypsy trail across the country, through the Malvern woods and come out on the other side of them, quite near Wiltney. It's only half an hour's walk, while around by the Malvern Road it's an hour. What a lovely afternoon this is!"

It was a lovely afternoon—such an afternoon as only September can produce when summer has stolen back for one more day of dream and glamour. Harvest fields drenched in sunshine lay all around them: the austere charm of northern firs made wonderful the ways over which they walked: goldenrod beribboned the fences and the sacrificial fires of willow-herb were kindled on all the burnt lands along the sequestered roads back among the hills. But they soon discovered that canvassing for subscriptions was not all fun—though, to be sure, as Ilse said, they found plenty of human nature for their essays.

There was the old man who said "Humph" at the end of every remark Emily made. When finally asked for a subscription he gruffly said "No."

"I'm glad you didn't say 'Humph' this time," said Emily. "It was getting monotonous."

The old fellow stared—then chuckled.

"Are ye any relation to the proud Murrays? I worked at a place they call New Moon when I was young and one of the Murray gals—Elizabeth her name was—had a sort of high-and-lofty way o' looking at ye, just like yours."

"My mother was a Murray."

"I was thinkin' so—ye bear the stamp of the breed. Well, here's two dollars an' ye kin put my name down. I'd ruther see the special edition 'fore I subscribe. I don't favour buying bearskins afore I see the bear. But it's worth two dollars to see a proud Murray coming down to askin' old Billy Scott fer a subscription."

"Why didn't you slay him with a glance?" asked Ilse as they walked away.

Emily was walking savagely, with her head held high and her eyes snapping.

"I'm out to get subscriptions, not to make widows. I didn't expect it would be all plain sailing."

There was another man who growled all the way through Emily's explanations—and then, when she was primed for refusal, gave her five subscriptions.

"He likes to disappoint people," she told Ilse, as they went down the lane. "He would rather disappoint them agreeably than not at all."

One man swore volubly—"not at anything in particular, but just at large," as Ilse said; and another old man was on the point of subscribing when his wife interfered.

"I wouldn't if I was you, Father. The editor of that paper is an infidel."

"Very impident of him, to be sure," said "Father," and put his money back in his wallet.

"Delicious!" murmured Emily when she was out of ear-shot. "I must jot that down in my Jimmy-book."

As a rule the women received them more politely than the men, but the men gave them more subscriptions. Indeed, the only woman who subscribed was an elderly dame whose heart Emily won by listening sympathetically to a long account of the beauty and virtues of the said elderly lady's deceased pet Thomas-cat—though it must be admitted that she whispered aside to Ilse at its conclusion,

"Charlottetown papers please copy."

Their worst experience was with a man who treated them to a tirade of abuse because his politics differed from the politics of the *Times* and he seemed to hold them responsible for it. When he halted for breath Emily stood up.

"Kick the dog—then you'll feel better," she said calmly, as she stalked out. Ilse was white with rage.

"Could you have believed people could be so detestable?" she exploded. "To rate *us* as if we were responsible for the politics of the *Times!* Well—*Human Nature from Canvasser's Point of View* is to be the subject of my essay. I'll describe that man and picture myself telling him all the things I wanted to and didn't!"

Emily broke into laughter—and found her temper again.

"*You* can. *I* can't even take that revenge—my promise to Aunt Elizabeth binds me. I shall have to stick to facts. Come, let's not think of the brute. After all, we've got quite a lot of subscriptions already—and there's a clump of white birches in which it is reasonably certain a dryad lives—and that cloud over the firs looks like the faint, golden ghost of a cloud."

"Nevertheless, I should have liked to reduce that old vampire to powder," said Ilse.

At the next place of call, however, their experience was pleasant and they were asked to stay for supper. By sunset they had done reasonably well in the matter of subscriptions and had accumulated enough private jokes and by-words to furnish fun for many moons of reminiscence. They decided to canvass no more that night. They had not got quite as far as Hunter's Creek but Emily thought it would be safe to make a cross-cut from where they were. The Malvern woods were not so very extensive and no matter where they came out on the northern side of them, they would be able to see Wiltney.

They climbed a fence, went up across a hill pasture field feathered with asters, and were swallowed up by the Malvern woods, crossed and recrossed by dozens of trails. The world disappeared behind them and they were alone in a realm of wild beauty. Emily thought the walk through the woods all too short, though tired Ilse, whose foot had turned on a pebble earlier in the day, found it unpleasantly long. Emily liked everything about it—she liked to see that shining gold head of Ilse's slipping through the grey-green trunks, under the long, swaying boughs—she liked the faint dream-like notes of sleepy birds—she liked the little wandering, whispering, tricksy wind o' dusk among the tree crests—she liked the incredibly delicate fragrance of wood flowers and growths—she liked the little ferns that brushed Ilse's silken ankles—she liked that slender, white, tantalising thing which gleamed out for a moment adown the dim vista of a winding path—was it a birch or a wood-nymph? No matter—it had given her that stab of poignant rapture she called "the flash" —her priceless thing whose flitting, uncalculated moments were worth cycles of mere existence. Emily wandered on, thinking all of the loveliness of the road and nothing of the road itself, absently following limping Ilse, until at last the trees suddenly fell away before them and they found themselves in the open, with a wild sort of little pasture before them, and beyond, in the clear afterlight, a long, sloping valley, rather bare and desolate, where the farmsteads had no great appearance of thrift or comfort.

"Why—where are we?" said Ilse blankly. "I don't see anything like Wiltney."

Emily came abruptly out of her dreams and tried to get her bearings. The only landmark visible was a tall spire on a hill ten miles away.

"Why, there's the spire of the Catholic church at Indian Head," she said flatly. "And that must be Hard-scrabble Road down there. We must have taken a wrong turning somewhere, Ilse—we've come out on the east side of the woods instead of the north."

"Then we're five miles from Wiltney," said Ilse despairingly. "I can never walk that far—and we can't go back through those woods—it will be pitch dark in a quarter of an hour. What on earth can we do?"

"Admit we're lost and make a beautiful thing of it," said Emily, coolly.

"Oh, we're lost all right, to all intents and purposes," moaned Ilse, climbing feebly up on the tumbledown fence and sitting there, "but I don't see how we're going to make it beautiful. We can't stay here all night. The only thing to do is to go down and see if they'll put us up at any of those houses. I don't like the idea. If that's Hardscrabble Road the people are all poor— and *dirty*. I've heard Aunt Net tell weird tales of Hardscrabble Road."

"Why can't we stay here all night?" said Emily.

Ilse looked at Emily to see if she meant it—saw that she did.

"Where can we sleep? Hang ourselves over this fence?"

"Over on that haystack," said Emily. "It's only half finished—Hardscrabble fashion. The top is flat—there's a ladder leaning against it—the hay is dry and clean— the night is summer warm—there are no mosquitoes this time of year—we can put our raincoats over us to keep off the dew. Why not?"

Ilse looked at the haystack in the corner of the little pasture—and began to laugh assentingly.

"What will Aunt Ruth say?"

"Aunt Ruth need never know it. I'll be sly for once with a vengeance. Besides, I've always longed to sleep out in the open. It's been one of the secret wishes I believed were for ever unattainable, hedged about as I am with aunts. And now it has tumbled into my lap like a gift thrown down by the gods. It's really such good luck as to be uncanny."

"Suppose it rains," said Ilse, who, nevertheless, found the idea very alluring.

"It won't rain—there isn't a cloud in sight except those great fluffy rose-and-white ones piling up over Indian Head. They're the kind of clouds that always make me feel that I'd love to soar up on wings as eagles and swoop right down into the middle of them."

It was easy to ascend the little haystack. They sank down on its top with sighs of content, realising that they were tireder than they had thought. The stack was built of the wild, fragrant grasses of the little pasture, and yielded an indescribably alluring aroma, such as no cultivated clover can give. They could see nothing but a great sky of faint rose above them, pricked with early stars, and the dim fringe of tree-tops around the field. Bats and swallows swooped darkly above them against the paling western gold—delicate fragrances exhaled from the mosses and ferns just over the fence under the trees—a couple of aspen poplars in the corner talked in silvery whispers, of the gossip of the woods. They laughed together in sheer lawless pleasure. An ancient enchantment was suddenly upon them, and the white magic of the sky and the dark magic of the woods wove the final spell of a potent incantation.

"Such loveliness as this doesn't seem real," murmured Emily. "It's so wonderful it *hurts* me. I'm afraid to speak out loud for fear it will vanish. Were we vexed with that horrid old man and his beastly politics today, Ilse? Why, he doesn't exist—not in *this* world, anyway. I hear the Wind Woman running with soft, soft footsteps over the hill. I shall always think of the wind as a personality. She is a shrew when she blows from the north—a lonely seeker when she blows from the east— a laughing girl when she comes from the west—and tonight from the south a little grey fairy."

"How do you think of such things?" asked Ilse.

This was a question which, for some mysterious reason, always annoyed Emily.

"I don't think of them—they *come*," she answered rather shortly.

Ilse resented the tone.

"For heaven's sake, Emily, don't be such a crank!" she exclaimed.

For a second the wonderful world in which Emily was at the moment living, trembled and wavered like a disturbed reflection in water. Then——

"Don't let's quarrel *here*," she implored. "One of us might push the other off the haystack."

Ilse burst out laughing. Nobody can really laugh and keep angry. So their night under the stars was not spoiled by a fight. They talked for a while in whispers, of school girl secrets and dreams and fears. They even talked of getting married some time in the future. Of course they shouldn't have, but they *did*. Ilse, it appeared, was slightly pessimistic in regard to her matrimonial chances.

"The boys like me as a pal but I don't believe any one will ever really fall in love with me."

"Nonsense," said Emily reassuringly. "Nine out of ten men will fall in love with you."

"But it will be the tenth I'll want," persisted Ilse gloomily.

And then they talked of almost everything else in the world. Finally, they made a solemn compact that whichever one of them died first was to come back to the other if it were possible. How many such compacts have been made! And has even one ever been kept?

Then Ilse grew drowsy and fell asleep. But Emily did not sleep—did not want to sleep. It was too dear a night to go to sleep, she felt. She wanted to lie awake for the pleasure of it and think over a thousand things.

Emily always looked back to that night spent under the stars as a sort of milestone. Everything in it and of it ministered to her. It filled her with its beauty, which she must later give to the world. She wished that she could coin some magic word that might express it.

The round moon rose. Did an old witch in a high-crowned hat ride past it on a broomstick? No, it was only a bat and the little tip of a hemlock tree by the fence. She made a poem on it at once, the lines singing themselves through her consciousness without effort. With one side of her nature she liked writing prose best—with the other she liked writing poetry. This side was uppermost tonight and her very thoughts ran into rhyme. A great, pulsating star hung low in the sky over Indian Head. Emily gazed on it and recalled Teddy's old fancy of his previous existence in a star. The idea seized on her imagination and she spun a dream life, lived in some happy planet circling round that mighty, far-off sun. Then came the northern lights— drifts of pale fire over the sky—spears of light, as of empyrean armies—pale, elusive hosts retreating and advancing. Emily lay and watched them in rapture. Her soul was washed pure in that great bath of splendour. She was a high priestess of loveliness assisting at the divine rites of her worship—and she knew her goddess smiled.

She was glad Ilse was asleep. Any human companionship, even the dearest and most perfect, would have been alien to her then. She was sufficient unto herself, needing not love nor comradeship nor any human emotion to round out her felicity. Such moments come rarely in any life, but when they do come they are inexpressibly wonderful—as if the finite were for a second infinity—as if humanity were for a space uplifted into divinity—as if all ugliness had vanished, leaving only flawless beauty. Oh—beauty—Emily shivered with the pure ecstasy of it. She loved it—it filled her being tonight as never before. She was afraid to move or breathe lest she break the current of beauty that was flowing through her. Life seemed like a wonderful instrument on which to play supernal harmonies.

"Oh, God, make me worthy of it—oh, make me worthy of it," she prayed. Could she ever be worthy of such a message—could she dare try to carry some of the loveliness of that "dialogue divine" back to the everyday world of sordid market-place and clamorous street? She *must* give it—she could not keep it to herself. Would the world listen—understand—feel? Only if she were faithful to the trust and gave out that which was committed to her, careless of blame or praise. High priestess of beauty—yes, she would serve at no other shrine!

She fell asleep in this rapt mood—dreamed that she was Sappho springing from the Leucadian rock—woke to find herself at the bottom of the haystack with Ilse's startled face peering down at her. Fortunately so much of the stack had slipped down with her that she was able to say cautiously,

"I think I'm all in one piece still."

13
Haven

When you have fallen asleep listening to the hymns of the gods it is something of an anti-climax to be wakened by an ignominious tumble from a haystack. But at least it had aroused them in time to see the sunrise over Indian Head, which was worth the sacrifice of several hours of inglorious ease.

"Besides, I might never have known what an exquisite thing a spider's web beaded with dew is," said Emily. "Look at it—swung between those two tall, plumy grasses."

"Write a poem on it," jeered Ilse, whose alarm made her fleetingly cross.

"How's your foot?"

"Oh, it's all right. But my hair is sopping wet with dew."

"So is mine. We'll carry our hats for a while and the

sun will soon dry us. It's just as well to get an early start. We can get back to civilisation by the time it's safe for us to be seen. Only we'll have to breakfast on the crackers in my bag. It won't do for us to be looking for breakfast, with no rational account to give of where we spent the night. Ilse, swear you'll never mention this escapade to a living soul. It's been beautiful—but it will remain beautiful just as long as only we two know of it. Remember the result of your telling about our moonlit bath."

"People have such beastly minds," grumbled Ilse, sliding down the stack.

"Oh, *look* at Indian Head. I could be a sun worshipper this very moment."

Indian Head was a flaming mount of splendour. The far-off hills turned beautifully purple against the radiant sky. Even the bare, ugly Hardscrabble Road was transfigured and luminous in hazes of silver. The fields and woods were very lovely in the faint pearly lustre.

"The world is always young again for just a few moments at the dawn," murmured Emily.

Then she pulled her Jimmy-book out of her bag and wrote the sentence down!

They had the usual experiences of canvassers the world over that day. Some people refused to subscribe, ungraciously: some subscribed graciously: some refused to subscribe so pleasantly that they left an agreeable impression: some consented to subscribe so unpleasantly that Emily wished they had refused. But on the whole they enjoyed the forenoon, especially when an excellent early dinner in a hospitable farmhouse on the Western Road filled up the aching void left by a few crackers and a night on a haystack.

"S'pose you didn't come across any stray children today?" asked their host.

"No. Have any been lost?"

"Little Allan Bradshaw—Will Bradshaw's son, downriver at Malvern Point—has been missing ever since

Tuesday morning. He walked out of the house that morning, singing, and hasn't been seen or heard of since."

Emily and Ilse exchanged shocked glances.

"How old was he?"

"Just seven—and an only child. They say his poor ma is plumb distracted. All the Malvern Point men have been s'arching for him for two days, and not a trace of him kin they discover."

"What can have happened to him?" said Emily, pale with horror.

"It's a mystery. Some think he fell off the wharf at the Point—it was only about a quarter of a mile from the house and he used to like sitting there and watching the boats. But nobody saw anything of him 'round the wharf or the bridge that morning. There's a lot of marshland west of the Bradshaw farm, full of bogs and pools. Some think he must have wandered there and got lost and perished—ye remember Tuesday night was terrible cold. *That's* where his mother thinks he is—and if you ask *me*, she's right. If he'd been anywhere else he'd have been found by the s'arching parties. They've combed the country."

The story haunted Emily all the rest of the day and she walked under its shadow. Anything like that always took almost a morbid hold on her. She could not bear the thought of the poor mother at Malvern Point. And the little lad—where was he? Where had he been the previous night when she had lain in the ecstasy of wild, free hours? That night had not been cold—but Wednesday night had. And she shuddered as she recalled Tuesday night, when a bitter autumnal wind-storm had raged till dawn, with showers of hail and stinging rain. Had he been out in that—the poor lost baby?

"Oh, I can't *bear* it!" she moaned.

"It's dreadful," agreed Ilse, looking rather sick, "but *we* can't do anything. There's no use in thinking of it.

Oh"—suddenly Ilse stamped her foot—"I believe Father used to be right when he didn't believe in God. Such a hideous thing as *this*—how could it happen if there *is* a God—a *decent* God, anyway?"

"God hadn't anything to do with *this*," said Emily. "You *know* the Power that made last night couldn't have brought about this monstrous thing."

"Well, He didn't prevent it," retorted Ilse—who was suffering so keenly that she wanted to arraign the universe at the bar of her pain.

"Little Allan Bradshaw may be found yet—he *must* be," exclaimed Emily.

"He won't be found alive," stormed Ilse. "No, don't talk to me about God. And don't talk to me of this. I've got to forget it—I'll go crazy if I don't."

Ilse put the matter out of her mind with another stamp of her foot and Emily tried to. She could not quite succeed but she forced herself to concentrate superficially on the business of the day, though she knew the horror lurked in the back of her consciousness. Only once did she really forget it—when they came around a point on the Malvern River Road and saw a little house built in the cup of a tiny bay, with a steep grassy hill rising behind it. Scattered over the hill were solitary, beautifully shaped young fir-trees like little green, elongated pyramids. No other house was in sight. All about it was a lovely autumnal solitude of grey, swift-running, windy river, and red, spruce-fringed points.

"That house belongs to me," said Emily.

Ilse stared.

"To you?"

"Yes. Of course, I don't *own* it. But haven't you sometimes seen houses that you knew belonged to you no matter who owned them?"

No, Ilse hadn't. She hadn't the least idea what Emily meant.

"I know who owns that house," she said. "It's Mr.

Scobie of Kingsport. He built it for a summer cottage. I heard Aunt Net talking of it the last time I was in Wiltney. It was finished a few weeks ago. It's a pretty little house, but too small for me. *I* like a big house—I don't want to feel cramped and crowded—especially in summer."

"It's hard for a big house to have any personality," said Emily thoughtfully. "But little houses almost always have. That house is full of it. There isn't a line or a corner that isn't eloquent, and those casement windows are lovable—especially that little one high up under the eaves over the front door. It's absolutely smiling at me. Look at it glowing like a jewel in the sunshine out of the dark shingle setting. The little house is greeting us. You dear friendly thing, I love you—I understand you. As Old Kelly would say, 'may niver a tear be shed under your roof.' The people who are going to live in you must be nice people or they would never have *thought* you. If I lived in you, beloved, I'd always stand at that western window at evening to wave to some one coming home. That is just exactly what that window was built for—a frame for love and welcome."

"When you get through with talking to your house we'd better hurry on," warned Ilse. "There's a storm coming up. See those clouds—and those sea-gulls. Gulls never come up this far except before a storm. It's going to rain any minute. We'll not sleep on a haystack tonight, Friend Emily."

Emily loitered past the little house and looked at it lovingly as long as she could. It *was* such a dear little place with its dubbed-off gables and rich, brown shingle tints, and its general intimate air of sharing mutual jokes and secrets. She turned around half a dozen times to look upon it, as they climbed the steep hill, and when at last it dipped below sight she sighed.

"I hate to leave it. I have the oddest feeling, Ilse, that it's *calling* to me—that I ought to go back to it."

"Don't be silly," said Ilse impatiently. "There—it's sprinkling now! If you hadn't poked so long looking at your blessed little hut we'd have been out on the main road now, and near shelter. Wow, but it's cold!"

"It's going to be a dreadful night," said Emily in a low voice. "Oh, Ilse, where is that poor little lost boy tonight? I wish I knew if they had found him."

"Don't!" said Ilse savagely. "Don't say another word about him. It's awful—it's hideous—but what can *we* do?"

"Nothing. That's the dreadful thing about it. It seems wicked to go on about our own business, asking for subscriptions, when that child is not found."

By this time they had reached the main road. The rest of the afternoon was not pleasant. Stinging showers came at intervals: between them the world was raw and damp and cold, with a moaning wind that came in ominous sighing gusts under a leaden sky. At every house where they called they were reminded of the lost baby, for there were only women to give or refuse subscriptions. The men were all away searching for him.

"Though it isn't any use *now*," said one woman gloomily, "except that they may find his little body. He can't have lived this long. I jest can't eat or cook for thinking of his poor mother. They say she's nigh crazy—I don't wonder."

"They say old Margaret McIntyre is taking it quite calmly," said an older woman, who was piecing a log-cabin quilt by the window. "I'd have thought she'd be wild, too. She seemed real fond of little Allan."

"Oh, Margaret McIntyre has never got worked up about anything for the past five years—ever since her own son Neil was frozen to death in the Klondyke. Seems as if her feelings were frozen then, too—she's been a little mad ever since. *She* won't worry none over this—she'll just smile and tell you she spanked the King."

Both women laughed. Emily, with the story-teller's nose, scented a story instantly, but though she would fain have lingered to hunt it down Ilse hustled her away.

"We *must* get on, Emily, or we'll never reach St. Clair before night."

They soon realised that they were not going to reach it. At sunset St. Clair was still three miles away and there was every indication of a wild evening.

"We can't get to St. Clair, that's certain," said Ilse. "It's going to settle down for a steady rain and it'll be as black as a million black cats in a quarter of an hour. We'd better go to that house over there and ask if we can stay all night. It looks snug and respectable—though it certainly is the jumping-off place."

The house at which Ilse pointed—an old whitewashed house with a grey roof—was set on the face of a hill amid bright green fields of clover aftermath. A wet red road wound up the hill to it. A thick grove of spruces shut it off from the gulf shore, and beyond the grove a tiny dip in the land revealed a triangular glimpse of misty, white-capped, grey sea. The near brook valley was filled with young spruces, dark-green in the rain. The grey clouds hung heavily over it. Suddenly the sun broke through the clouds in the west for one magical moment. The hill of clover meadows flashed instantly into incredibly vivid green. The triangle of sea shimmered into violet. The old house gleamed like white marble against the emerald of its hilly background, and the inky black sky over and around it.

"Oh," gasped Emily, "I never saw anything so wonderful!"

She groped wildly in her bag and clutched her Jimmy-book. The post of a field-gate served as a desk—Emily licked a stubborn pencil and wrote feverishly. Ilse squatted on a stone in a fence corner and waited with ostentatious patience. She knew that when a certain look appeared on Emily's face she was not to be dragged away until she was ready to go. The sun had vanished and the rain was beginning to fall again when Emily put her Jimmy-book back into her bag, with a sigh of satisfaction.

"I *had* to get it, Ilse."

"Couldn't you have waited till you got to dry land and wrote it down from memory?" grumbled Ilse, uncoiling herself from her stone.

"No—I'd have missed some of the flavour then. I've got it all now—and in just exactly the right words. Come on—I'll race you to the house. Oh, smell that wind—there's nothing in all the world like a salt sea-wind—a savage salt sea-wind. After all, there's something delightful in a storm. There's always *something*—deep down in me—that seems to rise and leap out to meet a storm—wrestle with it."

"I feel that way sometimes—but not tonight," said Ilse. "I'm tired—and that poor baby——"

"Oh!" Emily's triumph and exultation went from her in a cry of pain. "Oh—Ilse—I'd forgotten for a moment—how could I? *Where* can he be?"

"Dead," said Ilse harshly. "It's better to think so—than to think of him alive still—out tonight. Come, we've got to get in somewhere. The storm is on for good now—no more showers."

An angular woman panoplied in a white apron so stiffly starched that it could easily have stood alone, opened the door of the house on the hill and bade them enter.

"Oh, yes, you can stay here, I reckon," she said, not inhospitably, "if you'll excuse things being a bit upset. They're in sad trouble here."

"Oh—I'm sorry," stammered Emily. "We won't intrude—we'll go somewhere else."

"Oh, we don't mind *you*, if you don't mind *us*. There's a spare room. You're welcome. You can't go on in a storm like this—there isn't another house for some ways. I advise you to stop here. I'll get you a bit of supper—I don't live here—I'm just a neighbour come to help 'em out a bit. Hollinger's my name—Mrs. Julia Hollinger. Mrs. Bradshaw ain't good for anything—you've heard of her little boy mebbe."

"Is this where—and—he—hasn't—been found?"

"No—never will be. I'm not mentioning it to her"—with a quick glance over her shoulder along the hall—"but it's my opinion he got in the quicksands down by the bay. That's what *I* think. Come in and lay off your things. I s'pose you don't mind eating in the kitchen. The room is cold—we haven't the stove up in it yet. It'll have to be put up soon if there's a funeral. I s'pose there won't be if he's in the quicksand. You can't have a funeral without a body, can you?"

All this was very gruesome. Emily and Ilse would fain have gone elsewhere—but the storm had broken in full fury and darkness seemed to pour in from the sea over the changed world. They took off their drenched hats and coats and followed their hostess to the kitchen, a clean, old-fashioned spot which seemed cheerful enough in lamp-light and fire-glow.

"Sit up to the fire. I'll poke it a bit. Don't mind Grandfather Bradshaw—Grandfather, here's two young ladies that want to stay all night."

Grandfather stared stonily at them out of little, hazy, blue eyes and said not a word.

"Don't mind him"—in a pig's whisper—"he's over ninety and he never was much of a talker. Clara—Mrs. Bradshaw—is in there"—nodding towards the door of what seemed a small bedroom off the kitchen. "Her brother's with her—Dr. McIntyre from Charlottetown. We sent for him yesterday. He's the only one that can do anything with her. She's been walking the floor all day but we've got her persuaded to lie down a bit. Her husband's out looking for little Allan."

"A child *can't* be lost in the nineteenth century," said Grandfather Bradshaw, with uncanny suddenness and positiveness.

"There, there now, Grandfather, I advise *you* not to get worked up. And this is the twentieth century now. He's still living back there. His memory stopped a few years ago. What might your names be? Burnley? Starr? From Blair Water? Oh, then you'll know the Murrays? Niece? Oh!"

Mrs. Julia Hollinger's "Oh" was subtly eloquent. She had been setting dishes and food down at a rapid rate on the clean oil-cloth on the table. Now she swept them aside, extracted a table-cloth from a drawer of the cupboard, got silver forks and spoons out of another drawer, and a handsome pair of salt and pepper shakers from the shelves.

"Don't go to any trouble for us," pleaded Emily.

"Oh, it's no trouble. If all was well here you'd find Mrs. Bradshaw real glad to have you. She's a very kind woman, poor soul. It's awful hard to see her in such trouble. Allan was all the child she had, you see."

"A child can't be *lost* in the nineteenth century, I tell you," repeated Grandfather Bradshaw, with an irritable shift of emphasis.

"No—no," soothingly, "of course not, Grandfather. Little Allan'll turn up all right yet. Here's a hot cup o' tea for you. I advise you to drink it. *That*'ll keep him quiet for a bit. Not that he's ever very fussy—only everybody's a bit upset—except old Mrs. McIntyre. Nothing ever upsets *her*. It's just as well, only it seems to me real unfeeling. 'Course, she isn't just right. Come, sit in and have a bite, girls. Listen to that rain, will you? The men will be soaked. They can't search much longer tonight—Will will soon be home. I sorter dread it—Clara'll go wild again when he comes home without little Allan. We had a terrible time with her last night, pore thing."

"A child can't be lost in the *nineteenth* century," said Grandfather Bradshaw—and choked over his hot drink in his indignation.

"No—nor in the twentieth neither," said Mrs.

Hollinger, patting him on the back. "I advise you to go to bed, Grandfather. You're tired."

"I am *not* tired and I will go to bed when I choose, Julia Hollinger."

"Oh, very well, Grandfather. I advise you not to get worked up. I think I'll take a cup o' tea in to Clara. Perhaps she'll take it now. She hasn't eaten or drunk since Tuesday night. How can a woman stand that—I put it to you?"

Emily and Ilse ate their supper with what appetite they could summon up, while Grandfather Bradshaw watched them suspiciously, and sorrowful sounds reached them from the little inner room.

"It is wet and cold tonight—where is he—my little son?" moaned a woman's voice, with an undertone of agony that made Emily writhe as if she felt it herself.

"They'll find him soon, Clara," said Mrs. Hollinger, in a sprightly tone of artificial comfort. "Just you be patient—take a sleep, I advise you—they're bound to find him soon."

"They'll never find him." The voice was almost a scream now. "He is dead—he is dead—he died that bitter cold Tuesday night so long ago. O God, have mercy! He was such a little fellow! And I've told him so often not to speak until he was spoken to—he'll never speak to me again. I wouldn't let him have a light after he went to bed—and he died in the dark, alone and cold. I wouldn't let him have a dog—he wanted one so much. But he wants nothing now—only a grave and a shroud."

"I can't endure this," muttered Emily. "I *can't*, Ilse. I feel as if I'd go mad with horror. I'd rather be out in the storm."

Lank Mrs. Hollinger, looking at once sympathetic and important, came out of the bedroom and shut the door.

"Awful, isn't it! She'll go on like that all night. Would you like to go to bed? It's quite airly, but mebbe you're tired an' 'ud ruther be where you can't hear her, pore soul. She wouldn't take the tea—she's scared the doctor put a sleeping pill in it. She doesn't want to sleep till he's found, dead or alive. If he's in the quicksands o' course he never *will* be found."

"Julia Hollinger, you are a fool and the daughter of a fool, but surely even you must see that a child *can't* be lost in the nineteenth century," said Grandfather Bradshaw.

"Well, if it was anybody but you called me a fool, Grandfather, I'd be mad," said Mrs. Hollinger, a trifle tartly. She lighted a lamp and took the girls upstairs. "I hope you'll sleep. I advise you to get in between the blankets though there's sheets on the bed. They wuz all aired today, blankets *and* sheets. I thought it'd be better to air 'em in case there was a funeral. I remember the New Moon Murrays wuz always particular about airing their beds, so I thought I'd mention it. Listen to that wind. We'll likely hear of awful damage from this storm. I wouldn't wonder if the roof blew off this house tonight. Troubles never come singly. I advise you not to git upset if you hear a noise through the night. If the men bring the body home Clara'll likely act like all possessed, pore thing. Mebbe you'd better turn the key in the lock. Old Mrs. McIntyre wanders round a bit sometimes. She's quite harmless and mostly sane enough but it gives folks a start."

The girls felt relieved as the door closed behind Mrs. Hollinger. She was a good soul, doing her neighbourly duty as she conceived it, faithfully, but she was not exactly cheerful company. They found themselves in a tiny, meticulously neat "spare room" under the sloping eaves. Most of the space in it was occupied by a big comfortable bed that looked as if it were meant to be slept in, and not merely to decorate the room. A little four-paned window, with a spotless white muslin frill, shut them in from the cold, stormy night that was on the sea.

"Ugh," shivered Ilse, and got into the bed as speedily as possible. Emily followed her more slowly, forgetting about the key. Ilse, tired out, fell asleep almost immediately, but Emily could not sleep. She lay and suffered, straining her ears for the sound of footsteps. The rain dashed against the window, not in drops, but sheets, the wind snarled and shrieked. Down below the hill she heard the white waves ravening along the dark shore. Could it be only twenty-four hours since that moonlit, summery glamour of the haystack and the ferny pasture? Why, that must have been in another world.

Where was that poor lost child? In one of the pauses of the storm she fancied she heard a little whimper overhead in the dark as if some lonely little soul, lately freed from the body, were trying to find its way to kin. She could discover no way of escape from her pain: her gates of dream were shut against her: she could not detach her mind from her feelings and dramatise them. Her nerves grew strained and tense. Painfully she sent her thoughts out into the storm; seeking, striving to pierce the mystery of the child's whereabouts. He *must* be found—she clenched her hands—he *must*. That poor mother!

"O God, let him be found, *safe*—let him be found, *safe*," Emily prayed desperately and insistently, over and over again—all the more desperately and insistently because it seemed a prayer so impossible of fulfilment. But she reiterated it to bar out of her mind terrible pictures of swamp and quicksand and river, until at last she was so weary that mental torture could no longer keep her awake, and she fell into a troubled slumber, while the storm roared on and the baffled searchers finally gave up their vain quest.

14
The Woman Who Spanked the King

The wet dawn came up from the gulf in the wake of
the spent storm and crept greyly into the little
spare room of the whitewashed house on the hill.
Emily woke with a start from a troubled dream of
seeking—and finding—the lost boy. But where she had
found him she could not now remember. Ilse was still
asleep at the back of the bed, her pale-gold curls lying
in a silken heap on the pillow. Emily, her thoughts still
tangled in the cobweb meshes of her dream, looked
around the room—and thought she must be dreaming
still.

By the tiny table, covered with its white, lace-trimmed
cloth, a woman was sitting—a tall, stout, old woman,
wearing over her thick grey hair a spotless white widow's
cap, such as the old Highland Scotchwomen still wore
in the early years of the century. She had on a dress of
plum-coloured drugget with a large, snowy apron, and
she wore it with the air of a queen. A neat blue shawl
was folded over her breast. Her face was curiously
white and deeply wrinkled but Emily, with her gift for
seeing essentials, saw instantly the strength and vivacity
which still characterised every feature. She saw, too,
that the beautiful, clear blue eyes looked as if their
owner had been dreadfully hurt sometime. This must
be the old Mrs. McIntyre of whom Mrs. Hollinger had
spoken. And if so, then old Mrs. McIntyre was a very
dignified personage indeed.

Mrs. McIntyre sat with her hands folded on her lap,

191

looking steadily at Emily with a gaze in which there was something hard to define—something just a little strange. Emily recalled the fact that Mrs. McIntyre was supposed to be not "quite right." She wondered a little uneasily what she should do. Ought she to speak? Mrs. McIntyre saved her the trouble of deciding.

"You will be having Highlandmen for your forefathers?" she said, in an unexpectedly rich, powerful voice, full of the delightful Highland accent.

"Yes," said Emily.

"And you will be Presbyterian?"

"Yes."

"They will be the only decent things to be," remarked Mrs. McIntyre in a tone of satisfaction. "And will you please be telling me what your name is? Emily Starr! That will be a fery pretty name. I will be telling you mine—it is Mistress Margaret McIntyre. I am no common person—I am the woman who spanked the King."

Again Emily, now thoroughly awake, thrilled with the story-teller's instinct. But Ilse, awakening at the moment, gave a low exclamation of surprise. Mistress McIntyre lifted her head with a quite regal gesture.

"You will not be afraid of me, my dear. I will not be hurting you although I will be the woman who spanked the King. That is what the people say of me—oh, yess—as I walk into the church. 'She iss the woman who spanked the King.'"

"I suppose," said Emily hesitatingly, "that we'd better be getting up."

"You will not be rising until I haf told you my tale," said Mistress McIntyre firmly. "I will be knowing as soon as I saw you that you will be the one to hear it. You will not be having fery much colour and I will not be saying that you are fery pretty—oh, no. But you will be having the little hands and the little ears—they will be the ears of the fairies, I am thinking. The girl with you there, she iss a fery nice girl and will make a fery fine wife for a handsome man—she is clefer, oh, yess—

but you haf the way and it is to you I will be telling my story."

"Let her tell it," whispered Ilse. "I'm dying of curiosity to hear about the King being spanked."

Emily, who realised that there was no "letting" in the case, only a matter of lying still and listening to whatever it seemed good to Mistress McIntyre to say, nodded.

"You will not be having the twa talks? I will be meaning the Gaelic."

Spellbound, Emily shook her black head.

"That iss a pity, for my story will not be sounding so well in the English—oh, no. You will be saying to yourself the old woman iss having a dream, but you will be wrong, for it iss the true story I will be telling you—oh, yess. I spanked the King. Of course he would not be the King then—he could be only a little prince and no more than nine years old—just the same age as my little Alec. But it iss at the beginning I must be or you will not be understanding the matter at all at all. It wass all a long, long time ago, before ever we left the Old Country. My husband would be Alistair McIntyre and he would be a shepherd near the Balmoral Castle. Alistair was a fery handsome man and we were fery happy. It wass not that we did not quarrel once in a while—oh, no, that would be fery monotonous. But when we made up it is more loving than ever we would be. And I would be fery good-looking myself. I will be getting fatter and fatter all the time now but I wass fery slim and peautiful then—oh, yess, it iss the truth I will be telling you though I will be seeing that you are laughing in your sleeves at me. When you will be eighty you will be knowing more about it.

"You will be remembering maybe that Queen Victoria and Prince Albert would be coming up to Balmoral efery summer and bringing their children with them, and they would not be bringing any more servants than they could help, for they would not be wanting fuss and pother, but just a quiet, nice time like common folks. On Sundays they would be walking down sometimes to the church in the glen to be hearing Mr. Donald MacPherson preach. Mr. Donald MacPherson wass fery gifted in prayer and he would not be liking it when people would come in when he wass praying. He would be apt to be stopping and saying, 'O Lord, we will be waiting until Sandy Big Jim hass taken his seat'—oh, yess. I would be hearing the Queen laugh the next day—at Sandy Big Jim, you will be knowing, not at the minister.

"When they will be needing some more help at the Castle, they just sent for me and Janet Jardine. Janet's husband wass a gillie on the estate. She would be always saying to me, 'Good-morning, *Mistress* McIntyre' when we would be meeting and I would be saying, 'Good-morning, *Janet*,' just to be showing the superiority of the McIntyres over the Jardines. But she wass a fery good creature in her place and we would be getting on fery well together when she would not be forgetting it.

"I wass fery good friends with the Queen—oh, yess. She wass not a proud woman whatefer. She would be sitting in my house at times and drinking a cup of tea and she would be talking to me of her children. She wass not fery handsome, oh, no, but she would be having a fery pretty hand. Prince Albert wass fery fine looking, so people would be saying, but to my mind Alistair wass far the handsomer man. They would be fery fine people, whatefer, and the little princess and princesses would be playing about with my children efery day. The Queen would be knowing they were in good company and she would be easier in her mind about them than I wass—for Prince Bertie was the daring lad if efer there wass one—oh, yess, and the tricky one—and I would be worrying all the time for the fear he and Alec would be getting into a scrape. They would be playing every day together—and quarrelling, too. And it would not always be Alec's fault either. But it wass Alec that would be getting the scolding, poor lad. Somebody would haf to be scolded and you will be knowing that I could not be scolding the prince, my dear.

"There wass one great worry I will be having—the burn behind the house in the trees. It wass fery deep and swift in places and if a child should be falling in he would be drowned. I would be telling Prince Bertie and Alec time after time that they must nefer be going near the banks of the burn. They would be doing it once or twice for all that and I would be punishing Alec for it, though he would be telling me that he did not want to go and Prince Bertie would be saying, 'Oh, come on, there will not be any danger, do not be a coward,' and Alec, he would be going because he would be thinking he had to do what Prince Bertie wanted, and not liking fery well either to be called a coward, and him a McIntyre. I would be worrying so much over it that I would not be sleeping at nights. And then, my dear, one day Prince Bertie would be falling right into the deep pool and Alec would be trying to pull him out and falling in after him. And they would haf been drowned together if I had not been hearing the skirls of them when I would be coming home from the Castle after taking some buttermilk up for the Queen. Oh, yess, it is quick I will be taking in what had happened and running to the burn and it will not be long before I wass fishing them out, fery frightened and dripping. I will be knowing something had to be done and I was tired of blaming poor Alec, and besides it will be truth, my dear, that I wass fery, fery mad and I wass not thinking of princes and kings, but just of two fery bad little boys. Oh, it iss the quick temper I will be always having—oh, yess. I will be picking up Prince Bertie and turning him over my knee: and I will be giving him a sound spanking on the place the Good Lord will be making for spanks in princes as well as in common children. I will be spanking him *first* because he wass a prince. Then I spanked Alec and they made music together, for it wass fery angry I was and I will be doing what my hands will be finding to do with all my might, as the Good Book says.

"Then when Prince Bertie had gone home—fery mad—I will be cooling off and feeling a bit frightened. For I will not be knowing just how the Queen will be taking it, and I will not be liking the thought of Janet Jardine triumphing over me. But it iss a sensible woman Queen Victoria wass and she will be telling me next day that I did right: and Prince Albert will be smiling and joking to me about the laying on of hands. And Prince Bertie would not be disobeying me again about going to the burn—oh, no—and he could not be sitting down fery easy for some time. As for Alistair, I had been thinking he would be fery cross with me, but it will always be hard telling what a man will think of anything—oh, yess—for he would be laughing over it, too, and telling me that a day would come when I could be boasting that I had spanked the King. It wass all a long time ago now, but nefer will I be forgetting it. She would be dying two years ago and Prince Bertie would be the king at last. When Alistair and I came to Canada the Queen will be giving me a silk petticoat. It wass a fery fine petticoat of the Victoria tartan. I haf nefer worn it, but I will be wearing it once—in my coffin, oh, yess. I will be keeping it in the chest in my room and they will be knowing what it iss for. I will be wishing Janet Jardine could have known that I wass to be buried in a petticoat of the Victoria tartan, but she hass been dead for a long while. She wass a fery good sort of creature, although she wass not a McIntyre."

Mistress McIntyre folded her hands and held her peace. Having told her story she was content. Emily had listened avidly. Now she said:

"Mrs. McIntyre, will you let me write that story down, and publish it?"

Mistress McIntyre leaned forward. Her white, shrivelled face warmed a little, her deep-set eyes shone.

"Will you be meaning that it will be printed in a paper?"

"Yes."

Mistress McIntyre rearranged her shawl over her breast with hands that trembled a little.

"It iss strange how our wishes will be coming true at times. It iss a pity that the foolish people who will be saying there iss no God could not be hearing of this. You will be writing it out and you will be putting it into proud words——"

"No, no," said Emily quickly. "I will not do that. I may have to make a few changes and write a framework, but most of it I shall write exactly as you told it. I could not better it by a syllable."

Mistress McIntyre looked doubtful for a moment—then gratified.

"It iss only a poor, ignorant body I am, and I will not be choosing my words fery well, but maybe you will be knowing best. You haf listened to me fery nicely and it is sorry I am to have kept you so long with my old tales. I will be going now and letting you get up."

"Have they found the lost child?" asked Ilse eagerly.

Mistress McIntyre shook her head, composedly.

"Oh, no. It is not finding him in a hurry they will be. I will be hearing Clara skirling in the night. She iss the daughter of my son Angus. He will be marrying a Wilson and the Wilsons will always be making a stramash over eferything. The poor thing will be worrying that she was not good enough to the little lad, but it would always be spoiling him she wass, and him that full of mischief. I will not be of much use to her—I haf not the second sight. You will be having a bit of that yourself, I am thinking, oh, yess."

"No—no," said Emily, hurriedly. She could not help recalling a certain incident of her childhood at New Moon, of which she somehow never liked to think.

Old Mistress McIntyre nodded sagely and smoothed her white apron.

"It will not be right for you to be denying it, my dear, for it iss a great gift and my Cousin Helen four times removed will be having it, oh, yess. But they will not be finding little Allan, oh, no. Clara will be loving him too much. It iss not a fery good thing to be loving any one too much. God will be a jealous God, oh, yess; it is Margaret McIntyre who knows it. I will be having six sons once, all fery fine men and the youngest would be Neil. He wass six-feet-two in hiss stockings and there would be none of the others like him at all. There would be such fun in him—he would always be laughing, oh, yess, and the wiling tongue of him would be coaxing the birds off the bushes. He will be going to the Klondyke and he will be getting frozen to death out there one night, oh, yess. He will be dying while I wass praying for him. I haf not been praying since. Clara will be feeling like that now—she will be saying God does not hear. It iss a fery strange thing to be a woman, my dears, and to be loving so much for nothing. Little Allan wass a fery pretty baby. He will be having a fat little brown face and fery big blue eyes, and it is a pity he will not be turning up, though they will not be finding my Neil in time, oh, no. I will be leaving Clara alone and not vexing her with comforting. I wass always the great hand to leave people alone—without it would be when I spanked the King. It iss Julia Hollinger who will be darkening council by words without knowledge. It iss the foolish woman she iss. She would be leaving her husband because he will not be giving up a dog he liked. I am thinking he wass wise in sticking to the dog. But I will always be getting on well with Julia because I will have learned to suffer fools gladly. She will enjoy giving advice so much and it will not be hurting me whatefer because I will never be taking it. I will be saying good-bye to you now, my dears, and it iss fery glad I am to haf seen you and I will be wishing that trouble may nefer sit on your hearthstones. And I will not be forgetting either that you listened to me very polite, oh, yess. I will not be of much importance to anybody now—but once I spanked the King."

15
"The Thing That Couldn't"

W hen the door had closed behind Mistress Mc-Intyre, the girls got up and dressed rather laggingly. Emily thought of the day before her with some distaste. The fine flavour of adventure and romance with which they had started out had vanished, and canvassing a country road for subscriptions had suddenly become irksome. Physically, they were both tireder than they thought.

"It seems like an age since we left Shrewsbury," grumbled Ilse as she pulled on her stockings.

Emily had an even stronger feeling of a long passage of time. Her wakeful, enraptured night under the moon had seemed in itself like a year of some strange soul-growth. And this past night had been wakeful also, in a very different way, and she had roused from her brief sleep at its close with an odd, rather unpleasant sensation of some confused and troubled journey—a sensation which old Mistress McIntyre's story had banished for a time, but which now returned as she brushed her hair.

"I feel as if I had been wandering—somewhere—for hours," she said. "And I dreamed I found little Allan—but I don't know where. It was horrible to wake up feeling that I *had* known just immediately before I woke and had forgotten."

"I slept like a log," said Ilse, yawning. "I didn't even

dream. Emily, I want to get away from this house and this place as soon as I can. I feel as if I were in a nightmare—as if something horrible were pressing me down and I couldn't escape from it. It would be different if I could *do* anything—help in any way. But since I can't, I just want to escape from it. I forgot it for a few minutes while the old lady was telling her story—heartless old thing! *She* wasn't worrying one bit about poor little lost Allan."

"I think she stopped worrying long ago," said Emily dreamily. "That's what people mean when they say she isn't right. People who don't worry a little never *are* right—like Cousin Jimmy. But that was a great story. I'm going to write it for my first essay—and later on I'll see about having it printed. I'm sure it would make a splendid sketch for some magazine, if I can only catch the savour and vivacity she put into it. I think I'll jot down some of her expressions right away in my Jimmy-book before I forget them."

"Oh, drat your Jimmy-book!" said Ilse. "Let's get down—and eat breakfast if we have to—and get away."

But Emily, revelling again in her story-teller's paradise, had temporarily forgotten everything else.

"Where *is* my Jimmy-book?" she said impatiently. "It isn't in my bag—I know it was here last night. Surely I didn't leave it on that gate-post!"

"Isn't that it over on the table?" asked Ilse.

Emily gazed blankly at it.

"It can't be—it *is*—how did it get there? I *know* I didn't take it out of the bag last night."

"You must have," said Ilse indifferently.

Emily walked over to the table with a puzzled expression. The Jimmy-book was lying open on it, with her pencil beside it. Something on the page caught her eye suddenly. She bent over it.

"Why don't you hurry and finish your hair?" demanded Ilse a few minutes later. "I'm ready now—

for pity's sake, tear yourself from that blessed Jimmy-book for long enough to get dressed!"

Emily turned around, holding the Jimmy-book in her hands. She was very pale and her eyes were dark with fear and mystery.

"Ilse, look at this," she said in a trembling voice.

Ilse went over and looked at the page of the Jimmy-book which Emily held out to her. On it was a pencil sketch, exceedingly well done, of the little house on the river shore to which Emily had been so attracted on the preceding day. A black cross was marked on a small window over the front door and opposite it, on the margin of the Jimmy-book, beside another cross, was written:

"Allan Bradshaw is here."

"What does it mean?" gasped Ilse. "Who did it?"

"I—don't know," stammered Emily. "The writing—is *mine.*"

Ilse looked at Emily and drew back a little.

"You must have drawn it in your sleep," she said dazedly.

"I can't draw," said Emily.

"Who else could have done it? Mistress McIntyre couldn't—you know she couldn't. Emily, I never heard of such a strange thing. Do you think—do you think—he can be there?"

"How could he? The house must be locked up—there's no one working at it now. Besides, they must have searched all around there—he would be looking out of the window—it wasn't shuttered, you remember—calling—they would have seen—heard—him. I suppose I must have drawn that picture in my sleep— though I can't understand how I did it—because my mind was so filled with the thought of little Allan. It's so strange—it frightens me."

"You'll have to show it to the Bradshaws," said Ilse.

"I suppose so—and yet I hate to. It may fill them with a cruel false hope again—and there *can't* be anything in it. But I daren't risk *not* showing it. *You* show it—I can't, somehow. The thing has upset me—I feel frightened—childish—I could sit down and cry. If he *should* have been there—since Tuesday—he would be dead of starvation."

"Well, they'd *know*—I'll show it, of course. If it should turn out—Emily, you're an uncanny creature."

"Don't talk of it—I can't bear it," said Emily, shuddering.

There was no one in the kitchen when they entered it, but presently a young man came in—evidently the Dr. McIntyre of whom Mrs. Hollinger had spoken. He had a pleasant, clever face, with keen eyes behind his glasses, but he looked tired and sad.

"Good-morning," he said. "I hope you had a good rest and were not disturbed in any way. We are all sadly upset here, of course."

"They haven't found the little boy?" asked Ilse.

Dr. McIntyre shook his head.

"No. They have given up the search. He cannot be living yet—after Tuesday night and last night. The swamp will not give up its dead—I feel sure that is where he is. My poor sister is broken-hearted. I am sorry your visit should have happened at such a sorrowful time, but I hope Mrs. Hollinger has made you comfortable. Grandmother McIntyre would be quite offended if you lacked for anything. She was very famous for her hospitality in her day. I suppose you haven't seen her. She does not often show herself to strangers."

"Oh, we have seen her," said Emily absently. "She came into our room this morning and told us how she spanked the King."

Dr. McIntyre laughed a little.

"Then you have been honored. It is not to every one Grandmother tells that tale. She's something of an Ancient Mariner and knows her predestined listeners. She is a little bit strange. A few years ago her favourite son, my Uncle Neil, met his death in the Klondyke under sad circumstances. He was one of the Lost Patrol. Grandmother never recovered from the shock. She has never *felt* anything since—feeling seems to have been killed in her. She neither loves nor hates nor fears nor hopes—she lives entirely in the past and experiences only one emotion—a great pride in the fact that she once spanked the King. But I am keeping you from your breakfast—here comes Mrs. Hollinger to scold me."

"Wait a moment please, Dr. McIntyre," said Ilse hurriedly. "I—you—we—there is something I want to show you."

Dr. McIntyre bent a puzzled face over the Jimmy book.

"What is this? I don't understand——"

"We don't understand it, either—Emily drew it in her sleep."

"In her sleep?" Dr. McIntyre was too bewildered to be anything but an echo.

"She *must* have. There was nobody else—unless your Grandmother can draw."

"Not she. And she never saw this house—it's the Scobie cottage below Malvern Bridge, isn't it?"

"Yes. We saw it yesterday."

"But Allan can't be *there*—it's been locked for a month—the carpenters went away in August."

"Oh—I know," stammered Emily. "I was thinking so much of Allan before I went to sleep—I suppose it's only a dream—I don't understand it at all—but we *had* to show it to you."

"Of course. Well, I won't say anything to Will or Clara about it. I'll get Rob Mason from over the hill and we'll run down and have a look around the cottage. It would be odd if—but it couldn't possibly be. I don't see how we can get into the cottage. It's locked and the windows are shuttered."

"This one—over the front door—isn't."

"No, but that's a closet window at the end of the upstairs hall. I was over the house one day in August when the painters were at work in it. The closet shuts with a spring lock, so I suppose that is why they didn't put a shutter on that window. It's high up, close to the ceiling, I remember. Well, I'll slip over to Rob's and see about this. It won't do to leave any stone unturned."

Emily and Ilse ate what breakfast they could, thankful that Mrs. Hollinger let them alone, save for a few passing remarks as she came and went at work.

"Turrible night last night—but the rain is over. I never closed an eye. Pore Clara didn't either, but she's quieter now—sorter despairing. I'm skeered for her mind—her Grandmother never was right after she heard of *her* son's death. When Clara heard they weren't going to search no more she screamed once and laid down on the bed with her face to the wall—hain't stirred since. Well, the world has to go on for other folks. Help yourselves to the toast. I'd advise ye not to be in too much of a hurry starting out till the wind dries the mud a bit."

"I'm not going to go until we find out if—" whispered Ilse inconclusively.

Emily nodded. She could not eat, and if Aunt Elizabeth or Aunt Ruth had seen her they would have sent her to bed at once with orders to stay there—and they would have been quite right. She had almost reached her breaking-point. The hour that passed after Dr. McIntyre's departure seemed interminable. Suddenly they heard Mrs. Hollinger, who was washing milk-pails at the bench outside the kitchen door, give a sharp exclamation. A minute later she rushed into the kitchen, followed by Dr. McIntyre, breathless from his mad run from Malvern Bridge.

"Clara must be told first," he said. "It is her right."

He disappeared into the inner room. Mrs. Hollinger dropped into a chair, laughing and crying.

"They've found him—they've found little Allan—on the floor of the hall closet—in the Scobie cottage!"

"Is—he—living?" gasped Emily.

"Yes, but no more—he couldn't even speak—but he'll come round with care, the doctor says. They carried him to the nearest house—that's all the doctor had time to tell me."

A wild cry of joy came from the bedroom—and Clara Bradshaw, with dishevelled hair and pallid lips, but with the light of rapture shining in her eyes, rushed through the kitchen—out and over the hill. Mrs. Hollinger caught up a coat and ran after her. Dr. McIntyre sank into a chair.

"I couldn't stop her—and I'm not fit for another run yet—but joy doesn't kill. It would have been cruel to stop her, even if I could."

"Is little Allan all right?" asked Ilse.

"He will be. The poor kid was at the point of exhaustion, naturally. He wouldn't have lasted for another day. We carried him right up to Dr. Matheson at the Bridge and left him in his charge. He won't be fit to be brought home before tomorrow."

"Have you any idea how he came to be there?"

"Well, he couldn't tell us anything, of course, but I think I know how it happened. We found a cellar window about half an inch open. I fancy that Allan was poking about the house, boy fashion, and found that this window hadn't been fastened. He must have got entrance by it, pushed it almost shut behind him and then explored the house. He had pulled the closet door tight in some way and the spring lock made him a prisoner. The window was too high for him to reach or he might have attracted attention from it. The white plaster of the closet wall is all marked and scarred with his vain attempts to get up to the window. Of course, he must have shouted, but nobody has ever been near enough the house to hear him. You know, it stands in that bare little cove with nothing near it where a child could be hidden, so I suppose the searchers did not pay much attention to it. They didn't search the river banks until yesterday, anyhow, because it was never thought he would have gone away down there alone, and by yesterday he was past calling for help."

"I'm so—happy—since he's found," said Ilse, winking back tears of relief.

Grandfather Bradshaw suddenly poked his head out of the sitting-room doorway.

"I told ye a child *couldn't* be lost in the nineteenth century," he chuckled.

"He *was* lost, though," said Dr. McIntyre, "and he wouldn't have been found—in time—if it were not for this young lady. It's a very extraordinary thing."

"Emily is—psychic," said Ilse, quoting Mr. Carpenter.

"Psychic! Humph! Well, it's curious—very. I don't pretend to understand it. Grandmother would say it was second sight, of course. Naturally, she's a firm believer in that, like all the Highland folk."

"Oh—I'm sure I haven't second sight," protested Emily. "I must just have dreamed it—and got up in my sleep—but, then, I can't draw."

"Something used you as an instrument then," said Dr. McIntyre. "After all, Grandmother's explanation of second sight is just as reasonable as anything else, when one is compelled to believe an unbelievable thing."

"I'd rather not talk of it," said Emily, with a shiver. "I'm so glad Allan has been found—but *please* don't tell people about my part in it. Let them think it just occurred to you to search inside the Scobie house. I—I couldn't bear to have this talked of all over the country."

When they left the little white house on the windy hill the sun was breaking through the clouds and the harbour waters were dancing madly in it. The landscape was full of the wild beauty that comes in the wake of a spent storm and the Western Road stretched before them in loop and hill and dip of wet, red allurement; but Emily turned away from it.

"I'm going to leave it for my next trip," she said. "I can't go canvassing today, somehow. Friend of my heart, let's go to Malvern Bridge and take the morning train to Shrewsbury."

"It—was—awfully funny—about your dream," said Ilse. "It makes me a little afraid of you, Emily—somehow."

"Oh, don't be afraid of me," implored Emily. "It was only a coincidence. I was thinking of him so much—and the house took possession of me yesterday—"

"Remember how you found out about Mother?" said Ilse, in a low tone. "You *have* some power the rest of us haven't."

"Perhaps I'll grow out of it," said Emily desperately. "I hope so—I don't *want* to have any such power—you don't know how I feel about it, Ilse. It seems to me a terrible thing—as if I were marked out in some uncanny way—I don't feel *human*. When Dr. McIntyre spoke about *something* using me as an instrument, I went cold all over. It seemed to me that while *I* was asleep some *other* intelligence must have taken possession of my body and drawn that picture."

"It was *your* writing," said Ilse.

"Oh, I'm not going to talk of it—or *think* of it. I'm going to forget it. Don't ever speak of it to me again, Ilse."

16
Driftwood

"Shrewsbury,
"October 3, 19—

"I have finished canvassing my allotted portion of our fair province—I have the banner list of all the canvassers—and I have made almost enough out of my commissions to pay for my books for my whole Junior year. When I told Aunt Ruth this she did *not* sniff. I consider that a fact worth recording.

"Today my story, *The Sands of Time*, came back from *Merton's Magazine*. But the rejection slip was typewritten, not printed. Typewriting doesn't seem *quite* as insulting as print, some way.

> " 'We have read your story with interest, and regret to say that we cannot accept it for publication at the present time.'

"If they meant that 'with interest,' it is a little encouragement. But were they only trying to soften the blow?

"Ilse and I were notified recently that there were nine vacancies in the *Skull and Owl* and that we had been put on the list of those who might apply for membership. So we did. It is considered a great thing in school to be a Skull and Owl.

"The Junior year is in full swing now, and I find the work very interesting. Mr. Hardy has several of our classes, and I like him as a teacher better than any one since Mr. Carpenter. He was very much interested in my essay, *The Woman Who Spanked the King*. He gave it first place and commented on it specially in his class criticisms. Evelyn Blake is sure, naturally, that I copied it out of something, and feels certain she has read it somewhere before. Evelyn is wearing her hair in the new pompadour style this year and I think it is very unbecoming to her. But then, of course, the only part of Evelyn's anatomy I like is her back.

"I understand that the Martin Clan are furious with me. Sally Martin was married last week in the Anglican church here, and the *Times* editor asked me to report it. Of course, I went—though I *hate* reporting weddings. There are so many things I'd *like* to say sometimes that can't *be* said. But Sally's wedding was pretty and so was she, and I 'sent in quite a nice report of it, I thought, specially mentioning the bride's beautiful bouquet of 'roses and orchids'—the first bridal bouquet of orchids ever seen in Shrewsbury. I wrote as plain as print and there was no excuse whatever for that wretched typesetter on the *Times* turning 'orchids' into *sardines*. Of course, anybody with any sense would have known that it was only a printer's error. But the Martin clan have taken into their heads the absurd notion that I wrote *sardines* on purpose for a silly joke—because, it seems, it has been reported to them that I said once I was tired of the conventional reports of weddings and would like to write just one along different lines. I *did* say it—but my craving for originality would hardly lead me to report the bride as carrying a bouquet of sardines! Nevertheless, the Martins *do* think it, and Stella Martin didn't invite me to her thimble party—and Aunt Ruth says she doesn't wonder at it—and Aunt Elizabeth says I shouldn't have been so careless. *I!* Heaven grant me patience!

"October 5, 19—

"Mrs. Will Bradshaw came to see me this evening. Luckily Aunt Ruth was out—I say luckily, for I don't want Aunt Ruth to find out about my dream and its part in finding little Allan Bradshaw. This may be 'sly,' as Aunt Ruth would say, but the truth is that, sly or not sly, I could *not* bear to have Aunt Ruth sniffing and wondering and pawing over the incident.

"Mrs. Bradshaw came to thank me. It embarrassed me—because, after all, what had *I* to do with it? I don't want to think of or talk of it at all. Mrs. Bradshaw says little Allan is all right again, now, though it was a week after they found him before he could sit up. She was very pale and earnest.

"'He would have died there if you hadn't come, Miss Starr—and *I* would have died. I couldn't have gone on living—not knowing—oh, I shall never forget the horror of those days. I *had* to come and try to utter a little of my gratitude—you were gone when I came back that morning—I felt that I had been very inhospitable—'

"She broke down and cried—and so did I—and we had a good howl together. I am very glad and thankful that Allan was found, but I shall never like to think of the way it happened.

"New Moon,
"October 7, 19—

"I had a lovely walk and prowl this evening in the pond graveyard. Not exactly a cheerful place for an evening's ramble, one might suppose. But I always like to wander over that little westward slope of graves in the gentle melancholy of a fine autumn evening. I like to read the names on the stones and note the ages and think of all the loves and hates and hopes and fears that lie buried there. It was beautiful—and not sad. And all around were the red ploughed fields and the frosted, ferny woodsides and all the old familiar things I have loved—and love more and more it seems to me, the older I grow. Every week-end I come home to New Moon these things seem dearer to me—more a part of me. I love *things* just as much as *people*. I think Aunt Elizabeth is like this, too. That is why she will not have anything changed at New Moon. I am beginning to understand her better. I believe she likes me now, too. I was only a duty at first, but now I am something more.

"I stayed in the graveyard until a dull gold twilight came down and made a glimmering spectral place of it. Then Teddy came for me and we walked together up the field and through the Tomorrow Road. It is really a Today Road now, for the trees along it are above our heads, but we still call it the Tomorrow Road—partly out of habit and partly because we talk so much on it of *our* tomorrows and what we hope to do in them.

Somehow, Teddy is the only person I like to talk to about my tomorrows and my ambitions. There is no one else. Perry scoffs at my literary aspirations. He says, when I say anything about writing books, 'What is the good of that sort of thing?' And of course if a person can't see 'the good' for himself you can't explain it to him. I can't even talk to Dean about them—not since he said so bitterly one evening, 'I hate to hear of your tomorrows—they cannot by *my* tomorrows.' I think in a way Dean doesn't like to think of my growing up—I *think* he has a little of the Priest jealousy of sharing *anything*, especially friendship, with any one else—or with the world. I feel thrown back on myself. Somehow, it has seemed to me lately that Dean isn't interested any longer in my writing ambitions. He even, it seems to me, ridicules them slightly. For instance, Mr. Carpenter was delighted with my *Woman Who Spanked the King*, and told me it was excellent; but when Dean read it he smiled and said, 'It will do very well for a school essay, but—' and then he smiled again. It was not the smile I liked, either. It had 'too much Priest in it,' as Aunt Elizabeth would say. I felt—and feel—horribly cast down about it. It seemed to say, 'You can scribble amusingly, my dear, and have a pretty knack of phrase-turning; but I should be doing you an unkindness if I let you think that such a knack meant a very great deal.' If this is true—and it very likely is, for Dean is so clever and knows so much—then I can never accomplish anything worth while. I won't *try* to accomplish anything—I *won't* be just a 'pretty scribbler.'

"But it's different with Teddy.

"Teddy was wildly elated tonight—and so was I when I heard his news. He showed two of his pictures at the Charlottetown exhibition in September, and Mr. Lewes, of Montreal, has offered him fifty dollars apiece for them. That will pay his board in Shrewsbury for the winter and make it easier for Mrs. Kent. Although *she* wasn't glad when he told her. She said, 'Oh, yes, you think you are independent of me now'—and cried. Teddy was hurt, because he had never thought of such a thing. Poor Mrs. Kent. She must be very lonely. There is some strange barrier between her and her kind. I haven't been to the Tansy Patch for a long, long time. Once in the summer I went with Aunt Laura, who had heard Mrs. Kent was ill. Mrs. Kent was able to be up and she talked to Aunt Laura, but she never spoke to me, only looked at me now and then with a queer, smouldering fire in her eyes. But when we rose to come away, she spoke once—and said,

" 'You are very tall. You will soon be a woman—and stealing some other woman's son from her.'

"Aunt Laura said, as we walked home, that Mrs. Kent had always been strange, but was growing stranger.

" 'Some people think her mind is affected,' she said.

" 'I don't think the trouble is in her mind. She has a sick soul,' I said.

" 'Emily, dear, that is a dreadful thing to say,' said Aunt Laura.

"I don't see why. If bodies and minds can be sick, can't souls be, too? There are times when I feel as certain as if I had been told it that Mrs. Kent got some kind of terrible soul-wound some time, and it has never healed. I wish she didn't hate me. It hurts me to have Teddy's mother hate me. I don't know why this is. Dean is just as dear a friend as Teddy, yet I wouldn't care if all the rest of the Priest clan hated me.

"October 19, 19—

"Ilse and the other seven applicants were elected Skulls and Owls. I was black-beaned. We were notified to that effect Monday.

"Of course, I know it was Evelyn Blake who did it. There is nobody else who would do it. Ilse was furious: she tore into pieces the notification of her election and sent the scraps back to the secretary with a scathing repudiation of the *Skull and Owl* and all its works.

"Evelyn met me in the cloakroom today and assured me that she had voted for both Ilse and me.

" 'Has any one been saying you did not?' I asked, in my best Aunt Elizabethan manner.

" 'Yes—Ilse has,' said Evelyn peevishly. 'She was very insolent to me about it. Do you want to know who I *think* put the black bean in?'

"I looked Evelyn straight in the eyes.

" 'No, it is not necessary. I *know* who put it in'—and I turned and left her.

"Most of the Skulls and Owls are very angry about it—especially the Skulls. One or two Owls, I have heard, hoot that it is a good pill for the Murray pride. And, of course, several Seniors and Juniors who were not among the favoured nine are either gloatingly rejoiced or odiously sympathetic.

"Aunt Ruth heard of it today and wanted to know *why* I was black/beaned.

"New Moon,
"November 5, 19—

"Aunt Laura and I spent this afternoon, the one teaching, the other learning, a certain New Moon tradition—to wit, how to put pickles into glass jars in patterns. We stowed away the whole big crockful of new pickles, and when Aunt Elizabeth came to look them over she admitted she could not tell those which Aunt Laura had done from mine.

"This evening was very delightful. I had a good time with myself, out in the garden. It was lovely there tonight with the eerie loveliness of a fine November evening. At sunset there had been a wild little shower of snow, but it had cleared off, leaving the world just lightly covered, and the air clear and tingling. Almost all the flowers, including my wonderful asters, which were a vision all through the fall, were frozen black two weeks ago, but the beds still had white drifts of alyssum all around them. A big, smoky-red hunter's moon was just rising above the tree-tops. There was a yellow-red glow in the west behind the white hills on which a few dark trees grew. The snow had banished all the strange deep sadness of a dead landscape on a late fall evening, and the slopes and meadows of old New Moon farm were transformed into a wonderland in the faint, early moonlight. The old house had a coating of sparkling snow on its roof. Its lighted windows glowed like jewels. It looked exactly like a picture on a Christmas card. There was just a suggestion of grey-blue chimney smoke over the kitchen. A nice reek of burning autumn leaves came from Cousin Jimmy's smouldering bonfires in the lane. My cats were there, too, stealthy, goblin-eyed, harmonising with the hour and the place. The twilight—appropriately called the cats' light—is the only time when a cat really reveals himself. Saucy Sal was thin and gleaming, like the silvery ghost of a pussy. Daff was like a dark-grey, skulking tiger. He certainly gives the world assurance of a cat: he doesn't condescend to every one—and he never talks too much. They pounced at my feet and tore off and frisked back and rolled each other over— and were all so a part of the night and the haunted place that they didn't disturb my thoughts at all. I walked up and down the paths and around the dial and the summer-house in exhilaration. Air such as I breathed then always makes me a little drunk, I verily believe. I laughed at myself for feeling badly over not being elected an *Owl*. An Owl! Why, I felt like a young eagle, soaring sunward. All the world was before me to see and learn, and I exulted in it. The future was mine—and the past, too. I felt as if I had been alive here always—as if I shared in all the loves and lives of the old house. I felt as if I would live always—always—

always—I was sure of immortality then. I didn't just believe it—I *felt* it.

"Dean found me there: he was close beside me before I was aware of his presence.

"'You are smiling,' said Dean. 'I like to see a woman smiling to herself. Her thoughts must be innocent and pleasant. Has the day been kind to you, dear lady?'

"'Very kind—and this evening is its best gift. I'm *so* happy tonight, Dean—just to be alive makes me happy. I feel as if I were driving a team of stars. I wish such a mood could last, I feel so sure of myself tonight—so sure of my future. I'm not afraid of *anything*. At life's banquet of success I may not be the guest of honor, but I'll be among those present.'

"'You looked like a seeress gazing into the future as I came down the walk,' said Dean, 'standing here in the moonlight, white and rapt. Your skin is like a narcissus petal. You could dare to hold a white rose against your face—very few women can dare that. You aren't really very pretty, you know, Star, but your face makes people think of beautiful things—and that is a far rarer gift than mere beauty.'

"I like Dean's compliments. They are always different from anybody else's. And I like to be called a woman.

"'You'll make me vain,' I said.

"'Not with your sense of humour,' said Dean. 'A woman with a sense of humour is never vain. The most malevolent bad fairy in the world couldn't bestow two such drawbacks on the same christened babe.'

"'Do you call a sense of humour a drawback?' I asked.

"'To be sure it is. A woman who has a sense of humour possesses no refuge from the merciless truth about herself. She cannot think herself misunderstood. She cannot revel in self-pity. She cannot comfortably damn any one who differs from her. No, Emily, the woman with a sense of humour isn't to be envied.'

"This view of it hadn't occurred to me. We sat down on the stone bench and thrashed it out. Dean is not going away this winter. I am glad—I would miss him horribly. If I can't have a good spiel with Dean at least once a fortnight, life seems faded. There's so much *colour* in our talks; and then at times he can be so eloquently quiet. Part of the time tonight he was like that: we just sat there in the dream and dusk and quiet of the old garden and *heard* each other's thoughts. Part of the time he told me tales of old lands and the gorgeous bazaars of the East. Part of the time he asked me about myself, and my studies and my doings. I like a man who gives me now and then a chance to talk about myself.

"'What have you been reading lately?' he asked.

"'This afternoon, after I finished the pickles, I read several of Mrs. Browning's poems. We have her in our English work this year, you know. My favourite poem is *The Lay of the Brown Rosary*—and I am much more in sympathy with *Onora* than Mrs. Browning was.'

"'You would be,' said Dean. 'That is because you are a creature of emotion yourself. *You* would barter heaven for love, just as *Onora* did.'

"'I will not love—to love is to be a slave,' I said.

"And the minute I said it I was ashamed of saying it—because I knew I had just said it to sound clever. I don't really believe that to love is to be a slave—not with Murrays, anyhow. But Dean took me quite seriously.

"'Well, one must be a slave to *something* in this kind of a world,' he said. 'No one is free. Perhaps, after all, O daughter of the Stars, love is the easiest master—easier than hate—or fear—or necessity—or ambition—or pride. By the way, how are you getting on with the love-making parts of your stories?'

"'You forget—I can't write stories just now. When I can—well, you know long ago you promised you would teach me how to make love artistically.'

"I said it in a teasing way, just for a joke. But Dean seemed suddenly to become very much in earnest.

" 'Are you ready for the teaching?' he said, bending forward.

"For one crazy moment I really thought he was going to kiss me. I drew back—I felt myself flushing— all at once I thought of Teddy. I didn't know what to say—I picked up Daff—buried my face in his beautiful fur—listened to his inner purring. At that opportune moment Aunt Elizabeth came to the front door and wanted to know if I had my rubbers on. I hadn't—so I went in—and Dean went home. I watched him from my window, limping down the lane. He seemed very lonely, and all at once I felt terribly sorry for him. When I'm with Dean he's such good company, and we have such good times that I forget there must be another side to his life. I can fill only such a little corner of it. The rest must be very empty.

"November 14, 19—

"There is a fresh scandal about Emily of New Moon plus Ilse of Blair Water. I have just had an unpleasant interview with Aunt Ruth and must write it all out to rid my soul of bitterness. Such a tempest in a teapot over nothing! But Ilse and I *do* have the worst luck.

"I spent last Thursday evening with Ilse studying our English literature together. We did an evening of honest work and I left for home at nine. Ilse came out to the gate with me. It was a soft, dark, gentle, starry night. Ilse's new boarding-house is the last house on Cardigan Street, and beyond it the road veers over the little creek bridge into the park. We could see the park, dim and luring, in the starlight.

" 'Let's go for a walk around it before you go home,' proposed Ilse.

"We went: of course, I shouldn't have: I should have come right home to bed, like any good consumptive.

But I had just completed my autumnal course of cod-liver emulsion—ugh!—and thought I might defy the night air for once. So—we went. And it was delightful. Away over the harbour we heard the windy music of the November hills, but among the trees of the park it was calm and still. We left the road and wandered up a little side trail through the spicy fragrant evergreens on the hill. The firs and pines are always friendly, but they tell you no secrets as maples and poplars do: they never reveal their mysteries—never betray their long-guarded lore—and so, of course, they are more interesting than any other trees.

"The whole hillside was full of nice, elfish sounds and cool, elusive night smells—balsam and frosted fern. We seemed to be in the very heart of a peaceful hush. The night put her arms around us like a mother and drew us close together. We told each other everything. Of course, next day I repented me of this—though Ilse is a very satisfactory confidante and never betrays anything, even in her rages. But then it is not a Murray tradition to turn your soul inside out, even to your dearest friend. But darkness and fir balsam make people do such things. And we had lots of fun, too—Ilse is such an exhilarating companion. You've never dull a moment in her company. Altogether we had a lovely walk and came out of the park feeling dearer to each other than ever, with another beautiful memory to share. Just at the bridge we met Teddy and Perry coming off the Western Road. They'd been out for a constitutional hike. It happens to be one of the times Ilse and Perry are on speaking terms, so we all walked across the bridge together and then they went their way and we went ours. I was in bed and asleep by ten o'clock.

"But somebody saw us walking across the bridge. Next day it was all through the school: day after that all through the town: that Ilse and I had been prowling in the park with Teddy Kent and Perry Miller till twelve o'clock at night. Aunt Ruth heard it and summoned me to the bar of judgment tonight. I told her the whole story, but of course she didn't believe it.

" 'You know I was home at a quarter to ten last Thursday night, Aunt Ruth,' I said.

" 'I suppose the time was exaggerated,' admitted Aunt Ruth. 'But there must have been *something* to start such a story. There's no smoke without *some* fire. Emily, you are treading in your mother's footsteps.'

" 'Suppose we leave my mother out of the question— she's dead,' I said. 'The point is, Aunt Ruth, do you believe me or do you not?'

" 'I don't believe it was as bad as the report,' Aunt Ruth said reluctantly. 'But you have got yourself talked about. Of course, you must expect that, as long as you run with Ilse Burnley and off-scourings of the gutter like Perry Miller. Andrew wanted you to go for a walk in the park last Friday evening and you refused—I heard you. That would have been too respectable, of course.'

" 'Exactly,' I said. 'That was the very reason. There's no fun in anything that's too respectable.'

" 'Impertinence, Miss, is not wit,' said Aunt Ruth.

"I didn't mean to be impertinent, but it does annoy me to have Andrew flung in my teeth like that. Andrew is going to be one of my problems. Dean thinks it's great fun—*he* knows what is in the wind as well as I do. He is always teasing me about my red-headed young man—my r.h.y.m. for short.

" 'He's almost a rhyme,' said Dean.

." 'But never a poem,' said I.

"Certainly poor, good, dear Andrew is the stodgiest of prose. Yet I'd like him well enough if the whole Murray clan weren't literally throwing him at my head. They want to get me safely engaged before I'm old enough to elope, and who so safe as Andrew Murray?

"Oh, as Dean says, nobody is free—never, except just for a few brief moments now and then, when the flash comes, or when, as on my haystack night, the soul slips over into eternity for a little space. All the rest of our years we are slaves to something—traditions—conventions—ambitions—*relations*. And sometimes, as tonight, I think that last is the hardest bondage of all.

                              "New Moon,
                              "December 3, 19—

"I am here in my own dear room, with a fire in my little fireplace by the grace of Aunt Elizabeth. An open fire is always lovely, but it is ten times lovelier on a stormy night. I watched the storm from my window until darkness fell. There is a singular charm in snow coming gently down in slanting lines against dark trees. I wrote a description of it in my Jimmy-book as I watched. A wind has come up since and now my room is full of the soft forlorn sigh of snow, driving through Lofty John's spruce wood. It is one of the loveliest sounds in the world. Some sounds *are* so exquisite—far more exquisite than anything *seen*. Daff's purr there on my rug, for instance—and the snap and crackle of the fire—and the squeaks and scrambles of mice that are having a jamboree behind the wainscot. I love to be alone in my room like this. I like to think even the mice are having a good time. And I get so much pleasure out of all my little belongings. They have a meaning for me they have for no one else. I have never for one moment felt at home in my room at Aunt Ruth's, but as soon as I come *here* I enter into my kingdom. I love to read here—dream here—sit by the window and shape some airy fancy into verse.

"I've been reading one of Father's books tonight. I always feel so beautifully near to Father when I read his books—as if I might suddenly look over my shoulder and see him. And so often I come across his pencilled notes on the margin and they seem like a message from him. The book I'm reading tonight is a wonderful one—wonderful in plot and conception—wonderful in its grasp of motives and passions. As I read it I feel humbled and insignificant—which is good for me. I say to myself, 'You poor, pitiful, little creature, did you ever imagine *you* could write? If so, your delusion is now stripped away from you forever and you behold yourself in your naked paltriness.' But I shall recover from this state of mind—and believe again that I *can* write a little—and go on cheerfully producing sketches and poems until I can do better. In another year and a half my promise to Aunt Elizabeth will be over and I can write stories again. Meanwhile—patience! To be sure, I get a bit weary at times of saying 'patience and perseverance.' It is hard not to see all at once the results of those estimable virtues. Sometimes I feel that I want to tear around and be as impatient as I like. But not tonight. Tonight I feel as contented as a cat on a rug. I would purr if I knew how.

"December 9, 19—

"This was Andrew-night. He came, all beautifully groomed up, as usual. Of course, I like a boy who gets himself up well, but Andrew really carries it too far. He always seems as if he had just been starched and ironed and was afraid to move or laugh for fear he'd crack. When I come to think of it, I've never heard Andrew give a hearty laugh yet. And I *know* he never hunted pirate gold when he was a boy. But he's good and sensible and tidy, and his nails are always clean, and the bank manager thinks a great deal of him. And he likes cats—in their place! Oh, I don't deserve such a cousin!"

"January 5, 19—

"Holidays are over. I had a beautiful two weeks at old white-hooded New Moon. The day before Christmas I had *five acceptances*. I wonder I didn't go crazy. Three of them were from magazines who don't pay anything, but subscriptions, for contributions. But the others were accompanied by *checks*—one for two dollars for a poem and one for ten dollars for my *Sands of Time*, which has been taken at last—my first story acceptance. Aunt Elizabeth looked at the checks and said wonderingly:

" 'Do you suppose the bank will really pay you *money* for those?'

"She could hardly believe it, even after Cousin Jimmy took them to Shrewsbury and cashed them.

"Of course, the money goes to my Shrewsbury expenses. But I had no end of fun planning how I would have spent it if I had been free to spend.

"Perry is on the High School team who will debate with the Queen's Academy boys in February. Good for Perry—it's a great honour to be chosen on that team. The debate is a yearly occurrence and Queen's has won for three years. Ilse offered to coach Perry on the elocution of his speech and she is taking no end of trouble with him—especially in preventing him from saying '*devil*opement' when he means 'development.' It's awfully good of her, for she really doesn't like him. I do hope Shrewsbury will win.

"We have *The Idylls of the King* in English class this term. I like some things in them, but I detest Tennyson's *Arthur*. If I had been *Guinevere* I'd have boxed his ears—but I wouldn't have been unfaithful to him for *Lancelot*, who was just as odious in a different way. As for *Geraint*, if I had been *Enid* I'd have *bitten* him. These 'patient Griseldas' deserve all they get. Lady Enid, if you had been a Murray of New Moon you would have kept your husband in better order and he would have liked you all the better for it.

"I read a story tonight. It ended unhappily. I was wretched until I had invented a happy ending for it. I shall always end *my* stories happily. I don't care whether it's 'true to life' or not. It's true to life as it *should be* and that's a better truth than the other.

"Speaking of books. I read an old one of Aunt Ruth's the other day—*The Children of the Abbey*. The heroine fainted in every chapter and cried quarts if any one looked at her. But as for the trials and persecutions she underwent, in spite of her delicate frame, their name was Legion and no fair maiden of these degenerate days could survive half of them—not even the newest of new women. I laughed over the book until I amazed Aunt Ruth, who thought it a very sad volume. It is the only novel in Aunt Ruth's house. One of her beaux gave it to her when she was young. It seems impossible to think that Aunt Ruth ever had beaux. Uncle Dutton seems an unreality, and even his picture on the crêpe-draped easel in the parlour cannot convince me of his existence.

"January 21, 19—

"Friday night the debate between Shrewsbury High and Queen's came off. The Queen's boys came up believing they were going to come, see, and conquer—and went home like the proverbial dogs with carefully adjusted tails. It was really Perry's speech that won the debate. He was a wonder. Even Aunt Ruth admitted for the first time that there was something in him. After it was over he came rushing up to Ilse and me in the corridor.

" 'Didn't I do great, Emily?' he demanded. 'I knew it was in me, but I didn't know if I could get it out. When I got up at first I felt tongue-tied—and then I saw *you*, looking at me as if you said, "You can—you *must*"—and I went ahead full steam. *You* won that debate, Emily.'

"Now wasn't that a nice thing to say before Ilse, who had worked for hours with him and drilled and slaved? Never a word of tribute to *her*—everything to me who hadn't done a thing except look interested.

"'Perry, you're an ungrateful barbarian,' I said—and left him there, with his jaw dropping. Ilse was so furious she cried. She has never spoken to him since—and that ass of a Perry can't understand why.

"'What's she peeved about now? I *thanked* her for all her trouble at our last practice,' he says.

"Certainly, Stovepipe Town has its limitations.

"February 2, 19—
"Last night Mrs. Rogers invited Aunt Ruth and me to dinner to meet her sister and brother-in-law, Mr. and Mrs. Herbert. Aunt Ruth had her Sunday scallops in her hair and wore her brown velvet dress that reeked of moth-balls and her big oval brooch with Uncle Dutton's hair in it; and I put on my ashes-of-roses and Princess Mena's necklace and went, quivering with excitement, for Mr. Herbert is a member of the Dominion Cabinet and a man who stands in the presence of kings. He has a massive, silver head and eyes that have looked into people's thoughts so long that you have an uncanny feeling that they can see right into your soul and read motives you don't dare avow even to yourself. His face is a most interesting one. There is so much in it. All the varied experiences of his full, wonderful life had written it over. One could tell at sight that he was a born leader. Mrs. Rogers let me sit beside him at dinner. I was afraid to speak—afraid I'd say something stupid—afraid I'd make some ludicrous mistake. So I just sat quiet as a mouse and listened adoringly. Mrs. Rogers told me today that Mr. Herbert said, after we had left,

"'That little Starr girl of New Moon is the best conversationalist of any girl of her age I ever met.'

"So even great statesmen—but there—I won't be horrid.

"And he *was* splendid: he was wise and witty and humorous. I felt as if I were drinking in some rare, stimulating, mental wine. I forgot even Aunt Ruth's mothballs. What an event it is to meet such a man and take a peep through his wise eyes at the fascinating game of empire building!

"Perry went to the station today to get a glimpse of Mr. Herbert. Perry says he will be just as great a man some day. But, no. Perry can—and I believe will—go far—climb high. But he will be only a successful politician— never a statesman. Ilse flew into me when I said this.

"'I hate Perry Miller," she fumed, 'but I hate snobbery worse. *You're* a snob, Emily Starr. You think just because Perry comes from Stovepipe Town that he can never be a great man. If he had been one of the sacred Murrays you would see no limits to his attainments!'

"I thought Ilse was unfair, and I lifted my head haughtily.

"'After all,' I said, 'there *is* a difference between New Moon and Stovepipe Town.'"

17
"If a Body Kiss a Body"

It was half-past ten o'clock and Emily realised with a sigh that she must go to bed. When she had come in at half-past nine from Alice Kennedy's thimble party, she had asked permission of Aunt Ruth to sit up an hour later to do some special studying. Aunt Ruth had consented reluctantly and suspiciously and had gone to bed herself, with sundry warnings regarding candles and matches. Emily had studied diligently for forty-five minutes and written poetry for fifteen. The poem burned for completion, but Emily resolutely pushed her portfolio away.

At that moment she remembered that she had left her Jimmy-book in her school-bag in the dining-room. This would never do. Aunt Ruth would be down before her in the morning and would inevitably examine the book-bag, find the Jimmy-book and read it. There were things in that Jimmy-book it was well Aunt Ruth should not see. She must slip down and bring it up.

Very quietly she opened her door and tiptoed downstairs, in anguish at every creaking step. Aunt Ruth, who slept in the big front bedroom at the other end of the hall, would surely hear those creaks. They were enough to waken the dead. They did not waken Aunt Ruth, however, and Emily reached the dining-room, found her book-bag, and was just going to return when she happened to glance at the mantelpiece. There, propped up against the clock, was a letter for her which had evidently come by the evening mail—a nice thin letter with the address of a magazine in the corner. Emily set her candle on the table, tore open the letter, found the acceptance of a poem and a check for three dollars. Acceptances—especially acceptances with checks—were still such rare occurrences with our Emily that they always made her a little crazy. She forgot Aunt Ruth—she forgot that it was nearing eleven o'clock: she stood there entranced, reading over and over the brief editorial note—brief, but, oh, how sweet! "Your charming poem"—"we would like to see more of your work"—oh, yes, indeed, they *should* see more of it.

Emily turned with a start. Was that a tap at the door? No—at the window. Who? What? The next moment she was aware that Perry was standing on the side verandah, grinning at her through the window.

She was at it in a flash and without pausing to think, still in the exhilaration of her acceptance, she slipped the catch and pushed the window up. She knew where

Perry had been and was dying to know how he had got along. He had been invited to dinner with Dr. Hardy, in the fine Queen Street house. This was considered a great honour and very few students ever received it. Perry owed the invitation to his brilliant speech at the interschool debate. Dr. Hardy had heard it and decided that here was a coming man.

Perry had been enormously proud of the invitation and had bragged of it to Teddy and Emily—not to Ilse, who had not yet forgiven him for his tactlessness on the night of the debate. Emily had been pleased, but had warned Perry that he would need to watch his step at Dr. Hardy's. She felt some qualms in regard to his etiquette, but Perry had felt none. *He* would be all right, he loftily declared. Perry perched himself on the window-sill and Emily sat down on the corner of the sofa, reminding herself that it could be only for a minute.

"Saw the light in the window as I went past," said Perry. "So I thought I'd just take a sneak round to the side and see if it was you. Wanted to tell you the tale while it was fresh. Say, Emily, you were right—r-i-g-h-t! I should smile. I wouldn't go through this evening again for a hundred dollars."

"How *did* you get along?" asked Emily anxiously. In a sense, she felt responsible for Perry's manners. Such as he had he had acquired at New Moon.

Perry grinned.

"It's a heart-rending tale. I've had a lot of conceit taken out of me. I suppose you'll say that's a good thing."

"You could spare some," said Emily coolly.

Perry shrugged his shoulders.

"Well, I'll tell you all about it if you won't tell Ilse or Teddy. I'm not going to have *them* laughing at me. I went to Queen Street at the proper time—I remembered all you'd said about boots and tie and nails and hand-kerchief and I was all right outside. When I got to the house my troubles began. It was so big and splendid I felt queer—not afraid—I wasn't afraid *then*—but just a bit as if I was ready to jump—like a strange cat when you try to pat it. I rang the bell; of course, it stuck and kept on ringing like mad. I could hear it away down the hall, and thinks I, 'They'll think I don't know any better than to keep on ringing it till somebody comes,' and that rattled me. The maid rattled me still more. I didn't know whether I ought to shake hands with her or not."

"Oh, Perry!"

"Well, I *didn't*. I never was to a house where there was a maid like that before, all dolled up with a cap and finicky little apron. She made me feel like thirty cents."

"*Did* you shake hands with her?"

"No."

Emily gave a sigh of relief.

"She held the door open and I went in. I didn't know what to do then. Guess I'd have stood there till I took root, only Dr. Hardy himself come—came—through the hall. *He* shook hands and showed me where to put my hat and coat and then he took me into the parlour to meet his wife. The floor was as slippery as ice—and just as I stepped on the rug inside the parlour door it went clean from under me and down I went and slid across the floor, feet foremost, right to Mrs. Hardy. I was on my back, not on my stomach, or it would have been quite the proper Oriental caper, wouldn't it?"

Emily couldn't laugh.

"Oh, *Perry!*"

"Great snakes, Emily, it wasn't my fault. All the etiquette in the world couldn't have prevented it. Of course, I felt like a fool, but I got up and laughed. Nobody else laughed. They were all decent. Mrs. Hardy was smooth as wax—hoped I hadn't hurt myself, and Dr. Hardy said *he* had slipped the same way more than once after they had given up their good old carpets and taken to rugs and hardwood. I was scared to move, so I sat down in the nearest chair, and there was a dog on it—Mrs. Hardy's Peke. Oh, I didn't kill it— *I* got the worst scare of the two. By the time I had made port in another chair the sw— perspiration was just pouring down my face. Some more folks arrived just then, so that kind of took the edge off me, and I had time to get my bearings. I found I had about ten pairs of hands and feet. And my boots were too big and coarse. Then I found myself with my hands in my pockets, *whistling*."

Emily began to say, "Oh, Perry," but bit it off and swallowed it. What was the use of saying *anything*?

"I knew *that* wasn't proper, so I stopped and took my hands out—and began to bite my nails. Finally, I put my hands underneath me and sat on 'em. I doubled my feet back under my chair, and I sat like that till we went out to dinner—sat like that when a fat old lady waddled in and all the other fellows stood up. I didn't—didn't see any reason for it—there was plenty of chairs. But later on it occurred to me that it was some etiquette stunt and I ought to have got up, too. Should I?"

"Of course," said Emily, wearily. "Don't you remember how Ilse used to rag you about that very thing?"

"Oh, I'd forgotten—Ilse was always jawing about something. But live and learn. I won't forget again, you bet. There were three or four other boys there—the new French teacher and a couple of bankers—and some ladies. I got out to dinner without falling over the floor and got into a chair between Miss Hardy and the aforesaid old lady. I gave one look over that table—and then, Emily, I knew what it was to be afraid at last, all right. I never knew it before, honest. It's an awful feeling. I was in a regular funk. I used to think you carried fierce style at New Moon when you had company, but I never saw anything like that table—and everything so dazzling and glittering, and enough forks and spoons and things at one place to fit everybody out. There was a piece of bread folded in my napkin and it fell out and went skating over the floor. I could feel myself turning red all over my face and neck. I s'pose you call it blushing. I never blushed afore—before—that I remember. I didn't know whether I ought to get up and go and pick it up or not. Then the maid brought me another one. I used the wrong spoon to eat my soup with, but I tried to remember what your Aunt Laura said about the proper way to eat soup. I'd get on all right for a few spoonfuls—then I'd get interested in something somebody was saying—and go *gulp*."

"Did you tilt your plate to get the last spoonful?" asked Emily despairingly.

"No, I was just going to when I remembered it wasn't proper. I hate to lost it, too. It was awful good soup and I was hungry. The good old dowager next to me *did*. I got on pretty well with the meat and vegetables, except once. I had packed a load of meat and potatoes on my fork and just as I lifted it I saw Mrs. Hardy eyeing it, and I remembered I oughtn't to have loaded up my fork like that—and I jumped—and it all fell off in my napkin. I didn't know whether it would be etiquette to scrape it up and put it back on my plate so I left it there. The pudding was all right—only I et it with a spoon—my soup spoon—and every one else et theirs with a fork. But it tasted just as good one way as another and I was getting reckless. You always use spoons at New Moon to eat pudding."

"Why didn't you watch what the others did and imitate them?"

"Too rattled. But I'll say this—for all the style, the eats weren't a bit better than you have at New Moon—no, nor as good, by a jugful. Your Aunt Elizabeth's cooking would knock the spots off the Hardy's every time—and they didn't give you too much of anything! After the dinner was over we went back to the parlour—*they* called it living-room—and things weren't so bad. I didn't do anything out of the way except knock over a bookcase."

"Perry!"

"Well, it was wobbly. I was leaning against it talking to Mr. Hardy, and I suppose I leaned too hard, for the blooming thing went over. But, righting it and getting the books back seemed to loosen me up and I wasn't so tongue-tied after that. I got on not too bad—only every once in a long while I'd let slip a bit of slang, before I could catch it. I tell you, I wished I'd taken your advice about talking slang. Once the fat old lady agreed with something I'd said—she had sense if she *did* have three chins—and I was so tickled to find her on my side that I got excited and said to her, 'You bet your boots' before I thought. And I guess I bragged a bit. *Do* I brag too much, Emily?"

This question had never presented itself to Perry before.

"You *do*," said Emily candidly, "and it's *very* bad form."

"Well, I felt kind of cheap after I'd done it. I guess I've got an awful lot to learn yet, Emily. I'm going to buy a book on etiquette and learn it off by heart. No more evenings like this for me. But it was better at the last. Jim Hardy took me off to the den and we played checkers and I licked him dizzy. Nothing wrong with my checker etiquette, I tell *you*. And Mrs. Hardy said my speech at the debate was the best she had ever heard for a boy of my age, and she wanted to know what I meant to go in for. She's a great little dame and has the social end of things down fine. That is one reason I want you to marry me when the time comes, Emily—I've got to have a wife with brains."

"Don't talk nonsense, Perry," said Emily, haughtily.

"'Tisn't nonsense," said Perry, stubbornly. "And it's time we settled *something*. You needn't turn up your nose at me because you're a Murray. I'll be worth marrying some day—even for a Murray. Come, put me out of my misery."

Emily rose disdainfully. She had her dreams, as all girls have, the rose-red one of love among them, but Perry Miller had no share in those dreams.

"I'm *not* a Murray—and I'm going upstairs. Goodnight."

"Wait half a second," said Perry, with a grin. "When the clock strikes eleven I'm going to kiss you."

Emily did not for a moment believe that Perry had the slightest notion of doing anything of the kind—which was foolish of her, for Perry had a habit of always doing what he said he was going to do. But, then, he had never been sentimental. She ignored his remark, but lingered a moment to ask another question about the Hardy dinner. Perry did not answer the question: the clock began to strike eleven as she asked it—he flung his legs over the window-sill and stepped into the room. Emily realised too late that he meant what he said. She had only time to duck her head and Perry's hearty, energetic smack—there was nothing subtle about Perry's kisses—fell on her ear instead of her cheek.

At the very moment Perry kissed her and before her indignant protest could rush to her lips two things happened. A gust of wind swept in from the verandah and blew the little candle out, *and* the dining-room door opened and Aunt Ruth appeared in the doorway, robed in a pink flannel nightgown and carrying another candle, the light of which struck upward with gruesome effect on her set face with its halo of crimping-pins.

This is one of the places where a conscientious biographer feels that, in the good old phrase, her pen cannot do justice to the scene.

Emily and Perry stood as if turned to stone. So, for a moment, did Aunt Ruth. Aunt Ruth had expected to find Emily there, writing, as she had done one night a month previously when Emily had had an inspiration at bedtime and had slipped down to the warm dining-room to jot it in a Jimmy-book. But *this*! I must admit it *did* look bad. Really, I think we can hardly blame Aunt Ruth for righteous indignation.

Aunt Ruth looked at the unlucky pair.

"What are you doing here?" she asked Perry.

Stovepipe Town made a mistake.

"Oh, looking for a round square," said Perry off-handedly, his eyes suddenly becoming limpid with mischief and lawless roguery.

Perry's "impudence"—Aunt Ruth called it that, and, really, I think he *was* impudent—naturally made a bad matter worse. Aunt Ruth turned to Emily.

"Perhaps *you* can explain how you came to be here, at this hour, kissing this fellow in the dark?"

Emily flinched from the crude vulgarity of the question as if Aunt Ruth had struck her. She forgot how much appearances justified Aunt Ruth, and let a perverse spirit enter into and possess her. She lifted her head haughtily.

"I have no explanation to give to such a question, Aunt Ruth."

"I didn't think you would have."

Aunt Ruth gave a very disagreeable laugh, through which a thin, discordant note of triumph sounded. One might have thought that, under all her anger, something pleased Aunt Ruth. It *is* pleasant to be justified in the opinion we have always entertained of anybody. "Well, perhaps you will be so good as to answer some questions. How did this fellow get here?"

"Window," said Perry laconically, seeing that Emily was not going to answer.

"I was not asking *you*, sir. Go," said Aunt Ruth, pointing dramatically to the window.

"I'm not going to stir a step out of this room until I see what you're going to do to Emily," said Perry stubbornly.

"I," said Aunt Ruth, with an air of terrible detachment, "am not going to do anything to Emily."

"Mrs. Dutton, be a good sport," implored Perry coaxingly. "It's all my fault—honest! Emily wasn't one bit to blame. You see, it was this way—"

But Perry was too late.

"I have asked my niece for an explanation and she has refused to give it. I do not choose to listen to yours."

"But—" persisted Perry.

"You had better go, Perry," said Emily, whose face was flying danger signals. She spoke quietly, but the Murrayest of all Murrays could not have expressed a more definite command. There was a quality in it Perry dared not disregard. He meekly scrambled out of the window into the night. Aunt Ruth stepped forward and shut the window. Then, ignoring Emily utterly, she marched her pink flanneled little figure back upstairs.

Emily did not sleep much that night—nor, I admit, did she deserve to. After her sudden anger died away, shame cut her like a whip. She realised that she had behaved very foolishly in refusing an explanation to Aunt Ruth. Aunt Ruth had a right to it, when such a situation developed in her own house, no matter how hateful and disagreeable she made her method of demanding it. Of course, she would not have believed a word of it; but Emily, if she had given it, would not have further complicated her false position.

Emily fully expected she would be sent home to New Moon in disgrace. Aunt Ruth would stonily decline to keep such a girl any longer in her house—Aunt Elizabeth would agree with her—Aunt Laura would be heartbroken. Would even Cousin Jimmy's loyalty stand the strain? It was a very bitter prospect. No wonder Emily spent a white night. She was so unhappy that every beat of her heart seemed to hurt her. And again I say, most unequivocally, she deserved it. I haven't one word of pity or excuse for her.

18
Circumstantial Evidence

At the Saturday morning breakfast-table Aunt Ruth preserved a stony silence, but she smiled cruelly to herself as she buttered and ate her toast. Any one might have seen clearly that Aunt Ruth was enjoying herself—and, with equal clearness, that Emily was *not*. Aunt Ruth passed Emily the toast and marmalade with killing politeness, as if to say,

"I will not abate one jot or tittle of the proper thing. I may turn you out of my house, but it will be your own fault if you go without your breakfast."

After breakfast Aunt Ruth went uptown. Emily suspected that she had gone to telephone to Dr. Burnley a message for New Moon. She expected when Aunt Ruth returned to be told to pack her trunk. But still Aunt Ruth spoke not. In the middle of the afternoon Cousin Jimmy arrived with the double-seated box-sleigh. Aunt Ruth went out and conferred with him. Then she came in and at last broke her silence.

"Put on your wraps," she said. "We are going to New Moon."

Emily obeyed mutely. She got into the back seat of the sleigh and Aunt Ruth sat beside Cousin Jimmy in front. Cousin Jimmy looked back at Emily over the collar of his fur coat and said, "Hello, Pussy," with just a shade too much of cheerful encouragement. Evidently Cousin Jimmy believed something very serious had happened, though he didn't know what.

It was not a pleasant drive through the beautiful

greys and smokes and pearls of the winter afternoon. The arrival at New Moon was not pleasant. Aunt Elizabeth looked stern—Aunt Laura looked apprehensive.

"I have brought Emily here," said Aunt Ruth, "because I do not feel that I can deal with her alone. You and Laura, Elizabeth, must pass judgment on her behaviour yourselves."

So it was to be a domestic court, with her, Emily, at the bar of justice. Justice—would she get justice? Well, she would make a fight for it. She flung up her head and the colour rushed back into her face.

They were all in the sitting-room when she came down from her room. Aunt Elizabeth sat by the table. Aunt Laura was on the sofa ready to cry. Aunt Ruth was standing on the rug before the fire, looking peevishly at Cousin Jimmy, who, instead of going to the barn as he should have done, had tied the horse to the orchard fence and had seated himself back in the corner, determined, like Perry, to see what was going to be done to Emily. Ruth was annoyed. She wished Elizabeth would not always insist on admitting Jimmy to family conclaves when he desired to be present. It was absurd to suppose that a grown-up child like Jimmy had any right there.

Emily did not sit down. She went and stood by the window, where her black head came out against the crimson curtain as softly and darkly clear as a pine-tree against a sunset of spring. Outside a white, dead world lay in the chilly twilight of early March. Past the garden and the Lombardy poplars the fields of New Moon looked very lonely and drear, with the intense red streak of lingering sunset beyond them. Emily shivered.

"Well," said Cousin Jimmy, "let's begin and get it over. Emily must want her supper."

"When you know what *I* know about her, you will think she needs something besides supper," said Mrs. Dutton tartly.

"I know all any one need know about Emily," retorted Cousin Jimmy.

"Jimmy Murray, you are an ass," said Aunt Ruth, angrily.

"Well, we're cousins," agreed Cousin Jimmy pleasantly.

"Jimmy, be silent," said Elizabeth, majestically. "Ruth, let us hear what you have to say."

Aunt Ruth told the whole story. She stuck to facts, but her manner of telling them made them seem even blacker than they were. She really contrived to make a very ugly story of it, and Emily shivered again as she listened. As the telling proceeded Aunt Elizabeth's face became harder and colder, Aunt Laura began to cry, and Cousin Jimmy began to whistle.

"He was kissing her *neck*," concluded Aunt Ruth. Her tone implied that, bad as it was to kiss on ordinary places for kissing, it was a thousand-fold more scandalous and disgraceful to kiss the neck.

"It was my ear, really," murmured Emily, with a sudden impish grin she could not check in time. Under all her discomfort and dread, there was *Something* that was standing back and *enjoying* this—the drama, the comedy of it. But this outbreak of it was most unfortunate. It made her appear flippant and unashamed.

"Now, I ask you," said Aunt Ruth, throwing out her pudgy hands, "if you can expect me to keep a girl like her any longer in my house?"

"No, I don't think we can," said Elizabeth slowly.

Aunt Laura began to sob wildly. Cousin Jimmy brought down the front legs of his chair with a bang.

Emily turned from the window and faced them all.

"I want to explain what happened, Aunt Elizabeth."

"I think we have heard enough about it," said Aunt Elizabeth icily—all the more icily because of a certain bitter disappointment that was filling her soul. She had been gradually becoming very fond and proud of Emily, in her reserved, undemonstrative Murray way: to find her capable of such conduct as this was a terrible blow to Aunt Elizabeth. Her very pain made her the more merciless.

"No, that won't do now, Aunt Elizabeth," said Emily quietly. "I'm too old to be treated like that. You *must* hear my side of the story."

The Murray look was on her face—the look Elizabeth knew and remembered so well of old. She wavered.

"You had your chance to explain last night," snapped Aunt Ruth, "and you wouldn't do it."

"Because I was hurt and angry over your thinking the worst of me," said Emily. "Besides, I knew *you* wouldn't believe me."

"I would have believed you if you had told the truth," said Aunt Ruth. "The reason you wouldn't explain last night was because you couldn't think up an excuse for your conduct on the spur of the moment. You've had time to invent something since, I suppose."

"Did you ever know Emily to tell a lie?" demanded Cousin Jimmy.

Mrs. Dutton opened her lips to say "Yes." Then closed them again. Suppose Jimmy should demand a specific instance? She felt sure Emily had told her— fibs—a score of times, but what proof had she of it?

"*Did* you?" persisted that abominable Jimmy.

"I am not going to be catechised by you." Aunt Ruth turned her back on him. "Elizabeth, I've always told you that girl was deep and sly, haven't I?"

"Yes," admitted poor Elizabeth, rather thankful that there need be no indecision on *that* point. Ruth had certainly told her so times out of number.

"And doesn't this show I was right?"

"I'm—afraid—so." Elizabeth Murray felt that it was a very bitter moment for her.

"Then it is for *you* to decide what is to be done about the matter," said Ruth triumphantly.

"Not yet," interposed Cousin Jimmy resolutely. "You haven't given Emily the ghost of a chance to explain.

That's no fair trial. Now let her talk for ten minutes without interrupting her once."

"That is only fair," said Elizabeth with sudden resolution. She had a mad, irrational hope that, after all, Emily might be able to clear herself.

"Oh—well—" Mrs. Dutton yielded ungraciously and sat herself down with a thud on old Archibald Murray's chair.

"Now, Emily, tell us what really happened," said Cousin Jimmy.

"Well, upon my word!" exploded Aunt Ruth. "Do you mean to say *I* didn't tell what really happened?"

Cousin Jimmy lifted his hand.

"Now—now—you had your say. Come, Pussy."

Emily told her story from beginning to end. Something in it carried conviction. Three of her listeners at least believed her and felt an enormous load lifted from their minds. Even Aunt Ruth, deep down in her heart, knew Emily was telling the truth, but she would not admit it.

"A very ingenious tale, upon my word," she said derisively.

Cousin Jimmy got up and walked across the floor. He bent down before Mrs. Dutton and thrust his rosy face with its forked beard and child-like brown eyes under his shock of grey curls, very close to hers.

"Ruth Murray," he said, "do you remember the story that got around forty years ago about you and Fred Blair? *Do* you?"

Aunt Ruth pushed back her chair. Cousin Jimmy followed her.

"Do you remember that you were caught in a scrape that looked far worse than this? *Didn't* it?"

Again poor Aunt Ruth pushed back her chair. Again Cousin Jimmy followed.

"Do you remember how mad you were because people wouldn't believe you? But your father believed you—*he* had confidence in his own flesh and blood. *Hadn't* he?"

Aunt Ruth had reached the wall by this time and had to surrender at discretion.

"I—I—remember well enough," she said shortly.

Her cheeks were a curdled red. Emily looked at her interestedly. *Was* Aunt Ruth trying to blush? Ruth Dutton was, in fact, living over some very miserable months in her long past youth. When she was a girl of eighteen she had been trapped in a very ugly situation. And she had been innocent—absolutely innocent. She had been the helpless victim of a most impish combination of circumstances. Her father had believed her story and her own family had backed her up. But her contemporaries had believed the evidence of known facts for years—perhaps believed it yet, if they ever thought about the matter. Ruth Dutton shivered over the remembrance of her suffering under the lash of scandal. She no longer dared to refuse credence to Emily's story but she could not yield gracefully.

"Jimmy," she said sharply, "will you be good enough to go away and sit down? I suppose Emily *is* telling the truth—it's a pity she took so long deciding to tell it. And I'm sure that creature *was* making love to her."

"No, he was only asking me to marry him," said Emily coolly.

You heard three gasps in the room. Aunt Ruth alone was able to speak.

"Do you intend to, may I ask?"

"No. I've told him so half a dozen times."

"Well, I'm glad you had that much sense. Stovepipe Town, indeed!"

"Stovepipe Town had nothing to do with it. Ten years from now Perry Miller will be a man whom even a Murray would delight to honour. But he doesn't happen to be the type I fancy, that's all."

Could *this* be Emily—this tall young woman coolly giving her reasons for refusing an offer of marriage—

and talking about the "types" she fancied? Elizabeth—Laura—even Ruth looked at her as if they had never seen her before. And there was a new respect in their eyes. Of course they knew that Andrew was—was—well, in short, that Andrew *was*. But years must doubtless pass before Andrew would—would—well, *would*! And now the thing had happened already with another suitor—happened "half a dozen times" mark you! At that moment, although they were quite unconscious of it, they ceased to regard her as a child. At a bound she had entered their world and must henceforth be met on equal terms. There could be no more family courts. They *felt* this, though they did not perceive it. Aunt Ruth's next remark showed it. She spoke almost as she might have spoken to Laura or Elizabeth, if she had deemed it her duty to admonish them.

"Just suppose, Em'ly, if any one passing had seen Perry Miller sitting in that window at that hour of the night?"

"Yes, of course. I see your angle of it perfectly, Aunt Ruth. All I want is to get you to see *mine*. I was foolish to open the window and talk to Perry—I see that now. I simply didn't think—and then I got so interested in the story of his mishaps at Dr. Hardy's dinner that I forgot how time was going."

"Was Perry Miller to dinner at *Dr. Hardy's*?" asked Aunt Elizabeth. This was another staggerer for her. The world—the Murray world—must be literally turned upside-down if Stovepipe Town was invited to dinner on Queen Street. At the same moment Aunt Ruth remembered with a pang of horror that Perry Miller had seen her in her pink flannel nightgown. It hadn't mattered before—he had been only the help-boy at New Moon. *Now* he was Dr. Hardy's guest.

"Yes. Dr. Hardy thinks he is a very brilliant debater and says he has a future," said Emily.

"Well," snapped Aunt Ruth, "*I* wish you would stop prowling about my house at all hours, writing novels.

If you had been in your bed, as you should have been, this would never have happened."

"I wasn't writing novels," cried Emily. "I've never written a word of fiction since I promised Aunt Elizabeth. I wasn't writing *anything*. I told you I just went down to get my Jimmy-book."

"*Why* couldn't you have left that where it was till morning?" persisted Aunt Ruth.

"Come, come," said Cousin Jimmy, "don't start up another argument. I want my supper. You girls go and get it."

Elizabeth and Laura left the room as meekly as if old Archibald Murray himself had commanded it. After a moment Ruth followed them. Things had not turned out just as she anticipated; but, after all, she was resigned. It would not have been a nice thing for a scandal like this concerning a Murray to be blown abroad, as must have happened if a verdict of guilty had been found against Emily.

"So *that's* settled," said Cousin Jimmy to Emily as the door closed.

Emily drew a long breath. The quiet, dignified old room suddenly seemed very beautiful and friendly to her.

"Yes, thanks to you," she said, springing across it to give him an impetuous hug. "Now, scold me, Cousin Jimmy, scold me *hard*."

"No, no. But it *would* have been more prudent *not* to have opened that window, wouldn't it now, Pussy?"

"Of course it would. But prudence is such a shoddy virtue at times, Cousin Jimmy. One is ashamed of it—one likes to just go ahead and—and——"

"And hang consequences," supplied Cousin Jimmy.

"Something like that," Emily laughed. "I hate to go mincing through life, afraid to take a single long step for fear somebody is watching. I want to 'wave my wild tail and walk by my wild lone.' There wasn't a bit of real harm in my opening that window and talking to

Perry. There wasn't even any harm in his trying to kiss me. He just did it to tease me. Oh, I *hate* conventions. As you say—hang consequences."

"But we can't hang 'em, Pussy—that's just the trouble. They're more likely to hang us. I put it to you, Pussy—suppose—there's no harm in supposing it— that you were grown up and married and had a daughter of your age, and you went downstairs one night and found as Aunt Ruth found you and Perry. *Would* you like it? *Would* you be well pleased? Honest, now?"

Emily stared hard at the fire for a moment.

"No, I wouldn't," she said at last. "But then—that's different. I wouldn't *know*."

Cousin Jimmy chuckled.

"That's the point, Pussy. Other people can't *know*. So we've got to watch our step. Oh, I'm only simple Jimmy Murray, but I can see we have to watch our step. Pussy, we're going to have roast spare-ribs for supper."

A savoury whiff crept in from the kitchen at that very moment—a homely, comfortable odour that had nothing in common with compromising situations and family skeletons. Emily gave Cousin Jimmy another hug.

"Better a dinner of herbs where Cousin Jimmy is than roast spare-ribs and Aunt Ruth therewith," she said.

19
"Airy Voices"

"April 3, 19—

"There *are* times when I am tempted to believe in the influence of evil stars or the reality of unlucky days. Otherwise how can such diabolical things happen as do happen to well-meaning people? Aunt Ruth has only just begun to grow weary of recalling the night she found Perry kissing me in the dining-room, and now I'm in another ridiculous scrape.

"I will be honest. It was not dropping my umbrella which was responsible for it, neither was it the fact that I let the kitchen mirror at New Moon fall last Saturday and crack. It was just my own carelessness.

"St. John's Presbyterian church here in Shrewsbury became vacant at New Year's and has been hearing candidates. Mr. Towers of the *Times* asked me to report the sermons for his paper on such Sundays as I was not in Blair Water. The first sermon was good and I reported it with pleasure. The second one was harm-less, very harmless, and I reported it without pain. But the third, which I heard last Sunday, was ridiculous. I said so to Aunt Ruth on the way home from church and Aunt Ruth said, 'Do you think *you* are competent to criticise a sermon?'

"Well, yes, I do!

"That sermon was a most inconsistent thing. Mr. Wickham contradicted himself half a dozen times. He mixed his metaphors—he attributed something to St. Paul that belonged to Shakespeare—he committed al-most every conceivable literary sin, including the unpardonable one of being deadly dull. However, it was my business to report the sermon, so report it I did. Then I had to do something to get it out of my system, so I wrote, for my own satisfaction, an analysis of it. It was a crazy but delightful deed. I showed up all the inconsistencies, the misquotations, the weaknesses and the wobblings. I enjoyed writing it—I made it as pointed and satirical and satanical as I could—oh, I admit it was a very vitriolic document.

"Then I handed *it* into the *Times* by mistake!

"Mr. Towers passed it over to the typesetter without reading it. He had a touching confidence in my work, which he will never have again. It came out the next day.

"I awoke to find myself infamous.

"I expected Mr. Towers would be furious; but he is only mildly annoyed—and a little amused at the back of it. It isn't as if Mr. Wickham had been a settled minister here, of course. Nobody cared for him or his sermon and Mr. Towers is a Presbyterian, so the St. John's people can't accuse him of wanting to insult *them*. It is poor Emily B. on whom is laid the whole burden of condemnation. It appears most of them think I did it 'to show off.' Aunt Ruth is furious, Aunt Elizabeth outraged, Aunt Laura grieved, Cousin Jimmy alarmed. It is such a shocking thing to criticise a minister's sermon. It is a Murray tradition that ministers' sermons—Presbyterian ministers' especially— are sacrosanct. My presumption and vanity will yet be the ruin of me, so Aunt Elizabeth coldly informs me. The only person who seems pleased is Mr. Carpenter. (Dean is away in New York. I know *he* would like it, too.) Mr. Carpenter is telling every one that my 'report' is the best thing of its kind he ever read. But Mr. Carpenter is suspected of heresy, so his commendation will not go far to rehabilitate me.

"I feel wretched over the affair. My mistakes worry me more than my sins sometimes. And yet, an unholy something, 'way back in me, is grinning over it all. Every word in that 'report' was true. And more than true—appropriate. *I* didn't mix my metaphors.

"Now, to live this down!

"April 20, 19—

"'Awake thou north wind and come thou south. Blow upon my garden that the spices thereof may flow out.'

"So chanted I as I went through the Land of Uprightness this evening—only I put 'woods' in place of garden. For spring is just around the corner and I have forgotten everything but gladness.

"We had a grey, rainy dawn but sunshine came in the afternoon and a bit of April frost tonight—just enough to make the earth firm. It seemed to me a night when the ancient gods might be met with in the lonely places. But I saw nothing except some sly things back among the fir copses that *may* have been companies of goblins, if they weren't merely shadows.

"(I wonder why *goblin* in such an enchanting word and *gobbling* such an ugly one. And why is *shadowy* suggestive of all beauty while umbrageous is so ugly?)

"But I heard all kinds of fairy sounds and each gave me an exquisite vanishing joy as I went up the hill. There is always something satisfying in climbing to the top of a hill. And that is a hill-top I love. When I reached it I stood still and let the loveliness of the evening flow through me like music. How the Wind Woman was singing in the bits of birchland around me—how she whistled in the serrated tops of the trees against the sky! One of the thirteen new silver moons of the year was hanging over the harbour. I stood there and thought of many, many beautiful things—of wild, free brooks running through starlit April fields—of rippled grey-satin seas—of the grace of an elm against the moonlight—of roots stirring and thrilling in the earth—owls laughing in darkness—a curl of foam on a long sandy shore—a young moon setting over a dark hill—the grey of gulf storms.

"I had only seventy-five cents in the world but Paradise isn't bought with money.

"Then I sat down on an old boulder and tried to put those moments of delicate happiness into a poem. I caught the shape of them fairly well, I think—but not their soul. It escaped me.

"It was quite dark when I came back and the whole character of my Land of Uprightness seemed changed. It was eerie—almost sinister. I would have run if I could have dared. The trees, my old well-known friends, were strange and aloof. The sounds I heard were not the cheery, companionable sounds of daytime—nor the friendly, fairy sounds of the sunset—they were creeping and weird, as if the life of the woods had suddenly developed something almost hostile to me—something at least that was furtive and alien and unacquainted. I could fancy that I heard stealthy footsteps all around me—that strange eyes were watching me through the boughs. When I reached the open space and hopped over the fence into Aunt Ruth's back yard I felt as if I were escaping from some fascinating but not altogether hallowed locality—a place given over to Paganism and the revels of satyrs. I don't believe the woods are ever wholly Christian in the darkness. There is always a lurking life in them that dares not show itself to the sun but regains its own with the night.

"'You should not be out in the damp with that cough of yours,' said Aunt Ruth.

"But it wasn't the damp that hurt me—for I *was* hurt. It was that little fascinating whisper of something unholy. I was afraid of it—and yet I loved it. The beauty I had loved on the hill-top seemed suddenly quite tasteless beside it. I sat down in my room and wrote another poem. When I had written it I felt that I had exorcised something out of my soul and Emily-in-the-Glass seemed no longer a stranger to me.

"Aunt Ruth has just brought in a dose of hot milk and cayenne pepper for my cough. It is on the table before me—I have to drink it—and it has made both Paradise and Pagan-land seem very foolish and unreal!

"May 25, 19—
"Dean came home from New York last Friday and that evening we walked and talked in New Moon

garden in a weird, uncanny twilight following a rainy day. I had a light dress on and as Dean came down the path he said,

"'When I saw you first I thought you were a wild, white cherry-tree—like *that'*—and he pointed to one that was leaning and beckoning, ghost-fair in the dusk, from Lofty John's bush.

"It was such a beautiful thing that just to be distantly compared to it made me feel very well pleased with myself, and it was lovely to have dear old Dean back again. So we had a delightful evening, and picked a big bunch of Cousin Jimmy's pansies and watched the grey rainclouds draw together in great purple masses in the east, leaving the western sky all clear and star-powdered.

"'There is something in your company,' said Dean, 'that makes stars seem starrier and pansies purpler.'

"Wasn't that nice of him! How is it that his opinion of me and Aunt Ruth's opinion of me are so very different?

"He had a little flat parcel under his arm and when he went away he handed it to me.

"'I brought you that to counteract Lord Byron,' he said.

"It was a framed copy of the 'Portrait of Giovanna Degli Albizzi, wife of Lorenzo Tornabuoni Ghirlanjo'—a Lady of the Quatro Cento. I brought it to Shrewsbury and have it hanging in my room. I love to look at the Lady Giovanna—that slim, beautiful young thing with her sleek coils of pale gold and her prim little curls and her fine, high-bred profile (*did* the painter flatter her?) and her white neck and open, unshadowed brow, with the indefinable air over it all of saintliness and remoteness and fate—for the Lady Giovanna died young.

"*And* her embroidered velvet sleeves, slashed and puffed, very beautifully made and fitting the arm perfectly. The Lady Giovanna must have had a good dressmaker and, in spite of her saintliness, one thinks she was quite aware of the fact. I am always wishing that she would turn her head and let me see her full face.

"Aunt Ruth thinks she is queer-looking and evidently doubts the propriety of having her in the same room with the jewelled chromo of Queen Alexandra.

"I doubt it myself.

"June 10, 19—

"I do all my studying now by the pool in the Land of Uprightness, among those wonderful, tall, slender trees. I'm a Druidess in the woods—I regard trees with something more than love—worship.

"And then, too, trees, unlike so many humans, always improve on acquaintance. No matter how much you like them at the start you are sure to like them much better further on, and best of all when you have known them for years and enjoyed intercourse with them in all seasons. I know a hundred dear things about these trees in the Land of Uprightness that I didn't know when I came here two years ago.

"Trees have as much individuality as human beings. Not even two spruces are alike. There is always some kink or curve or bend of bough to single each one out from its fellows. Some trees love to grow sociably together, their branches twining, like Ilse and me with our arms about each other, whispering interminably of their secrets. Then there are more exclusive groups of four or five—clan-Murray trees; and there are hermits of trees who choose to stand apart in solitary state and who hold commune only with the winds of heaven. Yet these trees are often the best worth knowing. One feels it is more of a triumph to win their confidence than that of easier trees. Tonight I suddenly saw a great, pulsating star resting on the very crest of the big fir that stands alone in the eastern corner and I had a sense of two majesties meeting that will abide with me for days and enchant everything—even classroom routine and dishwashing and Aunt Ruth's Saturday cleaning.

"June 25, 19—

"We had our history examination today—the Tudor period. I've found it very fascinating—but more because of what isn't in the histories than of what *is*. They don't—they *can't* tell you what you would really like to know. What did Jane Seymour think of when she was awake in the dark? Of murdered Anne, or of pale, forsaken Katherine? Or just about the fashion of her new ruff? Did she ever think she had paid too high for her crown or was she satisfied with her bargain? And was she happy in those few hours after her little son was born—or did she see a ghostly procession beckoning her onward with them? Was Lady Jane Gray 'Janie' to her friends and did she *ever* have a fit of temper? What did Shakespeare's wife actually think of him? And was any man ever *really* in love with Queen Elizabeth? I am always asking questions like this when I study that pageant of kings and queens and geniuses and puppets put down in the school curriculum as 'The Tudor Period.'

"July 7, 19—

"Two years of High School are over. The result of my exams was such as to please even Aunt Ruth, who condescended to say that she always knew I could study if I put my mind to it. In brief, I led my class. And I'm pleased. But I begin to understand what Dean meant when he said real education was what you dug out of life for yourself. After all, the things that have taught me the most these past two years have been my wanderings in the Land of Uprightness, and my night on the haystack, and the Lady Giovanna, and the old woman who spanked the King, and trying to write nothing but *facts*, and things like that. Even rejection slips and hating Evelyn Blake have taught me something. Speaking of Evelyn—she failed in her exams and will have to take her senior year over again. I am truly sorry.

"That sounds as if I were a most amiable, forgiving creature. Let me be perfectly frank. I am sorry she didn't pass, because if she had she wouldn't be in school next year.

"July 20, 19—

"Ilse and I go bathing every day now. Aunt Laura is always very particular about seeing that we have our bathing suits with us. I wonder if she ever heard any faint, far-off echoes of our moonlit petticoatedness.

"But so far our dips have been in the afternoon. And afterwards we have a glorious wallow on sunwarm, golden sands, with the gauzy dunes behind us stretching to the harbour, and the lazy blue sea before us, dotted over with sails that are silver in the magic of the sunlight. Oh, life is good—good—good. In spite of three rejection slips that came today. Those very editors will be *asking* for my work some day! Meanwhile Aunt Laura is teaching me how to make a certain rich and complicated kind of chocolate cake after a recipe which a friend of hers in Virginia sent her thirty years ago. Nobody in Blair Water has ever been able to get it and Aunt Laura made me solemnly promise I would never reveal it.

"The real name of the cake is Devil's Food but Aunt Elizabeth will not have it called that.

"Aug. 2, 19—

"I was down seeing Mr. Carpenter this evening. He has been laid up with rheumatism and one can see he is getting old. He was very cranky with the scholars last year and there was some protest against keeping him on, but it was done. Most of the Blair Water people have sense enough to realise that with all his crankiness Mr. Carpenter is a teacher in a thousand.

"'One can't teach fools amiably,' he growled, when the trustees told him there were complaints about his harshness.

"Perhaps it was his rheumatism that made Mr. Carpenter rather crusty over the poems I took to him for criticism. When he read the one I had composed that April night on a hill-top he tossed it back to me—'a pretty little gossamer thing,' he said.

"And I had really thought the poem expressed in some measure the enchantment of that evening. How I must have failed! "Then I gave him the poem I had written after I had come in that night. He read it over twice, then he deliberately tore it into strips.

"'Now—*why*?' I said, rather annoyed. 'There was nothing wrong about that poem, Mr. Carpenter.'

"'Not about its body,' he said. 'Every line of it, taken by itself, might be read in Sunday School. But its *soul*—what mood were you in when you wrote that, in heaven's name?'

"'The mood of the Golden Age,' I said.

"'No—of an age far before that. That poem was sheer Paganism, girl, though I don't think you realise it. To be sure, from the point of view of literature it's worth a thousand of your pretty songs. All the same, that way danger lies. Better stick to your own age. You're part of it and can possess it without its possessing you. Emily, there was a streak of diabolism in that poem. It's enough to make me believe that poets *are* inspired—by some spirits outside themselves. Didn't you feel *possessed* when you wrote it?'

"'Yes,' I said, remembering. I felt rather glad Mr. Carpenter had torn the poem up. I could never have done it myself. I have destroyed a great many of my poems that seemed trash on successive readings, but this one never seemed so and it always brought back the strange charm and terror of that walk. But Mr. Carpenter was right—I feel it.

"He also berated me because I happened to mention I had been reading Mrs. Hemans' poems. Aunt Laura has a cherished volume, bound in faded blue and gold, with an inscription from an admirer. In Aunt Laura's youth it was the thing to give your adored a volume of poetry on her birthday. The things Mr. Carpenter said about Mrs. Hemans were not fit to write in a young lady's diary. I suppose he is right in the main—yet I *do* like some of her poems. Just here and there comes a line or verse that haunts me for days, delightfully.

" *'The march of the hosts as Alaric passed'*

is one—though I can't give any *reason* for my liking it—one never *can* give reasons for enchantment—and another is,

" *'The sounds of the sea and the sounds of the night*
Were around Clotilde as she knelt to pray
In a chapel where the mighty lay
On the old Provençal shore.'

"That isn't great poetry—but there's a bit of magic in it for all that—concentrated in the last line, I think. I never read it without feeling that *I* am Clotilde, kneeling there—'on the old Provençal shore'—with the banners of forgotten wars waving over me.

"Mr. Carpenter sneered at my 'liking for slops' and told me to go and read the Elsie books! But when I was coming away he paid me the first personal compliment I ever had from him.

" 'I like that blue dress you've got on. And you know how to wear it. That's good. I can't bear to see a woman badly dressed. It hurts me—and it must hurt God Almighty. I've no use for dowds and I'm sure He hasn't. After all, if you know how to dress yourself it won't matter if you do like Mrs. Hemans.'

"I met Old Kelly on the way home and he stopped and gave me a bag of candy and sent his 'rispicts to *him.*'

"August 15, 19—

"This is a wonderful year for columbines. The old orchard is full of them—all in lovely white and purple and fairy blue and dreamy pink colour. They are half wild and so have a charm no real tamed garden flower ever has. And what a name—*columbine* is poetry itself. How much lovelier the common names of flowers are than the horrid Latiny names the florists stick in their catalogues. Heartsease and Bride's Bouquet, Prince's Feather, Snap-dragon, Flora's Paint Brush, Dusty Millers, Bachelor's Buttons, Baby's Breath, Love-in-a-mist—oh, I love them all.

"September 1, 19—

"Two things happened today. One was a letter from Great-aunt Nancy to Aunt Elizabeth. Aunt Nancy has never taken any notice of my existence since my visit to Priest Pond four years ago. But she is still alive, ninety-four years old, and from all accounts quite lively yet. She wrote some sarcastic things in her letter, about both me and Aunt Elizabeth; but she wound up by offering to pay all my expenses in Shrewsbury next year, including my board to Aunt Ruth.

"I am very glad. In spite of Aunt Nancy's sarcasm I don't mind feeling indebted to her. *She* has never nagged or patronised me—or did anything for me because she felt it her 'duty.' 'Hang duty,' she said in her letter. 'I'm doing this because it will vex some of the Priests, and because Wallace is putting on too many airs about "helping to educate Emily." I dare say you feel yourself that you've done virtuously. Tell Emily to go back to Shrewsbury and learn all she can—but to hide it and show her ankles.' Aunt Elizabeth was horrified at this and wouldn't show me the letter. But Cousin Jimmy told me what was in it.

"The second thing was that Aunt Elizabeth informed me that, since Aunt Nancy was paying my expenses, she, Aunt Elizabeth, felt that she ought not to hold me any longer to my promise about writing fiction. I was, she told me, free to do as I chose about that matter.

"'Though I shall never approve of your writing fiction,' she said, gravely. 'At least I hope you will not neglect your studies.'

"Oh, no, dear Aunt Elizabeth, I won't neglect them. But I feel like a released prisoner. My fingers tingle to grasp a pen—my brain teems with plots. I've a score of fascinating dream characters I want to write about. Oh, if there only were not such a chasm between *seeing* a thing and getting it down on paper!

"'Ever since you got that check for a story last winter Elizabeth's been wondering if she oughtn't to let you write,' Cousin Jimmy told me. 'But she couldn't bring herself to back down till Aunt Nancy's letter gave her the excuse. Money makes the Murray mare go, Emily. Want some more Yankee stamps?'

"Mrs. Kent has told Teddy he can go for another year. After that he doesn't know what will happen. So we are going back and I am so happy that I want to write it in Italics.

"September 10, 19—

"I have been elected president of the Senior class for this year. *And* the *Skulls and Owls* sent me a notice that I had been elected a member of their august fraternity without the formality of an application.

"Evelyn Blake, by the way, is at present laid up with tonsillitis!

"I accepted the presidency—but I wrote a note to the

Skull and Owl declining membership with awful politeness.

"After black-beaning me last year, indeed!

"October 7, 19—

"There was great excitement today in class when Dr. Hardy made a certain announcement. Kathleen Darcy's uncle, who is a Professor of McGill, is visiting here, and he has taken it into his head to offer a prize for the best poem, written by a pupil of Shrewsbury High School—said prize being a complete set of Parkman. The poems must be handed in by the first of November, and are to be 'not less than twenty lines, and no more than sixty.' Sounds as if a tape measure was the first requisite. I have been wildly hunting through my Jimmy-books tonight and have decided to send in *Wild Grapes*. It is my second best poem. *A Song of Sixpence* is my best, but it has only fifteen lines and to add any more would spoil it. I think I can improve *Wild Grapes* a bit. There are two or three words in it I've always been dubious about. They don't exactly express fully what I want to say, but I can't find any others that do, either. I wish one could coin words, as I used to do long ago when I wrote letters to Father and just invented a word whenever I wanted one. But then, Father would have understood the words if he had ever seen the letters— while I am afraid the judges in the contest wouldn't.

"*Wild Grapes* should certainly win the prize. This isn't conceit or vanity or presumption. It's just *knowing*. If the prize were for mathematics Kath Darcy should win it. If it were for beauty Hazel Ellis would win it. If it were for all round proficiency, Perry Miller—for elocution, Ilse—for drawing, Teddy. But since it is for poetry, E. B. Starr is the one!

"We are studying Tennyson and Keats in Senior Literature this year. I like Tennyson but sometimes he enrages me. He is beautiful—not *too* beautiful, as Keats is—the Perfect Artist. But he never lets us forget the artist—we are always conscious of it—he is never swept away by some splendid mountain torrent of feeling. Not he—he flows on serenely between well-ordered banks and carefully laid-out gardens. And no matter how much one loves a garden one doesn't want to be cooped up in it *all* the time—one likes an excursion now and then into the wilderness. At least Emily Byrd Starr does—to the sorrow of her relations.

"Keats *is* too full of beauty. When I read his poetry I feel stifled in roses and long for a breath of frosty air or the austerity of a chill mountain peak. But, oh, he has *some* lines—

> " *'Magic casements opening on the foam*
> *Of perilous seas, in faërylands forlorn'*—

"When I read them I always feel a sort of despair! *What* is the use of trying to do what *has* been done, once and for all?

"But I found some other lines that inspire me—I have written them on the index-page of my new Jimmy-book.

> " *'He ne'er is crowned*
> *With immortality who fears to follow*
> *Where airy voices lead.'*

"Oh, it's true. We must follow our 'airy voices,' follow them through every discouragement and doubt and disbelief till they lead us to our City of Fulfilment, wherever it may be.

"I had four rejections in the mail today, raucously shrieking failure at me. Airy Voices grow faint in such a clamour. But I'll hear them again. And I *will* follow—I will not be discouraged. Years ago I wrote a 'vow'—I found it the other day in an old packet in my cupboard—

that I would 'climb the Alpine Path and write my name on the scroll of fame.'

"I'll keep on climbing!

"October 20, 19—

"I read my *Chronicles of an Old Garden* over the other night. I think I can improve it considerably, now that Aunt Elizabeth has lifted the ban. I wanted Mr. Carpenter to read it, but he said,

"'Lord, girl, I can't wade through all that stuff. My eyes are bad. What is it—a book? Jade, it will be time ten years from now for you to be writing books.'

"'I've got to practice,' I said indignantly.

"'Oh, practice—practice—but don't try out the results on me. I'm too old—I really am, Jade. I don't mind a short—a very short story—now and then—but let a poor old devil off the books.'

"I might ask Dean what he thinks of it. But Dean *does* laugh now at my ambitions—very cautiously and kindly—but he *does* laugh. And Teddy thinks everything I write perfect, so he's no use as a critic. I wonder—I wonder if any publisher would accept *The Chronicles*? I'm sure I've seen books of the kind that weren't *much* better.

"'November 11, 19—

"This evening I spent 'expurgating' a novel for Mr. Towers' use and behoof. When Mr. Towers was away in August on his vacation the sub-editor, Mr. Grady, began to run a serial in the *Times* called *A Bleeding Heart*. Instead of getting A. P. A. stuff, as Mr. Towers always does, Mr. Grady simply bought the reprint of a sensational and sentimental English novel at the Shoppe and began publishing it. It was very long and only about half of it has appeared. Mr. Towers saw that it would run all winter in its present form. So he bade me take it and cut out 'all unnecessary stuff.' I have followed instructions mercilessly—'cutting out' most of the kisses and embraces, two-thirds of the love making and all the descriptions, with the happy result that I have reduced it to about a quarter of its normal length; and all I can say is may heaven have mercy on the soul of the compositor who has to set it in its present mutilated condition.

"Summer and autumn have gone. It seems to me they go more quickly than they used to. The goldenrod has turned white in the corners of the Land of Uprightness and the frost lies like a silver scarf on the ground o' mornings. The evening winds that go 'piping down the valleys wild' are heart-broken searchers, seeking for things loved and lost, calling in vain on elf and fay. For the fairy folk, if they be not all fled afar to the southlands, must be curled up asleep in the hearts of the firs or among the roots of the ferns.

"And every night we have murky red sunsets flaming in smoky crimson across the harbour, with a star above them like a saved soul gazing with compassionate eyes into pits of torment where sinful spirits are being purged from the stains of earthly pilgrimage.

"Would I dare to show the above sentence to Mr. Carpenter? I would *not*. Therefore there is something fearfully wrong with it.

"I know what's wrong with it, now that I've written it in cold blood. It's 'fine writing.' And yet it's just what I felt when I stood on the hill beyond the Land of Uprightness tonight and looked across the harbour. And who cares what this old journal thinks?

"December 2, 19—
"The results of the prize poem competition were

announced today. Evelyn Blake is the winner with a poem entitled *A Legend of Abegweit*.

"There isn't anything to say—so I say it.

"Besides, Aunt Ruth has said everything!

                                          "December 15, 19—

"Evelyn's prize poem was printed in the *Times* this week with her photograph and a biographical sketch. The set of Parkman is on exhibition in the windows of the Booke Shoppe.

"*A Legend of Abegweit is* a fairly good poem. It is in ballad style, and rhythm and rhyme are correct—which could not be said of any other poem of Evelyn's I've ever seen.

"Evelyn Blake has said of everything of mine she ever saw in print that she was sure I copied it from somewhere. I hate to imitate her—but I *know* that *she* never wrote that poem. It isn't any expression of *her* at all. She might as well have imitated Dr. Hardy's handwriting and claimed it as her own. Her mincing copperplate script is as much like Dr. Hardy's black, forcible scrawl as that poem is like *her*.

"Besides, though *A Legend of Abegweit* is fairly good it is *not* as good as *Wild Grapes*.

"I am not going to say so to any one but down it goes in this journal. Because it's *true*.

                                            "Dec. 20, 19—

"I showed *A Legend of Abegweit* and *Wild Grapes* to Mr. Carpenter. When he had read them both he said, 'Who were the judges?'

"I told him.

"'Give them my compliments and tell them they're asses,' he said.

"I feel comforted. I won't tell the judges—or any

one—that they're asses. But it soothes me to know they are.

"The strange thing is—Aunt Elizabeth asked to see *Wild Grapes* and when she had read it she said,

" '*I* am no judge of poetry, of course, but it seems to me that *yours* is of a *higher order.*'

"Jan. 4, 19—

"I spent the Christmas week at Uncle Oliver's. I didn't like it. It was too noisy. I would have liked it years ago but they never asked me then. I had to eat when I wasn't hungry—play parchesi when I didn't want to—talk when I wanted to be silent. I was never alone for one moment all the time I was there. Besides, Andrew is getting to be such a nuisance. And Aunt Addie was odiously kind and motherly. I just felt all the time like a cat who is held on a lap where it doesn't want to be and gently, firmly stroked. I had to sleep with Jen, who is my first cousin and just my age, and who thinks in her heart I'm not half good enough for Andrew but is going to try with the blessing of God, to make the best of it. Jen is a nice, sensible girl and she and I are friendish. That is a word of my own coining. Jen and I are more than mere acquaintances but not really friendly. We will always be friendish and never more than friendish. We don't talk the same language.

"When I got home to dear New Moon I went up to my room and shut the door and revelled in solitude.

"School opened yesterday. Today in the Booke Shoppe I had an internal laugh. Mrs. Rodney and Mrs. Elder were looking over some books and Mrs. Rodney said,

" 'That story in the *Times*—*A Bleeding Heart*—was the strangest one I ever read. It wandered on, chapter after chapter, for weeks, and never seemed to get anywhere, and then it just finished up in eight chapters *lickety-split*. I can't understand it.'

"I could have solved the mystery for her but I didn't."

20
In the Old John House

When *The Woman Who Spanked the King* was accepted and published by a New York magazine of some standing, quite a sensation was produced in Blair Water and Shrewsbury, especially when the incredible news was whispered from lip to lip that Emily had actually been paid forty dollars for it. For the first time her clan began to take her writing mania with some degree of seriousness and Aunt Ruth gave up, finally and for ever, all slurs over wasted time. The acceptance came at the psychological moment when the sands of Emily's faith were running rather low. All the fall and winter her stuff had been coming back to her, except from two magazines whose editors evidently thought that literature was its own reward and quite independent of degrading monetary considerations. At first she had always felt dreadfully when a poem or story over which she had agonised came back with one of those icy little rejection slips or a few words of faint praise—the "but" rejections, Emily called these, and hated them worse than the printed ones. Tears of disappointment *would* come. But after a time she got hardened to it and didn't mind—so much. She only gave the editorial slip the Murray look and said "I will succeed." And never at any time had she any *real* doubt that she would. Down, deep down, something told her that her time would come. So, though she flinched momentarily at each rejection, as from the flick of a whip, she sat down and—wrote another story.

Still, her inner voice had grown rather faint under so many discouragements. The acceptance of *The Woman Who Spanked the King* suddenly raised it into a joyous paean of certainty again. The check meant much, but the storming of that magazine much more. She felt that she was surely winning a foothold. Mr. Carpenter chuckled over it and told her it really was "absolutely good."

"The best in this story belongs to Mistress McIntyre," said Emily ruefully. "I can't call it mine."

"The setting is yours—and what you've added harmonises perfectly with your foundation. And you didn't polish hers up too much—*that* shows the artist. Weren't you tempted to?"

"Yes. There were so many places I thought I *could* improve it a good deal."

"But you didn't try to—*that* makes it yours," said Mr. Carpenter—and left her to puzzle his meaning out for herself.

Emily spent thirty-five of her dollars so sensibly that even Aunt Ruth herself couldn't find fault with her budget. But with the remaining five she bought a set of Parkman. It was a much nicer set than the prize one—which the donor had really picked out of a mail-order list—and Emily felt much prouder of it than if it had been the prize. After all, it was better to earn things for yourself. Emily has those Parkmans yet—somewhat faded and frayed now, but dearer to her than all the other volumes in her library. For a few weeks she was very happy and uplifted. The Murrays were proud of her, Principal Hardy had congratulated her, a local elocutionist of some repute had read her story at a concert in Charlottetown. And, most wonderful of all, a far-away reader in Mexico had written her a letter telling her what pleasure *The Woman Who Spanked the King* had given him. Emily read and re-read that letter until she knew it off by heart, and slept with it under her pillow. No lover's missive was ever more tenderly treated.

Then the affair of the old John house came up like a thunder-cloud and darkened all her cerulean sky.

There was a concert and "pie social" at Derry Pond one Friday night and Ilse had been asked to recite. Dr. Burnley took Ilse and Emily and Perry and Teddy over in his big, double-seated sleigh, and they had a gay and merry eight miles' drive through the soft snow that was beginning to fall. When the concert was half over, Dr. Burnley was summoned out. There was sudden and serious illness in a Derry Pond household. The doctor went, telling Teddy that he must drive the party home. Dr. Burnley made no bones about it. They might have silly rules about chaperonage in Shrewsbury and Charlottetown, but in Blair Water and Derry Pond they did not obtain. Teddy and Perry were decent boys— Emily was a Murray—Ilse was no fool. The doctor would have summed them up thus tersely if he had thought about it at all.

When the concert was over they left for home. It was snowing very thickly now and the wind was rising rapidly, but the first three miles of the road were through sheltering woods and were not unpleasant. There was a wild, weird beauty in the snow-coated ranks of trees, standing in the pale light of the moon behind the storm-clouds. The sleigh-bells laughed at the shriek of the wind far overhead. Teddy managed the doctor's team without difficulty. Once or twice Emily had a strong suspicion that he was using only one arm to drive them. She wondered if he had noticed that evening that she wore her hair really "up" for the first time—in a soft ebon "Psyche knot" under her crimson hat. Emily thought again that there was something quite delightful about a storm.

But when they left the woods their troubles began. The storm swooped down on them in all its fury. The winter road went through the fields and wound and twisted and doubled in and out and around corners and spruce groves—a road that would "break a snake's back," as Perry said. The track was already almost obliterated with the drift and the horses plunged to their knees. They had not gone a mile before Perry whistled in dismay.

"We'll never make Blair Water tonight, Ted."

"We've got to make somewhere," shouted Ted. "We can't camp *here*. And there's no house till we get back to the summer road, past Shaw's hill. Duck under the robes, girls. You'd better get back with Ilse, Emily, and Perry will come here with me."

The transfer was effected, Emily no longer thinking storms quite so delightful. Perry and Teddy were both thoroughly alarmed. They knew the horses could not go much farther in that depth of snow—the summer road beyond Shaw's hill would be blocked with drift—and it was bitterly cold on those high, bleak hills between the valleys of Derry Pond and Blair Water.

"If we can only get to Malcolm Shaw's we'll be all right," muttered Perry.

"We'll never get that far. Shaw's hill is filled in by this time to the fence-tops," said Teddy. "Here's the old John house. Do you suppose we could stay here?"

"Cold as a barn," said Perry. "The girls would freeze. We must try to make Malcolm's."

When the plunging horses reached the summer road, the boys saw at a glance that Shaw's hill was a hopeless proposition. All traces of track were obliterated by drifts that were over the fence-tops. Telephone-posts were blown down across the road and a huge, fallen tree blocked the gap where the field road ran out to it.

"Nothing to do but go back to the old John house," said Perry. "We can't go wandering over the fields in the teeth of this storm, looking for a way through to Malcolm's. We'd get stuck and freeze to death."

Teddy turned the horses. The snow was thicker than ever. Every minute the drift deepened. The track was entirely gone, and if the old John house had been very far away they could never have found it. Fortunately, it was near, and after one last wild flounder through the unbroken drift around it, during which the boys had to get out and scramble along on their own feet, they reached the comparative calm of the little cleared space in the young spruce woods, wherein stood the old John house.

The "old John house" had been old when, forty years before, John Shaw had moved into it with his young bride. It had been a lonely spot even then, far back from the road, and almost surrounded by spruce woods. John Shaw had lived there five years; then his wife died; he had sold the farm to his brother Malcolm and gone West. Malcolm farmed the land and kept the little barn in good repair, but the house had never been occupied since, save for a few weeks in winter when Malcolm's boys camped there while they "got out" their firewood. It was not even locked. Tramps and burglars were unknown in Derry Pond. Our castaways found easy entrance through the door of the tumbledown porch and drew a breath of relief to find themselves out of the shrieking wind and driving snow.

"We won't freeze anyhow," said Perry. "Ted and I'll have to see if we can get the horses in the barn and then we'll come back and see if we can't make ourselves comfortable. I've got matches and I've never been stumped yet."

Perry met no great difficulties in making good his boast. His lighted match revealed a couple of half-burned candles in squat tin candlesticks, a cracked and rusty but still quite serviceable old Waterloo stove, three chairs, a bench, a sofa, and a table.

"What's the matter with this?" demanded Perry.

"They'll be awfully worried about us at home, that's all," said Emily, shaking the snow off her wraps.

"Worry won't kill them in one night," said Perry. "We'll get home tomorrow somehow."

"Meanwhile, this is an adventure," laughed Emily. "Let's get all the fun out of it we can."

Ilse said nothing—which was very odd in Ilse. Emily,

looking at her, saw that she was very pale and recalled that she had been unusually quiet ever since they had left the hall.

"Aren't you feeling all right, Ilse?" she asked anxiously.

"I'm feeling all wrong," said Ilse, with a ghastly smile. "I'm—I'm sick as a dog," she added, with more force than elegance.

"Oh, Ilse——"

"Don't hit the ceiling," said Ilse impatiently. "I'm not beginning pneumonia or appendictis. I'm just plain *sick*. That pie I had at the hall was too rich, I suppose. It's turned my little tummy upside down. O—w—w."

"Lie down on the sofa," urged Emily. "Perhaps you'll feel better then."

Ilse, shuddering and abject, cast herself down. A "sick stomach" is not a romantic ailment or a very deadly one, but it certainly takes the ginger out of its victim for the time being.

The boys, finding a box full of wood behind the stove, soon had a roaring fire. Perry took one of the candles and explored the little house. In a small room opening off the kitchen was an old-fashioned wooden bedstead with a rope mattress. The other room—it had been Almira Shaw's parlour in olden days—was half filled with oat-straw. Upstairs there was nothing but emptiness and dust. But in the little pantry Perry made some finds.

"There's a can of pork and beans here," he announced, "and a tin box half full of crackers. I see our breakfast. I s'pose the Shaw boys left them here. And what's this?"

Perry brought out a small bottle, uncorked and sniffed it solemnly.

"Whiskey, as I'm a living sinner. Not much, but enough. Here's your medicine, Ilse. You take it in some hot water and it'll settle your stomach in a jiffy."

"I hate the taste of whiskey," moaned Ilse. "Father never uses it—he doesn't believe in it."

"Aunt Tom does," said Perry, as if that settled the matter. "It's a sure cure. Try it and see."

"But there isn't any water," said Ilse.

"You'll have to take it straight, then. There's only about two tablespoons in the bottle. Try it. It won't kill you if it doesn't cure you."

Poor Ilse was really feeling so abjectly wretched that she would have taken anything, short of poison, if she thought there was any chance of its helping her. She crawled off the sofa, sat down on a chair before the fire and swallowed the dose. It was good, strong whiskey— Malcolm Shaw could have told you that. And I think there was really more than two tablespoonfuls in the bottle, though Perry always insisted that there wasn't. Ilse sat huddled in her chair for a few minutes longer, then she got up and put her hand uncertainly on Emily's shoulder.

"Do you feel worse?" asked Emily, anxiously.

"I'm—I'm drunk," said Ilse. "Help me back to the sofa, for mercy's sake. My legs are going to double up under me. Who was the Scotchman up at Malvern who said he never got drunk but the whiskey always settled in his knees? But mine's in the head, too. It's spinning round."

Perry and Teddy both sprang to help her and between them a very wobbly Ilse made safe port on the sofa again.

"Is there anything we can do?" implored Emily.

"Too much has already been done," said Ilse with preternatural solemnity. She shut her eyes and not another word would she say in response to any entreaty. Finally it was deemed best to let her alone.

"She'll sleep it off, and, anyway, I guess it'll settle her stomach," said Perry.

Emily could not take it so philosophically. Not until Ilse's quiet breathing half an hour later proved that she was really asleep could Emily begin to taste the flavour of their "adventure." The wind threshed about the old house and rattled the windows as if in a fury over their escape from it. It was very pleasant to sit before the stove and listen to the wild melody of defeated storm—very pleasant to think about the vanished life of this old dead house, in the years when it had been full of love and laughter—very pleasant to talk of cabbages and kings with Perry and Teddy, in the faint glow of candlelight—very pleasant to sit in occasional silences, staring into the firelight, which flickered alluringly over Emily's milk-white brow and haunting, shadowy eyes. Once Emily, glancing up suddenly, found Teddy looking at her strangely. For just a moment their eyes met and locked—only a moment—yet Emily was never really to belong to herself again. She wondered dazedly what had happened. Whence came that wave of unimaginable sweetness that seemed to engulf her, body and spirit? She trembled—she was afraid. It seemed to open such dizzying possibilities of change. The only clear idea that emerged from her confusion of thought was that she wanted to sit with Teddy before a fire like this every night of their lives—and then a fig for the storms! She dared not look at Teddy again, but she thrilled with a delicious sense of his nearness; she was acutely conscious of his tall, boyish straightness, his glossy black hair, his luminous dark-blue eyes. She had always known she liked Teddy better than any other male creature in her ken—but *this* was something apart from liking altogether—this sense of belonging to him that had come in that significant exchange of glances. All at once she seemed to know why she had always snubbed any of the High School boys who wanted to be her beau.

The delight of the spell that had been suddenly laid on her was so intolerable that she must break it. She sprang up and went over to the window. The little hissing whisper of snow against the blue-white frost crystals on the pane seemed softly to scorn her bewilderment. The three big haystacks, thatched with snow, dimly visible at the corner of the barn, seemed to be shaking their shoulders with laughter over her predicament. The fire in the stove reflected out in the clearing seemed like a mocking goblin bonfire under the firs. Beyond it, through the woods, were unfathomable spaces of white storm. For a moment Emily wished she were out in them—there would be freedom there from this fetter of terrible delight that had so suddenly and inexplicably made her a prisoner—her, who hated bonds.

"Am I falling in love with Teddy?" she thought. "I won't—I won't."

Perry, quite unconscious of all that had happened in the wink of an eye to Teddy and Emily, yawned and stretched.

"Guess we'd better hit the hay—the candles are about done. I guess that straw will make a real good bed for us, Ted. Let's carry enough out and pile it on the bedstead in there to make a comfortable roost for the girls. With one of the fur rugs over it, it won't be so bad. We ought to have some high old dreams tonight—Ilse especially. Wonder if she's sober yet?"

"I've a pocket full of dreams to sell," said Teddy, whimsically, with a new, unaccountable gaiety of voice and manner. "What d'ye lack? What d'ye lack? A dream of success—a dream of adventure—a dream of the sea—a dream of the woodland—any kind of a dream you want at reasonable prices, including one or two unique little nightmares. What will you give me for a dream?"

Emily turned around—stared at him for a moment—then forgot thrills and spells and everything else in a wild longing for a Jimmy-book. As if his question, "What will you give me for a dream?" had been a magic formula opening some sealed chamber in her brain, she saw unrolling before her a dazzling idea for a story—complete even to the title—*A Seller of Dreams.* For the rest of that night Emily thought of nothing else.

The boys went off to their straw couch, and Emily, after deciding to leave Ilse, who seemed comfortable, on the sofa as long as she slept, lay down on the bed in the small room. But not to sleep. She had never felt less like sleeping. She did not want to sleep. She had forgotten that she had been falling in love with Teddy— she had forgotten everything but her wonderful idea; chapter by chapter, page by page, it unrolled itself before her in the darkness. Her characters lived and laughed and talked and did and enjoyed and suffered— she saw them on the background of the storm. Her cheeks burned, her heart beat, she tingled from head to foot with the keen rapture of creation—a joy that sprang fountain-like from the depths of being and seemed independent of all earthly things. Ilse had got drunk on Malcolm Shaw's forgotten Scotch whiskey, but Emily was intoxicated with immortal wine.

21
Thicker Than Water

Emily did not sleep until nearly morning. The storm had ceased and the landscape around the old John house had a spectral look in the light of the sinking moon when she finally drifted into slumber, with a delightful sense of accomplishment—for she had finished thinking out her story. Nothing remained now except to jot its outlines down in her Jimmy-book. She would not feel safe until she had them in black and white. She would not try to write it yet—oh, not for years. She must wait until time and experience had made of her pen an instrument capable of doing justice to her conception—for it is one thing to pursue an idea through an ecstatic night and quite another to get it down on paper in a manner that will reproduce a tenth of its original charm and significance.

Emily was wakened by Ilse, who was sitting on the side of her bed, looking rather pale and seedy, but with amber eyes full of unconquerable laughter.

"Well, I've slept off my debauch, Emily Starr. And my tummy's all right this morning. Malcolm's whiskey *did* settle it—though I think the remedy is worse than the disease. I suppose you wondered why I wouldn't talk last night."

"I thought you were too drunk to talk," said Emily candidly.

Ilse giggled.

"I was too drunk *not* to talk. When I got to that sofa, Emily, my giddiness passed off and I *wanted* to talk—oh, golly, but I wanted to talk! And I wanted to say the silliest things and tell everything I ever knew or thought. I'd just enough sense left to know I mustn't say those things or I'd make a fool of myself for ever—and I felt that if I said *one* word it would be like taking a cork out of a bottle—*everything* would gurgle out. So I just buttoned my mouth up and wouldn't say the one word. It gives me a chill to think of the things I *could* have said—and before Perry. You'll never catch your little Ilse going on a spree again. I'm a reformed character from this day forth."

"What I can't understand," said Emily, "is how such a small dose of *anything* could have turned your head like that."

"Oh, well, you know Mother was a Mitchell. It's a notorious fact that the Mitchells can't take a teaspoonful of booze without toppling. It's one of their family kinks. Well, rise up, my love, my fair one. The boys are getting a fire on and Perry says we can dope up a fair meal from the pork and beans and crackers. I'm hungry enough to eat the cans."

It was while Emily was rummaging in the pantry in

search of some salt that she made a great discovery. Far back on the top shelf was a pile of dusty old books— dating back probably to the days of John and Almira Shaw—old, mildewed diaries, almanacs, account books. Emily knocked the pile down and when she was picking it up discovered that one of the books was an old scrapbook. A loose leaf had fallen out of it. As Emily replaced it, her eyes fell on the title of a poem pasted on it. She caught it up, her breath coming quickly. *A Legend of Abegweit*—the poem with which Evelyn had won the prize! Here it was in this old, yellowed scrapbook of twenty years' vintage—word for word, except that Evelyn had cut out two verses to shorten it to the required length.

"And the two best verses in it," thought Emily, contemptuously. "How like Evelyn! She has simply no literary judgment."

Emily replaced the books on the shelf, but she slipped the loose leaf into her pocket and ate her share of breakfast very absently. By this time men were on the roads breaking out the tracks. Perry and Teddy found a shovel in the barn and soon had a way opened to the road. They got home finally, after a slow but uneventful drive, to find the New Moon folks rather anxious as to their fate and mildly horrified to learn that they had had to spend the night in the old John house.

"You might have caught your deaths of cold," said Elizabeth, severely.

"Well, it was Hobson's choice. It was that or freeze to death in the drifts," said Emily, and nothing more was said about the matter. Since they had got home safe and nobody had caught cold, what more *was* there to say? That was the New Moon way of looking at it.

The Shrewsbury way was somewhat different. But the Shrewsbury way did not become apparent immediately. The whole story was over Shrewsbury by Monday night—Ilse told it in school and described her drunken orgy with great spirit and vivacity, amid shrieks of laughter from her classmates. Emily, who had called, for the first time, on Evelyn Blake that evening, found Evelyn looking quite well pleased over something.

"Can't you stop Ilse from telling that story, my dear?"

"What story?"

"Why, about getting drunk last Friday night—the night you and she spent with Teddy Kent and Perry Miller in that old house up at Derry Pond," said Evelyn smoothly.

Emily suddenly flushed. There was *something* in Evelyn's tone—the innocent fact seemed all at once to take on shades of a sinister significance. Was Evelyn being deliberately insolent?

"I don't know why she shouldn't tell the story," said Emily, coldly. "It was a good joke on her."

"But you know how people will talk," said Evelyn, gently. "It's all rather—unfortunate. Of course, you couldn't help being caught in the storm—I suppose— but Ilse will only make matters worse. She is so indiscreet—haven't you *any* influence over her, Emily?"

"I didn't come here to discuss that," said Emily, bluntly. "I came to show you something I found in the old John house."

She held out the leaf of the scrapbook. Evelyn looked at it blankly for a moment. Then her face turned a curious mottled purple. She made an involuntary movement as if to snatch the paper, but Emily quickly drew it back. Their eyes met. In that moment Emily felt that the score between them was at last even.

She waited for Evelyn to speak. After a moment Evelyn did speak—sullenly:

"Well, what are you going to do about it?"

"I haven't decided yet," said Emily.

Evelyn's long, brown, treacherous eyes swept up to Emily's face with a crafty, seeking expression.

"I suppose you mean to take it to Dr. Hardy and disgrace me before the school?"

"Well, you deserve it, don't you?" said Emily, judicially.

"I—I wanted to win that prize because Father promised me a trip to Vancouver next summer if I won it," muttered Evelyn, suddenly crumpling. "I—I was crazy to go. Oh, *don't* betray me, Emily—Father will be furious. I—I'll give you the Parkman set—I'll do anything— only don't——"

Evelyn began to cry. Emily didn't like the sight.

"I don't want your Parkman," she said, contemptuously. "But there is one thing you must do. You will confess to Aunt Ruth that it was you who drew that moustache on my face the day of the English exam and not Ilse."

Evelyn wiped away her tears and swallowed something.

"That was only a joke," she sobbed.

"It was no joke to lie about it," said Emily, sternly.

"You're so—so—*blunt*." Evelyn looked for a dry spot on her handkerchief and found one. "It was all a joke. I just ran back from the Shoppe to do it. I thought, of course, you'd look in the glass when you got up. I d-didn't suppose you'd g-go to class like that. And I didn't know your Aunt took it so seriously. Of course— I'll tell her—if you'll—if you'll——"

"Write it out and sign it," said Emily, remorselessly.

Evelyn wrote it out and signed it.

"You'll give me—*that*," she pleaded, with an entreating gesture towards the scrapbook leaf.

"Oh, no, I'll keep this," said Emily.

"And what assurance have I that you won't tell— some day—after all?" sniffed Evelyn.

"You have the word of a Starr," said Emily, loftily.

She went out with a smile. She had finally conquered in the long duel. And she held in her hand what would finally clear Ilse in Aunt Ruth's eyes.

Aunt Ruth sniffed a good deal over Evelyn's note and was inclined to ask questions as to how it had been extorted. But not getting much satisfaction out of Emily on this score and knowing that Allan Burnley had been sore at her ever since her banishment of his daughter, she secretly welcomed an excuse to recall it.

"Very well, then. I told you Ilse could come here when you could prove to my satisfaction that she had not played that trick on you. You have proved it, and I keep my word. I am a just woman," concluded Aunt Ruth—who was, perhaps, the most unjust woman on the earth at that time.

So far, well. But if Evelyn wanted revenge she tasted it to the full in the next three weeks, without raising a finger or wagging a tongue to secure it. All Shrewsbury burned with gossip about the night of the storm—insinuations, distortions, wholesale fabrications. Emily was so snubbed at Janet Thompson's afternoon tea that she went home white with humiliation. Ilse was furious.

"I wouldn't mind if I *had* been rip-roaring drunk and had the fun of it," she vowed with a stamp of her foot. "But I wasn't drunk enough to be happy—only just drunk enough to be silly. There are moments, Emily, when I feel that I could have a gorgeous time if I were a cat and these old Shrewsbury dames were mice. But let's keep our smiles pinned on. I really don't care a snap for them. This will soon die out. We'll fight."

"You can't fight insinuations," said Emily, bitterly.

Ilse did not care—but Emily cared horribly. The Murray pride smarted unbearably. And it smarted worse and worse as time went on. A sneer at the night of the storm was published in a rag of a paper that was printed in a town on the mainland and made up of "spicy" notes sent to it from all over the Maritimes. nobody ever confessed to reading it, but almost everybody knew everything that was in it—except Aunt Ruth, who wouldn't have handled the sheet with the tongs. No names were mentioned, but every one knew who was referred to, and the venomous innuendo of the thing was unmistakable. Emily thought she would die of shame. And the worst sting was that it was so vulgar and ugly—and had made that beautiful night of laughter and revelation and rapturous creation in the old John house vulgar and ugly. She had thought it would always be one of her most beautiful memories. And now this!

Teddy and Perry saw red and wanted to kill somebody, but whom could they kill? As Emily told them, anything they said or did would only make the matter worse. It was bad enough after the publication of that paragraph. Emily was not invited to Florence Black's dance the next week—the great social event of the winter. She was left out of Hattie Denoon's skating party. Several of the Shrewsbury matrons did not see her when they met her on the streets. Others set her a thousand miles away by bland, icy politeness. Some young men about town grew oddly familiar in look and manner. One of them, with whom she was totally unacquainted, spoke to her one evening in the Post Office. Emily turned and looked at him. Crushed, humiliated as she was, she was still Archibald Murray's granddaughter. The wretched youth was three blocks away from the Post Office before he came to himself and knew where he was. To this day he has not forgotten how Emily Byrd Starr's eyes looked when she was angry.

But even the Murray look, while it might demolish a concrete offender, could not scotch scandalous stories. Everybody, she felt morbidly, believed them. It was reported to her that Miss Percy of the library said she had always distrusted Emily Starr's smile—she had always felt sure it was deliberately provocative and alluring. Emily felt that she, like poor King Henry, would never smile again. People remembered that old Nancy Priest had been a wild thing seventy years ago—and hadn't there been some scandal about Mrs. Dutton herself in her girlhood? What's bred in the bone, you understand. Her mother had eloped, hadn't she? And Ilse's mother? Of course, she had been killed by falling into the old Lee well, but who knew what she would have done if she hadn't? Then there was that old story of bathing on Blair Water sandshore *au naturel.* In short, you didn't see ankles like Emily's on proper girls. They simply didn't have them.

Even harmless, unnecessary Andrew had ceased to call on Friday nights. There *was* a sting in this. Emily thought Andrew a bore and dreaded his Friday nights. She had always meant to send him packing as soon as he gave her an opportunity. But for Andrew to go packing of his own accord had a very different flavour, mark you. Emily clenched her hands when she thought of it.

A bitter report came to her ears that Principal Hardy had said she ought to resign from the presidency of the Senior Class. Emily threw up her head. Resign? Confess defeat and admit guilt? Not she!

"I could knock that man's block off," said Ilse. "Emily Starr, don't let yourself worry over this. What does it matter what a lot of doddering old donkeys think? I hereby devote them to the infernal gods. They'll have their maws full of something else in a month and they'll forget this."

"*I*'ll never forget it," said Emily, passionately. "To my dying day I'll remember the humiliation of these weeks. And now—Ilse, Mrs. Tolliver has written asking me to give up my stall at the St. John's bazaar."

"Emily Starr—she hasn't!"

"She has. Oh, of course, she cloaks it under an excuse that she'd like a stall for her cousin from New York, who is visiting her—but *I* understand. And it's 'Dear Miss Starr'—look you—when it was 'Dearest Emily' a few weeks ago. Everybody in St. John's will know why I've been asked to step out. And she almost went to her knees to Aunt Ruth to let me take the stall. Aunt Ruth didn't want to let me."

"What will your Aunt Ruth say about this?"

"Oh, that's the worst of it, Ilse. She'll have to know now. She's never heard a word of this since she's been laid up with her sciatica. I've lived in dread of her finding out—for I know it will be hideous when she does. She's getting about now, so of course she'd soon hear it, anyway. And I haven't the spirit to stand up to her, Ilse. Oh, it all seems like a nightmare."

"They've got such mean, narrow, malicious, beastly little minds in this town," said Ilse—and was straightway comforted. But Emily could not ease her tortured spirit by a choice assortment of adjectives. Neither could she write out her misery and so rid herself of it. There were no more jottings in her Jimmy-book, no further entries in her journal, no new stories or poems. The flash never came now—never would come again. There would never again be wonderful little secret raptures of insight and creation which no one could share. Life had grown thin and poor, tarnished and unlovely. There was no beauty in anything—not even in the golden-white March solitudes of New Moon, when she went home for the weekend. She had longed to go home, where no one believed ill of her. No one at New Moon had heard anything of what was being whispered in Shrewsbury. But their very ignorance tortured Emily. Soon they *would* know; they would be hurt and grieved over the fact that a Murray, even an innocent Murray, had become a target for scandal. And who knew how they would regard Ilse's mishap with Malcolm's Scotch? Emily felt it almost a relief to go back to Shrewsbury.

She imagined slurs in everything Principal Hardy said—covert insults in every remark or look of her schoolmates. Only Evelyn Blake posed as friend and defender, and this was the most unkindest cut of all. Whether alarm or malice was behind Evelyn's pose, Emily did not know—but she did know that Evelyn's parade of friendship and loyalty and staunch belief in the face of overwhelming evidence, was something that seemed to smirch her more than all the gossip could. Evelyn went about assuring every one that *she* wouldn't believe one word against "poor dear Emily." Poor dear Emily could have cheerfully watched her drown—or thought she could.

Meanwhile, Aunt Ruth, who had been confined to her house for several weeks with sciatica and had been so crusty with it that neither friends nor enemies had dared to hint anything to her of the gossip concerning her niece, was beginning to take notice. Her sciatica had departed and left her faculties free to concentrate on other things. She recalled that Emily's appetite had been poor for days and Aunt Ruth suspected that she had not been sleeping. The moment this suspicion occurred to Aunt Ruth she took action. Secret worries were not to be tolerated in her house.

"Emily, I want to know what is the matter with you," she demanded, one Saturday afternoon when Emily, pale and listless, with purple smudges under her eyes, had eaten next to nothing for dinner.

A little colour came into Emily's face. The hour she had dreaded so was upon her. Aunt Ruth must be told all. And Emily felt miserably that she had neither the courage to endure the resultant heckling nor the spirit to hold her own against Aunt Ruth's whys and wherefores. She knew so well how it would all be: horror over the John house episode—as if anybody could have helped it: annoyance over the gossip—as if Emily were responsible for it: several assurances that she had always expected something like this: and then intolerable weeks of reminders and slurs. Emily felt a sort of mental nausea at the whole prospect. For a minute she could not speak.

"What have you been doing?" persisted Aunt Ruth.

Emily set her teeth. It was unendurable, but it must be endured. The story had to be told—the only thing to do was to get it told as soon as possible.

"I haven't done anything wrong, Aunt Ruth. I've just done something that has been misunderstood."

Aunt Ruth sniffed. But she listened without interruption to Emily's story. Emily told it as briefly as possible, feeling as if she were a criminal in the witness box with Aunt Ruth as judge, jury, and prosecuting attorney all in one. When she had finished she sat in silence waiting for some characteristic Aunt Ruthian comment.

"And what are they making all the fuss about?" said Aunt Ruth.

Emily didn't know exactly what to say. She stared at Aunt Ruth.

"They—they're thinking—and saying all sorts of horrible things," she faltered. "You see—down here in sheltered Shrewsbury they didn't realise what a storm it was. And then, of course, every one who repeated the story coloured it a little—we were *all* drunk by the time it filtered through Shrewsbury."

"What exasperates me," said Aunt Ruth, "is to think you told about it in Shrewsbury at all. Why on earth didn't you keep it all quiet?"

"That would have been *sly*." Emily's demon suddenly prompted her to say this. Now that the story was out she felt a rebound of spirit that was almost laughter.

"Sly! It would have been common sense," snorted Aunt Ruth. "But, of course, Ilse couldn't hold her tongue. I've often told you, Emily, that a fool friend is ten times more dangerous than an enemy. But what are you killing yourself worrying for? *Your* conscience is clear. This gossip will soon die out."

"Principal Hardy says I ought to resign from the presidency of the class," said Emily.

"Jim Hardy! Why, his Father was a hired boy to my Grandfather for years," said Aunt Ruth in tones of ineffable contempt. "Does Jim Hardy imagine that *my niece* would behave improperly?"

Emily felt herself all at sea. She thought she really must be dreaming. Was this incredible woman Aunt Ruth? It couldn't be Aunt Ruth. Emily was up against one of the contradictions of human nature. She was learning that you may fight with your kin—disapprove of them—even hate them, but that there is a bond between you for all that. Somehow, your very nerves and sinews are twisted with theirs. Blood is always thicker than water. Let an outsider attack—that's all. Aunt Ruth had at least one of the Murray virtues—loyalty to clan.

"Don't worry over Jim Hardy," said Aunt Ruth. "I'll soon settle him. I'll teach people to keep their tongues off the Murrays."

"But Mrs. Tolliver has asked me to let her cousin take my stall in the bazaar," said Emily. "You know what that means."

"I know that Polly Tolliver is an upstart and a fool," retorted Aunt Ruth. "Ever since Nat Tolliver married his stenographer, St. John's Church hasn't been the same place. Ten years ago she was a barefooted girl running round the back streets of Charlottetown. The cats themselves wouldn't have brought her in. Now she puts on the airs of a queen and tries to run the church. I'll soon clip *her* claws. She was pretty thankful a few weeks ago to have a Murray in her stall. It was a rise in the world for *her*. Polly Tolliver, forsooth. What is this world coming to?"

Aunt Ruth sailed upstairs, leaving a dazed Emily looking at vanishing bogies. Aunt Ruth came down again, ready for the warpath. She had taken out her crimps, put on her best bonnet, her best black silk, and her new sealskin coat. Thus arrayed she skimmed uptown to the Tolliver residence on the hill. She remained there half an hour closeted with Mrs. Nat Tolliver. Aunt Ruth was a short, fat, little woman, looking very dowdy and old-fashioned in spite of new bonnet and sealskin coat. Mrs. Nat was the last word in fashion and elegance, with her Paris gown, her lorgnette and her beautifully marcelled hair—marcels were just coming in then and Mrs. Nat's was the first in Shrewsbury. But the victory of the encounter did not perch on Mrs.

Tolliver's standard. Nobody knows just what was said at that notable interview. Certainly Mrs. Tolliver never told. But when Aunt Ruth left the big house Mrs. Tolliver was crushing her Paris gown and her marcel waves among the cushions of her davenport while she wept tears of rage and humiliation; and Aunt Ruth carried a note in her muff to Mrs. Tolliver's "Dear Emily," saying that her cousin was not going to take part in the bazaar and would "Dear Emily" be so kind as to take the stall as at first planned. Dr. Hardy was next interviewed, and again Aunt Ruth went, saw, conquered. The maid in the Hardy household heard and reported one sentence of the confab, though nobody ever believed that Aunt Ruth really said to stately, spectacled Dr. Hardy,

"I know you're a fool, Jim Hardy, but for heaven's sake pretend you're not for five minutes!"

No, the thing was impossible. Of course, the maid invented it.

"You won't have much more trouble, Emily," said Aunt Ruth on her return home. "Polly and Jim have got their craws full. When people see you at the bazaar they'll soon realise what way the wind blows and trim their sails accordingly. I've a few things to say to some other folks when opportunity offers. Matters have come to a pretty pass if decent boys and girls can't escape freezing to death without being slandered for it. Don't you give this thing another thought, Emily. Remember, you've got a family behind you."

Emily went to her glass when Aunt Ruth had gone downstairs. She tilted it at the proper angle and smiled at Emily-in-the-Glass—smiled slowly, provocatively, alluringly.

"I wonder where I put my Jimmy-book," thought Emily. "I must add a few more touches to my sketch of Aunt Ruth."

22
"Love Me, Love My Dog"

When Shrewsbury people discovered that Mrs. Dutton was backing her niece, the flame of gossip that had swept over the town died down in an incredibly short time. Mrs. Dutton gave more to the various funds of St. John's Church than any other member—it was a Murray tradition to support your church becomingly. Mrs. Dutton had lent money to half the business men in town—she held Nat Tolliver's note for an amount that kept him wakeful o' nights. Mrs. Dutton had a disconcerting knowledge of family skeletons—to which she had no delicacy in referring. Therefore, Mrs. Dutton was a person to be kept in good humour, and if people had made the mistake of supposing that because she was very strict with her niece, it was safe to snub that niece, why, the sooner they corrected that mistake the better for all concerned.

Emily sold baby jackets and blankets and bootees and bonnets in Mrs. Tolliver's stall at the big bazaar and wheedled elderly gentlemen into buying them, with her now famous smile: everybody was nice to her and she was happy again, though the experience had left a scar. Shrewsbury folks in after years said that Emily Starr had never really forgiven them for having talked about her—and added that the Murrays never did forgive, you know. But forgiveness did not enter into the matter. Emily had suffered so horribly that henceforth the sight of any one who had been connected with her suffering was hateful to her. When Mrs.

284

Tolliver asked her, a week later, to pour tea at the reception she was giving her cousin, Emily declined politely, without troubling herself to give any excuse. And something in the tilt of her chin, or in the level glance of her eyes, made Mrs. Tolliver feel to her marrow that she was still Polly Riordan of Riordan Alley, and would never be anybody else in the sight of a Murray of New Moon.

But Andrew was welcomed quite sweetly when he somewhat sheepishly called the following Friday night. It may be that he felt a little doubtful of his reception, in spite of the fact that he was sealed of the tribe. But Emily was markedly gracious to him. Perhaps she had her own reasons for it. Again, I call attention to the fact that I am Emily's biographer, not her apologist. If she took a way to get even with Andrew which I may not approve, what can I do but deplore it? For my own satisfaction, however, I may remark in passing that I do think Emily went too far when she told Andrew—after his report of some compliments his manager had paid him—that he was certainly a wonder. I cannot even excuse her by saying that she spoke in sarcastic tones. She did not: she said it most sweetly with an upward glance followed by a downward one that made even Andrew's well-regulated heart skip a beat. Oh, Emily, Emily!

Things went well with Emily that spring. She had several acceptances and checks, and was beginning to plume herself on being quite a literary person. Her clan began to take her scribbling mania somewhat seriously. Checks were unanswerable things.

"Emily has made fifty dollars by her pen since New Year's," Aunt Ruth told Mrs. Drury. "I begin to think the child has an easy way of making a living."

An easy way! Emily, overhearing this as she went through the hall, smiled and sighed. What did Aunt Ruth—what did any one know of the disappointments and failures of the climbers on Alpine Paths? What did she know of the despairs and agonies of one who *sees* but cannot *reach*. What did she know of the bitterness of one who conceives a wonderful tale and writes it down, only to find a flat and flavourless manuscript as a reward for all her toil? What did she know of barred doors and impregnable editorial sanctums? Of brutal rejection slips and the awfulness of faint praise? Of hopes deferred and hours of sickening doubt and self-distrust?

Aunt Ruth knew of none of these things, but she took to having fits of indignation when Emily's manuscripts were returned.

"Impudence *I* call it," she said. "Don't send that editor another line. Remember, you're a Murray!"

"I'm afraid he doesn't know that," said Emily, gravely.

"Then why don't you tell him?" said Aunt Ruth.

Shrewsbury had a mild sensation in May when Janet Royal came home from New York with her wonderful dresses, her brilliant reputation, and her chow dog. Janet was a Shrewsbury girl, but she had never been home since she had "gone to the States" twenty years ago. She was clever and ambitious and she had succeeded. She was the literary editor of a big metropolitan woman's magazine and one of the readers for a noted publishing house. Emily held her breath when she heard of Miss Royal's arrival. Oh, if she could only see her—have a talk with her—ask her about a hundred things she wanted to know! When Mr. Towers told her in an off-hand manner to go and interview Miss Royal and write it up for the *Times*, Emily trembled between terror and delight. Here was her excuse. But *could* she—had she assurance enough? Wouldn't Miss Royal think her unbearably presumptuous? How could *she* ask Miss Royal questions about her career and her opinion of the United States' foreign policy and reciprocity? She could never have the courage.

"We both worship at the same altar—but she is high

priestess and I am only the humblest acolyte," wrote Emily in her journal.

Then she indited a very worshipful letter to Miss Royal, and rewrote it a dozen times, asking permission to interview her. After she had mailed it she could not sleep all night because it occurred to her that she should have signed herself "yours truly" instead of "yours sincerely."

"Yours sincerely" smacked of an acquaintanceship that did not exist. Miss Royal would surely think her presuming.

But Miss Royal sent back a charming letter—Emily has it to this day.

> "Ashburn, Monday.
>
> "Dear Miss Starr:—
>
> "Of course you may come and see me and I'll tell you everything you want to know for Jimmy Towers (God rest his sowl, an' wasn't he my first beau!) and everything you want to know for yourself. I think half my reason for coming back to P.E.I. this spring was because I wanted to see the writer of *The Woman Who Spanked the King*. I read it last winter when it came out in *Roche's* and I thought it charming. Come and tell me all about yourself and your ambitions. You *are* ambitious, aren't you? And I think you're going to be able to realise your ambitions, too, and I want to help you if I can. You've got something I never had—real creative ability—but I've heaps of experience and what I've learned from it is yours for the asking. I *can* help you to avoid some snares and pitfalls, and I'm not without a bit of 'pull' in certain quarters. Come to Ashburn next Friday afternoon when 'school's out' and we'll have a heart-to-heart pow-pow.
>
> "Yours fraternally,
> "JANET ROYAL."

Emily thrilled to the ends of her toes when she read this letter. "Yours fraternally"—oh, heavenly! She knelt at her window and looked out with enraptured eyes into the slender firs of the Land of Uprightness and the dewy young clover fields beyond. Oh, was it possible that some day she would be a brilliant, successful woman like Miss Royal? That letter made it seem possible—made every wonderful dream seem possible. And on Friday—four more days—she was going to see and talk intimately with her high priestess.

Mrs. Angela Royal, who called to see Aunt Ruth that evening, didn't exactly seem to think Janet Royal a high priestess or a wonder. But then, of course, a prophetess is apt to have scant honour in her own country and Mrs. Royal had brought Janet up.

"I don't say but what she's got on well," she confided to Aunt Ruth. "She gets a big salary. But she's an old maid for all that. And as odd in some ways as Dick's hat-band."

Emily, studying Latin in the bay window, went on fire with indignation. This was nothing short of *lèse-majesté*.

"She is very fine looking yet," said Aunt Ruth. "Janet was always a nice girl."

"Oh, yes, she's nice enough. But I was always afraid she was too clever to get married, and I was right. And she's full of foreign notions. She's never on time for her meals—and it really makes me sick the fuss she makes over that dog of hers—Chu-Chin, she calls it. *He* rules the house. He does *exactly* as he likes and nobody dare say a word. My poor cat can't call her soul her own. Janet is so touchy about him. When I complained about him sleeping on the plush davenport she was so vexed she wouldn't speak for a day. That's a thing I don't like about Janet. She gets so high and mighty when she's offended. And she gets offended at things nobody else would dream of minding. And when she's offended with one she's offended with everybody. I hope nothing will upset her before you come on Friday, Emily. If she's out of humour she'll visit it on you. But I will say for her that she doesn't often get vexed and there's nothing mean or grudging about her. She'd work her fingers to the bone to serve a friend."

When Aunt Ruth had gone out to interview the grocer's boy, Mrs. Royal added hurriedly,

"She's greatly interested in you, Emily. She's always fond of having pretty, fresh girls about her—says it keeps her feeling young. She thinks your work shows real talent. If she takes a fancy to you it would be a great thing for you. But, for pity's sake, keep on good terms with that chow! If you offend *him*, Janet wouldn't have anything to do with you supposing you were Shakespeare himself."

Emily awoke Friday morning with the conviction that this was to be one of the crucial days of her life—a day of dazzling possibilities. She had had a terrible dream of sitting spellbound before Miss Royal, unable to utter one word except "Chu-Chin," which she repeated parrot-like whenever Miss Royal asked her a question.

It poured rain all the forenoon, much to her dismay, but at noon it cleared up brilliantly and the hills across the harbour scarfed themselves in fairy blue. Emily hurried home from school, pale with the solemnity of the occasion. Her toilet was an important rite. She must wear her new navy-blue silk—no question about that. It was positively long and made her look fully grown up. But how should she do her hair? The Psyche knot had more distinction, suited her profile, and showed to better advantage under her hat. Besides, perhaps a bare forehead made her look more intellectual. But Mrs. Royal had said that Miss Royal liked pretty girls. Pretty, therefore, she must be at all costs. The rich black hair was dressed low on her forehead and crowned by the new spring hat which Emily had dared to buy with her latest check, in spite of Aunt Elizabeth's disapproval and Aunt Ruth's unvarnished statement that a fool and her money were soon parted. But Emily was glad now that she had bought the hat. She *couldn't* have gone to interview Miss Royal in her plain black sailor. This hat was very becoming with its cascade of purple violets that fell from it over the lovely, unbroken waves of hair, just touching the milk-whiteness of her neck. Everything about her was exquisitely neat and dainty: she looked—I like the old phrase—as if she had just stepped from a band-box. Aunt Ruth, prowling about the hall, saw her coming downstairs and realised, with something of a shock, that Emily was a young woman.

"She carries herself like a Murray," thought Aunt Ruth.

The force of commendation could no further go, though it was really from the Starrs that Emily had inherited her slim elegance. The Murrays were stately and dignified, but stiff.

It was quite a little walk to Ashburn, which was a fine old white house set far back from the street amid great trees. Emily went up the gravel walk, edged with its fine-fringed shadows of spring, as a worshipper approaching a sacred fane. A fairly large, fluffy white dog was sitting half-way up the gravel walk. Emily looked at him curiously. She had never seen a chow dog. She decided that Chu-Chin was handsome, but not clean. He had evidently been having a glorious time in some mud puddle, for his paws and breast were reeking. Emily hoped he would approve of her, but keep his distance.

Evidently he approved of her, for he turned and trotted up the walk with her, amiably waving a plumy tail—or rather a tail that would have been plumy had it not been wet and muddy. He stood expectantly beside her while she rang the bell, and as soon as the door was opened he made a joyous bound on the lady who stood within, almost knocking her over.

Mrs. Royal herself had opened the door. She had, as

Emily saw at once, no beauty, but unmistakable distinction, from the crown of her gold-bronze hair to the toes of her satin slippers. She was arrayed in some marvellous dress of mauve velvet and she wore pince-nez with tortoise-shell rims, the first of their kind to be seen in Shrewsbury.

Chu-Chin gave one rapturous, slobbery wipe at her face with his tongue, then rushed on into Miss Royal's parlour. The beautiful mauve dress was spotted from collar to hem with muddy paw-marks. Emily thought that Chu-Chin fully deserved Mrs. Royal's bad opinion and mentally remarked that if he were *her* dog he should behave better. But Miss Royal did not reprove him in any way, and perhaps Emily's secret criticism was subconsciously prompted by her instant perception that Miss Royal's greeting, while perfectly courteous, was very cold. From her letter Emily had somehow expected a warmer reception.

"Won't you come in and sit down?" said Miss Royal. She ushered Emily in, waved to a comfortable chair, and sat down on a stiff and uncompromising Chippendale one. Somehow, Emily, sensitive at all times and abnormally so just now, felt that Miss Royal's selection of a chair was ominous. Why hadn't she sunk chummily into the depths of the big velvet morris? But there she sat, a stately, aloof figure, having apparently paid not the slightest attention to the appalling mud-stains on her beautiful dress. Chu-Chin had jumped on the big plush davenport, where he sat, cockily looking from one to the other as if enjoying the situation. It was all too evident that, as Mrs. Royal had foreboded, something had "upset" Miss Royal, and Emily's heart suddenly sank like lead.

"It's—a lovely day," she faltered. She knew it was an incredibly stupid thing to say, but she had to say something when Miss Royal wouldn't say anything. The silence was too awful.

"Very lovely," agreed Miss Royal, not looking at

Emily at all but at Chu-Chin, who was thumping a beautiful silk and lace cushion of Mrs. Royal's with his wet tail. Emily hated Chu-Chin. It was a relief to hate him, since as yet she did not dare to hate Miss Royal. But she wished herself a thousand miles away. Oh, if she only hadn't that little bundle of manuscripts on her lap! It was so evident what it was. She would never dare to show one of them to Miss Royal. Was this outraged empress the writer of that kind, friendly letter? It was impossible to believe it. This must be a nightmare. Her dream was "out" with a vengeance. She felt crude and bread-and-buttery and ignorant and dowdy—and young! Oh, so horribly young!

The moments passed—not so very many, perhaps, but seeming like hours to Emily. Her mouth was dry and parched, her brain paralysed. She couldn't think of a solitary thing to say. A horrible suspicion flashed across her mind that, since writing her letter, Miss Royal had heard the gossip about the night in the old John house and that her altered attitude was the result.

In her misery Emily squirmed in her chair and her little packet of manuscripts slipped to the floor. Emily stooped to retrieve it. At the same moment Chu-Chin made a flying leap from the davenport at it. His muddy paws caught the spray of violets hanging from Emily's hat and tore it loose. Emily let go of her packet and clutched her hat. Chu-Chin let go of the violets and pounced on the packet. Then, holding that in his mouth, he bolted out of the open glass door leading to the garden.

"Oh, what a relief it would be to tear my hair," thought Emily violently.

That diabolical chow had carried off her latest and best story and a number of choice poems. Heaven knew what he would do with them. She supposed she would never see them again. But, at least, there was fortunately now no question of showing them to Miss Royal.

Emily no longer cared whether Miss Royal was in a bad humour or not. She was no longer desirous of pleasing her—a woman who would let her dog behave like that to an invited guest and never reprove him! Nay, she even seemed to be amused at his antics. Emily was sure she had detected a fleeting smile on Miss Royal's arrogant face as she looked at the ruined violets scattered over the floor.

There suddenly popped into Emily's mind a story she had heard of Lofty John's father, who was in the habit of telling his wife,

"When people do be after snubbing you, Bridget, pull up your lip, Bridget, pull up your lip."

Emily pulled up her lip.

"A very playful dog," she said sarcastically.

"Very," agreed Miss Royal composedly.

"Don't you think a little discipline would improve him?" asked Emily.

"No, I do not think so," said Miss Royal meditatively.

Chu-Chin returned at this moment, capered about the room, knocked a small glass vase off a taboret with a whisk of his tail, sniffed at the ensuing fragments, then bounded up on the davenport again, where he sat panting. "Oh, what a good dog am I!"

Emily picked up her note-book and pencil.

"Mr. Towers sent me to interview you," she said.

"So I understand," said Miss Royal, never taking her eyes off her worshipped chow.

Emily: "May I trouble you to answer a few questions?"

Miss Royal, with exaggerated amiability: "Charmed."

(Chu-Chin, having saved enough breath, springs from the davenport and rushes through the half-opened folding doors of the dining-room.)

Emily, consulting note-book and recklessly asking the first question jotted down therein: "What do you think will be the result of the Presidential election this fall?"

Miss Royal: "I never think about it."

(Emily, with compressed lips, writes down in her

notebook: "She never thinks about it." Chu-Chin reappears, darts through parlour and out into the garden, carrying a roast chicken in his mouth.)

Miss Royal: "There goes my supper."

Emily, checking off first question: "Is there any likelihood that the United States Congress will look favourably on the recent reciprocity proposals of the Canadian Government?"

Miss Royal: "Is the Canadian Government making reciprocity proposals? I never heard of them."

(Emily writes, "She never heard of them." Miss Royal refits her pince-nez.)

Emily, thinks: "With a chin and a nose like that you'll look very witch-like when you grow old." *Says:* "Is it your opinion that the historical novel has had its day?"

Miss Royal languidly: "I always leave my opinions at home when I take a holiday."

(Emily writes, "She always leaves her opinions home when she takes a holiday," and wishes savagely she could write her own description of this interview, but knows Mr. Towers wouldn't print it. Then consoles herself by remembering that she has a virgin Jimmy-book at home and takes a wicked delight in thinking of the account that will be written in it that night. Chu-Chin enters. Emily wonders if he could have eaten the chicken in that short time. Chu-Chin, evidently feeling the need of some dessert, helps himself to one of Mrs. Royal's crocheted tidies, crawls under the piano with it and falls to chewing rapturously.)

Miss Royal, fervently: "*Dear* dog!"

Emily, suddenly inspired: "What do you think of chow dogs?"

Miss Royal: "The most adorable creatures in the world."

Emily, to herself: "So you've brought *one* opinion with you." *To Miss Royal:* "I do not admire them."

Miss Royal, with an icy smile: "It is evident that your taste in dogs must be quite different from mine."

Emily, to herself: "I wish Ilse were here to call you names for me."

(A large, motherly grey cat passes across the door-step outside. Chu-Chin bolts out from under the piano, shoots between the legs of a tall plant stand, and pursues the flying cat. The plant stand has gone over with a crash and Mrs. Royal's beautiful rex begonia lies in ruins on the floor, amid a heap of earth and broken pottery.)

Miss Royal, unsympathetically: "Poor Aunt Angela! Her heart will be broken."

Emily: "But that doesn't matter, does it?"

Miss Royal, gently: "Oh, no; not at all."

Emily, consulting note-book: "Do you find many changes in Shrewsbury?"

Miss Royal: "I find a good many changes in the people. The younger generation does not impress me favourably."

(Emily writes this down. Chu-Chin again reappears, evidently having chased the cat through a fresh mud puddle, and resumes his repast of the tidy, under the piano.)

Emily shut her note-book and rose. Not for any number of Mr. Towers would she prolong this inter-view. She looked like a young angel, but she was thinking terrible things. And she hated Miss Royal—oh, how she hated her!

"Thank you, that will be all," she said, with a haughtiness quite equal to Miss Royal's. "I'm sorry to have taken so much of your time. Good-afternoon."

She bowed slightly and went out to the hall. Miss Royal followed her to the parlour door.

"Hadn't you better take your dog, Miss Starr?" she asked sweetly.

Emily paused in the act of shutting the outer door and looked at Miss Royal.

"Pardon me."

"I said, hadn't you better take your dog?"

"My *dog*?"

"Yes. He hasn't quite finished the tidy, to be sure, but you might take it along. It won't be much good to Aunt Angela now."

"He—he—isn't *my* dog," gasped Emily.

"Not your dog? Whose dog is he then?" said Miss Royal.

"I—I thought he was yours—your chow," said Emily.

23
An Open Door

Miss Royal looked at Emily for a moment. Then she seized her wrist, shut the door, drew her back to the parlour, and firmly pushed her down into the morris chair. This done, Miss Royal threw herself on the muddy davenport and began to laugh—long and helplessly. Once or twice she rocked herself forward, gave Emily's knee two wild whacks, then rocked back and continued to laugh. Emily sat, smiling faintly. Her feelings had been too deeply harrowed to permit of Miss Royal's convulsions of mirth, but already there was glimmering in her mind a sketch for her Jimmy-book. Meanwhile, the white dog, having chewed the tidy to tatters, spied the cat again, and again rushed after her.

Finally Miss Royal sat erect and wiped her eyes.

"Oh, this is priceless, Emily Byrd Starr—priceless! When I'm eighty I'll recall this and howl over it. Who will write it up, you or I? But *who* does own that brute?"

"I'm sure I don't know," said Emily demurely. "I never saw him in my life before."

"Well, let's shut the door before he can return. And now, dear thing, sit here beside me—there's one clean spot here under the cushion. We're going to have our real talk now. Oh, I was so beastly to you when you were trying to ask me questions. I was *trying* to be beastly. Why didn't you throw something at me, you poor insulted darling?"

"I wanted to. But now I think you let me off very easily, considering the behaviour of my supposed dog."

Miss Royal went off in another convulsion.

"I don't know if I can forgive you for thinking that horrid curly white creature was my glorious red-gold chow. I'll take you up to my room before you go and you shall apologise to him. He's asleep on my bed. I locked him there to relieve dear Aunt Angela's mind about her cat. Chu-Chin wouldn't hurt the cat—he merely wants to play with her, and the foolish old thing runs. Now, you know, when a cat runs, a dog simply can't help chasing her. As Kipling tells us, he wouldn't be a proper dog if he didn't. If only that white fiend had confined himself to chasing the cat!"

"It is too bad about Mrs. Royal's begonia," said Emily, regretfully.

"Yes, that *is* a pity. Aunt Angela's had it for years. But I'll get her a new one. When I saw you coming up the walk with that dog frisking around you, of course I concluded he was yours. I had put on my favourite dress because it really makes me look almost beautiful— and I wanted you to love me; and when the beast muddied it all over and you never said a word of rebuke or apology, I simply went into one of my cold rages. I *do* go into them—I can't help it. It's one of my little faults. But I soon thaw out if now fresh aggrava- tion occurs. In this case fresh aggravation occurred every minute. I vowed to myself that if you did not even try to make your dog behave I would not suggest

that you should. And I suppose *you* were indignant
because I calmly let *my* dog spoil your violets and eat
your manuscripts?"

"I was."

"It's too bad about the manuscripts. Perhaps we can
find them—he can't really have swallowed them, but I
suppose he has chewed them to bits."

"It doesn't matter. I have other copies at home."

"And your questions! Emily, you were too delicious.
Did you really write down my answers?"

"Word for word. I meant to print them just so, too.
Mr. Towers had given me a list of questions for you,
but of course I didn't mean to fire them off point-blank
like that. I meant to weave them artfully into our
conversation as we went along. But here comes Mrs.
Royal."

Mrs. Royal came in, smiling. Her face changed as she
saw the begonia. But Miss Royal interposed quickly.

"Dearest Aunty, don't weep or faint—at least not
before you've told me who around here owns a white,
curly, utterly mannerless, devilish dog?"

"Lily Bates," said Mrs. Royal in a tone of despair.
"Oh, has she let that creature out again? I had a most
terrible time with him before you came. He's really just
a big puppy and he *can't* behave. I told her finally if I
caught him over here again I'd poison him. She's kept
him shut up since then. But now—oh, my lovely rex."

"Well, this dog came in with Emily. I supposed he
was her dog. Courtesy to a guest implies courtesy to
her dog—isn't there an old proverb that expresses it
more concisely? He embraced me fervently upon his
entrance, as my dearest dress testifies. He marked up
your davenport—he tore off Emily's violets—he chased
your cat—he overturned your begonia—he broke your
vase—he ran off with our chicken—ay, groan, Aunt
Angela, he did!—and yet I, determinedly composed
and courteous, said not a word of protest. I vow my

behaviour was worthy of New Moon itself—wasn't it, Emily?"

"You were just too mad to speak," said Mrs. Royal ruefully, fingering her wrecked begonia.

Miss Royal stole a sly glance at Emily.

"You see, I can't put anything over on Aunt Angela. She knows me too well. I admit I was not my usual charming self. But, Aunty darling, I'll get you a new vase and a new begonia—think of all the fun you'll have coaxing it along. Anticipation is always so much more interesting than realisation."

"*I'll* settle Lily Bates," said Mrs. Royal, going out of the room to look for a dustpan.

"Now, dear thing, let's gab," said Miss Royal, snuggling down beside Emily.

This was the Miss Royal of the letter. Emily found no difficulty in talking to *her*. They had a jolly hour and at the end of it Miss Royal made a proposition that took away Emily's breath.

"Emily, I want you to come back to New York with me in July. There's a vacancy on the staff of *The Ladies' Own*—no great thing in itself. You'll be sort of general handy man, and all odd jobs will be turned over to you—but you'll have a chance to work up. And you'll be in the centre of things. You can write—I realised that the moment I read *The Woman Who Spanked the King*. I know the editor of *Roche's* and I found out who you were and where you lived. That's really why I came down this spring—I wanted to get hold of you. You mustn't waste your life here—it would be a crime. Oh, of course, I know New Moon is a dear, quaint, lovely spot—full of poetry and steeped in romance. It was just the place for you to spend your childhood in. But you must have a chance to grow and develop and be yourself. You must have the stimulus of association with great minds—the training that only a great city can give. Come with me. If you do, I promise you that in ten years' time Emily Byrd Starr will be a name to conjure with among the magazines of America."

Emily sat in a maze of bewilderment, too confused and dazzled to think clearly. She had never dreamed of this. It was as if Miss Royal had suddenly put into her hand a key to unlock the door into the world of all her dreams, and hopes, and imaginings. Beyond that door was all she had ever hoped for of success and fame. And yet—and yet—what faint, odd, resentment stirred at the back of all her whirling sensations? Was there a sting in Miss Royal's calm assumption that if Emily did *not* go with her her name would forever remain unknown? Did the old dead-and-gone Murrays turn over in their graves at the whisper that one of their descendants could never succeed without the help and "pull" of a stranger? Or *had* Miss Royal's manner been a shade too patronising? Whatever it was it kept Emily from figuratively flinging herself at Miss Royal's feet.

"Oh, Miss Royal, that would be wonderful," she faltered. "I'd love to go—but I'm afraid Aunt Elizabeth will never consent. She'll say I'm too young."

"How old *are* you?"

"Seventeen."

"I was eighteen when I went. I didn't know a soul in New York—I had just enough money to keep me for three months. I was a crude, callow little thing—yet I won out. *You* shall live with me. I'll look after you as well as Aunt Elizabeth herself could do. Tell her I'll guard you like the apple of my eye. I have a dear, cozy, little flat where we'll be as happy as queens, with my adored and adorable Chu-Chin. You'll love Chu-Chin, Emily."

"I think I'd like a cat better," said Emily firmly.

"Cats! Oh, we couldn't have a cat in a flat. It wouldn't be amenable enough to discipline. You must sacrifice your pussies on the altar of your art. I'm sure you'll like living with me. I'm *very* kind and amiable, dearest, when I feel like it—and I generally do feel like it—and I never lose my temper. It freezes up occasionally, but, as I told you, it thaws quickly. I bear other people's misfortunes with equanimity. And I *never* tell any one she has a cold or that she looks tired. Oh, I'd really make an adorable housemate."

"I'm sure you would," said Emily, smiling.

"I never saw a young girl before that I wanted to live with," said Miss Royal. "You have a sort of luminous personality, Emily. You'll give off light in dull places and empurple drab spots. Now, *do* make up your mind to come with me."

"It is Aunt Elizabeth's mind that must be made up," said Emily ruefully. "If she says I can go I'll—"

Emily found herself stopping suddenly.

"Go," finished Miss Royal joyfully. "Aunt Elizabeth will come around. I'll go and have a talk with her. I'll go out to New Moon with you next Friday night. You *must* have your chance."

"I can't thank you enough, Miss Royal, so I won't try. But I must go now. I'll think this all over—I'm too dazzled just now to think at all. You don't know what this means to me."

"I think I do," said Miss Royal gently. "I was once a young girl in Shrewsbury, eating my heart out because I had no chance."

"But you made your own chance—and won out," said Emily wistfully.

"Yes—but I had to go away to do it. I could never have got anywhere here. And it was a horribly hard climb at first. It took my youth. I want to save you some of the hardships and discouragements. You will go far beyond what I have done—you can create—I can only build with the materials others have made. But we builders have our place—we can make temples for our gods and goddesses if nothing else. Come with me, dear Girl Emily, and I will do all I can to help you in every way."

"Thank you—thank you," was all Emily could say.

Tears of gratitude for this offer of ungrudging help and
sympathy were in her eyes. She had not received too
much of sympathy or encouragement in her life. It
touched her deeply. She went away feeling that she
must turn the key and open the magic door beyond
which now seemed to lie all the beauty and allurement
of life—if only Aunt Elizabeth would let her.

"I can't do it if she doesn't approve," decided Emily.

Half-way home she suddenly stopped and laughed.
After all, Miss Royal had forgotten to show her Chu-
Chin.

"But it doesn't matter," she thought, "because in the
first place I can't believe that, after this, I'll ever feel any
real interest in chow dogs. And in the second place I'll see
him often enough if I go to New York with Miss Royal."

24
A Valley of Vision

Would she go to New York with Miss Royal? That
was the question Emily had now to answer. Or
rather, the question Aunt Elizabeth must answer. For
on Aunt Elizabeth's answer, as Emily felt, everything
depended. And she had no real hope that Aunt Elizabeth
would let her go. Emily might look longingly towards
those pleasant, far-off, green pastures pictured by Miss
Royal, but she was quite sure she could never browse
in them. The Murray pride—and prejudice—would be
an impassable barrier.

Emily said nothing to Aunt Ruth about Miss Royal's
offer. It was Aunt Elizabeth's due to hear it first. She
kept her dazzling secret until the next week-end, when

Miss Royal came to New Moon, very gracious and pleasant, and the wee-est bit patronising, to ask Aunt Elizabeth to let Emily go with her.

Aunt Elizabeth listened in silence—a disapproving silence, as Emily felt.

"The Murray women have never had to work out for their living," she said coldly.

"It isn't exactly what you would call 'working out,' dear Miss Murray," said Miss Royal, with the courteous patience one must use to a lady whose viewpoint was that of an outlived generation. "Thousands of women are going into business and professional life, everywhere."

"I suppose it's all right for them if they don't get married," said Aunt Elizabeth.

Miss Royal flushed slightly. She knew that in Blair Water and Shrewsbury she was regarded as an old maid, and therefore a failure, no matter what her income and her standing might be in New York. But she kept her temper and tried another line of attack.

"Emily has an unusual gift for writing," she said. "I think she can do something really worth while if she gets a chance. She ought to have her chance, Miss Murray. You know there isn't any chance for that kind of work here."

"Emily has made ninety dollars this past year with her pen," said Aunt Elizabeth.

"Heaven grant me patience!" thought Miss Royal. Said Miss Royal,

"Yes, and ten years from now she may be making a few hundreds; whereas, if she comes with me, in ten years' time her income would probably be as many thousands."

"I'll have to think it over," said Aunt Elizabeth.

Emily felt surprised that Aunt Elizabeth had even consented to think it over. She had expected absolute refusal.

"She'll come round to it," whispered Miss Royal, when she went away. "I'm going to get you, darling Emily B. I know the Murrays of old. They always had an eye to the main chance. Aunty will let you come."

"I'm afraid not," said Emily ruefully.

When Miss Royal had gone Aunt Elizabeth looked at Emily.

"Would you like to go, Emily?"

"Yes—I think so—if you don't mind," faltered Emily. She was very pale—she did not plead or coax. But she had no hope—none.

Aunt Elizabeth took a week to think it over. She called in Ruth and Wallace and Oliver to help her. Ruth said dubiously,

"I suppose we ought to let her go. It's a splendid chance for her. It's not as if she were going alone—I'd never agree to that. Janet will look after her."

"She's too young—she's too young," said Uncle Oliver.

"It seems a good chance for her—Janet Royal has done well, they say," said Uncle Wallace.

Aunt Elizabeth even wrote to Great-aunt Nancy. The answer came back in Aunt Nancy's quavering hand:

"Suppose you let Emily decide for herself," suggested Aunt Nancy.

Aunt Elizabeth folded up Aunt Nancy's letter and called Emily into the parlour.

"If you wish to go with Miss Royal you may," she said. "I feel it would not be right for me to hinder you. We shall miss you—we would rather have you with us for a few years yet. I know nothing about New York. I am told it is a wicked city. But you have been brought up carefully. I leave the decision in your own hands. Laura, what are you crying about?"

Emily felt as if she wanted to cry herself. To her amazement she felt something that was *not* delight or pleasure. It was one thing to long after forbidden pastures. It seemed to be quite another thing when the bars were flung down and you were told to enter if you would.

Emily did not immediately rush to her room and write a joyous letter to Miss Royal—who was visiting friends in Charlottetown. Instead she went out into the garden and thought very hard—all that afternoon and all Sunday. During the week in Shrewsbury she was quiet and thoughtful, conscious that Aunt Ruth was watching her closely. For some reason Aunt Ruth did not discuss the matter with her. Perhaps she was thinking of Andrew. Or perhaps it was an understood thing among the Murrays that Emily's decision was to be entirely uninfluenced.

Emily couldn't understand why she didn't write Miss Royal at once. Of course she would go. Wouldn't it be terribly foolish not to? She would never have such a chance again. It *was* such a splendid chance—everything made easy—the Alpine Path no more than a smooth and gentle slope—success certain and brilliant and quick. Why, then, did she have to keep telling herself all this—why was she driven to seek Mr. Carpenter's advice the next week-end? And Mr. Carpenter would not help her much. He was rheumatic and cranky.

"Don't tell me the cats have been hunting again," he groaned.

"No. I haven't any manuscripts this time," said Emily, with a faint smile. "I've come for advice of a different kind."

She told him of her perplexity.

"It's such a splendid chance," she concluded.

"Of course it's a splendid chance—to go and be Yankeefied," grunted Mr. Carpenter.

"I wouldn't get Yankeefied," said Emily resentfully. "Miss Royal has been twenty years in New York and she isn't Yankeefied."

"Isn't she? I don't mean by Yankeefied what you think I do," retorted Mr. Carpenter. "I'm not referring to the silly girls who go up to 'the States' to work and come back in six months with an accent that would raise blisters on your skin. Janet Royal *is* Yankeefied—her outlook and atmosphere and style are all U.S. And I'm not condemning them—they're all right. But—she isn't a Canadian any longer—and that's what I wanted you to be—pure Canadian through and through, doing something as far as in you lay for the literature of your own country, keeping your Canadian tang and flavour. But of course there's not many dollars in that sort of thing yet."

"There's no chance to do *anything* here," argued Emily.

"No—no more than there was in Haworth Parsonage," growled Mr. Carpenter.

"I'm not a Charlotte Brontë," protested Emily. "She had genius—it can stand alone. I have only talent—it needs help—and—and—guidance."

"In short, pull," said Mr. Carpenter.

"So you think I oughtn't to go," said Emily anxiously.

"Go if you want to. To be quickly famous we must all stoop a little. Oh, go—go—I'm telling you. I'm too old to argue—go in peace. You'd be a fool not to—only fools do sometimes attain. There's a special Providence for them, no doubt."

Emily went away from the little house in the hollow with her eyes rather black. She met Old Kelly on her way up the hill and he pulled his plump nag and red chariot to a standstill and beckoned to her.

"Gurrl dear, here's some peppermints for you. And now, ain't it high time—eh—now, you know—" Old Kelly winked at her.

"Oh, I'm going to be an old maid, Mr. Kelly," smiled Emily.

Old Kelly shook his head as he gathered up his reins.

"Shure an' nothing like that will ever be happening to you. You're one av the folks God really loves—only don't be taking one av the Prastes now—never one av the Prastes, gurrl dear."

"Mr. Kelly," said Emily suddenly. "I've been offered a splendid chance—to go to New York and take a place on the staff of a magazine. I can't make up my mind. What do you think I'd better do?"

As she spoke she thought of the horror of Aunt Elizabeth at the idea of a Murray asking Old Jock

Kelly's advice. She herself was a little ashamed of doing it.

Old Kelly shook his head again.

"What do the b'ys around here be thinking av? But what does the ould lady say?"

"Aunt Elizabeth says I can do as I like."

"Then I guess we'll be laving it at that," said Old Kelly—and drove off without another word. Plainly there was no help to be had in Old Kelly.

"Why should I want help?" thought Emily desperately. "What has got into me that I can't make up my own mind? Why can't I *say* I'll go? It doesn't seem to me now that I *want* to go—I only feel I *ought* to want to go."

She wished that Dean were home. But Dean had not got back from his winter in Los Angeles. And somehow she could not talk the matter over with Teddy. Nothing had come of that wonderful moment in the old John house—nothing except a certain constraint that had almost spoiled their old comradeship. Outwardly they were as good friends as ever; but something was gone—and nothing seemed to be taking its place. She would not admit to herself that she was afraid to ask Teddy. Suppose he told her to go? That would hurt unbearably—because it would show that he didn't care whether she went or stayed. But Emily would not glance at this at all.

"Of course I'll go," she said aloud to herself. Perhaps the spoken word would settle things. "What would I do next year if I didn't? Aunt Elizabeth will certainly never let me go anywhere else alone. Ilse will be away—and Perry—Teddy too, likely. He says he's bound to go and do something to earn money for his art study. I *must* go."

She said it fiercely as if arguing against some invisible opponent. When she reached home in the twilight, no one was there and she went restlessly all over the house. What charm and dignity and fineness the old rooms had, with their candles and their ladder-backed chairs and their braided rugs! How dear and entreating was her own little room with its diamond paper and its guardian angel, its fat black rose-jar and its funny, kinky window pane! Would Miss Royal's flat be half so wonderful?

"Of course I'll go," she said again—feeling that if she could only have left off the "of course" the thing *would* have been settled.

She went out into the garden, lying in the remote, passionless beauty of early spring moonlight, and walked up and down its paths. From afar came the whistle of the Shrewsbury train—like a call from the alluring world beyond—a world full of interest, charm, drama. She paused by the old lichened sun-dial and traced the motto on its border, "So goes Time by." Time did go by—swiftly, mercilessly, even at New Moon, unspoiled as it was by any haste or rush of modernity. Should she not take the current when it offered? The white June lilies waved in the faint breeze—she could almost see her old friend the Wind Woman bending over them to tilt their waxen chins. Would the Wind Woman come to her in the crowded city streets? Could she be like Kipling's cat there?

"And I wonder if I'll ever have the flash in New York," she thought wistfully.

How beautiful was this old garden which Cousin Jimmy loved! How beautiful was old New Moon farm! Its beauty had a subtly romantic quality all its own. There was enchantment in the curve of the dark-red, dew-wet road beyond—remote, spiritual allurement in the Three Princesses—magic in the orchard—a hint of intriguing devilment in the fir wood. How could she leave this old house that had sheltered and loved her—never tell me houses do not love!—the graves of her kin by the Blair Water pond, the wide fields and haunted woods where her childhood dreams had been dreamed? All at once she knew she could not leave them—she knew she had never really wanted to leave them. *That* was why she had gone about desperately asking advice of impossible outsiders. She had really been hoping they would tell her not to go. That was why she had wished so wildly that Dean were home—he would certainly have told her not to go.

"I belong to New Moon—I stay among my own people," she said.

There was no doubt about this decision—she did not want any one to help her to it. A deep, inner contentment possessed her as she went up the walk and into the old house which no longer looked reproachfully at her. She found Elizabeth and Laura and Cousin Jimmy in the kitchen full of its candle magic.

"I am not going to New York, Aunt Elizabeth," she said. "I am going to stay here at New Moon with you."

Aunt Laura gave a little cry of joy. Cousin Jimmy said, "Hurrah!" Aunt Elizabeth knitted a round of her stocking before she said anything. Then——

"I thought a Murray would," she said.

Emily went straight to Ashburn Monday evening. Miss Royal had returned and greeted her warmly.

"I hope you've come to tell me that Miss Murray has decided to be reasonable and let you come with me, honeysweet."

"She told me I could decide for myself."

Miss Royal clapped her hands.

"Oh, goody, goody! Then it's all settled."

Emily was pale, but her eyes were black with earnestness and intense feeling.

"Yes, it's settled—I'm not going," she said. "I thank you with all my heart, Miss Royal, but I can't go."

Miss Royal stared at her—realised in a moment that it was not the slightest use to plead or argue—but began to plead and argue all the same.

"Emily—you can't mean it? Why can't you come?"

"I can't leave New Moon—I love it too much—it means too much to me."

"I thought you wanted to come with me, Emily," said Miss Royal reproachfully.

"I did. And part of me wants to yet. But away down under that another part of me will not go. Don't think me foolish and ungrateful, Miss Royal."

"Of course I don't think you're ungrateful," said Miss Royal, helplessly, "but I do—yes, I do think you are awfully foolish. You are simply throwing away your chances of a career. What can you ever do here that is worth while, child? You've no idea of the difficulties in your path. You can't get material here—there's no atmosphere—no——"

"I'll create my own atmosphere," said Emily, with a trifle of spirit. After all, she thought, Miss Royal's viewpoint was just the same as Mrs. Alec Sawyer's, and her manner *was* patronising. "And as for material—people *live* here just the same as anywhere else—suffer and enjoy and sin and aspire just as they do in New York."

"You don't know a thing about it," said Miss Royal, rather pettishly. "You'll never be able to write anything really worth while here—no big thing. There's no inspiration—you'll be hampered in every way—the big editors won't look farther than the address of P.E. Island on your manuscript. Emily, you're committing literary suicide. You'll realise that at three of the clock some white night, Emily B. Oh, I suppose, after some years you'll work up a clientele of Sunday School and agricultural papers. But will that satisfy you? You know it won't. And then the petty jealousy of these small prunes-and prisms places—if you do anything the people you went to school with can't do, some of them will never forgive you. And they'll all think you're the heroine of your own stories—especially if you portray her beautiful and charming. If you write a love story they'll be sure it's your own. You'll get so tired of Blair Water—you'll know all the people in it—what they are and can be—it'll be like reading a book for the twentieth time. Oh, I know all about it. 'I was alive before you were borned,' as I said when I was eight, to a playmate of six. You'll get discouraged—the hour of three o'clock will gradually overwhelm you—there's a three o'clock every night, remember—you'll give up—you'll marry that cousin of yours——"

"Never."

"Well, some one like him, then, and 'settle down' ——"

"No, I'll never 'settle down,'" said Emily decidedly. "Never as long as I live—what a stodgy condition!"

—"and you'll have a parlour like this of Aunt Angela's," continued Miss Royal relentlessly. "A mantelpiece crowded with photographs—an easel with an 'enlarged' picture in a frame eight inches wide—a red plush album with a crocheted doily on it, a crazy-quilt on your spare-room bed—a hand-painted banner in your hall—and, as a final touch of elegance, an asparagus fern will 'grace the centre of your dining-room table.'"

"No," said Emily gravely, "such things are not among the Murray traditions."

"Well, the spiritual equivalent of them, then. Oh, I can see your whole life, Emily, here in a place like this where people can't see a mile beyond their nose."

"I can see farther than that," said Emily, putting up her chin. "I can see to the stars."

"I was speaking figuratively, my dear."

"So was I. Oh, Miss Royal, I know life is rather cramped here in some ways—but the sky is as much mine as anybody's. I may not succeed here—but, if not, I wouldn't succeed in New York either. Some fountain of living water would dry up in my soul if I left the land I love. I know I'll have difficulties and discouragements here, but people have overcome far worse. You know that story you told me about Parkman—that for years he was unable to write for more than five minutes at a time—that he took three years to write one of his books—six lines per day for three years. I shall always remember that when I get discouraged. It will help me through any number of white nights."

"Well"—Miss Royal threw out her hands—"I give up. I think you're making a terrible mistake, Emily—but if in the years to come I find out I'm wrong I'll write and admit it. And if *you* find out you were wrong write me and admit it, and you'll find me as ready to help you as ever. I won't even say 'I told you so.' Send me any of your stories my magazine is fit for, and ask me for any advice I can give. I'm going right back to New York tomorrow. I was only going to wait till July to take you with me. Since you won't come I'm off. I detest living in a place where all they think is that I've played my cards badly, and lost the matrimonial game—where all the young girls—except *you*—are so abominably respectful to me—and where the old folks keep telling me I look so much like my mother. Mother was *ugly*. Let's say good-bye and make it snappy."

"Miss Royal," said Emily earnestly, "you do believe—don't you—that I appreciate your kindness? Your sympathy and encouragement have meant more to me—always will mean more to me than you can ever dream."

Miss Royal whisked her handkerchief furtively across her eyes and made an elaborate curtsey.

"Thank you for them kind words, lady," she said solemnly.

Then she laughed a little, put her hands on Emily's shoulders and kissed her cheek.

"All the good wishes ever thought, said, or written go with you," she said. "And I think it would be—nice—if any place would ever mean to me what it is evident New Moon means to you."

At three o'clock that night a wakeful but contented Emily remembered that she had never seen Chu-Chin.

25
April Love

"June 10, 19—

*"Y*esterday evening Andrew Oliver Murray asked Emily Byrd Starr to marry him.

"The said Emily Byrd Starr told him she wouldn't.

"I'm glad it's over. I've felt it coming for some time. Every evening Andrew has been here I've felt that he was trying to bring the conversation around to some serious subject, but I have never felt quite equal to the interview, and always contrived to sidetrack him with frivolity.

"Yesterday evening I went to the Land of Uprightness for one of the last rambles I shall have in it. I climbed the hill of firs and looked down over the fields of mist and silver in the moonlight. The shadows of the ferns and sweet wild grasses along the edge of the woods were like a dance of sprites. Away beyond the harbour, below the moonlight, was a sky of purple and amber where a sunset had been. But behind me was darkness— a darkness which, with its tang of fir balsam, was like a perfumed chamber where one might dream dreams and see visions. Always when I go into the Land of Uprightness I leave behind the realm of daylight and things known and go into the realm of shadow and mystery and enchantment where anything might happen—anything might come true. I can *believe* anything there—old myths—legends—dryads—fauns— leprechauns. One of my wonder moments came to me—it seemed to me that I got out of my body and was *free*—I'm sure I heard an echo of that 'random word' of the gods—and I wanted some unused language to express what I saw and felt.

"Enter Andrew, spic and span, prim and gentlemanly.

"Fauns—fairies—wonder moments—random words— fled pell-mell. No new language was needed now.

"'What a pity side-whiskers went out with the last generation—they would suit him so,' I said to myself in good plain English.

"I knew Andrew had come to say something special. Otherwise he would not have followed me into the Land of Uprightness, but have waited decorously in Aunt Ruth's parlour. I knew it had to come and I made up my mind to get it over and have done with it. The expectant attitude of Aunt Ruth and the New Moon folks has been oppressive lately. I believe they all feel quite sure that the real reason I wouldn't go to New York was that I couldn't bear to part with Andrew!

"But I was *not* going to have Andrew propose to me by moonlight in the Land of Uprightness. I might have been bewitched into accepting him. So when he said, 'It's nice here, let's stay here for a while—after all, I think there is nothing so pretty as nature,' I said gently but firmly that, though nature must feel highly flattered, it was too damp for a person with a tendency to consumption, and I must go in.

"In we went. I sat down opposite Andrew and stared at a bit of Aunt Ruth's crochet yarn on the carpet. I shall remember the colour and shape of that yarn to my dying day. Andrew talked jerkily about indifferent things and then began throwing out hints— he would get his managership in two years more—he believed in people marrying young—and so on. He floundered badly. I suppoe I could have made it easier for him but I hardened my heart, remembering how he had kept away in those dreadful weeks of the John house scandal. At last he blurted out,

" 'Emily, let's get married when—when—as soon as I'm able to.'

"He seemed to feel that he ought to say something more but didn't know just what—so he repeated 'just as soon as I'm able to' and stopped.

"I don't believe I even went through the motions of a blush.

" 'Why should we get married?' I said.

"Andrew looked aghast. Evidently this was not the Murray tradition of receiving a proposal.

" 'Why? Why? Because—I'd like it,' he stammered.

" '*I* wouldn't,' I said.

"Andrew stared at me for a few moments trying to take in the amazing idea that he was being refused.

" 'But *why*?' he asked—exactly in Aunt Ruth's tone and manner.

" 'Because I don't love you,' I said.

"Andrew *did* blush. I know he thought I was immodest.

" 'I—I—think—they'd all like it,' he stammered.

" '*I* wouldn't,' I said again. I said it in a tone even Andrew couldn't mistake.

"He was so surprised I don't think he felt anything *but* surprise—not even disappointment. He didn't know what to do or say—a *Murray* couldn't coax—so he got up and went out without another word. I thought he banged the door but afterwards I discovered it was only the wind. I wish he *had* banged the door. It would have saved my self-respect. It is mortifying to refuse a man and then discover that his main feeling is bewilderment.

"Next morning Aunt Ruth, evidently suspecting something amiss from the brevity of Andrew's call, asked me point blank what had happened. There's nothing subtle about Aunt Ruth. I told her just as point blankly.

" 'What fault have you to find with Andrew?' she asked icily.

" 'No fault—but he tastes flat. He has all the virtues

but the pinch of salt was left out' I said, with my nose in the air.

"'I hope you don't go farther and fare worse,' said Aunt Ruth ominously—meaning, as I knew, Stovepipe Town. I could have reassured Aunt Ruth on that point, also, had I chosen. Last week Perry came to tell me that he is going into Mr. Abel's office in Charlottetown to study law. It's a splendid chance for him. Mr. Abel heard his speech the night of the inter-school debate and has had his eye on him ever since, I understand. I congratulated him heartily. I really was delighted.

"'He'll give me enough to pay my board,' said Perry, 'and I guess I can rustle my clothes on some side line. I've got to hoe my own row. Aunt Tom won't help me. *You* know why.'

"'I'm sorry, Perry,' I said, laughing a little.

"'*Won't* you, Emily?' he said. 'I'd like this thing settled.'

"'It is settled,' I said.

"'I suppose I've made an awful ass of myself about you,' grumbled Perry.

"'You have,' I said comfortingly—but still laughingly. Somehow I've never been able to take Perry seriously any more than Andrew. I've always got the feeling that he just imagines he's in love with me.

"'You won't get a cleverer man than me in a hurry,' warned Perry. 'I'm going to climb high.'

"'I'm sure you will,' I said warmly, 'and nobody will be more pleased than your friend, Emily B.'

"'Oh, *friends*,' said Perry sulkily. 'It's not for a friend I want you. But I've always heard it was no use to coax a Murray. Will you tell me one thing? It isn't my funeral—but are you going to marry Andrew Murray?'

"'It isn't your funeral—but I'm *not*,' I said.

"'Well,' said Perry, as he went out, 'if you ever change your mind, let me know. It will be all right—if I haven't changed mine.'

"I have written the account of this exactly as it

happened. But—I have also written another account of it in my Jimmy-book as it *should* have happened. I find I am beginning to overcome my old difficulty of getting my dream people to make love fluently. In my imaginary account both Perry and I talked bee-yew-tifully.

"I think Perry really felt a little worse than Andrew did, and I felt sorry about it. I do like Perry so much as a chum and friend. I hate to disappoint him, but I know he will soon get over it.

"So I'll be the only one left at Blair Water next year. I don't know how I'll feel about that. I dare say I'll feel a little flat by times—perhaps at three o' the night I'll wish I had gone with Miss Royal. But I'm going to settle down to hard, serious work. It's a long climb to the crest of the Alpine Path.

"But I believe in myself, and there is always my world behind the curtain.

"New Moon,
"June 21, 19—

"As soon as I arrived home tonight I felt a decided atmosphere of disapproval, and realised that Aunt Elizabeth knew all about Andrew. She was angry and Aunt Laura was sorry; but nobody has said anything. At twilight I talked it over in the garden with Cousin Jimmy. Andrew, it seems, *has* been feeling quite badly since the numbness of shock wore off. His appetite has failed; and Aunt Addie indignantly wants to know if I expect to marry a prince or a millionaire since *her* son is not good enough for me.

"Cousin Jimmy thinks I did perfectly right. Cousin Jimmy would think I had done perfectly right if I had murdered Andrew and buried him in the Land of Uprightness. It's very nice to have *one* friend like that, though too many wouldn't be good for you.

*   *   *

"June 22, 19—

"I don't know which is worse—to have somebody you *don't* like ask you to marry him or *not* have some one you *do* like. Both are rather unpleasant.

"I have decided that I only imagined certain things in the old John house. I'm afraid Aunt Ruth was right when she used to say my imagination needed a curb. This evening I loitered in the garden. In spite of the fact that it was June it was cold and raw, and I felt a little lonely and discouraged and flat—perhaps because two stories of which I had hoped a good deal came back to me today. Suddenly I heard Teddy's signal whistle in the old orchard. Of course I went. It's always a case of 'Oh, whistle and I'll come to you, my lad' with me—though I would die before I would admit it to any one but my journal. As soon as I saw his face I knew he had some great news.

"He had. He held out a letter, 'Mr. Frederick Kent.' I never can remember that Teddy's name is Frederick—he can never be anything but Teddy to me. He has won a scholarship at the School of Design in Montreal—five hundred dollars for two years. I was instantly as excited as he was—with a queer feeling behind the excitement which was so compounded of fear and hope and expectancy that I couldn't tell which predominated.

" 'How splendid for you, Teddy!' I said, a little tremulously. 'Oh, I'm so glad! But your mother—what does she think of it?'

" 'She'll let me go—but she'll be very lonely and unhappy,' said Teddy, growing very sober instantly. 'I want her to come with me, but she won't leave the Tansy Patch. I hate to think of her living there all alone. I—I wish she didn't feel as she does about you, Emily. If she didn't—you could be such a comfort to her.'

"I wondered if it occurred to Teddy that I might need a little comforting too. A queer silence fell between us. We walked along the Tomorrow Road—it has grown so beautiful that one wonders if any tomorrow can make it more beautiful—until we reached the fence of the pond pasture and stood there under the grey-green gloom of the firs. I felt suddenly very happy and in those few minutes part of me planted a garden and laid out beautiful closets and bought a dozen solid silver teaspoons and arranged my attic and hemstitched a double damask tablecloth—and the other part of me just *waited*. Once I said it was a lovely evening—it wasn't—and a few minutes later I said it looked like rain—it didn't.

"But one *had* to say something.

" 'I'm going to work hard—I'm going to get everything possible out of those two years,' Teddy said at last, staring at Blair Water and at the sky and at the sandhills, and at the green leisurely meadows, and at everything but me. 'Then, perhaps, when they're up I'll manage to get to Paris. To go abroad—to see the masterpieces of great artists—to live in their atmosphere—to see the scenes their genius immortalised—all I've been hungry for all my life. And when I come back——'

"Teddy stopped abruptly and turned to me. From the look in his eyes I thought he was going to kiss me—I really did. I don't know what I would have done if I couldn't have shut my own eyes.

" 'And when I come back—' he repeated—stopped again.

" 'Yes?' I said. I don't deny to this my journal that I said it a trifle expectantly.

" 'I'll make the name of Frederick Kent mean something in Canada!' said Teddy.

"I opened my eyes.

"Teddy was looking at the dim gold of Blair Water and scowling. Again I had a feeling that night air was not good for me. I shivered, said a few polite commonplaces, and left him there scowling. I wonder if he was too shy to kiss me—or just didn't want to.

"I *could* care tremendously for Teddy Kent if I let myself—if he wanted me to. It is evident he doesn't want me to. He is thinking of nothing but success and ambition and a career. He has forgotten our exchange of glances in the old John house—he has forgotten that he told me three years ago, on George Horton's tombstone, that I was the sweetest girl in the world. He will meet hundreds of wonderful girls out in the world—he will never think of me again.

"So be it.

"If Teddy doesn't want me I won't want him. That is a Murray tradition. But then I'm only half Murray. There is the Starr half to be considered. Luckily I have a career and an ambition also to think about, and a jealous goddess to serve, as Mr. Carpenter once told me. I think she might not tolerate a divided allegiance.

"I am conscious of three sensations.

"On top I am sternly composed and traditional.

"Underneath that, something that would hurt horribly if I let it is being kept down.

"And underneath that again is a queer feeling of relief that I still have my freedom.

"June 26, 19—

"All Shrewsbury is laughing over Ilse's last exploit and half Shrewsbury is disapproving. There is a certain very pompous young Senior who acts as usher in St. John's Church on Sundays, who takes himself very seriously and whom Ilse hates. Last Sunday she dressed herself up as an old woman, borrowing the toggery from a poor relation of Mrs. Adamson's who boards with her—a long, full, black skirt, bordered with crape, a black mantle bordered with crape, a widow's bonnet, and a heavy crape widow's veil. Arrayed thus, she tottered down the street and paused wistfully at the church steps as if she couldn't possibly climb them. Young Pomposity saw her, and, having some decent instincts behind his pomposity, went gallantly to her assistance. He took her shaking, mittened hand—it *was* shaking all right—Ilse was in spasms of laughter behind her veil—and assisted her frail, trembling feet up the steps, through the porch, up the aisle and into a pew. Ilse murmured a broken blessing on him, handed him a tract, sat through the service and then tottered home. Next day, of course, the story was all through the school and the poor lad was so guyed by the other boys that all his pomposity oozed out—temporarily at least—under the torture. Perhaps the incident may do him a world of good.

"Of course I scolded Ilse. She is a glad, daring creature and counts no cost. She will always do whatever she takes it into her head to do, even if it were to turn a somersault in the church aisle. I love her—love her—love her; and what I will do without her next year I do not know. Our tomorrows will always be separated after this—and grow apart—and when we meet occasionally it will be as strangers. Oh, I know—I know.

"Ilse was furious over what she called Perry's 'presumption' in thinking I could ever marry him.

" 'Oh, it was not presumption—it was condescension,' I said, laughing. 'Perry belongs to the great ducal house of Carabas.'

" 'Oh, he'll succeed, of course. But there'll always be a flavor of Stovepipe Town about him,' retorted Ilse.

" 'Why have you always been so hard on Perry, Ilse?' I protested.

" 'He's such a cackling oaf,' said Ilse morosely.

" 'Oh, well, he's just at the age when a boy knows everything,' I said, feeling quite wise and elderly. 'He will grow more ignorant and endurable after a while,' I went on, feeling epigrammatic. 'And he has improved in these Shrewsbury years,' I concluded, feeling smug.

" 'You talk as if he were a cabbage,' fumed Ilse. 'For heaven's sake, Emily, don't be so superior and patronising!' "

"There are times when Ilse is good for me. I know I deserved that.

* * *

"June 27, 19—

"Last night I dreamed I stood in the old summer-house at New Moon and saw the Lost Diamond sparkling on the floor at my feet. I picked it up in delight. It lay in my hand for a moment—then it seemed to elude my grasp, flash through the air, leaving a long, slender trail of brilliance behind it, and become a star in the western sky, just above the edge of the world. 'It is my star—I must reach it before it sets,' I thought, and started out. Suddenly Dean was beside me—and he, too, was following the star. I felt I must go slowly because he was lame and could not go fast—and all the time the star sank lower and lower. Yet I felt I couldn't leave Dean. Then just as suddenly—things *do* happen like that in dreams—so nice—without a bit of trouble—Teddy was beside me, too, holding out his hands to me, with the look in his eyes I had seen twice before. I put my hands in his—and he drew me towards him—I was holding up my face—then Dean gave a bitter cry, 'My star has set.' I turned my head for just a glance—the star was gone—and I woke up in a dull, ugly, rainy dawn with no star—no Teddy—no kiss.

"I wonder what the dream meant—if it meant anything. I must not think it did. It is a Murray tradition not to be superstitious.

"June 28, 19—

"This is my last night in Shrewsbury. 'Good-bye, proud world, I'm going home'—tomorrow, when Cousin Jimmy is coming for me and my trunk in the old express wagon and I will ride back in that chariot of state to New Moon.

"These three Shrewsbury years seemed so long to me when I looked ahead to them. And now, looking back, they seem as yesterday when it has passed. I think I've won something in them. I don't use so many italics—I've acquired a little poise and self-control—I've got a bit of bitter, worldly wisdom—and I've learned to smile over a rejection slip. I think that has been the hardest lesson of all to learn—and doubtless the most necessary.

"As I look back over these three years some things stand out so much more clearly and significantly than others, as if they had a special meaning all their own. And not always the things one might expect either. For instance, Evelyn's enmity and even that horrible moustache incident seemed faded and unimportant. But the moment I saw my first poem in *Garden and Woodland*—oh, that *was* a moment—my walk to New Moon and back the night of the play—the writing of that queer little poem of mine that Mr. Carpenter tore up—my night on the haystack under the September moon—that splendid old woman who spanked the King—the moment in class when I discovered Keats' lines about the 'airy voices'—and that other moment in the old John house when Teddy looked into my eyes—oh, it seems to me these are the things I will remember in the halls of Eternity when Evelyn Blake's sneers and the John house scandal and Aunt Ruth's nagging and the routine of lessons and examinations have been for ever forgotten. And my promise to Aunt Elizabeth *has* helped me, as Mr. Carpenter predicted. Not in my diary perhaps—I just let myself *go* here—one must have a 'vent'—but in my stories and Jimmy-books.

"We had our class day exercises this afternoon. I wore my new cream organdy with the violets in it and carried a big bouquet of pink peonies. Dean, who is in Montreal on his way home, wired the florist here for a bouquet of roses for me—seventeen roses—one for each year of my life—and it was presented to me when I went up for my diploma. That was dear of Dean.

"Perry was class orator and made a fine speech. And he got the medal for general proficiency. It has been a stiff pull between him and Will Morris, but Perry has won out.

"I wrote and read the class day prophecy. It was very amusing and the audience seemed to enjoy it. I had another one in my Jimmy-book at home. It was much *more* amusing but it wouldn't have done to read it.

"I wrote my last society letter for Mr. Towers tonight. I've always hated that stunt but I wanted the few pennies it brought in and one mustn't scorn the base degrees by which one ascends young ambition's ladder.

"I've also been packing up. Aunt Ruth came up occasionally and looked at me as I packed but was oddly silent. Finally she said, with a sigh,

" 'I shall miss you awfully, Emily.'

"I never dreamed of her saying and feeling anything like that. And it made me feel uncomfortable. Since Aunt Ruth was so decent about the John house scandal I've felt differently towards her. But I couldn't say I'd miss her.

"Yet something had to be said.

" 'I shall always be very grateful to you, Aunt Ruth, for what you have done for me these past three years.'

" 'I've tried to do my duty,' said Aunt Ruth virtuously.

"I find I'm oddly sorry to leave this little room I've never liked and that has never liked me, and that long hill starred with lights—after all, I've had some wonderful moments here. And even poor dying Byron! But by no stretch of sentiment can I regret parting from Queen Alexandra's chromo, or the vase of paper flowers. Of course, the Lady Giovanna goes with me. She *belongs* in my room at New Moon. She has always seemed like an exile here. It hurts me to think I shall never again hear the night wind in the Land of Uprightness. But I'll have my night wind in Lofty John's bush; I think Aunt Elizabeth means to let me have a kerosene lamp to write by—my door at New

Moon shuts *tight*—and I will not have to drink cambric tea. I went at dusk tonight to that little pearly pool which has always been such a witching spot to linger near on spring evenings. Through the trees that fringed it faint hues of rose and saffron from the west stole across it. It was unruffled by a breath and every leaf and branch and fern and blade of grass was mirrored in it. I looked in—and saw my face; and by an odd twist of reflection from a bending bough I seemed to wear a leafy garland on my head— like a laurel crown.

"I took it as a good omen.

"Perhaps Teddy was only shy!"

ABOUT THE AUTHOR

L. M. MONTGOMERY's fascinating accounts of the lives and romances of Anne, Emily, and other well-loved characters have achieved long-lasting popularity the world over. Born in 1874 in Prince Edward Island, Canada, Lucy Maud showed an early flair for storytelling. She soon began to have her writing published in papers and magazines, and when she died in Toronto in 1942 she had written more than twenty novels and a large number of short stories. Most of her books are set in Prince Edward Island, which she loved very much and wrote of most beautifully. *Anne of Green Gables*, her most popular work, has been translated into thirty-six languages, made into a film twice, and has had continuing success as a stage play. Lucy Maud Montgomery's early home at Cavendish, P.E.I., where she is buried, is a much-visited historic site.